THE WAY HOME

"Do you remember when we were that much in love?" Winston's smooth voice interrupted her thoughts.

Marlena looked up at him and shook her head. "If they only knew what they were in for."

He dropped down on the blanket next to her. "It wasn't all bad, Marlena. If I had to do it over, I'd still fall in love with you. Everyone should experience that kind of love at least once."

She didn't know what to say. Why was Winston making this confession? "I'm not so sure, Winston. Love hurts."

He tilted her chin up. "Do you regret what we shared?"

She studied his soft, brown eyes. How could she regret loving this dear, dear man? She shook her head. "No," she whispered.

His hand caressed her chin, then her cheek. She thought he was going to kiss her and she had no idea how she would respond. He dropped his hand from her face before she had to decide.

TIMELESS LOVE

Look for these historical romances in the Arabesque line:

BLACK PEARL by Francine Craft (0236-0, $4.99)

CLARA'S PROMISE by Shirley Hailstock (0147-X, $4.99)

MIDNIGHT MOON by Mildred Riley (0200-X; $4.99)

SUNSHINE AND SHADOWS by Roberta Gayle (0136-4, $4.99)

THE WAY HOME

Angela Benson

Pinnacle Books
Kensington Publishing Corp.
http://www.pinnaclebooks.com

PINNACLE BOOKS are published by

Kensington Publishing Corp.
850 Third Avenue
New York, NY 10022

First Printing: March, 1997
10 9 8 7 6 5 4 3 2 1

Printed in the United States of America

Chapter 1

Marlena dabbed at the corners of her burgundy-painted lips, then stepped back and checked her reflection in the gold-framed mirror one last time. She didn't know why she was so nervous. She'd been to hundreds of parties in the last ten years—parties that would make this event seem like a backyard barbeque—but she'd never been this anxious.

She cast a quick glance behind her and after making sure she still had the bathroom to herself, she tugged on the thin straps of her short, black beaded dress. Why hadn't she noticed *before* that her breasts seemed as though they were about to fall out of the thing? She tugged one last time, then stopped.

What are you doing, Marlena Rhodes? she asked herself silently. This party is in your honor, given by people who watched you grow up. So what if some of them treated you like dirt then? Look where you have them now—groveling at your feet. You've done it, girl. You've made the residents of the elite Rosemont section of Gaines sit up and take notice.

Marlena dropped her hands from the thin straps of her dress. There was nothing wrong with what she wore. Accented with an ivory cameo choker and matching button cameo earrings, her ensemble suited the occasion perfectly. It displayed her feminine form with the understated elegance and subtle sexuality that had become her trademark. She dabbed at her lips once more, took a final deep breath, then turned on her three-inch heels and left the bathroom.

"We've been looking for you, dear," Mrs. Hampton said as soon as Marlena returned to the intimate gathering on the Hampton's expansive patio. The older woman wore a gray silk dress adorned with a single strand of pearls and matching earrings. "Come with me, the Browns are dying to meet you. You do remember them, don't you? They owned the car dealership when you left. Well, now they own four of them."

Marlena listened to the older woman and wished, not for the first time, that her mother could be here with her. Josie Rhodes would have loved this. She'd always wanted to be on the inside of Gaines's black society, but she'd never been granted entrance. Though she'd had the style, she hadn't had the money that would have made her acceptable to these people.

Marlena smiled appropriately as the Browns talked about themselves and questioned her about her practice. These were among the most shallow people she'd ever met. They weren't really interested in her, she knew; they were dazzled by her success. How many of the lawyers in Gaines got the opportunity to try a case before the Supreme Court and win? How many of the lawyers in Gaines had their faces splashed across the front page of every newspaper in the country after successfully representing a major entertainment figure in a murder case? None.

The only reason all these people were attending to her tonight was because she moved in circles they could only read about. From Washington, D.C., to Hollywood, California, from the White House to Denzel Washington's house, she'd been there, done that. She wished it meant as much to her as it did to these people.

"I hear you drive one of our cars, Marlena," Mr. Brown was saying. "Would you be interested in shooting a commercial for us?"

"Thanks for asking, Mr. Brown," she began, wondering how the man knew what kind of car she drove.

"Call me, Frank," he said, cutting her off. "I don't want an answer tonight. You think about it. Maybe you could give me the name of your business manager and I'll have my people talk to him."

Your people talk to my people. She wanted to laugh at the man's pompous arrogance. Instead, she opened her beaded purse and handed him a card with her manager's name on it.

She was about to say more when Mrs. Hampton took her arm again. "You can't monopolize our Marlena here, Frank," the older woman chided. "A lot of people want to meet one of Gaines's most famous natives."

Marlena smiled at the Brown couple, glad for Mrs. Hampton's interruption. For the first time tonight, she appreciated the older woman's snobbery.

Mrs. Hampton led her to the far edge of the patio where an older, brown-skinned, slightly graying man stood off to himself. "This is Reginald McCoy," Mrs. Hampton said, pushing Marlena closer to the attractive gentleman whose name and face she didn't recognize.

While Mrs. Hampton gave detailed biographies of each of them, Marlena noticed that Mr. McCoy's eyes couldn't stay away from her breasts. She appreciated a complimentary glance from an attractive man as well as the next woman, but there was something predatory about Mr. McCoy's stare which made her uncomfortable.

"I'll leave you two to get acquainted," Mrs. Hampton said, ending her spiel. Then she rushed off toward the other guests.

"Welcome home, Marlena," McCoy said, in a deep, husky tone that would have been sensual had his eyes not held the gleam of a cat about to pounce on its dinner.

After talking with McCoy for a few minutes, Marlena relaxed, thinking maybe she'd misjudged the man. He was a flirt, but certainly nothing more and she could flirt with the best of them.

When he leaned close to her and placed his hand on her bare shoulder in an intimate gesture, she knew it was time to end their conversation. She looked up at him to tell him so when she felt the presence she'd been alternately dreading and awaiting. Her lips parted slightly but no words came out.

McCoy took her parted lips as an invitation and the next thing she knew, the man had planted his lips firmly against hers.

Winston Taylor wasn't surprised when he saw his ex-fiancée lift her face for Reggie McCoy's kiss, but he was surprised at his body's reaction to it. He'd guessed from the intimate way McCoy had been caressing Marlena's bare shoulders that theirs was more than a friendly, welcome home conversation. Well, he told himself, Marlena was a grown woman and she was no longer his. She could do what she wanted, when she wanted, and with whom she wanted.

Maybe she *was* the money-hungry bitch his mother had always said she was, after all. She'd certainly zeroed in on Moneybags McCoy with haste. He wondered how many other men she'd seduced with her kisses.

Winston refused to stop his unkind thoughts about Marlena. It was much easier to hate her than it was to examine the other emotions she evoked in him. Unfortunately, his hatred did nothing to ease his desire.

He could still feel those full lips of hers against his. He remembered how soft and vulnerable she'd been in his arms. She'd worn a mask of indifference for the world, but she'd allowed him entrance into her soul and he'd felt blessed because of it. There was a time when he would have given his life for her. He'd loved her that much.

She hadn't loved him that much though. When she'd had to choose between a simple, though in no way lacking, life with him in Gaines and the lure of an extravagant lifestyle as a partner in one of D.C.'s top law firms, she'd gone for the gold and left him with a broken heart.

Well, he told himself, that was the past. Water under the bridge, as they said. She could strip naked and have sex with McCoy in the middle of Main Street if she wanted, but she wouldn't make a mockery of this party the town had planned for her and she wouldn't ruin his plans for his new project.

He ignored the flicker of jealousy in his belly and clamped down on the urge to punch McCoy's lights out. "Welcome home, Marlena," he said, when he stood no more than three feet away from the still-embracing couple. When Marlena moved to push McCoy away from her, he added, "No need to break up on my account. I just wish you would've waited until you got back to the hotel. The people of Gaines aren't used to such public displays of . . . ah . . . affection."

The gleam in McCoy's eyes over Marlena's head made Winston's hands to curl into fists at his side. The older man's message couldn't have been clearer. He already saw himself in Marlena's bed.

When Marlena finally stepped away from McCoy and turned to face Winston, he felt as though the wind had been knocked out of him. She was more beautiful now than she'd been when she'd walked out of his life ten years ago. He wanted to slip his fingers under the thin straps of her dress and slowly push the garment off her shoulders and down her body, leaving a trail of hot kisses in its path.

"Hello, Winston," she said through those full lips he wanted so much to caress with his own. "How have you been?"

"Fine," he said, amazed his vocal cords worked. "I don't have to ask how you are. You look wonderful." He cast a glance above her head at McCoy. "But I guess he's already told you that."

She smiled one of her rare smiles and he was again a teenager in the throes of first love. Though in those days Marlena rarely smiled, she'd always had a special smile for him. She wore that smile now. "A woman never tires of hearing she's beautiful. I'm sure you know that."

McCoy placed a proprietary arm across Marlena's shoulders again. "Maybe we should continue this conversation over dinner. Everyone else has gone in."

Winston pinned Marlena with a stare. "That's why I interrupted your fun. Mrs. Hampton sent me to get you," he lied.

McCoy's hand slid to Marlena's waist and he led her through

the patio doors and into the house. Winston walked behind them, his eyes glued to the foreign hand on the small of Marlena's back. He needed a drink and he needed one fast.

Marlena felt Winston's eyes boring into her back as McCoy escorted her into the house. She didn't have to guess what he was thinking. It had been in his eyes when she'd turned around and spoken to him. He'd thought she wanted McCoy's kiss when all she'd wanted was to slap the older man's face and get away from him.

Winston's presence had stopped her. She'd wanted to slap *him* when she realized what he thought. He should have known her better than to think she'd kiss a man she'd just met. Well, if that was how little he thought of her, she'd show him how right he was. She had purposed then to spend the rest of the evening with McCoy.

McCoy seated himself next to her at dinner as she'd known he would and she feigned interest in his conversation. When someone tapped him on his shoulder, she stole a glance down the table at Winston. When she'd first felt his presence, all the years between them had vanished, and she'd wanted to turn and hurl herself into the strong arms that had held her close so many times in the past. The years had come back in spades when she'd turned and seen his face. The disapproving frown set clearly in his strong, masculine features showed he hadn't had any such nostalgic thoughts.

She'd been disappointed he hadn't had even one good memory of them to make their first meeting in ten years special. What did you expect? she asked herself. That he would take one look at you and realize he still loved you? Get real, girl. Life has gone on—yours and his. You came here to put the past in its place. Well, he's helping you accomplish your goal.

Almost as if he'd heard her thinking, Winston turned and caught her looking at him. When he lifted his wine glass to her in mock toast, she quickly turned away.

McCoy said something to her but she couldn't concentrate

on his words. Her thoughts were still in the past. "I love you," Winston had said the day they'd parted. "Don't do this to us."

Her heart ached every time she remembered that day, but she'd had no choice. She'd had to end the relationship then or he would have ended it later—when he found out.

She cast another quick glance at him and noticed the gorgeous woman, whom she guessed was his date, seated next to him. Apparently, Winston's taste in women had changed over the years. Though he'd often told her how much he loved her dark skin and how he thought her short, short hair made her look sexy, his current date was a light-skinned beauty with long relaxed hair.

Her old insecurities kicked in and she wondered if Winston had ever really loved her. How could he have? She'd been a poor girl from the wrong side of town who'd had to struggle for everything she'd ever gotten. She'd worn the same clothes day after day and week after week. Of course, they'd been clean, pressed and repaired; she'd made sure of that. Ironically, people had often commented on her sense of fashion, not realizing her choice of classic styles which endured was because she couldn't afford to keep up with the latest trends.

The same could be said of her hair. Though she wore it short now because it was more manageable that way, she'd had to wear it cut short back then because she hadn't had the money for regular perms.

What had Winston Taylor, son of one of the wealthiest black men in Gaines, seen in her? He could have had any girl he wanted and he'd chosen her. She'd never understood why and she'd always thought that one day he'd ask himself the same question, decide he could do a lot better, and leave her.

Winston suffered through the dinner. He'd barely heard a word his date had said all night. All his thoughts centered around Marlena. He needed to talk to her about the project, he told himself as he made his excuses to his date and made his way across the room to Marlena.

"Do you mind if I borrow Marlena for a few minutes,

Reggie?'' he asked, when he reached her side. He wondered if the older man was really going to spend the night with her. ''I need to talk to her about some plans the council has on the table.''

McCoy smiled down at Marlena. ''Only if you promise to bring her back.''

Before Marlena could respond, Winston had taken her arm and was pulling her out of the dining room and into the Hampton's library. He closed the door behind them.

''You seem to be having a good time tonight,'' he said, with a little more of an edge in his voice than he'd planned. He couldn't help it though. The thought of Marlena in bed with McCoy made him angry.

She walked to the mahogany bookcases that lined the far wall and began fingering the books. ''This is a nice party. I *almost* feel welcome.''

''You sound surprised,'' he said, taking a seat on the leather couch in the middle of the room. ''Gaines is your home. Of course you're welcome here.''

She smiled what he'd always called her public smile because it didn't reach her eyes. ''Is it me they're welcoming, Winston, or the things I've done? Somehow I don't think I'd be as welcome without that Supreme Court case or that L.A. murder trial behind me.''

She sounded like the girl he'd loved: vulnerable, a bit insecure, yet strong and determined. She'd always felt she didn't belong, that she wasn't good enough, and though he'd tried to tell her she was wrong, she'd never really believed him. He'd thought her success would have given her the validation he hadn't been able to give, but it hadn't. Marlena still needed to prove her worth to herself and to the people of Gaines just as she'd felt she had to do years ago. ''It's what you wanted, isn't it?'' he asked. ''You wanted fame and recognition and now you have it. You should be happy that Gaines's finest has opened their arms to you. You've achieved your goal.''

He thought he saw a flicker of regret in her eyes but it was quickly replaced with boredom. ''What did you want to talk to me about?'' she asked, taking a seat in the leather Queen Anne chair next to the couch.

''Oh,'' he said, trying to focus on the project he wanted to talk to her about instead of on her smooth legs which screamed out to him when she crossed them. ''I'm working on a special project with the city council.''

''You've accomplished your goal then, too,'' she said, her words forcing his eyes back to her face. ''You always wanted to come back here and make a difference. A job on the council allows you to do that, doesn't it?''

''I'm trying,'' he said, leaning toward her. ''That's why I wanted to talk to you. I'm working on this project to get more Gaines High graduates to return here to live and work.''

''How can I help?'' she asked. ''I'm only here for a visit. I don't plan to live in Gaines ever again.''

He leaned back away from her. ''I wouldn't expect someone as prominent as yourself to be content here with a bunch of small town yahoos like us,'' he said with a sneer. ''But I had hoped you would lend your name and support to the project.''

''That's not what I meant, Winston.''

He waved his hand in the air. ''It doesn't matter. Just hear me out. The program, called *The Way Home*, has contacted all the major businesses within a forty-five-minute driving radius about professional job opportunities. We're in the process of matching those opportunities with the professions of some of our graduates. Once that's finished, we have to contact the graduates and convince them to come back here and interview for the positions.''

''You make it sound so simple, but why would anyone want to come back here? This town wasn't very friendly to a lot of us. Are you sure you aren't the only one who wants graduates to come back?''

Winston stood and pushed his hands into the pockets of his dress pants, making her smile. As he stood before her now in his dark gray pants and jacket with the light gray banded-collar shirt, he reminded her of the man she'd always loved. Her Winston had never been one to wear ties. It was comforting to know that he was still the same in some ways.

"The town needs to grow," he said. "Or it's going to die. Some people don't believe that, but I know it. I see it already. Most people who have the option, choose to leave Gaines, so we're left with a town full of people with no options."

"I never thought you were a snob, Winston."

He looked down at her. "I'm not. Don't take what I said the wrong way. I'm not complaining about the people who stay. My point is that for people to have hope, they need examples, they need role models. What role models are left for the people here? What examples do the kids have to follow? It's a much tougher world than it was when we were kids, Marlena."

"And you think this program . . ."

"*The Way Home,*" he supplied for her.

"And you think *The Way Home* will make a difference?"

He walked over and crouched down next to her and the memory of the day he'd proposed flashed in her mind. "We've got to do something before it's too late," he said. "I think *The Way Home* is worth a try. Will you help me?"

She looked into the sad puppy-dog eyes that had attracted her from the first and knew she wouldn't be able to refuse him. "What do you want me to do?"

"So you'll help?"

She got up from her chair and walked to the windows to keep from embarrassing herself by grinning in his face like some lovesick teenager. "You still haven't told me what you want me to do."

She felt him walk up behind her, and needing something to do with her hands, she pushed back the heavy velvet curtains and looked out on the Hampton's immaculate gardens.

"Two things," he said to her back. He was so close that she could feel his breath on her neck. "Both of them easy. First, I want you to contact some of the graduates about the program."

She stepped closer to the window, then turned around to face him. He wasn't as close as she'd thought. At least three feet separated them. "Sounds easy enough. What else?"

He turned on the puppy-dog smile again. God, that smile

should be registered as a lethal weapon. "You could go on a couple of interviews yourself."

"No way, Winston," she said, still fighting the teenage grin. She realized the years hadn't diminished Winston's power to affect her senses. "I'm not interested in interviewing for a job."

He took a step closer to her. "Look, it's not that bad. They really won't be interviews anyway. A few firms and businesses in the area have expressed a strong interest in talking to you. They want to wine and dine you. I hope you know that you can have any position in the state that you want just by saying the word."

"That's exactly the point," she said, going back to her chair. He'd gotten a bit too close for comfort. "I don't want any position in the state. I'm perfectly happy where I am."

He marched right behind her back to her chair. "I know that, but the people who want to meet you don't have to know it. Just go to dinner a few times and listen to their pitches. I wouldn't ask you to do this if it wasn't important, Marlena, but the program needs you. The companies and firms interested in talking to you have a lot of influence. They can help place a lot of candidates." He dropped down next to her chair again. "The council is threatening to pull its support from the project if you don't get involved."

Disappointment grabbed her heart. She should have known that he was only asking her because he had to. "I'm only going to be here a few weeks, Winston," she said, being deliberately vague. She'd planned to be away from the office for a month but she wasn't sure yet she wanted to spend the entire month in Gaines.

"Does that mean you'll do it?"

"I can't very well let the council pull the plug on the project. I'll do what I can, but I'm not moving back here."

"Great, Marlena," Winston said. Before she could respond, he surprised her by pulling her into his arms. She thought the embrace would be a brief hug of thanks, but it quickly progressed to something more as his hands caressed her back. Giving in to the moment, she pressed her lips against the side of his neck and inhaled the masculine scent of his cologne. Their closeness erased the ten years that separated them and they were young and in love once again.

Sensing he shared her feelings, she pulled back and looked into the eyes of the man who had loved her so well in the past. She didn't say anything because there was nothing to say. She lowered her eyelids and waited.

Winston knew he shouldn't do what he was about to do, but he also knew he was going to do it. He'd wanted to kiss her since he'd first seen her in McCoy's arms. He'd wanted to wipe that kiss from her mind and her body and make her forget the other man existed.

He touched his fingers to the corners of her eyes and she raised her eyes to his. He smiled at her, then slowly lowered his head to hers.

"There you are, Marlena," Mrs. Hampton said from the doorway. "Reginald is looking for you."

Winston cursed softly and dropped his hands from Marlena's face. "You'd better go join your date," he said. "I'm sure he doesn't think the evening is over yet."

Marlena jumped up and grabbed her purse, as shaken by what had almost happened as he was. Winston noticed that she was licking her lips when she left, much as she'd done in the past when he'd teased her and made her hot with passion.

He stood and straightened his jacket and his now tight pants. That he still wanted Marlena was the only thought on his mind when he left the library.

Chapter 2

Marlena leaned against the door to her suite in the modest Gaines Inn, relieved she'd finally gotten rid of McCoy. The man had actually thought he was spending the night with her. Men! Sometimes they could be the biggest jerks. What had she been thinking to dismiss her first impression of him? Not what, she answered herself, but who. She'd allowed thoughts of Winston to crowd her mind and affect her thinking.

She pushed away from the door, kicked off her heels, and went to the telephone, pausing to glance at her watch before picking up the receiver and dialing the seven digits.

"Hello," a tired woman's voice said into the phone.

"Cheryl, is that you?"

"Yes, this is Cheryl. Who's this?"

"It's Marlena, girl. How are you?"

"Marlena, is it really you? I heard you were coming to town. Why didn't you call me? Where are you?"

Cheryl's excitement made Marlena relax. This was the welcome she'd been waiting for. "I'm staying at the Gaines Inn. Why weren't you at the party tonight? I didn't call you because I expected to see you there."

Cheryl laughed. "You *have* been away a long time. There

are still two Gaineses. One for the blacks with money and the other for the rest of us. Your party tonight was given by the money crowd, the rest of us weren't invited.''

"Damn," Marlena said. "I hate this town."

"Oh, girl, it's not so bad. Hey, what are you doing? Why don't you come over? I know you have transportation."

Marlena looked at her watch again. She wanted to go over, but she didn't want to impose on Cheryl. "But it's so late."

"Late, nothing. You get over here. I just got in from pulling a double shift at work and I don't have to go back till Monday. We can have a sleepover like the money girls used to do."

Marlena giggled, feeling like a teenager again. "Are we gonna talk about *boys?*"

"What else? Now get over here. I can't wait to see you."

Marlena got directions to her friend's house and hung up the phone with a smile on her face. The short conversation with Cheryl had made her feel more welcome than that bourgeois dinner they'd billed as a Welcome Home party. She needed to see Cheryl. Her friend would make her feel like she was really and truly home.

Marlena quickly got out of her dress dudes and slipped on a pair of jeans and an old Howard sweatshirt that were perfect for a sleepover. She threw a few clothes and some toiletries in an overnight bag and headed out the door.

"You're lookin' good, girl," Cheryl said, stepping out of Marlena's embrace and giving her the once-over. "I just hope you didn't wear that outfit to your shindig tonight."

Marlena laughed a wide, open laugh, feeling secure and happy in her friend's home. "I wish. That would have given the stuffed shirts something to talk about all year."

"It would've served 'em right."

"Hey, where's Patrice? The last time I saw her she was practically a baby. It's been a long time."

"Ten years to be exact." Cheryl's eyes twinkled and looked like a teenager again. Her shoulder-length braids and the African-print shirt she wore indicated her politics hadn't changed over the years. "Can you believe that my baby is out on a date? It's a wonder my hair hasn't fallen out."

"She can't be any worse on you than you were on your mom."

Cheryl rolled her eyes toward the ceiling. "That's why I call Mama everyday and tell her how much I love her and appreciate her. Patrice is going to be the death of me."

Marlena plopped down on the worn but clean upholstered couch in Cheryl's family room. The small house her friend lived in was a big step above the projects where they'd been raised. Cheryl had done well for herself, even if the money people in Rosemont didn't realize it. "Well, I can't wait to see her again."

Cheryl glanced at the clock. "Her curfew is one o'clock on Fridays so she'll be out a while longer." Cheryl rubbed her hands together in anticipation. "That gives us some time to get in some juicy gossip before she gets here."

Marlena giggled again and Cheryl began to catch her up on the town news. They laughed and talked for what seemed like hours before Cheryl asked the question Marlena had known she would ask. "What did you think of Winston?"

Marlena remembered their embrace. She shrugged. "You tell me. I only spoke with him for a few minutes. I'd heard he was divorced."

"Best thing that ever happened to him," Cheryl said with an agreeing nod. "That Patty was a piece of work. I don't know what he saw in her in the first place. There was rebound going on there big time."

"What are you talking about?"

"You know, girl. Winston only married her to get over you. It didn't work though."

Marlena didn't agree with her friend's assessment. Though a part of her had thought the same thing when she'd first heard about Winston's quick marriage to her old nemesis, Patty Brock, she'd finally come to realize Winston had simply gone back to his first love.

Winston and Patty had dated from ninth grade until first semester senior year, almost four years. Patty had accused

Marlena of stealing Winston, although Patty and Winston had broken up months before she entered the picture. She'd actually been surprised when Winston had sought her out and had wondered if his pursuit of her was a rebound reaction.

"I thought he and Patty had a child," she said.

Cheryl shook her head and turned up her nose. "No way. Miss Priss probably didn't want to put her body through the strain."

Marlena was glad Patty hadn't had Winston's baby. She didn't stop to consider why. "Maybe Winston didn't want kids either." Even as she spoke, Marlena knew her words weren't true. Winston had told her more than once that he wanted a big family. He loved kids and always regretted being an only child. An only child herself, she'd shared his desire for children though she'd never agreed with the big family idea. Two or three kids would have been enough for her.

"No way," Cheryl said. "That man loves kids. You should see the ones hanging around his office. He coaches summer league ball, he's a Big Brother, and he's the voice of reason for every teenage boy in this town. Winston's one of the few really good guys in all of Gaines."

Marlena unfolded her legs and got up from the couch. "He's a man, Cheryl, not a saint."

"That's not what you used to say."

Marlena gave a hollow laugh. "I was a girl then and Winston was the guy I thought I could never have. I did think he was a saint. I thought he had to be to love me."

"You loved him very much one time, Marlena. Do you still love him?"

Marlena made herself at home and went into the kitchen for another glass of diet soda. "Winston will always have a special place in my heart."

"But do you still love him?"

Marlena shrugged. How did she feel about Winston? How did he feel about her? "I love him. I'll probably always love him. He was my first love."

"You aren't answering my question, girl, and I think I know why."

"You do, do you?" Marlena said, leaning against the kitchen door.

"I think you came back here to see if there was still a chance for the two of you. There is. Winston's never gotten over you."

Marlena turned away. She'd thought a lot about the past before deciding to come back. After the fanfare of her last trial and the breakup of her latest relationship, she'd needed to ground herself again. She'd thought she could do that by coming back to Gaines. Seeing Winston was only a by-product, she told herself.

"Did you hear what I said, Marlena? Winston's never gotten over you. You can find your way back to him if that's what you really want."

Marlena heard a car pull up before she could answer.

"That's Patrice," Cheryl said. "Get ready to meet the daughter of my dreams."

"I'm home," a soft, girlish voice called from the direction of the front door. "I'll be in in a minute."

Cheryl rolled her eyes again. "See what I mean? At home by one, but out on the porch until two."

Marlena laughed, relieved she'd been spared further probing into her feelings about Winston.

Winston piled his plate high with grits, cheese eggs, sausage, and biscuits with gravy from the sideboard before taking his seat next to his mother at the eight-foot dining room table. Her Saturday morning summons had been unavoidable, so he figured he might as well get a good meal out of it.

"You're going to make yourself sick, Winston," his mother said as she sipped from a cup of hot, black coffee. The coffee and a dried piece of toast were her breakfast. At sixty, Barbara Taylor still watched her waistline, and so did a lot of her male contemporaries. The attractive, perfectly groomed widow never lacked for male companionship. Admirers he would never have guessed had crawled out of the woodwork after his father's death five years ago.

"I only eat like this when I come home. Can I help it if

Martha is in love with me?" He cut into the gravy-soaked
biscuit with his fork and popped half of it into his mouth.
"Delicious," he said, licking his lips.

His mother lifted her nose in disdain. "I'm going to speak
to Martha *again.* She knows I don't want that type of food in
this house. One of these days that woman is going to go too
far."

"Leave her alone, Mother. Martha can prepare eggs benedict
for you and your genteel friends, but let her enjoy herself and
fix a down-home breakfast for me. I love it."

"All that grease and fat. I don't believe it, Winston. You
eat like somebody from the projects."

Winston loved his mother, but he hated her snobbery. It
wasn't as though she'd been born with money. To the contrary,
she'd been dirt poor when his well-to-do father had met and
fallen in love with her. From the way she acted now, he wondered if she'd erased all memory of her impoverished upbringing from her mind. "A lot of good people live in the projects,
Mother," he said, knowing it was futile to try to change her
mind, but refusing to allow her biased statement to go
unchecked.

"I guess you're referring to that Rhodes woman?" His
mother placed her cup in its saucer and dabbed at her lips with
her embroidered cloth napkin. "I was wondering when you'd
bring her up."

"No, I wasn't referring to *Marlena,*" he emphasized his ex-
fiancée's name, "but since *you* brought her up, yes, I think
she's the perfect example. She grew up in the projects and look
what she's accomplished."

"But I bet she still has the morals of an alley cat," his
mother murmured.

"Mother!" Winston shouted, lowering the fork that had been
halfway to his mouth.

"Don't 'Mother' me, Winston. I know what I'm talking
about. A good education and a good job can't change bad genes
and a poor upbringing. Have you forgotten what that . . . that
. . . woman did to you? How can you defend her?"

"I'm not defending her," Winston said, trying to keep his

temper in check. He hadn't forgotten that Marlena had dumped him without warning. He hadn't forgiven her either, but something inside him grew protective when his mother maligned her. It always had. "Marlena doesn't need defending. She never has."

"Just like her mother," Mrs. Taylor continued. "The apple sure didn't fall too far from the tree in that case."

Winston slammed his napkin on the table and pushed back in his chair. "That's it, Mother. I won't sit here and let you malign Marlena for no reason."

"No reason? You *have* forgotten, haven't you? You've forgotten that the girl who had accepted your marriage proposal walked out of your life without a second's hesitation after she got that big job offer."

Winston stood and pushed his chair to the table. He leaned on its back. "Look, Mother, that was ten years ago. You've got to let it go. I have. What's the use of holding a grudge? Marlena has moved ahead with her life and so have I."

His mother picked up her coffee cup again. "I heard that Mrs. Hampton found the two of you in the library last night."

Winston felt like a child again and he didn't like the feeling. "She didn't have to *find* us because we weren't hiding. We were having a private business discussion. Marlena is going to be working with me on *The Way Home.*"

Down went his mother's cup again. "You've got to be kidding? First, the town decides to give that woman a party and now you're inviting her to work on *The Way Home*? If all of you would just ignore her, she'd leave. But, no, you're treating her as if she's royalty and she's eating it up."

"You're not being rational," he said. What else could he say? How could he tell his mother he hated her when she talked this way? His father had been the only one capable of keeping her in line. He wished the older man were here now.

"I'm not being rational? You're the one who's not being rational. You must be thinking with something other than your head."

"That's it, Mother," he said. "I won't listen to this."

"I heard she was all over McCoy last night, too. That woman

can spot a rich man from a mile off. I wonder how many she had to sleep with to get her fancy title?'' His mother picked up her cup and sipped like an innocent debutante.

There was nothing more Winston could say. He turned and left his mother alone with her superior attitude and her condescending manner. He was glad she had looks, because he feared she'd be a lonely old woman if she had to rely on her personality for friendship.

When Winston pulled up in front of the Gaines Inn, the recently built three-story accommodation that was Gaines's only hotel, he told himself he was only there to schedule a Monday morning meeting with Marlena to discuss *The Way Home*. He refused to acknowledge that a part of him wanted to assure himself McCoy hadn't spent the night with her.

After ringing her room, Billy, the nineteen-year-old desk clerk whom Winston had coached in summer league baseball and whom he now considered a friend, turned to him. ''She's not answering.''

''Have you seen her this morning?'' Winston asked, though he knew Marlena's whereabouts were none of his business.

''No, sir,'' Billy answered with a formality that he reserved for his working hours.

''Does she have a car?''

''Sir?'' the young man asked.

''A car, Billy. Does she have one?''

He shrugged. ''I don't know.''

Winston leaned closer. ''Can't you check her registration record?''

''I don't know, Coach,'' the boy began. ''That's private information.''

Winston couldn't go farther. Billy had come a long way from his days as an up-and-coming juvenile delinquent. He couldn't allow the boy to do something he knew was wrong. He stood up straight. ''You're right, Billy. It is private. Why don't I just leave her a message?''

The boy smiled. "Sounds good to me." He reached under the counter and handed Winston a pad.

Winston scribbled a note asking Marlena to call him when she got in. *The Way Home* business, he added, wanting to make sure she understood he had no personal interest in seeing her.

He left the hotel knowing he was lying to himself and to her.

Marlena saw Winston pull away just as she drove into the hotel parking lot. What was he doing here? she wondered.

"Ms. Rhodes," Billy called when she entered the lobby. "You have a message."

Marlena walked to the desk, wondering who'd left her a note. She refused to consider Winston as the source of the missive.

Billy handed her the note and she knew from the scrawl that was supposed to be her name that Winston had indeed left the message. Her heart skipped a beat as she unfolded the paper.

Call me, it said. About *The Way Home*.

She crumpled the note in her hands and gave it back to Billy.

"Everything all right, Ms. Rhodes? You just missed Coach, ah, Mr. Taylor." He tossed the crumpled note in the garbage.

She smiled. "I'm fine. That's for giving me the note." She reached in her purse to give him a tip.

"There's no need for that," he said. "Me and Coach go way back. He'd kill me if he knew I took your money for giving you *his* note."

Marlena snapped her purse shut. "You're sure?" she asked.

"Positive. Just be sure to tell Coach I didn't take your money."

She smiled at the young man, wondering about the exact nature of his relationship with Winston. He certainly held Winston in high esteem. She shrugged. Who knew what bonded men and boys?

An hour later, Marlena stepped out of the shower to the sound of a ringing telephone. She grabbed one of the hotel's fluffy white towels, wrapped it around herself, and rushed to the phone next to the bed. She made a mental note to suggest the hotel add a phone in the bathroom. Though her suite—which she considered an oversized efficiency despite the hotel's suite label—lacked the amenities of her favorite lodgings, she only missed the bathroom phone.

"I'm not ready yet," she said when she picked up the receiver, thinking the caller was Cheryl. They'd planned to go over to the projects this morning and visit old friends.

"Marlena?"

She dropped down on the side of the bed. "Winston?"

"Did you get my note?" he asked.

She pulled the towel tighter around her. "I got it."

"Well?"

"Well what?"

"Can you make the meeting Monday morning?"

Marlena opened the nightstand table and pulled out her calendar. "Monday morning's bad for me. I'm speaking at the high school assembly. How about the afternoon? Say one o'clock?"

"Okay, one o'clock it is," he said.

"Okay," she repeated, waiting for him to hang up. When he didn't, she said his name.

"I'm still here," he said. "How does it feel to be back home?"

She pulled her legs up on the bed and slid up so she could rest her back against the headboard. "Great, now that I've seen Cheryl. I can't believe she wasn't invited to the party. Gaines certainly hasn't changed much over the years."

"Oh, I don't know. I think it's changed in some ways."

"All bad, I bet."

"I hope that's not so. I'd like to think some things have changed for the better."

"Such as?" she challenged, falling back into the old pattern of conversation she and Winston had shared.

"I'll have to let you see for yourself."

"What makes you think I'll stay that long?"

"This is your home. I don't understand how you've stayed *away* so long."

She sucked in her breath. He knew she'd always wanted to

come back. What he didn't know was that the option had been taken away from her the day after her mother's funeral. "Sometimes we're forced into certain decisions and situations, Winston," she said softly.

"And sometimes we lose sight of what's really important and go searching for material things of little value."

In the silence that lay between them, she thought about what could have been. If things had gone according to plan, she and Winston would be married with children by now. She'd wanted boys who looked like him and he'd agreed, saying girls who looked like her would drive him crazy when they became interested in boys. Things hadn't gone according to plan though and they'd spent the last ten years building separate lives, instead of building a family together.

"Look, Winston," she said, ending the trip down memory lane. "I have to hang up."

"Hot date?" he asked quickly.

"That's none of your business."

"This is a small town, Marlena. Everybody will know who you're seeing. There are no secrets in Gaines. You and McCoy should know that."

She didn't bother to tell him that her hot date was with Cheryl. She wouldn't be going anywhere or doing anything with McCoy. "Well, you listen to the old grapevine. I'm hanging up." She placed the receiver on the hook without waiting for his response.

Chapter 3

The past greeted Marlena with a thwap as she and Cheryl drove down Main Street from the Gaines Inn through the center of town, past Courthouse Square, and on toward Dusttown—the nickname given the eastside of Gaines during the early days because the only dirt roads in town had been the ones leading to and surrounding the predominately black community—where Main Street became Martin Luther King Boulevard. Marlena shook her head. Same road, different name. After all Dr. King had done, the people of Gaines couldn't even give the man an entire street.

The wooden shotgun houses that dotted the streets of MLK told her she was in Dusttown more than the green city sign in front of James Funeral Home that proclaimed the same. The house she and her mother, Josie, had lived in until they'd been fortunate enough to get an apartment in the housing project was still there, though it looked a lot worse now with its peeling and faded paint than it had when they'd lived there. When they'd moved to the projects she'd thought it was the best thing that ever happened to them, but time had proven her wrong. Sure the rooms were bigger and the appliances newer in the apartment, but there was something stifling about living in the projects—too many people with too much time on their hands living too close together. The originator of the housing project concept may have had good intentions but the implementation was a failure on massive terms.

"Still looks the same, doesn't it?" Cheryl asked as she turned the car off Martin Luther King and onto Holmes Street.

"In a lot of ways," Marlena responded, turning her thoughts from the philosophical to the realistic. "Rob's hasn't changed," she said, looking out the passenger window. A small white one-story building with Rob's Rib Shack written in red cursive letters across its front sat on the corner of Holmes and MLK. "Is the food still good?"

"The best. I thought we could have a late lunch there before we leave Dusttown. I only go about once a month. Pork ribs aren't exactly a staple in my diet."

Marlena laughed. "You're still on that 'almost' no pork regimen?"

Cheryl glanced over at her friend. "What do you think?" she asked with a smile.

"I think I'm too glad to see you again." She looked out of the passenger window at the stretch of boarded up houses along Holmes. "What's happened here?"

"Oh, you know," Cheryl said with a shrug. "People move. Some people think this is a bad area. We've had a problem with some of the kids down here so people are trying to get out."

Marlena shook her head. "What kind of problem? Not drugs." Drugs were a city problem, a D.C. problem; not a small town Gaines problem.

"There's talk. Gangs, definitely. Drugs, maybe."

"Makes me feel old," Marlena said.

Cheryl grinned at her. "You are old."

"That's not what I mean." Marlena's biggest worry growing up had been whether some mean classmate would make an ugly remark about Josie or whether she'd get new shoes before her old ones were too run over. The problems had seemed big then, but when compared to drugs and gangs, they didn't seem that big now.

Cheryl sobered. "I know, girl. I just thank God Patrice has a good head on her shoulders. Some of our classmates have had serious problems with their kids. Have you met Billy?"

"Billy?"

"The clerk at the hotel." Marlena nodded, and Cheryl continued, "That's Allison Woods's son. Hers and Tim Dawson's."

"Captain of the basketball team, Tim Dawson?"

Cheryl nodded.

"Now that was a fine brother. What's he doing?"

"That's the problem. He's doing nothing and Allison has had to raise the boy by herself. He got into some trouble a while back, but Winston helped him out."

Marlena's heart lurched at the mention of Winston's name. If she were honest with herself, she'd admit she'd been hungry for information about him since the Hampton's party, but had been reluctant to seek it out for fear Cheryl would get the wrong impression. "What kind of trouble did the boy get in and what did Winston do?"

Cheryl shrugged her shoulders. "I'm not sure. Something to do with a gun and some sports equipment. All I know is Winston fixed it and the boy hasn't been in trouble since."

Though she knew she had no right, Marlena felt proud that Winston had made a difference in the boy's life. "He was the boy's lawyer?"

"More than that. He was his friend. Like I told you, he's good with young people. He talks to them, he listens to them, he's there for them. He's such a good guy, Marlena. I can't believe you let him get away."

I didn't exactly let him get away, Marlena said to herself. "Winston and I weren't meant to be together, Cheryl."

"So you've said, but I'm still not convinced."

Marlena didn't want to talk about her past relationship with Winston so she deftly turned the conversation back to Allison Woods. "So how's Allison?"

"She's still Allison. It's hard for me to believe I was jealous of her in high school."

"You weren't the only one. Everybody was half-jealous of

Allison. She was Class Beauty every year, a cheerleader, and Homecoming Queen.''

Cheryl cut a glance at Marlena as the single-story red and white brick apartments of the public housing projects came into view. "Even you?"

"Please, girl. You know I was jealous."

Cheryl shook her head. "You never told me you were and you certainly didn't act like it."

"You didn't act like it either." She smiled at the memory. "As I remember, we spent most of our time talking about how silly she was."

Cheryl laughed. "Allison did act silly, but I don't think she really was. It was just her way of getting over."

Marlena remembered the high school Allison. Though the girl had lived in the projects along with her and Cheryl, she'd always worn the best clothes and had her hair professionally done. So what if she did just enough work to pass; she looked good, and when you're young, looking good meant a lot. "Are she and Tim still together?"

"**If you** can call it that. Tim drives one of those big rigs so **he's gone** more than he's here. Plus, they never got married. Five kids and they never got married. Allison should have shot his ass. I told her so, too."

When Cheryl stopped her car across the street from Marlena's old apartment, Marlena could swear she heard Josie's voice. "I don't want you coming up pregnant. You hear me, Marlena. Neither one of us need any babies."

The too-real memory made Marlena uncomfortable. "Ten years is a long time," she said aloud though she was talking to herself.

Cheryl squeezed her shoulder. "Not that long."

"Please. It's been eighteen years since high school and ten years since I was last in Gaines. That's a *very* long time. I still can't believe you have an almost-grown daughter. I'm old."

"It's a fact of life, girlfriend. You'd better get used to it."

"Right," Marlena said with a very unladylike snort. "I just had an awful thought."

"What?" Cheryl asked.

"You'll probably have grandchildren before I have kids. I'm definitely out of step with the class."

Cheryl moaned. "Don't even think about it. My becoming a grandmother is no laughing matter. Forget it, girl. Let's get out of this car and see who and what we can see."

"Where to first?" Marlena asked after she was out of car and standing on the sidewalk.

"Who knows? We'll play it by ear. People should be stirring by the time we make it back around the block." She looked down at the pink thong sandals Marlena had worn because they matched her shorts and tank top. "I hope those are comfortable shoes. Everybody has been talking about you and they all want to see the celebrity so we'll probably be down here for a while."

"I'm not a celebrity."

"You are to us," Cheryl said. "So you'd better get used to it. By the way, before you leave town you're going to have to tell me everything you can remember about Denzel's house."

Marlena opened her mouth to refuse her friend's request.

"Pretty please?" Cheryl begged. "If you tell me about Denzel, I'll tell you some juicy gossip about Mrs. Knowles."

"Our old history teacher?"

Cheryl's eyes sparkled as she nodded her head and rubbed her hands together. "Some real juicy gossip, too. In Mrs. Knowles's case, you definitely can't judge a book by it's cover."

Marlena laughed, her curiosity piqued by Cheryl's theatrics. "Deal. I'll tell you about Denzel's place if you tell me about Mrs. Knowles. And it had better be good, too."

Cheryl started walking and talking at the same time. As Marlena listened, she realized Mrs. Knowles's not-so-secret affair with the high school football coach was infinitely more interesting than a detailed description of Denzel's house. In terms of good gossip, Cheryl was going to get the short end of the stick.

As Cheryl had predicted by the time they made it around the block, people had started stirring. They were starting to come outside and sit on their cement porches or in gliders they had in their yards.

"Is that Mrs. Callaway?" Marlena asked inclining her head

in the direction of an apartment about fifty feet up the street from where they were standing.

Cheryl turned her head in the indicated direction. "That's her, all right. Let's go talk to her. I know she wants to see you."

Marlena and Cheryl marched over to Mrs. Callaway's yard. A hoard of flowers and plants greeted them. Shrubs lined the walkway, flowers of all colors filled a rectangular box in front of the porch, and potted plants covered almost every available space on the floor of the porch and the railing. Marlena wondered if Mrs. Callaway took care of·them herself. It seemed like a lot of work for the seventy-plus-year-old woman.

"Morning, Mrs. Callaway," Cheryl said with a bright smile and in a tone a few decibels higher than normal making Marlena wonder if Mrs. Callaway's hearing had gone bad. "I brought somebody to see you."

"Morning, Cheryl," the older woman said, standing up from her seat on the green and white glider and pressing a kiss to Cheryl's cheek. "I'm so glad to see you. How have you and that perfect little girl of yours been doing? I've missed you around here." Without waiting for Cheryl to answer her question, the older woman went on, "Now who's that you brought to see me? Is that Marlena, our movie star Marlena?"

Marlena stepped closer to the older woman, leaned in and kissed her jaw. "It's me, Mrs. Callaway, but I'm no movie star."

"We saw you on the television and in the newspaper. They were even talking about you on the radio. That's a movie star to me, girl. I know your mamma would be proud of you. Josie loved you something fierce, she did."

Marlena wished she had a prepared statement to give in response to the older woman's comment, but she didn't. Fortunately, Mrs. Callaway kept talking and she didn't have to say anything.

"That Josie was high-strung and full of fun. Too bad people around here didn't appreciate her. She was something special, your mother was. I sure do miss her," the older woman added almost as if to herself.

"I miss her, too, Mrs. Callaway," Marlena said and meant it. For all her mother's faults, Marlena never doubted her love while she was alive. It was only after she died and Marlena learned her secret that she'd doubted her mother's care. Those had been some hard days for the girl-woman who'd spent nearly all her life protecting her mother from the vicious attacks of people who despised her and her lifestyle.

"You were a good daughter, Marlena. Josie used to tell me that all the time. She knew you were going to make something out of yourself."

Again, Marlena didn't know what to say. She felt like an idiot. She'd tried court cases before hostile juries, so what was this nice, old woman doing to her? Making her remember, she answered for herself before giving Cheryl a pleading glance for help.

"We all did," Cheryl finally said when it became apparent Marlena wasn't going to respond. Marlena gave her a smile of thanks. "We all knew she'd make good. Too bad she had to leave Gaines to do it."

"Child, that's the way it is," the older woman agreed. "I've seen more young people grow up and leave here than I want to remember. I know why they have to leave, mind you, but I'm sure grateful for those like you who stay. This town would die without you, that Winston, and others like you."

Marlena's thoughts went to *The Way Home*. Maybe she and Winston needed to get Mrs. Callaway to work with them on the project.

"We're glad you're back, Marlena," Mrs. Callaway said, directing the conversation back to Marlena. "Are you going to be here for a while?"

Marlena shook her head, thankful for a question she could answer. "Not that long, Mrs. Callaway. Only about a month." It was only after Marlena said the words that she realized she'd made the decision to spend her entire vacation in Gaines.

The older woman glanced over at Cheryl. "You think we can convince her to stay?"

"I'm gonna try," Cheryl said, surprising Marlena. It was the first Cheryl had mentioned of wanting her to stay longer.

"Maybe we need some help from that Winston," the older woman said to a shocked Marlena. "Don't look so surprised. I have a good memory. You and that boy should be married with a house full of kids by now. How old are you anyway?"

"Thirty-five," Marlena answered.

"Never been married, either, have you?" At Marlena's nod, the older woman went on. "Just like I thought. You shouldda married that boy a long time ago. Sometimes I don't know what's in you young people's heads."

Marlena shot Cheryl another pleading glance, but this time she didn't get any help from her friend. "Things don't always work out the way we want, Mrs. Callaway."

"Don't I know it," the older woman went on. "I told Josie that she couldn't keep the two of you apart. I told that girl that, but she wouldn't listen. Sometimes that girl knew too much for her own good. I know why she didn't want it, but—"

"You know, Josie," Marlena interrupted, wondering how much the older woman knew about Josie's objections to her relationship with Winston but not wanting to find out in front of Cheryl. She wasn't ready yet to share that discovery with her friend. "Once she made up her mind about something, nobody could get her to change it."

The older woman didn't say anything for a moment and when she did Marlena was relieved she changed the subject. The three of them chatted on the porch for about an hour or so before Cheryl stood.

"Well, we've got to run, Mrs. Callaway," she said. "I promised a few of our old classmates that I'd bring Marlena by to see them today. I'll bring her back to see you before she leaves town though."

Marlena and Cheryl kissed the older woman's cheek, then stepped off the porch and back onto the sidewalk.

"That was fun," Marlena said. "I'm glad we stopped."

"Me, too," Cheryl said. "Now let's drop by Nancy's. She's living down here with her dad. He's been sick for the last year."

Marlena allowed Cheryl to lead the way to Nancy's house. Their friend had prepared lunch for them and though they tried to get out of it she refused to take no for an answer. After a couple of hours of reminiscing and eating good food, it was again time to leave.

"Why don't you stay for the ball game?" the light-skinned, somewhat heavy Nancy said.

"What game?" Marlena asked.

Cheryl slapped her hand across her forehead. "The softball game. I'd forgotten all about it. There's a game down here today." She turned to Nancy. "It starts at two, doesn't it?"

Nancy nodded. "Stay so we can go together. Marlena'll get to see a lot of old faces and we'll have a good time. What do you say?"

Cheryl looked at Marlena.

"I'm game, if you are," Marlena said.

Cheryl looked at Nancy. "I guess we're going then."

Winston knew exactly when Marlena got to the park. When he saw her, his breath caught in his throat. She was still the most beautiful woman he'd seen. From the very short waves on her small head to the what he knew were painted toe nails of her not-so-dainty feet, he found no fault in her. He knew other brothers complained about sisters with short hair, saying they liked to run their hands through long tresses, but not him. He loved Marlena's hair, always had. She'd probably look funny with long hair. He laughed to himself then corrected himself: Marlena would look gorgeous no matter how she wore her hair.

As Winston observed Marlena, he felt a pair of eyes fixed on him. He turned and wasn't surprised to find that those eyes belonged to his date, Miss Yolanda Underwood. A beautiful woman in her own right, Yolanda couldn't hold a candle to Marlena. They were night and day, literally. Yolanda was what some termed "high yellow" and Marlena was a deep, dark brown.

Winston smiled at Yolanda and she smiled back, but he wasn't naive enough to think that would be the end of it. Yolanda had questioned him endlessly about Marlena after the

Hamptons' party. He knew now that he would have done better had he told her about his past relationship with Marlena instead of letting her hear it through the grapevine.

Winston intended to turn his attention back to the game, but he caught sight of Marlena's pink tank top and he had to give her one last look, Yolanda or no Yolanda. He was only looking, he told himself. There was no law against looking.

"Coach."

Winston turned around at the sound of his name. "What's up, Billy?" he said, giving the young man a two-fisted handshake.

"Nothing, man. I was wondering if you knew Ms. Rhodes was here. I know you were looking for her this morning."

Winston needlessly pulled his baseball cap farther down on his head. "Yes, I saw her."

"She's lookin' good, isn't she?"

Winston frowned at the grin that appeared on the boy's face. "What's on your mind, Billy?"

The boy hooked his fingers in the waistband of his jeans. "The word is she used to be your lady. Not bad."

Winston shook his head, then waved the boy off. "You'd better get in position. The game's about to start."

"Don't want to talk about it, huh?" Billy looked up into the stands. "Don't look now, Coach, but I think Yolanda is going over to talk to Ms. Rhodes. Could be interesting."

"Billy!" Sometimes Winston wondered at the wisdom in allowing the boys to become so familiar with him, but only for a moment and only when they were dancing on his nerves as Billy was doing now. Most of the time, he cherished their friendship and appreciated them in his life as much, if not more, than they appreciated him in theirs.

"All right, already. I'm going. You'd better be careful, though. You know how women are."

"Billy, this is the last time."

"No need to get bent out of shape, Coach, especially since you have two women now." With those last words, the boy trotted off to his position in the outfield and Winston sneaked another peek into the stands. Sure enough, Yolanda had gotten up from her seat and was now standing in front of Marlena.

He wondered what she was up to, but he didn't have time to find out. The game started.

"Welcome back to Gaines, Marlena," Yolanda said, extending her hand. "I'm Yolanda."

Marlena looked up at the beauty she'd seen with Winston last night. It hadn't been the lighting, she told herself. Yolanda was as attractive in this hot sun as she had been in the Hampton's dining room. "Thank you," she said.

"Is anybody sitting here?" Yolanda asked, but Marlena guessed she didn't really want an answer since she was taking the seat even as she asked the question. "So how are you enjoying your visit?"

"I've only been here a day," Marlena answered. "But I'm having fun. Cheryl, Nancy, and I have been catching up." She turned to her friends. "You guys know Yolanda, don't you?" she asked.

Marlena saw the strained look that passed between her two friends. "We've seen her around," they said, before mumbling, "Hi."

Yolanda responded with a mere nod of her head. Marlena felt as though she was in the middle of a fight she hadn't known was going on.

"Winston and I are having the boys and some of our friends over for a cookout this evening, why don't you drop by. We'd love to have you."

Marlena didn't miss the woman's message. She'd made it loud and clear: Winston belonged to Yolanda. "I'm not sure what we have planned for tonight."

Yolanda stood and needlessly brushed at her still-creased shorts. "You can bring *them* too, if you like. There'll be plenty of food. We always have a lot on hand when the team comes by."

"You can bring them, too," Cheryl parroted after Yolanda headed back to her seat. "Who does she think she is?"

"Girl, you know who she thinks she is," Nancy filled in. "She thinks she's all that, but I've got a news flash for her."

"What's going on with you two?" Marlena said.

"Come off it, Marlena. That snobby b-witch is a trip. You saw how she totally looked over me and Nancy." Cheryl looked down her nose like one of the society matrons she'd seen satired on television. "Dahling, she's only interested in talking with you."

Marlena couldn't help it, she laughed. Yolanda had been a bit pretentious. "How long have she and Winston been an item?" she asked after her laughter subsided.

"Too long, if you ask me," Nancy said. "My guess is she wants the relationship to be more serious than it is. I hope you know that the only reason she came over here is because she saw Winston watching you."

Marlena shot a glance toward the field where Winston stood behind the umpire at home plate. He must have been upset about something because he was slapping his cap against his thigh. "Winston's not watching me."

"Not now," Cheryl said. "But he was before. And Miss Thang had to see it. She's some kinda trip. So are you gonna keep your hands off her man?"

"She didn't have to come all the way over hear to tell me that. I have no interest in Winston, at least, none beyond being a friend. Like I told you, the past is the past."

Marlena ignored the smirks that came across her friends' faces and turned her attention back to the game.

After Cheryl turned her late-model sedan off Holmes and onto MLK on the way out of Dusttown, she asked Marlena, "So how was it?"

"I had fun. I'm glad I came back home. This is just what I needed."

Cheryl brought the car to a stop at one of the town's four traffic lights. "Including Yolanda?"

"Including Yolanda," Marlena answered. "I'm no threat to her."

"Evidently she thinks you are."

Marlena cut a sidelong glance at her friend. "There is nothing between me and Winston and I wish you'd get that through your thick head.''

"You can't fault a girl for trying." Cheryl speeded through the light when it turned green. "I just don't think you and Winston are finished yet. You loved each other too much. I still can't believe you aren't married."

Marlena looked out the window, taking in the not-so-well-kept lawns of the homes that lined the street. "Believe it. We're not." She turned to her friend. "That was a long time ago, Cheryl. Winston and I are different people. We've had different experiences. We couldn't recapture what we had even if we wanted to."

"Do you want to?"

Marlena shrugged. She wanted to feel what she'd felt with Winston. She wanted to know that she could still love the way she'd loved then. If the last man in her life was right, she'd turned into a pretty cold woman. "I don't know."

"What's to know? Either you do or you don't."

"It's not that simple, Cheryl."

"Love never is."

Marlena shot another glance at her friend. "Are you speaking from experience?" she asked.

Cheryl shrugged. "Maybe."

"That's not good enough. Tell me, are you still in love with your ex?" Marlena had only met her friend's ex-husband once. He hadn't gone to school with them; Cheryl had met him at the factory in Leeds where she worked. They'd been married less than two years when they'd gotten divorced.

"I was never in love with him," Cheryl stated matter-of-factly. She turned the car onto her street and pulled into her driveway next to the red sports car already parked there.

"Then why did you marry him?"

Cheryl pointed to the porch where her daughter, Patrice, and Patrice's boyfriend sat on the swing. "So my baby would have a name."

Marlena knew her shock showed on her face and there was no way she could mask it.

"Close your mouth and get out," Cheryl said. "You have to meet the man in my daughter's life."

Marlena followed her friend to the porch. "Hi, Miss Marlena," Patrice said. "This is my boyfriend, Raymond."

The tall, lanky good-looking boy extended his hand. "Nice to meet you," he said. "Patrice says you went to school with her mother."

Marlena shook the boy's hand, impressed with his firm grip. "Yes, Cheryl and I went to school together back in the old days."

"Ahh," Patrice said, rolling her eyes. "You and Mama are just alike. I tell her she's not old and neither are you. You even wear hot clothes. I wish you'd get Mama to jazz up her wardrobe a little."

"Don't start, Patrice," Cheryl warned, needlessly straightening the bib of her knee-length denim overalls. "I'm not up for it today."

Again the teenager rolled her eyes. "Is it all right if we go to the movies?" she asked her mother.

"I promise I won't keep her out late, Mrs. Flakes," the boy said, taking Patrice's hand in his.

Cheryl sighed. "I know you won't, Raymond." She turned to her daughter. "Have you eaten dinner?"

"We're going to eat out. It's our anniversary. I told you."

It was Cheryl's turn to roll her eyes. "That you did. Well, don't stay out too late."

"We won't," Patrice said, practically pulling Raymond down the front steps after her.

Marlena watched as the young man held the car door open for the girl, smiled down at her, then ran around and got in the driver's seat.

"Young love," Cheryl grumbled.

"You don't like him?"

Cheryl shrugged. "He's a good kid, but they're too young to be so serious."

"We were serious at that age."

"And look what happened to us."

"Kids today are smarter than we were, Cheryl. Besides,

Patrice seems to have a good head on her shoulders and so does the boy. They'll be fine.''

Cheryl dropped down on the swing her daughter and friend had vacated and patted the seat next to her. Marlena sat down.

"You know,'' Cheryl began. "I never thought being a parent was this hard. You should have kids. They make you appreciate your mom more.''

"You may be right,'' Marlena said, thinking about the rocky relationship she and her mother had shared. Josie had never approved of her relationship with Winston. That was the one thing she and Winston's mother had had in common. Winston's father was the only one who'd seemed to understand and approve of the relationship.

Cheryl tapped her on the shoulder. "You were too hard on her, Marlena. She loved you and she didn't want you to get hurt.''

That's what Marlena had thought originally, but she was wrong. Her mother hadn't been concerned about her—not by a long shot. She just wished she'd known the reason for her mother's concern *before* she'd fallen in love with Winston. "I know Josie loved me, Cheryl, but she was a selfish woman sometimes.''

Cheryl just grunted.

"Okay, spit it out. I know you have something to say.''

Cheryl planted both her feet on the porch and stopped the gentle sway of the swing. "Sometimes a mother feels when her child is in over her head.'' She touched her chest. "She feels it here and she hurts almost as much as she thinks her child will hurt.''

"Are you talking about me and Josie or you and Patrice?''

"Maybe both. He's going to break her heart, Marlena. I know it. I just know it. His parents don't think she's good enough for him. Oh, she tries to pretend their opinion don't matter to her, but it does. I can see it in her eyes. She loves him so much and I just know he's going to break her heart.''

Marlena pulled the near-to-tears Cheryl into her arms. "You don't know that for sure. Give them a chance.''

Cheryl moved out of her friend's embrace, wiped her hands

down her tear-strained cheeks, and brushed her braids back off her face. "Sometimes I feel like it's my fault."

"That's ridiculous. You've been a great mother and Patrice is a great kid."

Cheryl shook her head. "No, I haven't. I got married because I was pregnant. I didn't go to college. And now my only child is being penalized for my mistakes. It's not her fault I haven't made much of my life. It's mine. I'm the reason she's not acceptable to his family. It's me. What if she blames me when she figures that out? What if she hates me?"

Marlena wanted to tell Cheryl that Patrice would never blame her or hate her, but the words wouldn't come. She still blamed her mother for her breakup with Winston, and her mother had been dead ten years. She no longer hated her, though God knows, she had for the first few years after her death.

All Marlena could do for Cheryl was to hold her and be her friend.

Chapter 4

Winston climbed the steps of Gaines's Friendship Baptist Church on Sunday morning, telling himself there was nothing wrong with attending two church services in one day. He'd done it before and, in all likelihood, he'd do it again. In his role as city councilman, he often had to attend service at Friendship *and* at his home church, Gaines United Methodist, to appeal to the townspeople on some issue or another.

You don't have an appeal to make today, he reminded himself.

Winston brushed aside the thought and pushed opened the church's massive oak door and entered the vestibule. Friendship was one of the oldest black churches in the state, founded in 1854, it had been an underground railroad stop, a reconstruction command control central, and a civil rights brainstorming site. Its congregation consisted of those Gaines residents who still felt church was a place to meet God and enjoy him. The loud clapping and shouts of Amen that Winston heard from the sanctuary confirmed it.

It also suggested the time was later than he'd thought. The services at Gaines U.M.E. lasted exactly one hour and by twelve-thirty the congregation was back home and dressed for the rest of the day's planned activities; Friendship was lucky if their prayer service was over by noon. He looked at his watch: eleven-fifty. Today was a lucky Sunday. Prayer service was over and the choir was up.

Winston peeked through the triangularly shaped glass in the swinging doors leading to the sanctuary. It was impossible to spot Marlena in the crowd that packed the church. With a hat adorning nearly every woman's head, he was fortunate to be able to see the pulpit.

The uniformed usher standing just inside the door saw him and pushed the door back so he could enter. He took the offered fan, courtesy of James Funeral Home, and the church bulletin and slid into the back pew next to the other latecomers. His baritone voice joined the choir in "Pass Me Not, O Gentle Savior."

When the song ended and the congregation sat down, Sister Morgan, a plump, pleasant-looking woman who was the church clerk, walked to the podium just in front, but to the left of the pulpit, and began reading the announcements. Winston quickly reached into his shirt pocket for a pen and jotted a short note on the back of his bulletin. He ripped the note off and motioned for the usher. When she leaned down to him, he slid the note into her white-gloved hand and whispered his instructions in her ear.

From her seat about midway in the church on the side facing the clerk, Marlena saw the usher hand the clerk what she assumed was a note. The action made her remember the days she'd served as a junior usher. She'd had to wear the same white dress, shoes, stockings, gloves, and hat. She wondered now as she had then why ushers dressed like nurses. Why couldn't they wear . . .

". . . special guest, but she's not really a guest, since she's a member of this church and has been since she was a little girl, Sister Marlena Rhodes," the clerk said, interrupting Marlena's thoughts. "Stand up for us, Sister Marlena."

Marlena didn't move until Cheryl poked her in the side with her elbow and whispered, "Go on. Stand up."

She stood and the clerk said, "Welcome home, Sister. We're glad to have you back. Do you want to say anything?"

Marlena wanted to shake her head, No, and sit back down, but the expectant look on Sister Morgan's face made her open her mouth. "It's good be back in my home church," she said. "I've missed Friendship."

She heard the murmurings of "We missed you, too" from the congregation and turned in a half-circle and smiled at the congregation. Her smile wavered just a tad when she glimpsed Winston in the back in his black suit, paisley tie, and white shirt. From a brief second, she wondered why he was here instead of at the Methodist Church where he and his family were members.

Marlena's attention was quickly drawn back to the clerk when the older woman said, "And I have a note here that says Sister Marlena will be working with Brother Winston on *The Way Home* project." The older woman smiled. "That's wonderful, Sister. Thank you for coming back to help us."

Pastor Reynolds rose from his seat in the pulpit and stood at the lectern. He beckoned to the back of the church. "Come on up here, Brother Winston," he said. "Everybody is not familiar with the program. Since *The Way Home* is your idea, you can explain it."

When Winston took Sister Morgan's place at the podium, he asked Marlena to join him. She wanted to decline, but again Cheryl nudged her forward. Winston took her hand when she reached him and pulled her closer. While he explained the project to the congregation, she thought of another time they'd stood together at this podium. It was the Sunday after her mother's funeral.

A chorus of Amen's told Marlena that Winston was finished, so she moved to go back to her seat. The pastor's voice stopped her.

"Why don't you two bless us with a song?" he asked. "It's been such a long time since you've ministered to us. And I do remember how the two of you could sing."

Again, the Amen's of the crowd pushed them onward.

"His Eye is On the Sparrow," Winston whispered and she nodded her head.

The same song they'd sung that Sunday, she thought.

Winston squeezed her hand in reassurance and she smiled up at him. He released her hand and took a seat at the piano.

Marlena didn't have time to worry about how her voice would sound. As Winston stroked the keys, the words to the song filled her mind and her heart and flowed out through her lips without any effort.

As she sang the last chorus, the congregation joined her. When she finished, there wasn't a dry eye in the church. Not even hers.

Winston waited for Marlena outside the church. He wanted to speak with her, but apparently so did everyone else.

"How you doing, Winston?" came Cheryl's sultry voice.

He turned and looked into the face of the smiling woman. The wide-brimmed blue hat she wore shadowed her face, but barely covered her hair, which hung in at least a hundred braids around her shoulders. "I'm good, Cheryl. How about you? I haven't seen you in a while."

She smiled the same open smile she'd worn since high school. "We're both pretty busy these days. *The Way Home* sounds *interesting. Very interesting.*"

There was something in the inflection of her voice when she'd said "interesting" that made him wonder what she meant. He was about to ask her when out of the corner of his eye, he saw Marlena coming toward them.

For the second time today, he drank in the picture she made in her black tam, black and white dress, and matching heels. How could she be more beautiful now than she'd been back then? And how, after all he'd suffered at her hands, could he be as drawn to her now as he'd been back then?

"Are you ready to go?" she asked Cheryl, after a mere nod to acknowledge his presence.

"In a minute," Cheryl said. She pointed toward the pastor.

"I need to speak to Pastor Reynolds first. I'll be back in a little bit."

Marlena turned to follow her, but Winston grabbed her hand. She looked first at his hand on hers, then at his face. He loosened his hold but he kept her hand in his.

"Do you worship here now?" she asked.

He shook his head, his eyes focused on her full, painted lips. She still wore the muted burgundy color that suited her so well. "I visit here occasionally," he answered. "But I'm still a member at Gaines United. Did you enjoy the service?"

She nodded and his eyes were drawn to her sexy neck. He still remembered how it felt to press his tongue against her smooth skin.

"It was wonderful," she said in answer to his question. "I didn't realize how much I missed the service, the singing, the excitement. There's nothing like it."

"No churches in D.C.?" he asked, not ready yet for their conversation to end.

"Churches, yes. Another Friendship, no. There's something special about this place. Gaines might have its problems, but Friendship isn't one of them. I've always felt loved and accepted here. Always."

He wondered if she meant she didn't feel accepted in D.C., but he didn't ask. "I know," he said. "You always said . . ." He stopped before he finished, then squeezed her hand.

"I know, Winston. I always said I wanted to get married here. As I said before, we don't always get what we want."

"And maybe we get what we want, realize we don't really want it, then drop it for something better."

He thought he saw disappointment and regret flicker in her eyes before she added, "And maybe there's no benefit in rehashing the past."

He dropped her hand, not sure why he'd been holding it in the first place. He didn't want Marlena back, he told himself, but he did want to understand why she'd walked out on him ten years ago. "Marlena," he began.

"Look," she said. "Cheryl's probably waiting for me. I'll see you tomorrow afternoon."

Winston watched her graceful movements as she walked over to where Cheryl stood with Pastor Reynolds. The pastor embraced her a final time and she and Cheryl headed for Cheryl's car.

He watched them until they were in the car and out of sight much as he'd watched her walk out of his life ten years ago. That day there'd been tears in his eyes and, as he remembered later, also in hers. He understood his tears, but what had she had to cry about? She'd been leaving him of her own choice.

Ten years later, her tears still haunted him. Why had she been crying? When his mind had been clear enough to remember anything other than the pain he'd felt, he'd been left with the memory of her tear-filled eyes. That vision stamped itself on his brain and wouldn't be erased.

He'd come up with a million reasons for her tears. Maybe she'd been crying because she felt guilty for the way she'd strung him along telling him she loved him and wanted to be his wife. Maybe she'd been crying because she felt sorry for him. Maybe she'd been crying because she was pregnant and didn't want him to know she was having an abortion. That last thought had caused him to wake up in a cold sweat on many a night.

They'd both decided they didn't want children until a few years after they were married and settled back in Gaines. Marlena had been adamant about no "seven-month" babies. She wasn't going to have people talking about her and her baby conceived outside the sanctity of marriage. He'd told her he could live with an accelerated timetable and even suggested they get married while still in school. Marlena had turned down the marriage idea, saying she wanted her degree first. She didn't want people to think he'd married beneath him, she'd said as if what people thought meant something to him. It didn't. All he'd wanted was her and her love.

He'd had both for a short time, at least. Then she had left and he'd had to learn to live without her. He'd tried but he wasn't certain how successful he'd been.

His marriage to Patty had been a disaster. He regretted marrying her, knowing he wasn't over his feelings for Marlena.

Not that he still loved Marlena—he couldn't after the way she'd treated him—but there was something unresolved with them. Almost as if they'd closed the book without reading the last chapter. That chapter and her tears had nagged at him over the years. Her tears most, because Marlena never cried.

Chapter 5

"Success means different things to different people," Marlena said, wrapping up her talk to the Gaines High auditorium of over three hundred students. "For me, success is not about money, or power. Success is about having dreams and having the courage to make those dreams come true. My wish for each one of you here today is that you would each have a dream, something you're passionate about, something you're willing to give your all for. Then I'd grant you the courage you need to take the steps necessary to make your dreams come true.

"And believe me, it *will* take courage. Courage to believe your dreams when *others* say they're impossible. Courage to believe your dreams when *you* begin to think they're impossible. Courage to hold onto your dreams when people or situations try to rip them from your arms. This morning I give you courage.

"Who am I to give you courage, you ask? Well," she continued, "I'm just a girl from the Gaines projects who dared to dream. I wasn't the smartest girl in my class or the prettiest or the nicest. But I had a dream that I could do more, go farther. I knew that my life could be more than it was. And the same is true for you. There's a big world out there beyond Gaines, a world where dreams come true. Don't be afraid to enter into it. Thank you.''

The applause started and Marlena stepped back from the podium. Principal Potter shook her hand and escorted her to her seat, then went back to the podium.

''Let's give another round of applause for Ms. Rhodes and her wonderful speech.'' The students joined the principal and the applause continued, making Marlena feel very uncomfortable. She didn't want the students to think she was something special. She wanted them to know that she was just like them. If she could achieve her dreams, so could they.

''Ms. Rhodes will be around to talk to the juniors and seniors in Mrs. Smith's English class for the rest of this morning and tomorrow afternoon,'' he continued. ''So have your questions ready. Now, you should all go to your second-period classes.''

As the students got up and began making their way back to class, Marlena stood and greeted a couple of her old teachers. Out of the corner of her eye, she saw Patrice and her boyfriend. When she turned fully in their direction, the young couple seemed to be in the middle of a spat. The young man said something then rushed out of the auditorium, leaving Patrice staring after him. Marlena said a few quick goodbyes, then headed for the teenager.

''Wait a minute, Patrice,'' she called to the girl who was about to leave the auditorium.

''Hi, Ms. Marlena,'' the young girl said, but there was no light in her eyes.

''Something wrong?''

The girl looked down at her shoes. ''Not really.''

Marlena tipped her chin up. ''Are you sure?''

''Oh, Ms. Marlena,'' the girl cried, dropping down in the end seat on the last row of the auditorium. She rested her face in her hands. ''It's Raymond. He's impossible.''

Marlena propped a hip against the arm of Patrice's chair and brushed her hand across the teen's soft, relaxed curls. ''What did he do, sweetheart? It can't be that bad.''

''Yes, it is,'' she corrected. ''You just don't know.''

"Then why don't you tell me?"

The girl finally lifted her head. "He wants me to go to church with him Sunday and then to his church picnic afterward."

Marlena didn't see what was so bad about the invitation and she said so.

"You don't understand. His parents hate me. They don't want me there."

Marlena's heart ached for the girl. "Have you told Raymond how you feel?"

The girl nodded slowly. "I told him, but he says we can't let them keep us apart. He says I should come because I love him and not stay away because I think they hate me. He doesn't understand."

Marlena continued to stroke the girl's head. She had no words of wisdom to give her.

"What do you think? Do you think I should go with him?"

Marlena stopped stroking the child's head. "It doesn't matter what I think. What do you think?"

"I don't know what to think. That's why I'm asking you. You're an adult. You're supposed to know this kind of stuff."

Marlena fought back a smile. "Are you in love with Raymond?"

"Of course, I love him. I love him so much it hurts."

"Then I think you know what you have to do."

Patrice slowly stood up. "I guess I do." She moved out into the aisle. "Thanks for listening."

Marlena fell in step with her. "Anytime."

When they reached the door and were about to go their separate ways, Marlena said, "Success in love is like success in anything else. You need courage to make your dreams come true. You can do it, Patrice. You and Raymond can do it."

Patrice smiled, looked over her shoulders quickly, then pulled Marlena in a quick embrace. "You're all right, you know?"

Marlena smiled, thinking the statement was the highest compliment the teenager could give her.

* * *

When Marlena arrived at the second-floor *The Way Home* office at two o'clock, the door was locked. "Damn," she muttered. "He could have waited."

She turned to leave. Just as she got to the door to the stairwell for the trek down, the door opened and out walked Winston.

"Hi," he said, smiling. He carried a grease-stained brown paper bag that smelled of barbeque sauce. "I went out for a bite to eat. I called the school, and they said you were still there so I thought I had time. You haven't been waiting long, have you?"

She shook her head. "I just got here."

"Well, come on then," he said, leading her back to the office. Once inside, he pointed her to the long folding table that spanned one side of the room. "Let's sit here. You don't mind if I eat while we talk, do you?"

She couldn't help it, she smiled. Winston looked like a kid today in his casual tan Dockers, brown leather loafers, white golf shirt, and trademark baseball cap. This one was tan. "You haven't changed a bit, have you, Winston?" she asked, reaching for his cap and pulling it off his head.

He grinned at her and the full effect of those bright thirty-twos almost made her heart stop. "Why mess with perfection?"

She slapped him on the arm with his cap. "Still as subtle as a sledgehammer."

He grunted, then pulled a gigantic sandwich out of the bag. She'd been right. It was barbeque. He took the sandwich in both his large hands and placed it to his lips. "Want some?" he asked. When she shook her head, he opened his mouth and bit off about a quarter of the sandwich in a single bite.

"When was the last time you ate?" she asked. "Last year?"

He licked away the barbeque sauce that had puddled at the corners of his mouth. "Can I help it if I have a big appetite? Anyway, I haven't gotten any complaints about the body recently."

She knew he wouldn't get any either. She didn't have to touch him to know he was rock-solid. In truth, she had yet to meet a man more attractive than him. It's those eyes, she said to herself. The small, sad, puppy-dog eyes were so at odds with his muscular, six-foot-plus frame that they drew you in every time. And then those ears. Any other man with ears that big would look like a rabbit, but not Winston. No, his big ears and his wide, almost flat nose, only made him look more virile, more in control.

"You don't have any complaints, do you?" he asked, stirring her out of her musings.

"Huh?"

He grinned. "The body. You've been checking it out. You don't have any complaints, do you?"

She wanted to tell him he was mistaken, that she hadn't been staring at him, but the gleam in his eyes told her he wouldn't believe her. "Not bad for a thirty-five-year-old, but I've seen better."

He frowned at her. "I bet you have," he said, then took another bite out of his sandwich. "Why didn't you get married?"

Because I haven't loved anyone since you. "The time never seemed right. My career took off so quickly that I didn't have time for much else."

He pushed the last of the sandwich in his mouth. "Then I guess you weren't lying." He rubbed the crumbs from his hands onto the brown paper bag, then balled up the bag and the sandwich wrappings.

"Lying about what?"

"When you told me your career wouldn't allow time for marriage. You didn't want to be tied down, you said."

She averted her eyes. That had been the biggest lie she'd ever told. More than anything she'd wanted to be tied down to Winston. "Why would you even think I was lying?"

He shrugged as if it no longer mattered. "Maybe there was another guy and you didn't want to tell me." He cleared his throat. "Okay, why don't we get down to business."

She wanted to tell him now as she'd told him then that there hadn't been anyone else. She'd loved only him. "I'm ready."

He walked to the metal desk in the center of the room and picked up a manila folder. When he sat back down at the table, he opened the folder and handed her the sheet on top. "Our first candidate."

She looked at the picture of Martin "Marty" Jones and immediately wondered how Cheryl would react to the news of her old boyfriend's return to town. "Why Marty?"

"He's a chemical engineer in plastics and the plastics factory in Chatham County is looking for a director of engineering. Marty's interested in the job, and they're interested in him. It's a perfect match."

She continued to look at Marty's photograph. "So you think they'll offer him the job, and he'll take it."

He nodded. "I'd bank on it. What's wrong? You have something against Marty?"

"Oh, no," she said. "I always liked Marty. He was a lot of fun back in high school." Marlena remembered the double-dating the two couples had done.

"Yeah, he was. I always thought he and Cheryl would get married, but I guess things happen."

She didn't have to look at him to know he was referring to the two of them as much as he was referring to Cheryl and Marty. "Why hasn't he come back to Gaines before now? Did he just go off to school and forget everybody?"

Winston lifted a brow at her. "Don't make him sound so cold. You did the same thing, remember?"

"Well, my case was different," she began.

Winston shook his head. "Not really. I think Marty never came back because Cheryl got pregnant and married so quickly after he left. He probably couldn't imagine living so close to her, her new husband, and their new baby. He loved Cheryl almost as much as I loved you."

Marlena placed the photo back on the table. Her heart felt as if someone had taken hold of it and squeezed. "Don't do this, Winston," she whispered.

"Do what?" he asked. "I did love you. Then I lost you but I got over it. Maybe Marty wasn't so lucky."

"You sure didn't waste much time getting married either," she commented.

He shrugged his broad shoulders. "What was the point? I

loved Patty and I married her. I always knew what I wanted. You were the one who was unsure."

She focused her eyes on Marty's resume. "I guess you always loved Patty," she murmured. Her heart stopped beating while she waited for his answer. When he didn't say anything, she looked up at him.

"Not always," he said when her gaze met his. "Definitely not always."

"When is he getting here?" Cheryl asked later that night as she cleaned off her kitchen counter, her back to Marlena. Marlena had offered to help but Cheryl wouldn't hear of it.

Marlena sighed. She'd thought telling Cheryl about Marty was the right thing to do. Now she wasn't so sure. "I'm not even sure he's coming. They have to make him a job offer and he has to take it."

Cheryl folded her dish cloth and placed it on the edge of the sink. Then she turned around and leaned against the counter. "But Winston thinks he's going to take it."

"He says Marty wants to come back home. He thinks Marty stayed away because you married somebody else. He also thinks Marty may still be in love with you."

"This can't be happening. Not now."

"I don't know why you're so upset. You and Marty were very much in love at one time. Maybe you can find that love again. Would that be so bad?"

"You don't understand," Cheryl said, turning around so Marlena could no longer see her face.

Marlena walked up behind her. "What don't I understand? What is it you're not telling me?"

Cheryl began to laugh, a cackling sound that hurt Marlena's ears.

Marlena put her hand on Cheryl's shoulder and turned her around. The tears in her friend's eyes stung her heart. "Tell me, Cheryl. What's wrong?"

"He's Patrice's father," Cheryl choked out.

Patrice's father, Marlena mouthed. "How can that be? Nathaniel is Patrice's father."

Cheryl glared at Marlena. "You're not stupid, girl. You know how it is."

"What are you saying, Cheryl?" Marlena asked, not liking the direction her mind was taking. "Tell me Marty is not Patrice's father."

"Oh, but he is," Cheryl said. She covered her face with her hands. "What am I going to do? Patrice doesn't know about him and he doesn't know about her."

Marlena's own secret tugged at her conscience. "I don't understand, Cheryl. Why didn't you tell Marty you were pregnant? Why did you marry Nathaniel?"

Cheryl pulled out one of her vinyl dinette chairs and sat down. "If Marty had known I was pregnant, he would've felt responsible. You know him. He would've done the right thing and married me."

"What's so wrong with that?"

Cheryl shook her head from side to side and misery filled her eyes. "I loved him, Marlena. God knows, I loved him. And I couldn't do that to him. He was the first one in his family to go to college. I couldn't let him give that up. He would've come to hate me. He might have even thought I'd gotten pregnant on purpose to keep him here."

"Oh, Cheryl," Marlena cried, reaching down to squeeze her friend's hand. "That wasn't your decision to make. You should have told him. You shouldn't have married Nathaniel and pretended Patrice was his." A sudden thought occurred to Marlena and she asked, "Is that why you and Nathaniel got divorced? Because he found out Patrice wasn't his?"

Cheryl wiped her hands down her face. "Nathaniel knew I was pregnant when he married me. He said it didn't matter."

"But he changed his mind after Patrice was born?"

Cheryl shook her head slowly. "I wish it had been that simple," she said as if she were talking to herself. "He left because he thought I was still in love with Marty."

"Was he right?"

Cheryl stood up and pushed her hands into the pockets of her loose-fitting jeans. "You know how it is with first loves, Marlena. I couldn't stop loving Marty. Not when I was carrying his baby and certainly not after she was born. Patrice might not look like Marty, but she has a lot of his ways."

Marlena wished there was something she could say or do to help her friend, but there wasn't. The time to pay the piper was nearing and Cheryl would have to pay up. "So what are you going to do?"

"I don't know. I don't know."

"You've got to tell Patrice he's her father," Marlena said softly, knowing her friend didn't want to hear the words but knowing they needed to be spoken.

"How can I tell her that I've been lying to her all her life? How can I tell her that the man she thinks is her father, isn't? How can I tell her that her father doesn't even know she's alive? She's going to hate me. They're both going to hate me."

Marlena leaned down and put her arms around Cheryl's shoulders. "You have to tell both of them. You don't have a choice."

Cheryl leaned back out of her friend's embrace. "Why do I have to tell them? Marty doesn't know. Why does he have to know?"

"You can't be serious, Cheryl. He's going to find out she's his daughter."

"How? Patrice doesn't look like him or any of his relatives. If she did, his relatives would have noticed and said something by now, but they haven't. They don't even speak to me. They still think I was two-timing Marty with Nathaniel. After all these years, they haven't forgiven me."

"It's wrong, Cheryl."

"But it's my decision and I choose not to tell them. And you can't tell them either."

Marlena bit her lip to keep from speaking. It *was* Cheryl's decision. And if she chose to make the wrong one, what could Marlena do?

"You're not going to tell me again how wrong I am?" Cheryl asked.

Marlena pushed out a long breath. "I want to, but I won't. You're right. It's your decision. I just hope you don't live to regret it."

Chapter 6

Winston rushed upstairs to *The Way Home* office, hoping he hadn't kept Marlena waiting *again*. A call from the courthouse had taken him away from their meeting yesterday before he could tell her about the party on Friday night.

When Winston opened the second-floor door, he saw Billy sitting on the floor outside the office. He didn't have to ask why the boy was there.

"Billy," he said and the boy looked up. The pain in his eyes made Winston hurt.

Billy stood up and looked in Winston's direction, but quickly lowered his eyes.

"Tim back in town?" Winston asked.

The boy nodded and stepped back so Winston could open the door. Once they were in the office, Winston dropped his briefcase on his desk and perched on its edge and waited.

Billy paced in front of him for at least five minutes without talking. Finally, he stopped pacing and asked, "Why does she do it? Why does she let him use her? It doesn't make sense."

Winston thought nineteen-year-old Billy sounded more like a nine-year-old as he asked the question. "We all do things that don't make a lot of sense, Billy. Don't be so hard on your mother. She's human and that means fallible. The important thing is that she loves you. You know that, don't you?''

Billy meet his gaze and Winston saw the tears in his eyes. The young man wiped at the tears with the back of his hand, then resumed his pacing. ''Yeah, I know she loves me, but . . .'' He stopped pacing and looked at Winston.

''But what?'' Winston probed. ''But you're angry with her?''

The boy resumed pacing. ''She's acting so stupid, Coach. She has to know he doesn't give a damn about her.''

Winston had often wondered about the relationship between Billy's mother and father but he'd given up trying to understand it. Though he agreed with Billy that Allison was doing herself a great disservice by putting up with Tim's garbage, there was nothing he could do since they were both adults. ''And you're angry with her?''

Billy stopped again. ''Hell, yes, I'm angry with her. She's acting like a . . . and she's so much better than that, Coach. She's pretty, she's fun, she's a great mother. She can do so much better than him. Why can't she see that?''

''Did you tell her again how it makes you feel when Tim drops in for a few days?''

Billy nodded. ''I told her and she said what she always says. That she loves him. That I'll understand one day when I love somebody. Well, I'm never gonna love anybody. Not like that. Not me.''

Big, tough words from a boy forced to grow up too fast. ''That's not the answer, Billy. Just because other people end up in bad relationships doesn't mean that you will.''

Billy stared at Coach as if daring him to name one stable relationship. Winston declined the challenge.

''How long is Tim going to be in town?'' Winston asked.

''Too long.'' At Winston's cocked brow, Billy added, ''A few days.''

Winston reached into his pants pocket and pulled out his key ring. He took off a key and handed it to Billy. ''You know the drill,'' he said.

Billy took the key. ''Thanks, Coach. It'll only be for a few days. He never stays any longer.''

"No problem, Billy. Did you tell your mother where you were going to be?

He nodded again. "I don't know why though. By now she should know."

Winston nodded. Since he had helped Billy through that trouble with the guns a couple of years back, the young man had fallen into the habit of staying with Winston on the nights his father was in town.

"Do you have to work tonight?" he asked Billy.

"Nah, you know Tuesdays are my off days."

"Okay, I should be home at a decent hour. Why don't we plan to eat dinner together. I'll cook."

Billy grabbed his throat and gagged. "Not that."

Winston smiled, glad some of the boy's anxiety had faded. "I'll see you tonight then."

"Thanks again, Coach. I owe you for this."

"Forget it and get out of here. Don't you have classes today?" Billy was enrolled in a nearby junior college and planned to attend the University of Georgia next year. He'd come a long way since his days of trouble.

"My first one's not until ten, but I'd better get moving." He extended his hand and Winston shook it. "Thanks, Coach."

Winston clapped Billy on the back and walked him to the door. "Don't forget dinner," he said as the boy took lanky steps down the hall.

Winston walked back into his office and sat down at his desk. How could Allison and Tim keep doing this to Billy? Couldn't they put the boy's needs above their own? From their actions, he guessed the answer was no.

At times like this Winston missed his father most. He would love to be able to go to him now and talk to him about Billy. His father had a knack for saying the right thing at just the right time. Winston hadn't met a man yet who was his equal— in integrity, love, or wisdom.

"Knock, knock."

The softly spoken words interrupted his thoughts and he raised his head to see Marlena standing in his office doorway.

"I hope I'm not too early," she said, almost shy in her manner.

Winston stood and walked around his desk, his eyes absorbing the picture she made in the gray dress and tailored black jacket. "No, you're not too early," he said, pointing to the couch. "Why don't you sit down? I would offer you some coffee, but I didn't get around to making it yet."

"That's all right," she said with a smile. "I had breakfast at the hotel." She paused. "Wasn't that Billy from the hotel I saw leaving as I was coming in?"

"Yes, he came to see me."

"Cheryl told me he was Allison and Tim's son. I didn't see the resemblance at first, but after she mentioned it I realized he looks exactly like Tim. He must be driving all the young girls crazy."

"You could say that," Winston said evasively.

"Is something the matter, Winston?" Marlena asked. "You seem a bit distracted this morning. If now's not good for you I can come back tomorrow."

He stared into her soft, brown eyes for a moment. "That won't be necessary. If I'm distracted, it's because I'm concerned about Billy. It's no secret he's having a hard time dealing with his parents' relationship. Sometimes it gets to me, that's all."

"Oh . . ." was all Marlena could think to say.

"You'd think parents would care more for their kids' feelings, wouldn't you?"

Marlena gave a self-deprecating smile. "You must have forgotten who you're talking to, Winston. My mother was Josie Rhodes, the *notorious* Josie Rhodes."

"Did it bother you that much, Marlena?"

She nodded.

"Why didn't you ever want to talk about it? I would have listened." When she didn't respond, Winston sighed deeply, then said, "I'm sorry. I shouldn't have brought it up."

"No, it's all right. Maybe you're right. Maybe I should have talked about it more."

Sensing the moment of intimacy had passed, Winston said,

"Thanks for coming by this morning. I'm sorry we were interrupted yesterday, but I had to get to the courthouse."

"Don't apologize. I'm an attorney. I know how things happen."

"I'm still sorry. I appreciate what you're doing for us and I don't want you to think I'm taking you for granted."

"Forget it, Winston. I want to do this." At his raised brow, she added, "I do. Cheryl and I went to Dusttown this past weekend so I see the need. It's amazing how much things change yet they're still very much the same."

Winston wiped his hands down his face. "If you focus on what *is*, you can become mighty depressed, but if you look at what could be, you get excited." He gave her a sheepish smile. "At least, I do."

"Don't you feel overwhelmed, Winston? *The Way Home* is just the beginning. It's going to take more than getting people to relocate here. It's going to take a change in the entire social structure of Gaines. I'm still not sure the town is ready."

The interest Marlena had taken in *The Way Home* pleased Winston. That she so quickly read the situation impressed and excited him. "It's doesn't matter if they're ready or not, Marlena, the time has come for people, and especially black people, to realize that we're all in this together: from the poorest person in Dusttown to the most respected person in Rosemont. If we don't pull together, we sink individually and I mean that literally. If this town dies, we all lose."

"So how do you intend to get people to work together?" Marlena asked.

Winston grinned. "Think about it. I know you aren't impressed with the way the Rosemont community has catered to you, but their reaction to you marks a major turning point for this town. You're part of the bridge that will bring the communities together. You're as comfortable in Dusttown and in South Gaines where Cheryl lives as you are in Rosemont. As people are faced with the reality of your accomplishments and the accomplishments of others like you, the myth that they're the privileged class by right of birth will crumble right before their eyes. It'll take time and it'll take more than one example, but it will happen. That's why *The Way Home* is so important.''

"So one of the goals of *The Way Home* is to show this town that success is not limited to the people of Rosemont, that success is not about where you're from but about where you want to go?''

"Exactly. It's starting with you and it's going to continue as we bring back more graduates. As I started telling you yesterday, Marty Jones is going to be our first candidate. We'll need to get a second one lined up fairly quickly. That's where I'm going to need your help.'' He got up and rifled through some files on his desk. "I've got a folder here somewhere with the paperwork on about eight other candidates. I'd like for you to go through them with me and make sure the work assignments are matched to the most appropriate candidates. After that's done, we can divide the candidates between us and start making phone calls. How does that sound?''

"As I said before, it sounds pretty easy and I want to help. Are you sure you don't also have some lawyerly work for me to do?''

He smiled because she did. "Well,'' he began. "Now that you mention it . . . I've been planning to draw up a boilerplate employment contract. If people are going to leave promising positions to come back here, I want them to have some guarantees and a safety net.''

"The good old pink parachute.''

"You got it. Would you mind drawing up something we can use?''

"No problem. I just need to make a phone call to my office.''

"Great! I appreciate your help on this, Marlena. As I told you, the Council was pretty adamant about having you involved in this.''

"I don't mind, Winston. It's the least I can do. Gaines is . . . ah . . . was my home, too.''

"Have you thought anymore about the other part of my request?''

She smiled. "I don't think a few cocktail parties will kill me. I guess I can do that, too.''

Winston didn't realize he'd been holding his breath until he released it. "You won't regret this, I promise. Are you free Friday night?"

Marlena laughed, a full, throaty sound that touched the chords of his heart. "You don't waste any time, do you?"

Winston dropped his head a little. "To be honest, I knew about this party Saturday night, but I was too scared to ask you about it."

"I don't believe you, Winston. I've never known you to be scared of anything."

"You just have selective memory. I'm been scared before. Sometimes with reason."

A tense silence followed his words and he knew she knew he was referring to their past breakup.

"If that's it?" Marlena said, ending the silence.

Winston stood when she did. "That's it. Along with my thanks."

She extended her hand and he folded it in his own. "I guess we're in business."

"I guess we are."

Two days later, Marlena rubbed her neck to relieve the tension brought on by reading through the candidate folders Winston had prepared.

"Tired?" Winston asked.

"Very. I didn't think this would be such hard work."

Winston looked at his watch. "We can knock off now. You probably want to rest up before going out this evening."

She didn't bother telling him that going out was having dinner with Cheryl. "Sounds good to me."

"Why—" A knock at the door interrupted Winston. "Come in," he called. "It's open."

Marlena recognized Patrice's boyfriend immediately.

"I'm sorry," the young man said. "I didn't know you were busy, Coach."

Winston waved the boy in. "We were finishing up. What can I do for you?"

The boy glanced at Marlena, then hesitated.

"I guess I'll leave you two alone," she said, concluding the boy wanted to speak privately with Winston. She picked up her purse from the table.

"You don't have to, Ms. Marlena. I'd like it if you stayed. Patrice likes you and maybe you could help us out."

"What's the problem?" Winston asked, concern causing his brow to wrinkle.

The boy slouched down in the chair Marlena had vacated. "Patrice is acting all crazy. She says she won't go to the church picnic with me because my folks hate her." He sighed. "They don't hate her. They just don't know her the way I do."

Winston looked over the boy's head at Marlena. She knew he recognized how much this young couple was like them at their age. "How can we help, Raymond?" he asked.

The boy leaned forward in his chair. "I was thinking that if you went to the picnic with us, she wouldn't be so scared. She'd know at least one person there liked her."

"Sure, I'll do that. I was going to the picnic anyway."

"And you'll sit with us and make her feel comfortable?"

Winston clapped the boy on his shoulders. "Of course. Patrice'll be the best-looking girl there. She'll need a chaperon."

Raymond groaned. "Don't even mention chaperon. I told her she should bring her mother and you'd have thought I said the house was on fire. Let's make this more like a double date than you being our chaperon." He glanced at Marlena, then quickly back to Winston. "I was thinking that since you aren't bringing anybody, you could bring Ms. Marlena. Patrice likes her and so does everybody else in town. With the two of you with us, Patrice is sure to be relaxed and that'll make her feel more welcome."

Winston and Raymond looked at Marlena. "Will you go with us?" the boy asked. "It would mean a lot to Patrice."

Marlena was torn between wanting to help Patrice and refusing to be Winston's unwanted date. They were already going to that cocktail party on Friday night. Two nights out in the same week could be one night too many. "Maybe Winston already has a date," she offered, thinking of Yolanda.

Winston opened his mouth to speak, but the boy beat him to it. Raymond pointed at Winston. "He's not seeing anybody special right now, so he wasn't planning on bringing a date. Isn't that right, Coach?"

Winston cleared his throat. "That's right, but you didn't have to put it that way. Ladies don't consider it an honor to go out with men that no one else wants."

"Oh," he said to Winston, then turned to Marlena. "A lot of women in Gaines want to go out with him. He's the most eligible bachelor around. How about it, will you go with us?"

"Maybe she already has a date for the picnic," Winston said.

"You don't, do you?" the boy asked.

Raymond's concern for Patrice, and Winston's obvious care and concern for Raymond brought a smile to Marlena's face. She wondered if he and the sons they'd planned to have would have been as close. "No, I don't and I'd love to go with you, Patrice and Winston."

"Great," the boy said, grinning. He seemed relaxed for the first time since he'd come in the office. "Just wait till I tell Patrice." He got up and practically ran to the door. "Thanks again," he said. "We're going to have a great time. I just know it." He closed the door and they heard his footsteps as he ran down the hall.

"How can his parents hate Patrice?" she asked, not really expecting an answer. "She's a wonderful girl, bright, pretty, kind. How can people be so shallow and so mean?"

"They don't hate her, Marlena. They think the two of them are too young to be so serious about each other."

She lifted a skeptical brow. "And it has nothing to do with the fact that Patrice's mother grew up in the projects and works in a factory, while Raymond's parents are second-generation physicians?"

Winston exhaled a deep breath. "That's part of it, but I'm sure they'll come around once they realize how serious the two of them are."

Marlena could only stare at him. "The way your mother

did with me? Come off it, Winston. Reality rarely changes bigotry.''

"Mother never hated you, Marlena. She didn't understand you. She would have loved you, if you'd given her a chance.''

Marlena knew Mrs. Taylor would never have accepted her. The woman would have done everything in her power to make Winston regret marrying her. "Look," she said, grabbing her purse again. "I'll see you tomorrow. I have to be at the school in the afternoon. Is it all right if I come by in the morning?''

"That's fine." He opened the desk drawer, removed a key and handed it to her. "Take this so you can get in if I'm not here.''

She dropped the key in her purse. "Thanks.''

"No," he said. "Thank you. I really appreciate what you're doing for *The Way Home and* for Patrice and Raymond.''

She shrugged. "It's the least I can do. Gaines was good to me in a lot of ways and I don't want to see it die. And as for Patrice and Raymond, well, maybe they'll be the ones who make it. You and I didn't. Marty and Cheryl didn't. Somebody has to prove that falling in love in Gaines doesn't automatically mean the relationship is doomed to failure.''

At six o'clock Friday night, Marlena sat, legs crossed, in the hotel lobby waiting for Winston to pick her up for the cocktail party. She told herself over and over that this wasn't a date. She and Winston were just two people driving together to an event to which they were both invited. It wasn't a date.

Then why did it feel like a date? Because the memories of every date she'd had with Winston filled her mind or because this *was* a date? She'd spent too much time getting dressed and she was too anxious about his response to the outfit she'd finally chosen. "Get a grip on yourself, girl," she told herself. "This is not a date.''

"Marlena, are you talking to yourself?" the deep voice sounded sweet to her ears.

She looked up and was greeted with a most handsome Winston decked out in a navy suit and what she guessed was his standard paisley tie. Hoping he hadn't heard what she'd said, she slid off the couch and stood up. "Just thinking out loud," she said with practiced ease.

He grinned. "Uh-huh. Are you ready to go?"

She wanted to make his grin disappear, but she settled for tossing him another fake smile. "As ready as I'm going to get."

"Okay, let's go then." He stepped back and let her out of the door before him, then directed her to his tan Lexus.

"Nice car," she said as she slid in and he held the door for her.

"It'll do," was his only comment.

"This is not a date," Winston murmured as he walked around to the driver's side. "This is not a date."

"What did you say?" Marlena asked as he slid behind the steering wheel.

"Oh, nothing." He hoped she hadn't heard what he was saying. "Just talking to myself. Do you want to hear some music?" He slipped in a Babyface CD without waiting for her response.

Winston took Main Street to the Lincoln Street turnoff for Athens Highway. Babyface's crooning was the only sound in the car.

"Feels funny, doesn't it?" Winston said after about six miles of silence and two tunes on the CD.

"I think familiar is a better word."

He sighed. "I don't think I was ever this nervous when we were dating. Except for that first date."

She smiled. "I never knew you were nervous. You always appeared so cool and in command. A very attractive trait."

He cut her a quick glance. "I was a good actor. The first time we went out I held the steering wheel with both of my hands so you wouldn't see them shake."

She started to laugh but her eyes went to his hands both of which were now on the steering wheel and she remembered the nights he hadn't used both hands to drive. Her laughter died in her throat. "My trick was to keep my hands primly folded on my lap."

He glanced her way again. "And if I remember correctly, you hugged the door all night." He chuckled. "I remember being afraid you were going to fall out of the car. You almost had me thinking you were afraid of me."

"Almost?" she asked, scooting away from the door just a tad. She didn't want him thinking he still made her nervous, especially since this wasn't even a date.

"Almost. Even back then, I was smart enough to know Marlena Rhodes didn't do anything she didn't want to do. If you had been afraid of me, you wouldn't have gone out with me."

"You think you knew me, huh?"

"Sure, I'd been watching you for a long time before I got the nerve to ask you out. I saw all the brothers you shot down and I had to build up my courage just in case you shot me down too."

Marlena had turned down lots of dates because she hadn't been free to trust the motives of most of the guys who asked her out. In the back of her mind, she always thought that her mother's reputation would make guys expect more from her than she was willing to give. "So why'd you ask me out?"

He shrugged his shoulders. "Attorney reasoning at work. If you turned me down, I could join the other guys in your reject pool, and if you said okay, I'd be one happy guy. At the time, I thought those were pretty good odds."

Winston still remembered the hammering in his chest the afternoon he'd asked her to go to the movies with him. When she'd said yes, he'd had to go to the bathroom so he could go high-five himself.

"That was a long time ago," she said, bringing his thoughts back to the present. "So tell me again about this event we're going to tonight."

Winston recognized her change of topic and decided to go along with it. A trip down memory lane served no purpose for either of them. "McCurdy and Lewis, one of the most established law firms in the southeast, has invited their more influential clients, some area corporate decision makers, and a few local politicians to meet you and talk about their participation in *The Way Home.*"

"You don't need me for that."

"Oh, yes, I do. McCurdy and Lewis would like to add your name to their door." He cut a glance at her. "You didn't hear it from me, but the word is they've been talking McCurdy, Rhodes and Lewis."

"You're kidding!"

He shook his head. "I told you. You're hot stuff around here and probably around a lot of other towns. Of course, McCurdy and Lewis don't really think they can get you, but they feel a strong need to try. That attorney reasoning at work again. They have a whole lot to gain and nothing to lose."

"You owe me, Winston," she said looking at his handsome profile. "My visit to Gaines was supposed to be a vacation. Parties where I'm on display are not my idea of a vacation."

"You must be used to it, especially since that L.A. trial."

She didn't think she'd ever be comfortable in the spotlight. She endured it because it was part of her job. "I'm used to it, but that doesn't mean I enjoy it. I was lucky to get the L.A. case and the publicity was invaluable, but I can live without the constant pandering of people who don't even know me. It's not very attractive."

"That's the price of fame," he said in a jocular vein. When she didn't laugh or even smile, he added, "I know this isn't how you planned to spend your vacation, but I'm glad for your help. I promise we won't stay long, but this could be an important night for *The Way Home.* A few of the company reps that'll be there tonight are leaning toward supporting the project. Tonight could push them over to our side."

Marlena heard the passion in Winston's voice as he spoke and she gained some insight into how personal *The Way Home* was for him. "I'll be on my best behavior," she said with her sugary public smile. "Those company reps won't know what hit them."

Chapter 7

"Great, Mr. Tompkins," Winston said, giving the president of Mainstream Dynamics, the largest producer of aeronautics products in the Southeast, a firm handshake. "I'll call you next week. You won't regret working with *The Way Home*."

"I don't expect I will, Mr. Taylor," the older gentlemen said. "Be sure to give my office a call." Winston watched as the man walked over to rejoin the circle around Marlena. She'd been surrounded by admirers all evening and more than once her throaty laughter had distracted him from a conversation he was having. He could say one thing for his ex-fiancée: she knew how to work a room.

He studied her from a distance and quickly noticed the slight droop in her almost-perfect smile. His lethal weapon was tired and he couldn't blame her. He moved over and joined her circle himself.

"The biggest case I had was the Rawlins murder trial more than ten years ago," George Madison of Madison Diversified Products, the country's third largest manufacturer of sports equipment, was saying.

Winston maneuvered until he was right next to Marlena. He was about to touch her elbow to alert her to his presence when she turned her head slightly and acknowledged him. Her eyes said it was time to go.

"Well, gentlemen," Winston said when Madison stopped to take a breath. "I promised Ms. Rhodes I'd have her back in Gaines early tonight. She has another engagement tomorrow morning."

The men clucked their regrets while at the same time expressing their pleasure at meeting her. More than one slipped her a business card and reminded her to keep in touch.

"Whew," Marlena said a few minutes later when they were back in Winston's car.

"Tired?"

"A little. I hope you don't mind if I take off my shoes. My feet are tired."

He grinned. "I don't know why you wear those high heels anyway."

She eased her feet out of her shoes and rotated each foot. "Ahh, that feels good."

"You and your three-inch heels."

"If you were as short as I am, I have no doubt you'd wear lifts to give yourself some height."

"Power shoes, huh?"

"You've got it," she said. "You're at a distinct disadvantage when you have to stare at a man's navel."

Winston chuckled. "You're not that short."

"Well, you know what I mean. I come across a lot of men who are almost Neanderthal in their thinking, and I need every advantage I can get."

In typical masculine fashion, Winston perused the firm arms and smooth skin exposed by the burgundy trapeze dress she wore. He decided not to tell her that those three-inch heels coupled with that dress inspired many thoughts—none of them professional.

She eyed him and he turned his glance away. "I know what you're thinking, Winston, but it's the world I work in. I can't control what men think and I'm not going to be responsible for their thoughts."

"I didn't say anything."

"But I know what you were thinking," she said again. "We both know that those important business men tonight thought as much about how I looked as about what I said. I don't even want to guess which they thought about more. It doesn't matter. What matters is *The Way Home*. How many converts did we get?"

"Seven."

"Is that good or bad?"

"Great. I was only expecting about four. They were all very impressed with you—with how you looked *and* with what you had to say. You've proven yourself as an attorney and they appreciated you as a woman. In other words, you had them eating out of the palm of your hand."

Her throaty laughter rang out. "Now you're exaggerating. But I knew it went well. I could feel the energy in the room. Do you know what I mean?"

He nodded. He knew exactly what she meant; he'd felt it too. She brought an excitement to the evening and the guests associated that excitement with *The Way Home*. He felt pride in their response to her as if her success was his. Residual feelings from their past relationship, he told himself. Nothing to worry about.

Sunday afternoon, Marlena found herself in Winston's company again. They weren't dating but they were certainly spending a lot of time together.

"Ms. Rhodes, Winston," Marlena looked up at the Ivy-league looking couple standing before her.

"Hi Gerald, Helen," Winston said. "Have you met Marlena?"

"No," Gerald said, "but we'd like to. We're Gerald and Helen Hill," he said to Marlena. "We've been out of town for the past week and we wanted to introduce ourselves. Though we've only been in Gaines a few years, we've come to think of it as home, so we wanted to welcome you back."

Marlena stood up and shook their hands. "It's nice to meet you. I've met your son, Raymond. You have a wonderful boy."

The man's chest puffed with pride at her words and the woman's smile widened. She knew these were people who cared deeply for their son. "He's a good son," Helen said.

"He and Patrice invited me to this picnic," Marlena added for good measure and was surprised by the obvious droop in Helen's smile and the deflation of Gerald's chest. There reactions made their feelings about Patrice and Raymond's relationship pretty clear.

"You know Patrice?" Helen asked.

"Oh, yes," Marlena said. "Patrice's mother and I are old friends. We grew up together."

"Well, isn't that something, dear," Gerald said. "It's such a small world."

"It sure is," Marlena agreed.

"Well, we'd better get back to our friends," Helen said. "It was nice meeting you."

Marlena sat back down on the blanket and Winston shook Gerald's hand.

"What was that all about?" Winston asked when the couple was out of earshot.

"You know what it was about. Those people have some nerve."

"Don't let them get to you, Marlena."

"I'm not thinking about myself. What about Raymond and Patrice?"

Marlena scanned the picnic area and found the young couple walking hand-in-hand across the grassy lane on the far side of the picnic area. To look at the young people, you'd think they didn't have a care in the world, that their only concern was how to love each other, but Marlena knew better. She knew the turmoil both children were in because of their parents' reaction to their love. She knew because she'd been there.

She'd do about anything to spare the teens the pain she was beginning to believe was going to find them. When news of Patrice's parentage became common knowledge, Raymond's parents would have a fit and they'd hold the information against the innocent girl. Marlena didn't understand the workings of an adult mind that could blame a child for the mistakes of her parents, but she knew that was exactly the kind of mind people like Raymond's parents had.

"Do you remember when we were that much in love?" Winston's smooth voice interrupted her thoughts.

She looked up at him and shook her head. "If they only knew what they were in for."

He dropped down on the blanket next to her. "It wasn't all bad, Marlena. If I had to do it over, I'd still fall in love with you. Everyone should experience that kind of love at least once."

She didn't know what to say. Why was Winston making this confession? "I'm not so sure, Winston. Love hurts."

He tilted her chin up. "Do you regret what we shared?"

She studied his soft, brown eyes. How could she regret loving this dear, dear man? She shook her head. "No," she whispered.

His hand caressed her chin, then her cheek. She thought he was going to kiss her and she had no idea how she should respond. He dropped his hand from her face before she had to decide. "Are you enjoying yourself?" he asked.

She shrugged. She really couldn't relax around these people. As with the party on Friday night, she felt as if she were on display. "About as much as I expected I would."

He leaned back on his elbow and plucked a blade of grass from the ground. "I don't understand you, Marlena."

"What's to understand?"

He trailed the blade of grass up her bare arm and shivers of desire shot through her body. "I don't understand why you let them get to you. Why does it even matter what they think?"

"It doesn't matter," she lied. She knew it shouldn't matter, but it did. It always had.

"When you walked out on me, it hurt. A lot. I hated you for a long time. A part of me still feels some of that hate, but there's also a part of me that understands why you felt you had to go. You needed to make a name for yourself and prove something to these people, and even to yourself."

He was right, she thought, but he only knew part of it. Her need to prove something to these people would never have forced her to walk away from him. Not by itself.

"But," he continued, "you give them too much power over how you feel. They're only people," he said. "And some of them aren't very nice people. They don't deserve the power you give them."

She lifted a brow at him. "Even your mother?"

He dropped the blade of grass. "Especially my mother. You didn't have to prove anything to her."

"She would have made our lives hell, Winston."

He shook his head so vehemently that she knew he believed he was right. "My mother's a very practical woman. She knew how much I loved you and she would have accepted you because you were my wife. Anyway, Dad accepted you. Mother wouldn't have crossed him."

"I'm sorry about your father, Winston," she said, remembering the sweet man who'd always had a smile for her. She'd chastised herself many times for not confronting him with his wife's venomous words. "I wanted to come back for the funeral, but I didn't think it was appropriate."

"I looked for you. Dad liked you a lot. He told me all the time how lucky I was to find you. He was pretty hurt by our breakup."

Marlena looked across the field and found Raymond and Patrice again. She couldn't look at Winston for fear he'd see the questions in her eyes. She wished again that she'd told Mr. Taylor what she'd learned. Maybe he could have helped her understand. "My absence wasn't part of a plan to hurt anybody, Winston. Not you. Not your dad."

"I miss him, you know. He was more than my dad. He was my friend. We shared everything."

Almost everything, Marlena corrected in her mind. "The perfect father," she murmured.

Winston laughed. "No, he wasn't perfect. No one is. But he was a good man, a good father, and he loved me. That was enough."

Marlena stood up, not wanting to continue this conversation. "I think I'll go say Hi to Mrs. Hampton. I haven't spoken to her all afternoon."

As Marlena walked away, she felt Winston's eyes on her.

He'd been the perfect gentlemen all afternoon. Not a single barb about the past. Instead, he'd been open about his feelings and caring of hers. She wondered how long his good spirits would last.

When Marlena finished talking to Mrs. Hampton, she turned and saw that Raymond and Patrice had joined Winston. She walked in their direction, hoping they were ready to go home. She'd smiled as much as she could for one day.

"I've been waiting to talk with you," the masculine voice said, making her skin crawl.

She turned and faced McCoy. "How are you?" she said a bit too brightly.

"Fine, now that I have the chance to talk to you. I've been trying to reach you at the hotel."

Marlena wondered why the man didn't take the hint. Did he really think she hadn't gotten his messages? "I've been busy catching up with old friends."

"So I see." McCoy inclined his head in Winston's direction. "Is he the reason I haven't heard from you?"

She didn't respond and let him draw his own conclusion. The tinge of guilt she felt for taking the excuse he supplied was a price she was more than willing to pay.

"If that's the way the wind blows, I'll have to cut my losses. You know how to reach me."

Marlena stared at the man's retreating back. Talk about arrogant, she thought.

"Well, hello, Marlena," a familiar voice said from behind her. She didn't have to turn around to know who it was. Mrs. Taylor came and stood in front of her. "Enjoying yourself?" the older woman asked.

"I was," Marlena said, her disdain for the woman obvious in the tightness of her voice.

Mrs. Taylor laughed, a soft, sweet sound Marlena was sure anybody in hearing distance thought was friendly laughter.

"If you'll excuse me, Mrs. Taylor," Marlena said, stepping around the woman who still hated her.

Mrs. Taylor grabbed her arm, effectively stopping her. "Not yet, dear. I have a few things to say to you."

Marlena snatched her arm away. "I think you said everything that needed to be said ten years ago. I can't imagine there's anything you need to add."

Mrs. Taylor's calm facade didn't waver. She stepped closer to Marlena. "Stay away from my son," she spat out. "Stay away from him."

It was Marlena's turn to laugh. "You can't bully me, Mrs. Taylor. I was a defenseless young woman then, but I'm not any longer. You'd better take your threats somewhere else." Marlena propped a finger against her chin. "I wonder what Winston would think if he knew about your threats."

The older woman's eyes flashed anger. "Don't even think about going to Winston. You think he hates you now. If he knew . . ."

Marlena had negotiated with enough sharks to know the woman let her voice drop off for dramatic effect. "Look, Mrs. Taylor, I didn't come back here to pick up where Winston and I left off. Gaines is my home. I have as much right to be here as you do." Her eyes scanned the area. Out of the more than one hundred people at the picnic, she guessed all but maybe ten lived in Rosemont. "As any of you do."

"You think so, do you?" Mrs. Taylor said, looking down her nose at the younger woman. "Personally, I think Gaines would be better off without the likes of you. You're just like your—"

"My mother is dead," Marlena said, interrupting the older woman. She'd taken all she was going to take today. "And if you want to keep her secrets in the grave with her, you'd better watch what you say. She *was* my mother."

The older woman smiled. "Just so we understand each other."

"Oh, I understand you, all right. You're a petty woman with no idea what it means to love and be loved." Marlena gave a derisive laugh. "And to think I used to respect you and want your friendship. But no more. You're a pathetic old woman who's unhappy and who wants everyone else to be unhappy. I pity you, Mrs. Taylor.''

Marlena turned away from the older woman, not waiting for her comment. By the time she reached Winston and the teenagers, she'd composed herself enough to wear a real smile.

''Hey,'' Patrice said when Marlena walked up. ''We're thinking about a movie. Coach says he'll go if you will. How about it?''

Marlena looked into the girl's bright eyes, glad the youngster had made it through the day without incident. ''He did, did he?''

''Sure he did,'' Raymond chimed in. ''Tell her, Coach.''

Winston grinned up at her. ''What I said was that I refuse to be the third wheel on their date.''

''So you be his date,'' Patrice said with a smile. ''From what I've heard today, it wouldn't be the first time.''

Marlena turned back to the girl. ''And what did you hear?''

''Oh, this and that,'' the girl teased. Her bright eyes twinkled with mischief.

''Mrs. Hampton told her you two dated in high school,'' Raymond explained.

''Just for a semester,'' Marlena clarified.

''But she also said you dated through college and law school,'' Patrice challenged. ''It must have been pretty serious. Was it?''

Marlena glanced at Winston, hoping he'd come to her rescue. He just shrugged. ''They've already cornered me.''

''So?'' Patrice prompted.

Marlena tweaked the teen's nose, determined not to rehash her past relationship with Winston. ''You ask too many questions. Now which movie are we going to see?''

Winston felt like a horny teenager on his first date with the girl of his dreams. He should have overridden Patrice's choice of movie and gone for the action flick. If he didn't know better, he'd swear the girl had chosen the movie because she'd known the effect it would have on him. He sneaked a glance down the row where she and Raymond sat away from the watchful eyes of him and Marlena. So much for a double date, he thought.

"It was a setup," Marlena whispered.

"A setup?" He'd obviously missed a lot of this movie. "What setup?"

Marlena tossed a handful of popcorn in her mouth. "Not the movie. Patrice and Raymond. They set us up."

"I was coming to that conclusion myself. What do they think they're doing?"

"Young love," Marlena said with a shrug. "They're in love and they want everyone else to be. You know how it is."

He certainly did. He and Marlena had gotten so bad in college that their friends had started staying in relationships just to keep them from trying to fix them up with someone new. "Remember Tommy Lane and Rebecca Askew?" he asked.

Marlena covered her mouth and laughed softly. "Do I? I can still hear her telling me she was never going out with us again." She poked Winston in the side with her elbow. "It was all your fault. You picked Tommy."

"How was I to know the guy was so stuck on himself?"

Marlena grunted. "How about when he spent more time checking his hair in the rearview mirror than he did talking to us?"

"It was too late then. The date was on. What did you want me to do, break the mirror?"

"That would have been a good idea."

"Right."

She laughed again. "It was so funny. Rebecca had to be the most narcissistic person I knew and here she'd met her match in Tommy. She probably would have liked him if he'd shared the mirror with her."

"Those two deserved each other. I think they were our best couple."

Marlena tossed more popcorn in her mouth. "Still, I was surprised when they started dating. Evidently he got a car with enough mirrors for both of them."

"Evidently," he said with a chuckle. "You know they're married, don't you?"

Marlena turned to him, her bright eyes stretched wide in the dark. "You're joking."

He shook his head. "They have a couple of kids, too."

"I can't believe it. Tommy and Rebecca. Talk about an unlikely couple."

"I couldn't believe it either, but I ran into him on a business trip to New York. That's where they live now. They even invited me over so I could meet the kids. They seem real happy."

"Tommy and Rebecca. Married. I never would've guessed."

The woman in front of them turned around and shushed them. They looked at each other and giggled, then they turned back to the screen and watched the rest of the love story in silence.

Chapter 8

Winston pulled into the vacant parking space on the side of the Gaines Inn, still feeling like a school boy on his first date. He glanced at Marlena out of the corner of his eye, wondering if she was wondering why he hadn't pulled up to the entrance and let her out there. Her profile told him nothing. Her eyes focused straight ahead, her jaw was relaxed, no evidence of tension on her part. Marlena was cooler than the lake in the winter.

"I had a good time," he said.

Her jaw tightened. Maybe she wasn't as unaffected as she appeared.

"So did I. Raymond and Patrice are good kids."

Not exactly the response he was looking for, he thought wryly. "Are you ready to go in?"

She jumped slightly and reached for the door. "Thanks for driving," she said.

He opened his door, remembering that she'd wanted to drive herself and glad he'd persuaded her it would be best if they rode together. "No problem."

When he reached her side of the car, she was already out. He tapped the automatic door lock then took her hand in his.

She hesitated and he thought she was going to remove her hand. She didn't.

They strolled to the hotel entrance in silence. He didn't know what to say, yet he wanted to say so much. He'd enjoyed being with her today. Talking about the past had helped him to accept it. He'd often wondered if he and Marlena could recapture what they'd had. Now, he knew he didn't want that.

He sneaked another glance at her as they walked past the desk. He lifted a hand to Billy. The young man smiled then said, "You have a few messages, Ms. Rhodes."

She glanced up at him and Winston released her hand so she could get her messages. He couldn't help but wonder who had left them.

He watched as she took about five notes from Billy. She looked up at the young man and he just shrugged. "He kept calling and he wanted to leave a message each time."

"Thanks, Billy," she said, stuffing the notes in the pockets of her navy walking shorts. "Have a good night."

Winston followed her to the elevator, then reached in front of her and pushed the up button. "McCoy?" he asked. The elevator doors opened before she could answer and they both stepped on. "Floor?"

He punched the number she gave him.

"You don't have to escort me all the way to the door," she said, her eyes focused on the pad of floor numbers.

"I know I don't have to. I want to. Humor me. It's part of my southern upbringing that I can't let go. If you take a girl out, you see her to her door."

She looked up at him. "Do you always do the right thing?"

He nodded, then ushered her off the elevator when it reached her floor. "I try."

When they arrived at her door, he extended his hand for her key and she gave it to him. He put it in the lock, pushed the door open, and walked in before her, turning on the lights and checking out the place. "Nice suite," he called from the sleeping area.

"What are you looking for, Winston? A burglar?"

He looked back and saw that she was laughing at him. "Like they say, better safe than sorry. Do you mind?"

She shook her head and dropped down on the couch in the sitting area. "Do your thing. I'll wait here until you tell me the coast is clear."

He didn't let her teasing stop him from checking her bathroom and sleeping area. He smiled at the clothes scattered across the bed, hoping they meant she'd had a hard time deciding what to wear for their outing today.

"All clear," he said when he was back in the sitting room with her.

Marlena sat up straight on the couch. "Now I can breathe easy," she said with a smile. "Do you really think all that was necessary? This is Gaines, remember?"

He pushed his hands in his pockets and stood in front of her. "Raymond mentioned that he and Patrice were going over to Athens Wednesday night to see *Ain't Misbehavin'* at the Morton."

"On a school night?" Marlena asked.

Winston sat on the couch next to her. "He asked if we'd go with them."

She peeked over at him. Though she would enjoy a visit to the historic theater, she didn't want him to feel obligated to spend time with her. "I'm not sure, Winston. Don't you have someone else you'd rather take?"

"Raymond told you I wasn't seeing anybody."

She'd heard what Raymond said, but she knew what she'd seen. "I met Yolanda and I know she was your date at the Hampton's and I assume she was your date at the ball game Saturday."

"Yolanda and I are friends; nothing more. I haven't seen her since the day of the ball game."

"Very good friends, I bet." She shrugged her shoulders slightly. "You don't have to lie to me, Winston."

"I'm not lying. Yolanda and I are just friends."

Marlena remembered the specifics of her conversation with the woman. "Your idea, not hers, I bet."

He didn't say anything. Marlena was right. Yolanda did

want their relationship to be more than it was, but he wasn't interested. A casual relationship he could handle, but Yolanda wanted it all, including the wedding band. He didn't. "How about the play?" he asked again. "You know, they're probably using the play as a cover to spend some time with us. Maybe they want to talk to us about something."

"Maybe they think they're matchmakers. Are you sure you want two starry-eyed teenagers taking control of your love life?"

He looked at her for a long minute, then stood. "I'm sorry," he said. "I shouldn't have pushed. You probably already have plans." He felt like a fool. He should have guessed she already had a date. The notes Billy had given her were probably from McCoy.

In no time, both of them were standing at her open door. "Thanks, Marlena. I had fun."

"You sound surprised," she said, her eyes shining. He wondered what she was thinking.

"I was. Even though we'd gone to the party together Friday, today was different. Today was more like it used to be between us."

"That was a long time ago, Winston."

He nodded, then raised his hand to cup her cheek. He smiled down into her brown eyes. "McCoy is a lucky man," he said, then turned and walked to the elevator, feeling her eyes on him the entire way.

Marlena's phone rang about an hour after Winston had left the hotel. Thinking the call was from him, she let the phone ring three times before picking it up.

"Hello," she said hesitantly, not sure what she wanted from a relationship with Winston.

"So how'd it go?" Cheryl's friendly voice asked.

Marlena relaxed and sat back on the bed, pulling her silk robe tighter around her. "It went. I think Patrice and Raymond had a good time."

"I know they did. It's all Patrice could talk about. She said

Raymond's parents even spent some time with y'all. How'd that go?''

After meeting Raymond's parents, Marlena had wondered if the boy was adopted. How could such a well-adjusted, level-headed young man come from parents so shallow? "I hope Patrice knows how pretentious they are. They should be glad she is interested in their son. It's hard to believe those people are Raymond's parents."

"I know what you mean. He's such a sweet kid. If it weren't for his folks, I'd be happy about him and Patrice. But I'm still not sure. I don't want my baby to get hurt."

"Patrice'll be fine, Cheryl. She's a lot stronger than you think."

"She's also not as strong as she pretends. She has such a soft heart and she's let all her defenses down where Raymond is concerned."

Marlena remembered the young couple walking hand-in-hand at the picnic. There was an openness and a genuineness to their relationship that Marlena envied. She wanted so much for the two of them to make it.

"I think she's sleeping with him," Cheryl was saying. "What do you think?"

Marlena didn't know what to think. She hadn't thought about it. She and Winston had been very much in love, but she'd decided not to sleep with him while they were in high school. A part of her reasoning was fear of repeating her mother's mistakes, the other was that she hadn't been really sure that Winston cared for her. The lingering insecurity about his past relationship with Patty had rested heavily on her mind. "I don't know. Have you talked with her?"

"We've had the birth control and the safe sex discussion a couple of times, but she didn't seem that interested either time. I hate to keep bringing it up for fear that if she's not having sex, all my instructions will push her into it."

Marlena heard her mother's "And don't go spreadin' your legs for every Tom, Dick, and Harry that comes along. You make sure you stay in control." She shook off the thought, knowing Cheryl's instructions had been given in saner terms.

"If you're concerned about it, why not have one final talk with her woman-to-woman. It'll make you feel better."

"You think so?"

Marlena nodded. "Do it for your own peace of mind. My instincts tell me that Patrice is a bright girl. If she's sexually active, I'm sure she's taking care of herself."

Cheryl grunted into the phone. "If only that were true. I was a bright girl, too, but look what happened to me. Marty and I were so in love that a lot of times we ignored the consequences."

"Love will make you do dumb stuff," Marlena agreed.

"Not you, Marlena. You did it all right. You went to college with your sweetheart. And look at you now. You have it all, girl. Everything we all wanted, you have."

"Not everything, Cheryl."

"If you're talking about a man, don't even try it. They're easy enough to find. I'm sure you could find one if you really wanted one. And a good one too. Not like the bums around here."

"Have you been seeing anybody?" Marlena asked, not wanting her love life, or lack of one, to become the topic of conversation.

"Not in the last couple of years. It seemed like such a waste of time. The guys at the factory all want to get in my pants. The ones I supervise think I'll go easier on them if they're giving it to me. And my peers thinks I should consider myself honored they want me. To hell with 'em all."

Marlena sighed. Here they were, two attractive and successful women, and what were they doing on a Sunday night? Complaining about men. "It's their loss."

"You got that right. Now, tell me about your date with Winston. I know you've been trying to make me forget my question."

Busted, Marlena thought. "It wasn't a real date."

"Patrice says you spent a lot of time alone at the picnic and then the woman in front of you in the movie had to tell you to be quiet. Sounds like a real date to me. Did he kiss you good night?"

"Of course not!"

"Did you want him to?"

"Of course not."

"Liar. I bet you did. You have to wonder if it'll be the same. If he'll taste the same. If the feelings you had then will come back."

"Are you talking about me and Winston or you and Marty?"

Cheryl sighed again. "Oh, I don't know, girl. I'm thinking so much my head's hurting. Do you know anything more about when or if Marty's coming to Gaines?"

"I know his interview is tentatively set for this Friday, but that's about it. Winston has been talking with him, not me."

"Friday?" Cheryl's voice raised an octave. "Why didn't you tell me?"

"I'm telling you now. I was waiting for you to ask about him. You told me pretty clearly to keep my nose out of your business."

"I didn't say that," Cheryl said. "I'd never say that."

"You didn't use those words, but you did tell me to mind my own business."

"You know what I meant. I want to know what's happening with Marty. I just don't want him to know that Patrice is his daughter. It'll only cause heartache for all of us."

Marlena knew Cheryl had her mind made up about keeping her secret, but she had to try once more to make her friend see that was a bad choice. "What if someone else tells them?"

"Who? Patrice is seventeen years old and nobody's told him or her. Nobody knows."

"What if your ex-husband told somebody?"

"Nathaniel would never tell. He loves Patrice and they're very close."

So much for that approach, Marlena thought. "Have you told him about Marty coming to town?"

"No. Why should I?"

"I don't believe you, Cheryl. You'd *better* tell him."

"As soon as you tell me when Marty's getting here, I'll tell him."

"Why are you being so difficult?"

"I'm not being difficult," her friend said. "Look, Raymond is leaving and I want to talk with Patrice some more before she goes to bed. I'll call you tomorrow."

Marlena hung up the phone full of worry for her friend. Cheryl was about to repeat the biggest mistake of her life. Marlena was sure of it. Her friend's secret was going to blow up right in her face.

Marlena's chirpy "Good morning" surprised Winston when he walked into *The Way Home* office at ten on Monday morning. "You're here bright and early," he said, admiring her fresh look in the yellow miniskirt and vest. The short-sleeved V-necked silk blouse she wore under the vest clung to her full breasts as she searched the drawers in the file cabinet next to the desk he'd had placed in the office for her. He glanced from her breasts to his hands and wondered how it would feel to touch those soft orbs again. They were bigger now than they had been then. He wondered if that was because . . .

"It's not so early. You're late."

He dropped his briefcase on his desk. "I had a court appearance this morning."

She closed the drawer, walked back to her desk and sat down. "What kind of case? How'd it go?"

He smiled at her interest. This was what they'd planned: sharing an office, working on projects together, being together. "Criminal. Teenager in trouble. It went fine. The judge is going to keep him in juvenile a couple of days to scare him. He's a good kid; he'll learn from this."

She smiled at him and his knees went weak. He wanted so much to pull her into his arms and kiss her until she begged for him to do more. "What?" he asked.

She propped her arms on the desk and rested her chin in her hands. "You."

"Me? What about me?"

"Do you have any idea how easy it was for me to fall in love with you? I tried not to, because I wasn't sure how you really felt, but I couldn't stop myself. I said, 'This guy is the real thing.' You were a good person then, and you're a good person now. I'm glad we're friends again.''

Friends, he thought, she considered them friends. For some reason, that didn't sit right with him.

"What's wrong?" she asked. "We *are* friends, aren't we?"

"Sure," he said, going around to sit at his desk. "Friends, buddies, lifelong pals. That's us."

She dropped her hand and raised her head. "Excuse me, I thought you wanted to be friends." He heard the hurt in her voice. "You never played these kinds of games in the past, Winston. Maybe I judged you honest too quickly."

Aw, hell. Look what he'd done now. "Look, Marlena. Of course, I want us to be friends. I'm glad we're building a friendship."

She eyed him skeptically. "But?"

The phone rang and he took advantage of the reprieve and picked it up, shrugging his shoulders.

"Marty," he said into the phone and Marlena went back to her files.

She knew what had upset Winston. She hadn't been sure until this morning, but now she knew that Winston wanted more than friendship. She didn't know whether the butterflies in her stomach were due to excitement or fear. Could they really build something new from the ashes of their past?

Not if his mother had anything to do with it, she told herself. No, Mrs. Taylor still didn't think Marlena was good enough for Winston. She'd let the older woman force her into walking away from Winston one time. Would she let her do it again?

Marlena glanced over at Winston as he chatted with Marty on the phone. He lived the life alone that they'd planned to live together. She wondered if he ever imagined what his life would be like if she were in it.

Winston hung up the phone. "It's final. Marty'll be here on Friday for the interview and he plans to stay around for a week or so and help with the program."

"You twisted his arm, I bet."

Winston grinned. "I didn't have to. I got the feeling he very much wanted to spend some time here. He asked about Cheryl."

She looked up at him with bright eyes. "What did he ask?"

"Nothing much. How she and Patrice were doing, if Cheryl was seeing anybody."

"Sounds to me like he asked a lot. That's interesting."

"Certainly is," Winston said, leaning back in his desk chair. "Seems Marty's got a lot more on his mind than *The Way Home*. What does Cheryl think about all this? Is she willing to give Marty another chance?"

"I don't know," Marlena lied, knowing fully well that Cheryl intended to stay as far away from Marty as possible.

"Do you know why they broke up?"

Marlena didn't want to discuss Cheryl and Marty because she knew she'd have to lie to Winston and she didn't want any more lies between them. "You'll have to ask Cheryl."

Winston leaned forward. "So you do know?"

She didn't say anything.

"Okay, I won't pry. But I think Marty wants to get back with her. She ought to give him a chance."

"You think so, huh?"

"Why not? Life's too short to hold a grudge. Look at us. We're *friends.*"

She didn't miss his emphasis on the word, friends. "Marty wants more than friendship."

He looked at her with eyes that scorched her skin. Then the phone rang. "You've got to start somewhere," he said before picking up the phone.

Chapter 9

Marlena missed Winston. He'd left after bringing her a barbeque sandwich for lunch, saying he had a court appearance this afternoon. She turned so her chair faced the windows, giving her a view of one side of Gaines's Courthouse Square. Not much work had been done on the county's center of government since she'd been away. Her eyes scanned the block. Not much maintenance had been done on any of the town's buildings, for that matter. Winston was right. The town was falling down around them.

She turned around in her chair and looked down at the recently drafted employment contract on her desk. Winston hadn't been talking about buildings when he'd said the town was dying. He'd been talking about people. She knew he was right about that, too.

What did young people in Gaines have to look forward to other than getting out? The town's only theater, The Dollar Show, played movies you could get on HBO. They'd had to drive twenty-five miles to the next town the other night to see a new release. Forget professional job opportunities. Most of the job opportunities here were in retail or hospitality. Not that those weren't worthy industries, but where was the balance?

Where were the high-tech businesses? Where were the growth occupations? They surely weren't in Gaines and that's why Gaines didn't have engineers and scientists.

Sure, Gaines had a black car dealership, a couple of black funeral homes, more than its share of hairdressers and barbers, loads of teachers and preachers, but only a few lawyers and even fewer physicians. Sadly, most of the people in those named positions had been in them when Marlena was a child. If they weren't still in the positions, their children had inherited them.

Where was the justice? she wondered. Those who had "it" passed it on, while those who didn't have "it," either never got it or had to leave Gaines to find it. Why did black people always have to leave? Why couldn't they stay and flourish?

A knock sounded on the door and Marlena looked up. "Come in," she said.

Patrice poked her head in the door. "Busy?"

Marlena stood and waved the young girl in, glad for the interruption. "Not too busy to talk to you. What's up?"

Patrice strode into the room, head held back and shoulders straight. Marlena admired the confidence she exuded in her flowered sundress and flat leather sandals.

"Why aren't you going to the play with us?" Patrice asked with a pout. "I'm not going if Coach brings Yo-lan-da."

Marlena tried not to smile at the girl's reference to Winston's date. "I'm sure she's a nice woman."

"Evidently you've never met her." Patrice sat in the chair in front of Marlena's desk and crossed her legs. "She's a nice woman, but only if you're in her circle. She doesn't like me. She doesn't even speak to me unless she's with Coach. I don't know what he sees in her anyway."

Probably that long hair and beautiful skin, Marlena thought. "There's no accounting for taste. So why did you drop by? I'm sure it wasn't to talk about Yolanda."

Patrice leaned her elbow on Marlena's desk. "I want to know why you aren't going with us."

"Because I have other plans," Marlena answered vaguely. "And because Winston and I don't need you and Raymond to play matchmaker for us."

Patrice grinned the grin of the young and invincible. "We couldn't help ourselves. You look like you belong together."

"We do, do we?"

The girl nodded. "And you dated in high school and college. Why did you break up anyway?"

"That's personal, Patrice."

The girl stood up and strolled to the window. "You and Coach were like me and Raymond, weren't you?" she asked softly.

Marlena looked at the young girl's back, so erect, so mature, but she was still a child. "What do you mean we were like you and Raymond?"

Patrice turned around and sat on the window seat. "You know what I mean. He lived in Rosemont and you lived in the projects. I bet his parents didn't like you any more than Raymond's parents like me." The girl lowered her head. "Why don't they like us?"

The girl's words tore at Marlena's heart. She wanted to strangle Raymond's parents and a few others who lived in the exclusive Rosemont section of town. Instead, she walked over and sat next to Patrice, placing her arm around the girl's shoulder. "I've been trying to figure that out for a very long time."

Patrice turned damp eyes up at her. "And you never figured it out?"

"I came up with a lot of possible answers, but none seemed reason enough for them not to like us."

"Then why don't they? We haven't done anything to them."

"You're right," Marlena said, wishing the young girl had never experienced cruelty and bigotry from members of her own race. "We haven't, but some people are cruel, Patrice. They can't be understood. Maybe they don't like people like us because they're angry at us. Maybe even a little envious."

"Angry at us?" the girl asked, disbelief in her eyes. "Why would they be angry at us? We didn't do anything to them. And there's definitely no reason for them to be envious."

"Think about it," Marlena said, remembering the cruel jokes Patty Brock and her friends had made about Josie. The taunts had been painful to hear back then. Unfortunately, Marlena still heard them in her mind. "We're as smart as they are. We make the same grades and we don't have as much time to study because we have to work. We have as much fun. We're just as happy. The only difference between us and them is their money.

"But their money hasn't made them better than us. It just allows them to buy nicer cars, nicer clothes, nicer houses," Marlena continued. "They're probably angry because they think the money should make them better and it doesn't. And they're probably envious because we don't have to spend all of our time worrying about somebody taking our money, or somebody having more money than us, or our money going away, the way they do."

"Do you really think so?" Patrice asked, obviously wanting to believe Marlena's words.

"I really do. But I also think we make them afraid."

"Afraid?"

"Yes." She tilted the girl's chin up. "They have to be. When they see us, they see themselves as they'd be without their money. And they know that without their money, people with money will treat them the same way they're treating us. I think that's enough to scare 'em, don't you?"

A little smile crossed Patrice's face. "You know, they go to church but I don't think they listen to the preacher when he says to treat people the way you want to be treated."

Marlena hugged Patrice to her. "No, I don't guess they listen to that part. But we have to remember that it's not all people with money. It's not Winston and it's not Raymond. It's just the people who aren't sure of themselves, the weak ones. Winston and Raymond are strong, so they don't have to put other people down."

"And you, too. You're strong. You started out with no money and now you're a big-time lawyer. You wear expensive clothes and I bet you drive a nice car and live in a big house. That makes you better than them. You started out with nothing and made something. Most of them started with something."

The girl's words encouraged Marlena's heart. Sometimes she forgot the odds she'd beaten to accomplish her dreams.

"You're strong, too, Patrice. You're strong because you work hard at home and at school. You're strong because you care about people. You're strong because you're loved and you know how to love. Those are the important things. Materials things come and go, but what's inside—the person you really are—is what counts."

Patrice sat silently in Marlena's arms for a long time. "I'm glad I stopped by this afternoon," she said.

Marlena smiled. "I'm glad you stopped by, too."

Patrice looked up at her with a devilish twinkle in her eyes. "Does that mean you've changed your mind about going to the play with us?"

Marlena watched Winston as he read the file in his hand. After only a little more than a week of working together, they'd fallen into a comfortable routine.

"You don't have to hang around here, Winston," she said. "I can lock up when I'm done."

He leaned back in his chair and rubbed one of his big hands across his neck. "I can hang around a while longer. Why don't you take off?"

"I thought you were going to the play with Patrice and Raymond tonight."

"They changed their plans, so I'm free tonight." He turned his attention back to the file.

"Yolanda out of town?" she asked as casually as she could and immediately wished she hadn't.

He looked up from the file. "No. Why do you ask?"

"No reason," she said with a shrug. "I just didn't think you'd let a change in Raymond and Patrice's plans change yours and Yolanda's."

He grinned a smug grin that made her want to hit him. "I told you Yolanda and I were friends. Nothing more. We don't go out that often."

She feigned interest in her open desk drawer. "It's none of my business. I shouldn't have mentioned it."

"Lena," he said softly, using the pet name he'd often called her. The name on his lips caressed her skin. "You're welcome to ask any questions you want."

She lifted her eyes to his trying to understand why he'd called her by that name. In the past, he'd only used it when they were closest. Lena was the name he called out when he came inside her. It was the name he called to let her know he wanted her. If he called her Lena when they were with other people, it meant he wanted and needed to be alone with her. Just hearing him utter the name now made her grown warm inside.

"I remember," he whispered from across the room.

She would have sworn that she felt his words against her lips. She parted her lips slightly as if to suck the words inside herself.

Winston pushed back his chair, got up, and stalked toward her, his eyes focused on her parted lips. She studied his six-foot physique, marveling at the tautness of his features and the warmth in his eyes. He'd come to her many times with the determination that now shone in his eyes and she'd never refused him. How could she have? He'd been her heart. She'd loved him more than she'd loved herself.

He came around her desk and kneeled down in front of her chair, placing his face at the same level as hers. "Lena," he said again and moved his mouth to hers.

When their lips touched, skyrockets shot off inside her stomach, her head, her heart, and she was sure she was going to die, or maybe she'd been dead and his kiss was bringing her back to life. She wasn't sure.

She told herself to push him away before things went too far. Instead she wound her arms around his neck and pulled him closer, fusing their mouths and their bodies. When he moaned his pet name for her again, she grew mushy inside and found it difficult to remain upright in her chair.

As if he knew what she was thinking, he pulled her out of the chair as he leaned back on the floor and rested his back against the carpet, their lips still fused and their bodies flush against each other. His large, strong hands massaged her buttocks and pulled her closer so she could feel him hard and long against her. She groaned his name.

"Lena," he managed to choke out again between kisses, his voice rough with passion. "I've missed you so much."

His words thrilled her and she showed him in the kiss. "I've missed you, too," she said when she was able to catch her breath. "You don't know how much."

He bucked against her and she moaned again. "Winston," she pleaded, needing something, needing him. "Please—"

Winston froze. What was he doing on the floor of his office with Marlena lying across him? He didn't have to search for an answer. He was doing what he'd dreamed of doing since the day of the Hamptons' party He wanted Marlena and from the pulsing in her body, she wanted him just as much.

"Winston," she called again.

He heard the need in her voice and it almost broke him.

Almost. He'd heard that tone before. It was the tone she'd used when he'd made love to her that last time, the desperate lovemaking of a man trying to hold on to a woman who no longer wanted or needed him. He'd shown her that night that she wanted him and she needed him, but she'd still left him the next morning. Though she'd had tears in her eyes, she'd walked out of his life and not looked back. He dropped his hands from her hips.

When she tensed against him, he felt like a bastard.

"Is something wrong?" she asked with caution.

He didn't want to hurt her, but he also didn't want to be hurt again. He could love Marlena—not the girl he'd loved ten years ago, but the woman she was now. It didn't take a lot of smarts to know they couldn't start a lasting relationship on the floor of this office. She deserved better and so did he.

"This isn't right, Marlena," he began. "We should—"

She quickly rolled off him and turned her back to him. "You don't have to say it." She straightened her now-rumpled blouse and pushed down her skirt which had risen up to her waist. "This shouldn't have happened." She gave a tight laugh, which he knew was fake. "I'm glad one of us came to our senses before we did something foolish."

He sat up behind her and placed a hand on her shoulder. She shook it off. "Look," she said. "I'm fine. Thanks for not letting me do something I'd regret in the morning."

His heart broke at the strength in her words. He knew what it took from her to say them. "It's not that, Lena," he said, deliberately using the pet name that had caused this entire scene. "I do want you, but not here and not like this. Not like you're some common—"

She turned and glared at him. "Like some common whore? Is that what you were going to say?"

"I care about you, Marlena," he said, wishing he could take back his earlier words, but knowing he couldn't. "You know I do."

"As much as you could care for any whore," she said through tight lips.

"Don't do this, Marlena. Don't twist my words. You know that's not what I meant. I care—"

"Forget it, Winston. None of this should have happened."

"I still have feelings for you," he said softly. "You have to know I do."

She got up and sat in her chair. "I *felt* the feeling you have for me"—she glanced at his crotch—"and believe me *it'll* go down."

"I'm not talking about sex, and you know it." He got up and stared down at her. "Why are you trying to make it ugly? It's never been ugly between us."

She forced her best smile on her face. "Look, Winston. You have me at a disadvantage here. In case you don't remember, I was just sprawled on top of you, begging you to make love to me. At least be a gentlemen, and give me time to regain my composure."

"Don't do this, Lena. Please don't do this."

"Don't call me that," she commanded through tight lips. "Don't ever call me that again. It used to mean something between us and now it doesn't, so don't use it."

"What if I want it to mean something?"

She shrugged. "Obviously, you don't. What were your words? Oh, yeah. You could have had me on the floor like a common whore, but you chose not to. Sorry, I don't give second chances.''

"You know I don't think of you as a whore. You know I don't.''

"It doesn't matter,'' she lied. She pushed her files into her desk drawer. "Look, if you're going to stay here, I think I'll get back to the hotel.''

"We need to talk about this, Marlena,'' he pleaded. "You can't just walk out.''

She picked up her purse, got out of her chair, and strode to the door. "Watch me.''

Winston stood rooted in his position wondering what had happened. "Damn,'' he said. "Maybe I should have made love to her.'' He shook his head. Making love to her would have been the worst thing he could have done. Marlena would have never forgiven herself if she'd let him take her on the office floor.

He knew both of them would have enjoyed the coupling, but he also knew the commonness of the act would have broken her. She'd grown older, stronger, and more confident in the years they'd been apart, but her sense of self was still weak around the edges.

"And you didn't help her much,'' his conscience told him.

Winston didn't know why he'd called her Lena. Today was the first time he'd even thought of using the name. He wished he could turn the clock back to the moment before the name had rolled off his tongue, but he couldn't. He'd told her he wanted her and then he'd rejected her. Now, he'd have to go through hell before she offered herself to him again.

He sighed, wondering if Marlena was worth it. He didn't have to wonder long.

Chapter 10

Marlena rushed back to the Gaines Inn and ran straight to the shower. She could no longer claim she'd come back to Gaines with no thoughts of regaining what she'd lost with Winston. Tonight had proven her a liar. She'd thrown herself at him. She still couldn't believe she'd done it.

It was Winston's fault. He'd called her "Lena," knowing what that name had meant between them in the past. He'd called her "Lena" and she'd responded as she always had, but this time, he hadn't meant it.

She still remembered how she'd felt when she'd realized his body was no longer responding to hers. Then the words he'd spoken, "Not like some common . . ."

She closed her eyes and let the warm water soothe the aches in her tired-from-sitting-and-reading muscles, wishing it could also ease the pain in her heart. She wrestled to keep memories of the awful conversation she'd had with Mrs. Taylor the day after her mother's funeral out of her mind, but she was too tired to put up much resistance.

"One day he'll find out what a whore you are," the cruel woman had told her with a disgusted smirk on her face. "As my old grandmother used to say, the truth will tell. And one day, Marlena, Winston will see you for the trash that you are. Mark my words."

The words sounded over and over in her mind. She pressed her hands to her ears to stop them, but the words burst through and resounded in her head, in her mind. As she slid to the floor of the shower stall, her tears mixing with the water streaming down her face, she wished she'd never come back to Gaines.

"If you leave now, you'll be running away," Cheryl said the next night. Marlena pushed the shopping cart while her friend loaded it with groceries.

"So?" Marlena had considered the alternatives and decided that running away was the easiest of them. Crying on the floor of her shower stall had been the lowest point of her life. Why should she stay in Gaines if all the visit did was cause her old insecurities to return? This trip was supposed to make her stronger, not weaker.

Cheryl tossed two loaves of multigrain bread in the cart. "You need to face your past, Marlena. Running away won't help you. You've tried it for ten years and it hasn't worked."

"You're a fine one to talk," Marlena said. "I don't see you facing your past."

Cheryl turned from the shelf of cake mixes and scanned the aisle, making sure no one was around. Then she glared at Marlena. "I don't believe you can stand there and compare our situations."

"And I can't believe you're telling me to face my past when you won't deal with your own."

Cheryl turned back to the shelf. "At least I'm not running away like you're planning to do."

Marlena sighed. She wanted to run away but she couldn't. The fighter in her knew running away would make her a coward. "I'm not leaving."

Cheryl turned around with wide eyes. "You're not? I thought you said—"

Marlena waved her friend's comment away. "I want to run,

but I can't. Not now. You're right. I ran once. I won't run any more.''

"That's what I wanted to hear. You make me proud, girl.''

Marlena folded her arms across her chest. "If I'm not going to run, then you can't either.''

Cheryl looked back at her friend. "I can't run. I live here.''

"Don't be a smart ass, Cheryl. You know what I mean. Not seeing Marty is the same as running. You have to see him and you have to tell him about Patrice.''

Cheryl turned back to the shelf without commenting. Marlena had to nudge her with the cart before she would look at her. "You know I'm right.''

"Maybe.''

"I know you're scared, Cheryl,'' Marlena said in a soft voice. "I'm scared, too. But if we do this together, it won't be so bad. I'll be there for you and you can be there for me. What do you say?''

Cheryl grimaced, but her lips soon turned up in a smile. "I say with a friend like you a person doesn't need many enemies.''

Marlena smiled back at her friend, glad they'd be there to support each other. "And I love you, too.''

Winston rushed up the stairs to *The Way Home* office, praying Marlena was there. He was bright enough to realize she'd been avoiding him the past couple of days and he knew why. He opened the door to the second-floor hallway. The kiss. The scene of the two of them on the floor in the office flashed across his mind and he groaned. What they had shared had been much more than a kiss.

He wanted to talk with Marlena about the episode, but she deliberately made herself scare. He'd had court appearances the last two mornings, and she'd been gone by the time he'd arrived in the office in the afternoon. She didn't return the calls he made to her, and he'd had to stop himself from going over there and demanding that she talk to him.

He turned the knob on the office door. No, he wouldn't invade her space for fear she'd leave town if he did. He'd give her time, a little time, to work through her emotions, but he wasn't going to let her get away from him. Not again.

Her head was bowed over some papers when he entered the office. They must have been very interesting papers because she didn't even look up. He took that time to study this woman who'd haunted him for more than ten years. She twirled a pencil in her hand while she read and he remembered she'd always done that when she studied.

Many a time, he'd pulled a pencil out of her hand, dragged her into his arms, and made passionate love to her. He smiled at the memory of the faint protests she'd given. He'd ignored them just as she'd wanted him to do. When she was in his arms, she was his. Nothing else had mattered to him or to her.

She looked up at him. "Hi, Winston," she said. "I didn't hear you come in."

"Must be pretty interesting reading." He inclined his head toward the papers in her hand.

"Oh, just more files. I think Cassandra Vines should be our next *The Way Home* candidate."

She gave him her evaluation of Cassandra's file.

"Sounds good," he said, distracted by the brightness of her eyes as she spoke. Her good mood made him want to talk about their relationship, but he didn't have much time. He checked his watch. He had no time. "I need a favor, Marlena."

"Sure," she said. "What is it?"

"I'm supposed to meet Marty's plane this afternoon and I can't do it. This case is taking up much more time than I'd planned. Do you think you can drive to Atlanta and pick him up? He can always take the shuttle, but I wanted to make his arrival something special."

She smiled and his heart did its usual flip flop. "No problem. I'll pick him up. Do you have his schedule?"

He opened his briefcase and removed Marty's itinerary. "Here," he said, handing it to her. "I really appreciate this. Maybe we can take him out tonight and invite Cheryl. I know he wants to see her." And I want to spend some time with you, he added silently.

Marlena turned her attention back to the file she'd been reading. "I'll see."

"You don't sound too optimistic about it. What? You don't think it's a good idea?"

She shook her head. "Oh, no. It's not that. It's just that I don't want to get in the matchmaking business. Marty and Cheryl will find each other soon enough."

Winston had a feeling there was something Marlena wasn't telling him, but he didn't have time to pursue it. He had to get back to the judge's chambers. "If you say so. Look, I have to run." He grabbed his briefcase and headed for the door. "Thanks for picking up Marty for me."

She nodded. "It's not a problem."

He put his hand on the door knob, then hesitated, feeling as if he should say something more. When no more words came, he opened the door. "Leave me a message if you change your mind about dinner," he said and stepped out of the office.

When Winston walked into Rob's Rib Shack later that night, the sight of Marlena and Marty huddled together laughing intimately made the hairs on his neck bristle. He marched over to them. "I see you made it in," he said, causing the two of them to look up at him. Neither had the decency to look embarrassed.

Marty rose from his seat and extended a hand. "Good to see you, man. It's been a long time."

Winston appraised the other man before speaking. Maybe he'd been wrong and nothing had been going on between Marty and Marlena. He took Marty's hand. "Good to see you, too. Sorry I couldn't meet you at the airport like we'd planned."

Marty grinned down at Marlena, then returned his gaze to Winston. "I consider it my good fortune. No offense, but I'd rather spend two hours looking at Marlena's beautiful face than at your ugly mug any day." Marty laughed at his own joke, then he sat back down.

Winston sat down, too. He turned to Marlena. "Thanks for picking him up for me," he said.

"No problem," was her reply. She smiled at Marty. "We had fun catching up on old times."

Winston wondered just how much fun they'd had, then chastised himself for behaving like a school boy. He cleared his throat. "Where's Cheryl?"

He didn't miss the quick glance Marlena shot Marty before answering his question. "She couldn't make it. She has to be at work pretty early in the morning."

Winston nodded, but something in Marlena's words made him not believe her. "Too bad."

"Hey," Marty chimed in. "I'm not complaining." He winked at Marlena. "Cheryl's loss is Marlena's gain."

Marlena shook her head but she smiled at Marty's words. Winston's guts clenched. "I'm gonna tell Cheryl you said that," she threatened.

Marty lifted his glass of beer to his lips. "Go right ahead. She needs to know I'm not waiting around for her."

Winston felt as if he'd missed an important part of the conversation. "Did you talk to Cheryl?" he asked Marty.

The other man shrugged his broad shoulders and Winston noticed he'd bulked up a lot since high school, not that Marty had ever been small. Winston couldn't help but pat his still-flat stomach as he tried to remember the last time he'd been to the gym.

Marty gave a grave sigh. "I made the mistake of calling her last night." His lips turned in a smirk. "She told me she wasn't interested in reliving the past and said we had nothing to talk about. So much for that."

Winston looked at Marlena. "What's up with Cheryl? It's not like her to be rude."

Marlena wished Winston hadn't put her on the spot. She had no idea what was up with Cheryl. Her friend hadn't even mentioned Marty's call to her. "Maybe she's busy."

"Right," Marty sneered. "Maybe she meant what she said. She has no desire to relive the past. Maybe she's right. I don't see the two of you trying to go back to those days."

Marlena looked down at the scattered remains of barbeque ribs and bread on her plate, refusing to meet Winston's gaze.

She didn't have to look at him to know he was staring at her, willing her to comment on Marty's statement. She didn't give in to his request.

"I'm sorry I brought it up," Winston said, not wanting to agree with Marty for fear he'd give his old friend the idea that Marlena was fair game when nothing could be farther from the truth. "Has Marlena filled you in on the work we have lined up for you while you're here?"

Marty released a friendly groan that made Marlena smile. She listened as Winston told Marty how he could help out at *The Way Home,* glad that her ex-fiancé had been smart enough to turn the conversation away from their personal lives and back to the primary reason they were all here: *The Way Home.*

After an hour or so of discussing the program and watching Winston eat the meal he'd finally ordered, the three of them were ready to call it a night.

"I'll drive you home," Winston said to Marty.

"There's no need," Marlena said, removing her shoulder bag from the back of her chair and placing it across her shoulder. "Since he's staying at the Gaines Inn, he can ride with me. Besides, all of his stuff is in my car. We came here straight from the airport."

Winston turned his gaze to Marty. "I thought you'd be staying with your sister?" Winston knew Marty's parents had retired a few years ago and moved back to the small Alabama town where they'd grown up.

"No way, man," Marty said. "I'm not even going to start that way. If I move in, she'll want to me stay. No, I'll stay at the hotel." He glanced at Marlena and grinned, making Winston wonder why he hadn't noticed before how stupid the grin looked spread across Marty's mug. "That way, I'll be close to a friendly face."

Too close, Winston thought. He stood up. "Okay, then. I guess I'll see you two in the morning."

Marlena stood and pushed her chair to the table. "We won't be in tomorrow morning, Winston," she said. "I'm driving Marty to his interview."

Winston could only stare at her. Why was she driving Marty to his interview?

"Wasn't that nice of her? Since I don't have a car, she offered to drive me."

"*The Way Home* will rent a car for you," Winston offered quickly. Too quickly.

Marty laughed. "I'd rather save *The Way Home* some money since this beautiful lady"—he draped an arm around Marlena's shoulders—"has offered to chauffeur me around. I may be dumb, but I'm not stupid."

"What you are is the biggest flirt in Gaines," Marlena said, smiling. "What's the town going to do with you?"

Winston watched as Marty tapped her pert nose, then said, "Make me a very happy man, I hope."

Marlena's throaty laughter was her response as she moved to the door with Marty's arm still draped across her shoulders. Winston followed them, his lips pursed tight. Marty was supposed to be making a play for Cheryl, not Marlena, he said to himself. He'd have to make a special point of speaking with the brother about the distribution of women.

Winston stood on the sidewalk while the couple climbed into Marlena's rented vehicle. Then he waved to them as they drove off. He shuffled back to his Bronco feeling like he'd missed the buzzer shot at the NBA finals.

First McCoy. Now Marty. What was Marlena doing? Casting her web over every available male in Gaines? He started his vehicle and slowly eased out into the empty street. A brilliant idea popped into his mind and he increased the pressure on the gas pedal. Five minutes later, he pulled into Cheryl's driveway.

He jumped out of the Bronco and rushed to the door. A sleepy-eyed Cheryl greeted him after a couple of presses on the doorbell and a few not-so-light taps on the door.

"What are you doing here, Winston? Is something wrong?"

For the first time, Winston considered the lateness of the hour. "No, nothing's wrong," he said. "Do you have a minute, Cheryl? I want to talk to you about something?"

"Who is it, Mom?" Winston heard Patrice call from the back of the house.

Cheryl yawned, then lifted her hand to cover her mouth. She looked over her shoulder. "Go back to bed, sweetheart. It's just Winston. He'll be leaving in a minute." She turned back to Winston. "Do you know what time it is? I've got to be at work at seven in the morning."

"It'll only take a couple of minutes," Winston said. "Come on, Cheryl. I promise I won't keep you long."

With reluctance, Cheryl unlocked her screen door and stood back so Winston could enter the house. "Just a couple of minutes." She walked back and sat down on her living room couch, pulling her robe tighter around her. After Winston was seated in the stuffed chair across from her, she asked, "Now what do you want to talk about this late at night?"

Winston didn't know how to begin. He probably should have thought out his plan a bit more before rushing over here. Well, he told himself, he was here now and he'd better make the best of it. "Marty came in tonight," he said.

Cheryl glanced down the hallway from where Patrice's voice had come before turning eyes filled with defiance to him. "So?"

"Why won't you see him?"

Cheryl jumped up from the couch and walked to the door. "This is none of your business, Winston," she said, pulling the door open. "You'd better leave."

Winston didn't move from his seat. "Not until I get some answers. Now, why won't you see him?"

Cheryl sighed. "Because I don't want to. Is that a good enough reason for you?"

Her anger surprised Winston. What did she have to be angry about? "He just wants to talk. Why won't you even talk to the man? You're the one who up and got married on him. If anybody deserves to be angry, it's Marty."

"Look," Cheryl said in a shouted whisper, her hands now on her hips and her feet tapping against the light brown carpet, "this is between me and Marty. He doesn't need you to run interference for him and I certainly don't need you to do it for me. I'd think you had enough on your hands with Marlena."

Winston's head jerked back at her statement. "You, look," he said, forcing himself to keep his voice down so Patrice wouldn't hear him. "If you don't at least talk to Marty, Marlena won't be on my hands anymore. She'll be *in* his."

Cheryl stopped tapping her feet. "What are you saying?"

Winston stood and walked to the door. He glared down at her, needing her to sense the urgency of the situation and to work with him so that neither one of them would lose the people they loved most. "I'm saying that Marty is looking for a substitute and maybe he thinks Marlena's it."

"What?" Cheryl sputtered.

"You heard me," Winston said, stepping out of the house. "You'd better make damn sure you don't want Marty anymore, because if you leave him to your friend, he may just decide he no longer wants you."

If Winston hadn't been so angry himself, he would've laughed at the surprise in Cheryl's eyes. Instead, all he could do was stomp off her porch and hustle back to his Bronco. He left her driveway with the satisfaction of knowing he wasn't the only one who wouldn't get any sleep tonight.

Chapter 11

Winston heard the footsteps in the hallway and quickly turned his attention from the office door back to the papers in front of him. No way would he let Marlena and Marty know he'd been waiting for them. He glanced down at his watch. Two o'clock. What did he care if they spent the entire day together? It was none of his business.

When the doorknob turned, Winston's heartbeat quickened and he told himself not to drill them with questions. It was none of his business, he told himself again.

"Winston, darling."

Winston uttered a soft curse, then looked up, a smile he didn't really feel plastered across his face. "Hi, Mother," he said, walking to the door to meet his mother and her friend. He gave her a quick kiss on the cheek, then extended his hand to the older, distinguished gentleman next to her who had been one of his father's closest friends. "Good to see you, Mr. Sanders."

"You, too, Winston," the older gentleman said, taking a seat in the chair next to Winston's mother. "We know you're busy so we'll get right to the point. Your mother and I are going to the symphony in Athens tonight. It's late notice, but we wondered if you and your lady friend would be interested in going with us.'' The older man pulled four tickets from his vest pocket. ''On me, of course.''

Winston wondered if Marlena would go with him. He could ask her. What's the worst thing she could do? Say no? He could handle that.

''Yes, dear,'' his mother added, crossing her legs and waving her recently manicured hand. ''I'd love to see Yolanda again. You haven't brought her to the house in a long while.''

Winston could only stare at his mother. He knew what she was doing and he didn't like it. ''I'm old enough to pick my own dates,'' he said rather harshly.

''Pardon me,'' his mother said, placing her hand across her chest as if she were offended. Winston would have been taken in by her act if he hadn't known it was solely for Mr. Sanders's benefit. ''I know you're old enough to pick your own dates. I was only letting you know how much I like Yolanda. There's no need to be so touchy about it.'' She flashed her eyelashes in Mr. Sanders' direction. ''Do you think I was out of line, Herman?''

Mr. Sanders fell for the bait as Winston had known he would. He watched the older man pat his mother's hand. ''No, Barbara, you didn't do anything wrong.'' He cast a stony glare at Winston. ''Your mother didn't mean any harm, Winston. There was no call to be rude to her. I think you owe her an apology.''

If Winston were one to roll his eyes, this would be the moment he'd do it. He closed his eyes briefly and prayed for patience. When he opened them, two faces stared at him: one still wore a stony glare, while the other looked on the verge of tears. His mother was a damn good actress. She knew as well as he did that the only reason she'd get her apology was because Winston refused to make a scene in front of Mr. Sanders. ''I'm sorry if I upset you, Mother. I didn't mean to.'' Winston's eyes sent her a message that said that poor excuse for an apology was all he was giving her.

''That's all right, dear'' she said, her tears drying up immediately. He wondered how she did that trick. She looked at Mr.

Sanders. "I think we should be going now, Herman. We've extended our invitation."

Mr. Sanders gave her a besotted smile and Winston felt sorry for the poor guy. His mother had him wrapped around her fingers. "You think you'll take us up on our offer, Winston?"

Winston looked at his mother, then back at Mr. Sanders. "Yes," he said. "I think I will."

"Good, good," Mr. Sanders said, getting up from his chair and assisting Winston's mother from hers at the same time. "We'll be leaving from your mother's house around six. We can all drive over together if that's all right with you. We'll make a night of it. After the symphony, we'll go to dinner."

"Thanks, Mr. Sanders," Winston said, getting up, too. "I think it's a great idea to ride over together and dinner sounds good." Winston placed a hand on the older man's shoulder and walked the couple to the door. He opened it and ushered them out, kissing his mother's cheek again before she left. "See you tonight, Mother," he said with a smile. "Me and my date."

Winston wished he had a camera to capture the look on his mother's face. Her expression clearly told him she was afraid he was going to do something to embarrass her.

"Okay, dear," she murmured, her eyes sending him all sorts of messages that he chose to ignore.

Winston closed the door behind the couple and leaned against it. Now all he had to do was get Marlena to go with him. That shouldn't be too difficult, he thought. No, not difficult at all. More like impossible. He grinned and rubbed his hands together. He was up to the challenge.

Marlena's good mood quickly vanished when she read the messages waiting for her at the hotel. Winston had called four times and Cheryl twice. She didn't know which call she dreaded returning most.

She sat down on the side of her bed and kicked off her pumps. The day had gone so well up to now. She'd had fun squiring Marty around. He'd made her laugh and she'd enjoyed it. They'd steered clear of painful topics, neither Cheryl's nor Winston's name had come up all day, though she was sure they had been on his mind as much as they'd been on hers.

She sighed as she picked up the phone and punched in the seven digits.

"Hello," Cheryl answered.

"I got your message," Marlena said tersely, not ready yet to be understanding. Cheryl should have told her about her conversation with Marty. "What did you want to talk about?"

"Winston dropped by last night."

"Oh."

"He told me to be careful about pushing Marty away. He said I might push him into someone else's arms."

Marlena could hear Winston saying something that outrageous. "He did, did he? That must have made you happy. Now you have another excuse for not telling him about Patrice. Though it's not like you were going to tell him anyway." She paused for effect. "Marty told Winston and me that he called you the other night."

"He did?"

"Yes, he did. He also told us that you said you didn't want to see him."

"Look, Marlena," Cheryl said. "I know you think I should tell him—"

Marlena began to grow weary with the conversation. "And if I remember correctly, you told me you would."

"You just don't know how hard it is or how scared I am. I could lose everything if I tell him."

"Think about what they'll lose if you don't tell them. Think about Patrice. What about when she's married with kids of her own? And Marty? Doesn't he deserve to know his grandkids? You've robbed him of his chance to know his daughter."

"You're not being fair, Marlena."

Marlena laughed a dry laugh that held no humor. Fair. She couldn't believe her friend had the nerve to mention fair.

"So how is he?" Cheryl asked.

Marlena could have maintained her anger if Cheryl had said anything else, but that question asked in such a quiet voice got to her. "He's fine. He looks good and he seems happy. He wears success well."

"Hmm. That's good."

Marlena debated telling Cheryl about the conversation she and Marty had on the way back from the airport. She didn't want to betray Marty's confidence, but at the same time she wanted her friend to understand what she was throwing away. "You hurt him when you said you didn't want to see him."

"I wasn't trying to hurt him."

"Sometimes good intentions backfire."

Cheryl sighed a long sigh. "I hear you, Marlena. I hear you. You think I should see him, don't you?"

"You know how I feel. You're my friend and I love you, but right is right. That's my last word on the subject. I refuse to get in the middle of your relationship with Marty. I'll only end up mad with you if I do."

"So, are you going out with Marty tonight?"

"No you don't, Cheryl. I'm not going to report Marty's activities back to you. If you want to see him, then see him, but don't use me to spy for you."

"I wasn't using you," her friend denied.

"What were you doing then?"

"Winston made it seem like Marty was interested in you."

Marlena laughed, this time a real laugh. "You're jealous! I don't believe it. You're jealous."

"No, I'm not."

Marlena kept laughing. "Yes, you are and you ought to be. Marty's a fine brother and I enjoyed spending the day with him."

"Good for you," Cheryl mumbled.

"He mentioned something about going out tonight. I think I'll call and see what his plans are. You don't mind, do you?"

"Why should I mind?" Cheryl asked, but Marlena knew she minded. "I bet Winston minds. I thought you were supposed to be dealing with your feelings for him. I don't see how you're going to do that if you're dating Marty."

"Winston hasn't exactly been beating down my door to take me out," she said. "I'm not sure he cares who I see."

"He cares, all right," Cheryl said quickly. "Why else would he come barging over here last night after Patrice and I were in bed? He doesn't want you seeing Marty."

Marlena was beginning to like the idea of going out with Marty more by the minute. She couldn't wait to tell him how Winston and Cheryl were reacting to their relationship. "Well, a little competition never hurt anybody. For all I know, Winston's seeing Yolanda. I can see Marty."

"So you're just using Marty?"

"Not really. I told you. I enjoy his company. All the better that it gets a rise out of Winston." And out of you, too, she added silently.

"You're too old to play games, Marlena," Cheryl said with such righteous indignation that Marlena almost laughed.

"I'm going to pretend you didn't say that, Ms. Game Player. Now, I've gotta go. I have to let Marty know I'm free tonight, after all."

Cheryl said goodbye and Marlena hung up. She'd get Marty and Cheryl back together if it was the last thing she did, she told herself. It wouldn't take much.

She reached for the phone to dial Marty's number, but it rang before she could pick it up. "Hello," she said, her voice full of cheer. That call to Cheryl had given her a charge.

"Hi, Marlena. Didn't you get my messages?" Winston's smooth voice asked.

"Yes, I got them. What did you want to talk to me about?"

"How'd it go with Marty today?"

Marlena smiled and leaned back on the bed. "We had a great time. Marty's a great guy. He was handsome in high school, but now—"

"Yeah, yeah," Winston interrupted and Marlena's smile grew wider. "Do you have any plans for tonight?"

"Not yet. I was about to phone Marty when you called. He mentioned something about getting together tonight."

He cursed under his breath. "I have tickets to the symphony in Athens. I thought you might like to go." He didn't see a need to mention they'd be going with his mother and her date.

"Well, I'll have to talk to Marty first."

He cursed again. "You don't have to call Marty. I thought you wanted him to get back with Cheryl. Going out with him is not going to make that happen. Maybe if he finds himself without a date, he'll disregard Cheryl's refusal to see him and get his butt over to her place."

"You may have a point," she said slowly.

"I know I have a point. I'll pick you up at five-forty-five." He hung up before she could say she wasn't going with him.

Winston strolled through the entrance of the Gaines Inn praying Marlena would be ready for their date. He thought about stopping at the desk, then decided against it when he saw the teasing grin on Billy's face. Now that the boy's father had left town again, Billy was back to his old self and that included teasing him about Marlena as he'd done at the baseball game over a week ago. He waved briefly and headed for the elevator, thinking his chances would be better if he met Marlena face-to-face.

He pressed the elevator button then stuffed his hands in his pockets while he waited. The golden doors slid open and he moved to get on. Marlena almost bumped into him.

He grinned like a school boy, glad she hadn't backed out of the date. "You look wonderful," he said and he meant it. The black off-the-shoulder midthigh dress she wore did as much for his libido as if she'd been wearing a negligee.

"Thank you," she said, giving him one of her rare smiles. She touched the lapel of his jacket. "You look pretty handsome yourself. Did you wear the tie for me?"

He placed his hand atop hers and said, "What can I say? I wanted to impress my date."

"Well, you did. I know how much you hate wearing a tie."

He placed his hand on the small of her back and led her out of the hotel and to his Bronco. Once they were both inside, she said, "Now this is you."

"The Bronco?"

"Yes, the engineers must have designed it with you in mind."

"I like it." He cast her a sidelong glance while they waited at the light. "I bet you drive a convertible. Foreign."

She smiled, thinking about the Mercedes convertible parked in her garage. "What makes you think that?"

He shifted gears and sent the Bronco through the light. He figured she'd bought the car not because she liked to drive it, but because of the success it symbolized; however, he knew enough about women to keep his thoughts on the subject to himself. "Maybe I'm psychic."

"Maybe you're guessing." She looked out the window, taking in the view of Main Street. When Winston passed the Lincoln Street turnoff for Athens Highway, Marlena turned to him. "I thought we were going to Athens."

"We have to make a stop first. Another couple is coming with us. Actually, we're going with them. They bought the tickets."

"Oh," she said, taking in the expansive two-story houses and large, well-manicured lawns that signaled their arrival in the exclusive Rosemont community. "I would have thought an R&B concert would be more to Patrice and Raymond's tastes."

"We're not going with Patrice and Raymond."

She turned to him with wide eyes when he turned onto his mother's street. "Doesn't your mother live on this street?" she asked cautiously.

He nodded. "Do you remember Herman Sanders?"

"Sure. He was a good friend of your father's, wasn't he? Is he going with us?"

"He and his date."

"Oh. That should be fun. I always liked Mr. Sanders."

"He liked you, too. He flirted with you a bit too much for me, but since he was so old, I didn't think I really had anything to worry about."

She laughed as he'd hoped she would. "He *was* a flirt, wasn't he? He's bringing his wife?"

"She died a couple of years before Dad. He's bringing his date."

"It's hard dating at thirty-five. I don't even want to think about dating after sixty."

"Maybe you won't have to. Maybe you and your husband will live to be a hundred."

"I have to get married first."

"Oh, you will," he said. "It's inevitable. My gender might be slow but we're not stupid."

Winston slowed in front of his mother's house and pulled into the circular drive behind Mr. Sanders's maroon Lincoln Town Car. "This is your mother's house," she said.

He put the Bronco in park and turned to her. "I know. Mother is Mr. Sander's date."

"We're going to the symphony with your mother?"

He nodded, hoping she wouldn't chicken out on him now. He wanted this evening to make up for the fiasco on the floor of his office. He wanted Marlena to know that he had the highest regard for her. "And dinner, too. That's not a problem, is it?"

"None at all," she said, lying through her teeth. She'd rather have a root canal than spend the evening with Winston's spiteful mother, but she'd be damned if she'd let the old witch make her stay home. "I'm sure we'll have an *interesting* evening."

Winston grinned at her, glad she'd chosen to face her fears. He knew how much his mother disliked Marlena and he knew how much that dislike had affected Marlena when they were dating before. He thought that facing his mother tonight would help Marlena become more confident in his mother's presence. "Before the evening is over, you'll probably be glad my mother is with us, while I'll want to drop her in the nearest river."

She laughed. "Why do you say that?"

"Because you're the most beautiful woman I've ever seen," he whispered, leaning closer to her. He touched his finger to her lips. "I want to kiss you so badly right now that my lips hurt."

A huge lump formed in Marlena's throat and she swallowed.

"Do you remember the first time I kissed you?" he asked, softly tracing her lips with his fingers.

Yes, she remembered the kiss. It was the third time he'd

taken her out. He'd driven her home after they'd spent the evening studying in the library. After he'd escorted her to the door, they'd spent a few awkward moments just looking at each other. She still hadn't believed she was really going out with Winston Taylor. She had known it was a dream that would end suddenly, leaving her with a broken heart.

The question in his eyes that night was the same as the question in his eyes tonight. He wanted to kiss her, but only if she wanted to kiss him. She'd wanted to kiss him that night so she'd inclined her head ever so slightly, giving him the signal he needed. She wanted to kiss him tonight, too, but not in front of his mother's house. She leaned away from him and his finger fell away from her lips.

"I remember," she said.

He smiled and a teasing warmth filled her insides. She was seventeen again.

"Good," he said. "Now let's get started with our double date."

Chapter 12

Marty turned the car Winston had rented for him onto Cheryl's street. He wondered again if he was doing the right thing. When he'd gotten the message Cheryl had left at the hotel asking him to call her, he'd decided to go a step farther and visit her. He hoped the visit didn't backfire on him. He looked at the house numbers on the mailboxes on the tidy street of small brick ranch-style homes. When he saw 1504, he took a deep breath and turned into the paved driveway. He quickly got out of the car, took long strides to the door, then rang the bell and waited for someone to answer. The open door and the sound of music from a radio or stereo that could be heard through the screened door told Marty someone was home.

As he leaned back against the brick column, he realized he'd left the hotel in such a rush that he hadn't changed out of the clothes he'd worn to his interview. He quickly removed his jacket and tie and undid the top buttons on his shirt. He looked back at his car, wondering if he had time to take the garments back there, then decided to stuff the tie in his pocket and throw the jacket over his shoulder. He hoped he looked casual and relaxed.

He rang the bell again and heard a familiar feminine voice yell, "Just a minute."

He smiled at the sound. How many times had he heard her say the same thing when he'd come to pick her up for one of their many dates? Then she'd lived in the projects, down the street from him. The modest home she now lived in was definitely a step up. Cheryl had done okay for herself—without him.

He saw her as soon as she turned the corner from what he assumed was the kitchen. She wore a pair of short cutoff jeans that hugged her hips and revealed the cute button navel in her still-flat stomach. Her faded "Free Mandela" T-shirt outlined the ample bust that still dominated his dreams.

When she saw him, she stopped in her tracks. He smiled because he had to. All the feelings he'd felt for her rushed back and he wondered how he'd managed to live without her. The hurt and the regrets vanished.

"Are you going to invite me in?" he asked. His words mobilized her and she strode to the door, her firm breasts bouncing with each step.

"I'm sorry," she said as she unlocked the screened door and pushed it open. "Come in."

He wanted to pull her into his arms and kiss her senseless, but he refrained. He was a patient man. He could wait. "You're looking good, Cheryl," he said because it was true.

She brushed her hand across the braid covering her head. "I look a mess. I didn't know you were coming over."

He grinned. It was either do that or kiss her. "You called. I came."

"Sit down," she said, picking up the magazines scattered on the couch and in the chair. "If you can find a spot."

Her nervousness erased his and he sat down on the couch. She kept standing. "Aren't you going to sit with me?" He patted the spot next to him, feeling pretty brave and confident about now. He figured she still had feelings for him if he made her this nervous.

"Oh," she said. "Sure." She sat on the far end of the couch. "So what have you been doing?"

He moved closer and her womanly scent filled his nostrils. "I had my interview today."

"Are you going to take the job?"

He smiled. She had always been his biggest supporter. "How do you know they offered me one?"

She looked as if that was the dumbest question she'd ever heard. "Didn't they?"

He nodded and moved a little closer. "And I'm seriously thinking about taking it."

"Good," she said.

"Why is it good? Do you want me back in Gaines?"

She stood up and folded her arms across her chest. "Gaines is your home. You can come back if you want."

He stood up too. He didn't want to play games with her. "You know why I'm coming back, don't you?"

She turned and looked into his eyes and he knew she knew. "Not really," she said.

"I can't get you out of my system. No other woman compares to you."

She lowered her arms. "I guess you've been through a lot of women."

He didn't want to discuss all the women who'd passed through is life. "I haven't been a monk, if that's what you're asking. It's been eighteen years."

"Oh," was all she said.

He knew they needed to talk about what had happened between them, why they had broken up, but he didn't want to hash that out now. All he wanted now was her. "I need to hold you, Cheryl. I really do. Is that all right?"

She didn't say anything, but she nodded her head. That was enough. In a flash she was in his arms and soon after that he was kissing her and she was kissing him back. The quick passion they'd shared before was still there. He knew from her response that the kiss wasn't going to satisfy either of them. He wanted to crawl inside her skin and from the way she pressed herself against him, he guessed she wanted the same thing. "I love you," he said. "I've always loved you."

She ended the kiss and for a second he wondered if he'd

misread her. Then she took his hand and led him down the hall. He didn't notice much in the room other than the bed. Her bed. He pulled her into his arms again and asked the only question he was going to ask. "Are you sure?"

"I never stopped loving you, Marty. I'm sure."

She still loved him. That was all he needed to hear. He pulled her back into his arms and resumed their kiss. As they kissed, they tugged and pulled at each other's clothes, needing to be closer. When they were both naked, he moved away from her. "Beautiful," he said in a thick voice. "You're so beautiful. My beautiful Cheryl, let me love you."

She did.

The shocked expression on Mrs. Taylor's face when Marlena entered her two-story brick traditional home on Winston's arm made Marlena determined to have a good time this evening. She flashed her brightest smile as Winston presented her to his mother and Mr. Sanders.

After a flimsy handshake and a muttered hello from Mrs. Taylor, Marlena found herself in the warm embrace of Mr. Sanders.

"It's so good to see you, young lady," he said, when she stepped out of his arms. "I'm sorry I missed that little wingding they held for you."

She squeezed the older man's hands. "It's good to see you, too, Mr. Sanders. Don't worry about missing that old party. Tonight more than makes up for your absence."

Winston, who had been speaking quietly with his mother, walked over and joined them. "Watch out, Mr. Sanders. Marlena is my date and I don't want you flirting with her."

The older man laughed. "Not to worry, my boy. I've got my own date tonight." He winked at Mrs. Taylor and Marlena guessed the woman wished the ground would open up and swallow every one of them but her. "We have a few minutes before we have to leave. Would either of you young people like a drink?" Mr. Sanders asked.

Marlena took her cue from Winston and shared a cocktail

with the older couple. She watched Mrs. Taylor out of the corner of her eye while Winston and Mr. Sanders made conversation. The older woman actually paled beneath her makeup. The thought of her passing out from disgust made Marlena smile.

"What are you thinking about?" Winston asked, tapping her lightly on her bare shoulder and causing a familiar tingling sensation.

"Just thinking," she said, still smiling.

"Are you enjoying yourself?"

She cast a quick glance at his mother. The older woman's discomfort still showed. "A lot more than your mother. Are you sure you want to ruin her evening?"

Winston grinned down at her. "No doubt about it. Mothers need a little shaking up every now and then. Who better to do it than their kids?"

"If you say so," she said, captivated by his masculine grin. At this point, she would have agreed with anything he said.

"We're about ready to go. Do you need to freshen up or anything?"

She appreciated his consideration, but shook her head.

He extended his arm to her and she took it. "Then it's time to get this show on the road."

The two couples made their way to Mr. Sanders' maroon Town Car. The older couple sat up front while she and Winston climbed into the back. The back seat was wide enough to accommodate another couple, but Winston didn't let that stop him from pulling Marlena to his side so that she sat in the curve of his arm.

"That's better," he said once she was settled. "You smell so good," he whispered against her ear.

She sucked in her breath and wondered how she was going to endure the long drive to Athens sitting so close to him. "Behave yourself," she told him. "Your mother's watching."

He placed his tongue ever so lightly against her ear. "I'm sure she's been in the back seat of a car before."

Marlena giggled like a school girl. "But I bet her date's mother wasn't in the front seat at the time."

"I knew it," he said, pulling away from her.

"Knew what?"

"I'd want to throw my mother in the nearest lake," he whispered. "I just didn't think it would happen so early in the evening."

"You're too bad," Marlena said as a feeling of contentment settled over her. She leaned closer to Winston.

Before Winston could comment, Mr. Sanders asked Marlena about her job in D.C. Winston listened as she told them about her latest case and all the celebrity surrounding it.

"How were you able to put up with those Hollywood types?" his mother asked, making a late entrance into the conversation. "They have no morals whatsoever. I know I couldn't stand to be around them."

Marlena caught the older woman's jab, but she didn't let it bother her. "I considered it my duty," she answered calmly. "You know, a light in darkness, that kind of thing."

Mrs. Taylor glanced back at her and Marlena could tell from the venom in her eyes that she wanted to make a snide retort. Only the presence of Mr. Sanders and Winston stopped her.

"Good for you, girl," Mr. Sanders said. "I've always wanted to go to Hollywood myself, but I never got around to it."

Marlena told them about the parties she'd attended and some of the celebrities she'd met.

"And after seeing all that you've seen, you decided to come back to Gaines. No place can beat home, can it?" Mr. Sanders asked.

"No, sir," she said. "Gaines isn't D.C. or New York or L.A. or Hollywood, but like they say, there's no place like home."

Mr. Sanders laughed, Winston squeezed her shoulders, Mrs. Taylor remained silent, and Marlena relaxed. There was definitely no place like home.

Cheryl propped her head on her folded arm and watched Marty sleep. He looked as content and fulfilled as she felt. They'd given each other some welcome. Her body still tingled from his intimate touches and erotic kisses. It was as if they'd never been apart. He still knew how to make her body scream and she hadn't forgotten a thing about his.

"Welcome home," she said when his eyelids fluttered open. She couldn't resist running her finger along his masculine jaw. He was still the handsomest man she'd ever seen. Sure, she knew everybody didn't share her opinion. Marty was too dark for some women, his face a bit too square for others, but to her, he was perfection.

"That was some welcome," he said with a leer. "How about a replay?"

She smiled down at him. "I don't know," she said. "Will you still respect me in the morning?"

He touched his hand to her face. "I meant what I said, Cheryl. I still love you."

"You don't have to say that." Though she loved hearing him say the words, she didn't want to raise her hopes and have them dashed later. For now it was enough that he wanted her as much as she wanted him, that he hadn't forgotten her, and that there was still a place in his heart that was hers. Love would come if they had enough time. She was sure of it.

"I'm not just saying the words. I mean them." He sat up in the bed, kicking the covers away, not embarrassed by his nakedness. "I guess I've always known that I still loved you."

She knew Marty wanted to talk, to clear the air their years apart had clouded, but she didn't. Not now. Now all she wanted was to be with him and pretend the years apart hadn't happened. She wanted to enjoy him and love him while she had the chance, because as soon as they started talking she feared the walls would go up and a lot of the old hurts would resurface.

Tonight was their night. She'd called Marty today because she'd known Patrice would be spending the night at her father's house, giving Cheryl and Marty the evening alone, probably the only time they'd have alone for a while. She'd planned on an evening of conversation and reacquaintance, but she'd gotten so much more. She didn't want to spoil it.

She ran her hand across his chest and he groaned as she'd known he would. She rewarded him with a lingering kiss.

He pulled her naked body across his and took control of the kiss, granting her the reprieve she wanted, at least for a little while.

When the double-dating couples were about midway through dinner, Marlena was reconsidering her "there's no place like home" spiel. Evidently, the evening had worn on Mrs. Taylor's nerves and she couldn't keep the animosity she felt toward Marlena hidden.

"What's the matter with you tonight?" Mr. Sanders asked with chastisement in his voice. "You've been practically rude to our Marlena here."

Mrs. Taylor picked up her wine glass and drained its contents. "I'm not being rude, am I, Marlena, darling?" she asked in a syrupy, but artificially sweet voice.

Marlena stared into the older woman's hate-filled eyes, then wiped her mouth with her cloth napkin. "She's not being rude at all, Mr. Sanders," she said, deliberately choosing not to respond to the older woman. "I've always understood and appreciated her quick wit. Sparring with Mrs. Taylor prepared me for dealing with hostile witnesses. The exercise proved invaluable."

The two men chuckled, but Mrs. Taylor looked as if she were about to make some biting remark. Winston stopped her by speaking first. "I've had a great time tonight, but I have an early morning tomorrow. I think I'll pass on dessert."

Marlena noticed that nobody pointed out to Winston that they were still having their meal. They were all as ready for this evening to end as he was; thanks to Mrs. Taylor.

The two couples ate the rest of their meal in a tense silence that was broken only when Mr. Sanders made some comment. Soon, they were out of the restaurant and back in the Town Car. Winston offered to drive back home, so the older couple sat in back while Marlena took her place next to Winston in front.

Marlena strapped herself in, but that didn't stop Winston from taking her arm and pulling her as close to him as her seatbelt would allow. She bet his action made Mrs. Taylor foam at the mouth.

"It takes two hands to drive, Winston," came Mrs. Taylor's comment not much later.

Winston looked up in the rearview mirror to catch his mother's gaze. He grinned. "I've been driving with one hand since I started dating. Don't worry. I'll get us home safely." He squeezed Marlena's shoulder. "There's too much valuable cargo onboard for me to be careless."

Mr. Sanders chuckled. "I know what you mean, boy. I've always wondered why people said you needed to keep both hands on the wheel. I sure could find better things to do with my other hand."

"Herman," Mrs. Taylor said. "Don't be so common."

"Aww, Barbara. I know for a fact that you spent many a night in the car with Albert and I know he only used one hand to drive."

"Herman!"

Marlena and Winston laughed.

"It's too late now, Mother. Your secret is out. Tell us more, Mr. Sanders."

"If you say one more word Herman Sanders," Winston's mother warned, "I'll never speak to you again."

"Now look what you've done, boy. You've got your date all cuddled close and now mine is threatening not to talk to me. What kind of friend are you?"

"Don't believe a word of what she says," Winston said. "She's all bark and no bite. Isn't that right, Mother?"

"I'm not talking to you either, Winston. I can't believe it. My own son has turned against me."

"Come on, Barbara," Mr. Sanders coaxed. "We're only having a little fun with you now."

"I'm not speaking to you, Herman, and I don't know if I'll ever speak to you again. I should have known this evening would end in disaster."

Marlena knew that last statement was for her, but she chose to ignore it. She could put up with Mrs. Taylor for the short ride back to Gaines.

"Well, boy, since your mother isn't talking to me, I guess you can put on some music. Maybe she'll be softened up by the time we get home."

Marlena heard a sound much like a slap then a muttered "ouch" from Mr. Sanders. She smiled and relaxed in Winston's embrace.

Chapter 13

By the time Winston pulled his Bronco into the hotel parking lot, Marlena had fallen asleep next to him. So much for my smooth charm, he thought. I'm so potent that I put her to sleep. His eyes moved from her innocent and beautiful face to her full breasts, which rose and fell as she breathed. Again, he wanted her. Again, he wasn't going to act on it.

He wanted more from Marlena than a sexual relationship, he admitted. He wanted to be a part of her life for a very long time and he wanted that life right here in Gaines where they both belonged. He had to make her want the same thing.

He kissed her lightly on the lips. "Wake up, sleepy head. We're home."

"Hmm," she murmured, but she didn't open her eyes.

He leaned across her and undid her seat belt. "You must have had a busy day," he said to her, knowing she couldn't hear him. "I hate to wake you, but I don't think you'd appreciate it if I carried you into the hotel. I wish I could take you to my house, but I don't think you'd appreciate that either."

He shook her shoulders slightly. "Sweetheart, wake up. You're home." When she still didn't wake up, Winston couldn't think of any other action to take. He leaned over and kissed her again. Unlike the previous kiss, this one gave vent to some of the desire he felt.

Her eyes remained closed as she instinctively lifted her arms around his neck. He gave himself to the kiss, telling himself that he wasn't really taking advantage of her.

When his hand moved to her breasts, she quickened and her eyes flew open. "Winston!" She dropped her arms from his neck and pulled away. "What are you doing?"

"I was trying to wake you up." He grinned at her bewildered expression. "It worked. Thanks for going with me tonight. I had a good time."

She rubbed her fingers across her lips, then quickly dropped them when she noticed that he watched her. "I had a good time, too."

"In spite of my mother?"

She nodded. "Believe it or not, your mother wasn't that bad." She had seen Mrs. Taylor behave much worse than she'd behaved tonight. "Any rudeness on her part was more than compensated for by Mr. Sanders's attentiveness. He's really a sweet old man."

"Hey, what about me? I'm not exactly beans and weenies."

She smiled. "And you too. It was a good evening. I'm glad I went."

"Does that mean you're up for doing it again?"

"I could probably handle it a couple of times a year."

"That's a start. What about an evening with just you and me? Do you think you could handle a date?"

She cocked her head to one side and gazed into his pure brown eyes, no longer able to deny her feelings for him. "I know I could."

His smile was her reward. "Good. So where do you want to go tomorrow night?"

"Eager, aren't we?"

"Not eager," he said sincerely. "Afraid you'll slip away from me again."

Her smile faltered at his reference to the past. "The only place I'm going is back to D.C."

"We'll see," he said.

"I *am* going back, Winston. D.C. is my home now."

He placed his finger against her ear and lightly caressed it. "Do you still have them?" he asked.

She didn't have to ask what he was talking about. "Always."

"Good. Wear them tomorrow. For me."

He'd given her gold stud earrings for a high school graduation present. The gift had been much too expensive, but he wouldn't take it back. He'd simply told her he loved her and she'd better get used to him showering her with gifts.

She hadn't worn the gold studs since the day she walked away from him. They held too many memories. Memories she had to keep out of her mind if she was going to stay away from him. That she'd brought them to Gaines was more proof she'd really come back to find him again. "I'll wear them."

"Good. Now I want one kiss to last me until I see you in the morning. You are coming to the office, aren't you?"

She nodded. "I might be late, though. You know I'm chauffeuring Marty around."

"Correction. You *were* chauffeuring Marty around. I took the liberty of renting a car for him. It was delivered to the Gaines Inn this afternoon."

"You didn't?"

"Oh, yes, I did. I don't want him to get used to having you around."

She gave an impish smile. "Afraid of the competition?"

He shook his head. "I really do want Marty to accept the job offer and I may ruin the deal if I have to deck him."

"You wouldn't," she said, her voice full of mirth.

"Since he now has his own car, we'll never find out. Now, back to a more important matter. Are you going to kiss me good night like a good girl?"

In answer, she leaned over and gave him a chaste peck on his smooth-shaven jaw.

"That wasn't a kiss."

"You said you wanted a good girl kiss, so I gave you one. Be careful what you ask for." She smiled, then turned and opened her door.

He stayed her arm. "Wait a minute. I'll help you down."

Winston rushed around to her side of the Bronco and lifted her out of her seat. He slowly slid her body down the length of his until her feet were on the ground.

"Thank you," she said breathlessly.

"Now, let's see if we can try that kiss again." He leaned his head down and she raised up on her toes. When their lips met, he groaned and lifted her into his arms again. She felt so good that he didn't want to ever let her go, though he knew he had to.

He slowly lifted his head and stared down into her bright eyes. "That's more like it," he said, allowing her feet to slide back down to the ground. "Now, let's get you safely inside the hotel before I lose control and take you back to my house." And to my bed where you belong, he added to himself.

He took her hand in his and led her into the lobby. When they reached the elevator, he pushed the button, then gazed down at her. "Don't look at me like that," he said.

"Like what?" she murmured, licking her tongue across her already kiss-swollen lips.

He groaned and shifted his feet in an effort to keep his body's response in check. "Like you want me to kiss you again."

The elevator doors opened before she could answer and he pushed her on. "You aren't coming up with me?" she asked with disappointment.

He shook his head. "If I go up, I won't be coming back down tonight. Is that what you want?"

Her eyes told him that was exactly what she wanted, but she shook her head. "I'll see you in the morning," she said as the elevator doors closed.

"If I live that long," he muttered to himself, then made for the doorway and the cold shower he knew awaited him when he got home.

Marty awoke later that night feeling smug and content. He'd always expected his reunion with Cheryl would be one of fireworks, but he could never have imagined the tenderness. and the protectiveness that would surround his heart when he held her in his arms. He looked down at her beautiful face and felt fortunate they'd been given another chance. Tightening his hold on her, he placed a kiss atop her head.

Cheryl was still his Cheryl. Then she'd worn an afro and now she sported braids. His little militant determined early that a perm would never go in her hair. He knew some men preferred straight hair they could run their fingers through, but he just preferred Cheryl. Her hair was her and he loved it. He'd had other women, women with permed hair, women with weaves, but none of them measured up to Cheryl.

"What are you thinking about?" her sleepy voice asked.

He kissed her upturned face. "You." Her broad smile forced him to give her another kiss.

"Hmm, that was good," she said, closing her eyes and licking her lips as if to savor his taste.

"There's more where that came from," he said.

She leaned up on his chest and stared into his eyes. "No way, buster. I'm not as young as I used to be. I need my rest and so do you."

"I'm not tired."

"You ought to be. We've been at it for a long time. What time is it anyway?"

She turned her head to the clock and his eyes followed her. She made some comment about the time but he didn't register it. His attention was directed at the photograph on the night stand next to the clock. He leaned over and picked it up. "Is this your daughter?"

He felt the tightness in her before she answered. "Yes, that's Patrice."

"She's a beauty," he said, staring at the picture. Cheryl's daughter, he thought, and the betrayal he'd felt all those years ago began to creep back.

"Thank you," Cheryl murmured.

"She looks a lot like you. Does she have any of her father's features?"

"Not really," she said, taking the photograph from him and placing it back on the nightstand. "She has his ways, but not his looks."

He looked back at the picture. He couldn't take his eyes off the girl. "How old is she?"

"Seventeen, last month. She'll be a senior in high school in the fall."

Marty mentally calculated the date of the child's conception. He loosened his hold on Cheryl.

"You knew I had a daughter, Marty," she said defensively. She moved off his chest and pulled the sheet up to cover her nakedness. This was the conversation she'd dreaded. Her reprieve was over.

"Were you sleeping with both of us at the same time?" he asked in a short, clipped tone.

What could she say? "No."

She heard him release a deep sigh and hoped that meant he believed her. "But as soon as I left, you jumped in the sack with him," he accused.

"That's not what happened," she said, hating the tone he used and hating the fear his tone made her feel. Where was the sensitive, tender man who'd just made such sweet love to her? The man who'd claimed only hours ago that he still loved her?

He sat up in the bed and threw his muscular legs over the side, presenting his taut back to her. "Then tell me what happened. How did you end up married to another man and carrying his baby?"

She closed her eyes against the pain and distance she heard in his voice. It hurt to know that he was cutting himself off from her. "Let's not spoil what we shared tonight, Marty."

"I'm not spoiling anything." He stood up and faced her in his naked glory, his arms folded across his chest like some African warrior. "I want some answers."

"It sounds like you want to punish me."

He stared at her for a long moment, eyes wide and nostrils flaring, then he dropped his arms and reached for his undershorts and slipped them on. Then he reached for his pants. "Are you seeing anybody now?" he asked.

She grabbed a handful of the sheet in her hand and squeezed

as his question pierced her heart. "How can you ask that after what we just shared?"

He yanked on his shirt and haphazardly buttoned it. "I want to know where I stand. We have a history of not communicating well. I don't want to repeat past mistakes. So, are you seeing anybody now?"

"No," she said through tight lips. "I'm not seeing anyone. I don't make a habit of sleeping with one man while I'm seeing another."

Still working at his buttons, he raised a brow, but he didn't say anything. She knew he was thinking that she'd slept with Nathaniel and him at the same time.

When he sat down on the bed to pull on his socks and shoes, she said, "I guess you're leaving."

"I think it's best."

"Best for who?"

Fully dressed, he stood up and stared at her. "For both of us. If I stay, I may say some things I'll regret later."

She nodded understanding while defeat filled her heart. "So much for being in love with me, huh?"

His dark eyes met hers. "Don't doubt that I love you, Cheryl, because I do, but that doesn't mean we don't have some problems to work through."

She hated herself for the relief she felt, knowing it reflected her need for this man. "Oh, I see. You're leaving because you want to work through our problems. Thanks for telling me. I thought you were escaping, but now I know you're working through our problems."

"Don't be sarcastic. You know what I mean."

"No, I don't."

He sighed again, then came and sat next to her on the bed. "I do love you," he said. "But it still hurts. I hate to think about you with another man. When I look at the picture of your daughter, all I can think is that she should be *our* daughter."

Cheryl's heart contracted as he spoke. She wanted to jump in and tell him that Patrice was his daughter, but he spoke before she could.

"But that's not the way it is," he went on. "The reality is

that though you told me you loved me and though you said you'd wait for me, you didn't. You married him almost as soon as I left town. How's that supposed to make me feel?"

Everything he said was true, but he didn't know the whole story. He didn't know that she'd done what she did for him, because she'd loved him so. How could she make him understand? She opened her mouth to try.

"Don't say anything," he said. "Not tonight. Just tell me this. Do you want to try again?"

She nodded. "More than anything. I know I've made some mistakes, Marty, but I've always loved you. Always."

He placed his hand against her smooth cheek and she read his love in his eyes. "I want so much to believe you, Cheryl."

She kissed the palm of his hand. "You can, Marty. I do love you. You'll never know how much."

He smiled and she had some hope that maybe they could work through this. "That's why I'm here. I've thought about you and what could have been between us every day. When Winston called about *The Way Home,* I thought it was an omen, a sign. There's hope for us, but we'll have to take it slow."

"It's a little too late for that, don't you think?" she said through the tears she knew were in her eyes.

"I didn't plan for this to happen," he said, wiping her tears with his fingers. "I came here to talk, to find out if seeing you made me realize I'd been loving a fantasy all these years." He kissed her lips lightly. "But as soon as I saw you, I knew that what I felt was real. Making love with you was as necessary as breathing."

She forced a smile. She'd needed him just as much, though she knew they'd shared the moment under artificial conditions. "Just be glad Patrice wasn't home or you wouldn't have been able to breathe."

The light in his eyes dimmed at the mention of Patrice's name. "She should have been my daughter, Cheryl. I should have been the one to see you grow big with pregnancy. We should have raised her together and she should have had brothers and sisters. A lot of them."

Tell him now, Cheryl, she commanded herself. Tell him. He wants children. He wants Patrice to be his. "Patrice is—"

"I know," he said, cutting her off. "Patrice is not my daughter and I'll have to deal with that. We have time. Now kiss me so I can get back to the hotel. If I stay any longer, Patrice will come home and find a man in her mother's bed."

He leaned over to kiss her, but she placed a hand on his chest. "Wait a minute, Marty. There's something I have to tell you."

He moved back. "Okay, tell me."

Cheryl was afraid to do what she was about to do, but she felt she had no choice. If she let Marty walk out of her house tonight without telling him the truth, she wasn't sure she'd ever have the courage to tell him. She took a deep breath, stared right into Marty's eyes, and put everything she loved on the line: "Patrice *is* your daughter."

Chapter 14

"What do you mean she's my daughter?" Marty asked, sure he'd heard wrong. Patrice couldn't be his daughter.

"She's your daughter," Cheryl repeated. "Yours and mine."

He dropped down on the side of the bed. "But how?" he asked, his mind in a fog. *Patrice was his daughter.* "How can this be?"

Cheryl covered her face with her hands, sighed again, then dropped her hands. "I was pregnant with your baby when I married Nathaniel."

"You were pregnant with *my* baby?" he repeated, knowing he was beginning to sound like a parrot. "You were pregnant with *my*"—he punched his finger to his chest—"baby and you married Nathaniel. What are you saying, Cheryl?"

She flinched and drew herself away from him. Just as she'd thought, the news was making Marty hate her. "You heard me, Marty. She's our daughter. You said you wanted her to be our daughter. Well, she is. I thought you'd be happy."

Marty leaped up from the bed. "Happy? What are you talking about? I'm supposed to be happy that you were pregnant with *my child, our child,* and you married another man? How is that supposed to make me happy?"

Cheryl told herself not to get upset. Marty wasn't lashing out at her exactly, he was reacting to her news. "I did it for you, don't you see?"

He shook his head and stared at her as if she were crazy. "I sure don't see. You were pregnant with my baby and you married Nathaniel *for me?* Surely you can come up with something better. How about aliens abducted you and forced you to marry him?"

Cheryl's anger simmered very close to be surface and if Marty didn't wipe that smirk off his face, he'd be the recipient of a large dose of it, she thought. "Don't be sarcastic. You were so excited about leaving for school. It was all you could talk about. If I had told you I was pregnant, what would you have done?"

"I would have married you the way we planned to do anyway. That's what I would have done. Didn't you know that?" His eyes filled with pain as he spoke.

She got up and went to comfort him, but when she tried to take his arm, he jerked it away. "I knew that's what you'd want to do," she explained, "but I couldn't let you make that sacrifice. Marty, you had a scholarship to Stanford. To *Stanford.* I couldn't let you give that up. Not because of me. I didn't want you saddled with a baby. What if your responsibility to us kept you from fulfilling your dreams? I couldn't take that chance. I knew you'd grow to resent me and the baby. I couldn't live with that."

Marty gave a harsh laugh that Cheryl had never heard before. "You thought I'd resent you and *my* baby? How do you think I feel now, Cheryl? How do you think I feel knowing you were pregnant with my baby and you didn't trust me enough to tell me? How do you think I feel knowing you willingly married another man and gave my child his name? How do you think I feel knowing I have a seventeen-year-old daughter whom I've never known, never even seen? How do you think all of that makes me feel?"

His words, his tone, his ragged face, all told her that she'd made the wrong the decision eighteen years ago. "I'm sorry,

Marty. I thought I was doing the right thing. I loved you so much." She reached for him again.

He stepped back. "You loved me?" He laughed that harsh laugh again. "Now that's a joke. How can you say you loved me after you've betrayed me the way you have?" He looked at her as if she were some insect he wanted to squash. "I don't even know who you are, Cheryl. You certainly aren't the woman I thought I was in love with."

Thought he was in love with her, the words echoed in her mind and strangled her hope. "What are you saying, Marty?"

He reached for his jacket. "Look, I've got to get out of here. I've got to get out of here."

"Don't," she pleaded. "Let's talk about this some more. You have to understand."

He stared at her and the emptiness in his eyes almost made her scream. Where was the love that had been present earlier? Where was the passion? "Marty," she began. "Please listen. You have to listen to me."

He shook his head. "I can't, Cheryl," he said, choking out the words. "I can't talk to you. I can't even bear to look at you. How could you do this to me? To us? How could you do it to our daughter?"

He gazed over at Patrice's lovely face, then turned his hard eyes back to Cheryl. "You're sure she's mine, aren't you?"

Cheryl crumpled against the bedcovers, his words a physical blow as much as an emotional one. "How could you ask me that? How could you?"

He shrugged, but kept his eyes fixed on her. "I don't know. Maybe you heard I had a little money now and thought you'd cut yourself in for a slice." His eyes scanned the quality, though not very expensive, furnishings in the room. "Not that you haven't done well for yourself. But maybe you decided you wanted to do a little better. Maybe you decided you wanted a big house in Rosemont and thought I'd could be your ticket to getting one."

His venom-filled words and hate-filled eyes defeated her. Just as she'd imagined, her news had made him hate her. She couldn't fight his hate. "I think you'd better leave," she said calmly.

He continued to stare at her. Finally, he shook his head then said, "You know, Cheryl, I have no idea how I ever loved you in the first place."

His words practically ripped her heart out of her chest, but she refused to let him know how beaten she was. She raised defiant eyes to him. "Get out of my house and don't ever come back."

Marlena heard the ringing phone as she unlocked her suite door. She quickly opened the door and rushed to the phone in the sleeping area expecting to hear Winston's smooth voice on the other end. "Miss me already?" she asked in a smooth voice of her own.

"I told you he'd hate me," came Cheryl's voice.

Marlena dropped down on the side of the bed, disappointed the call wasn't from Winston, but concerned about the tone of Cheryl's voice. "You told Marty?"

"And he responded just as I thought he would." Cheryl moaned. "Oh, Marlena, it was awful. Just awful."

"What did he say?"

"A lot. And a lot of it ugly. I can't even remember what he said, but I do remember him staring at me like I was a monster with two heads or something."

"It couldn't have been that bad."

"Please! It was worse. He hates me. I could see it in those dead eyes he fixed on me. He hates me."

"You don't know that for sure," Marlena said, trying to provide the encouragement her friend needed. "He's had a shock. Give him some time. He'll get over it and then you two can talk about it calmly."

"You didn't see him." Marlena heard the sniffle that followed her friend's words. "I've never seen him look that way."

Marlena felt for her friend. Though she had experienced betrayal and could imagine how Marty felt, she'd also been cast in the role of betrayer so she knew exactly where Cheryl was coming from. Neither role was one she wanted to play again. "Look, Cheryl," she said, "Do you want me to come over?"

Cheryl sniffled again. "That's not necessary. I'll be fine." She laughed, a forced sound in Marlena's ears. "Well, maybe not fine, but I'll make it through the night. I think I just need to let these tears come. I've held them inside for too long."

Marlena thought that was a good idea. Emotions held in too long tended to burst forth at the most inopportune time and in the most uncontrollable fashion. "I know you're hurt by Marty's response, but how do you feel about telling him? Do you think you did the right thing?"

Cheryl didn't answer immediately. She sniffled a few times, then she blew her nose. "You know, in a way, I feel relieved. I made a big mistake by not telling Marty about the baby back when I first found out I was pregnant. I guess I've always known I was wrong, but I couldn't bring myself to admit it. I've been carrying around a lot of guilt, so I guess, to answer your question, yeah, I feel some relief."

"I know you don't see it now, but you've accomplished a lot by telling Marty," Marlena said and her mind went immediately to her own secret. She'd told herself her actions, however misinterpreted, were done out of love. Was she as wrong as Cheryl had been? "You've helped Marty and you've helped yourself."

Cheryl sighed. "This means Patrice will have to be told."

"Patrice," Marlena repeated, thinking about the young girl for the first time. "She wasn't home when you and Marty had this discussion, was she?"

"Oh, no," Cheryl answered quickly. "She's spending the night with Nathaniel, the man she thinks is her father. Oh, God, this is really a mess. What have I done, Marlena?"

"Stop it, Cheryl. You've done what needed to be done and I'm proud of you. Now, don't worry about Patrice yet. You can't tell her about this until you and Marty work through it. So, try not to think about it."

"Easier said than done. She's all I can think about."

"Well, try to get some rest tonight. Are you sure you don't want me to come over?"

"I'm sure. I need this time alone to cry. I'll be fine."

"You're sure?"

"I told you I'm sure. Now stop worryin' about me. How did your evening go with Winston?"

Marlena knew Cheryl was trying to change the subject and while she debated whether to allow her to do so, a knock sounded on her door. She glanced at the clock and wondered who'd be visiting at this hour. Surely Winston hadn't changed his mind and decided to come up to her room after all, or had he?

"Can you hold on a minute, Cheryl?" she asked. "Somebody's at the door."

Marlena rushed to the door and looked out the peep hole. It was a much-worse-for-the-wear Marty. She opened the door and let him.

"You knew, didn't you?" he accused, stomping through her open door. "You knew Patrice was mine and you knew Cheryl had kept her from me. Can you believe she did this to me, Marlena? I loved her and this is how she repays me."

Marlena felt Marty's pain and helplessness but she wasn't sure she could do anything to ease either. "Why don't you sit down, Marty. I need to get off the phone."

Marty sat down, but he didn't say anything. Marlena wondered if her words had even registered.

She went back into the bedroom area and picked up the phone. "It's Marty."

"How is he?" Cheryl asked with concern.

Marlena glanced back at him sitting with his head down, his hands folded. "Not too well. He's pretty angry."

"That's an understatement," Cheryl muttered. "Look, I'm gonna hang up. Take care of Marty for me, Marlena. I love that guy more than I thought was possible."

Marlena's heart tightened. "He loves you, too. You've got to believe that."

"I'm trying," was all Cheryl would say before hanging up.

Marlena held the phone in her hand after her friend had hung up and wondered about the ramifications of Cheryl's revelation. Lives would be changed and hearts would be broken. She sighed, placed the phone on the hook, then got up to go back to Marty, hoping the healing that was sure to take place would make all the pain worth it.

Winston wanted to call Marlena as soon as he got home, but he forced himself to wait until after his shower. Now that he was showered and dressed, well, undressed, since he slept nude, he was ready to hear that soulful, sexy voice of hers. They weren't sleeping together tonight, but she could surely make his sleep a lot sounder.

He shifted his naked male frame against the headboard of his king-sized bed and picked up the phone, wondering what she wore to bed. The black negligee he'd bought for her birthday one year flashed in his mind. He crossed his legs and groaned.

Her phone rang for so long he wondered if the desk clerk had connected him to the wrong room. He knew Marlena couldn't be out. On the seventh ring, she picked up.

"Hello," the sleepy masculine voice said.

Winston sat up in the bed. "Marty?"

"Yeah. Who's this?"

What was Marty doing asleep in Marlena's room at this time of night? "This is Winston. Where's Marlena?"

Marty yawned. "I hear the shower," he said. "She must be in the shower."

Marlena was in the shower and Marty was asleep in her room. What was going on? "What are you doing in her room?" he asked.

Another yawn. "Sleeping, I guess. I stopped by to talk and I guess we both fell asleep."

More than anything Winston wanted to know where in Marlena's suite they'd fallen asleep but he managed to keep the question from escaping his lips.

"God," Marty said as Winston continued to mull over the possible sleeping arrangements. "I've never been so tired in all my life. I definitely needed that little nap."

Winston wanted to reach through the phone and punch Marty right in the nose. Did the guy have to rub it in? *He was so tired. He definitely needed a nap.* Winston didn't need a roadmap to figure out what had happened. "Hey, I'll let you get back to sleep or whatever."

"Okay, man. I'll tell Marlena you called."

"Yeah, you do that."

Winston slammed down the phone. An unbidden vision of Marlena clad in that black negligee in bed with a naked Marty formed in his mind. He closed his eyes to the vision. He didn't want to see Marlena in anybody's arms but his!

He got up from the bed and paced the room. Maybe the situation wasn't what it seemed, he reasoned. Yeah, and maybe Marlena didn't walk out on you ten years ago either. Face it, buddy, you've never been able to figure that woman out, so don't start trying to do it now.

Winston sat down on the side of the bed and dropped his head in his hands. He'd thought the night had gone well. Marlena had even agreed to go out with him again. Surely, she wouldn't have hopped in the sack with Marty immediately after leaving his arms.

Maybe he should have stayed and made love to her. She'd wanted him as much as he'd wanted her, but, no, he'd played the gentlemen and walked away. Marty hadn't. No, his old friend had walked in and taken advantage of a pump Winston had primed. He wanted to kill him.

Winston lay back on the bed and rested his folded hands across his bare stomach. He knew his mind was jumping to conclusions. There was no way Marlena would sleep with Marty, his rational self told him, if for no other reason than her allegiance to Cheryl. No, Marlena wasn't the kind of woman to steal a friend's man.

The ringing of his telephone interrupted his thoughts. Who the hell could this be? he wondered.

"Hello," he barked out. He didn't feel up to pretending he wanted to talk.

"Winston, are you all right? It's Marlena. Marty said you called."

He sat up. "Sorry I woke him up."

"That's all right," she said. "He needed to get up. If you hadn't called, I would have gotten him up when I got out of the shower."

Well, damn, she didn't even feel a need to lie about the situation. "I'm glad I could be of help."

"Is something wrong, Winston? You sound strange."

Strange. He'd say there was something strange about calling your woman's hotel room late at night and having a sleepy man pick up the phone. "Hey, I'm fine. I'm sorry I disturbed you and Marty. You could have waited until tomorrow to talk to me. I'm sure you have better things to do."

He heard her giggle and wondered what she found funny. "I don't believe you," she said.

"And I don't believe you. Look, I'm going to hang up. Marty must want you off the phone."

"Winston," she said, no more giggles in her voice. "Don't hang up."

"Why? Do you get off on having two men sniffing after you?"

She breathed a deep sigh and he wondered why she felt a need to keep her patience. "I should have let you hang up," she said. "Actually, I should hang up on you. I take it you think Marty and I have been doing more than talking tonight?"

"What am I supposed to think?" he shot back. Now that she'd voiced his thoughts, he felt rather foolish. Maybe he'd overreacted. Neither she nor Marty were trying to hide anything.

She sighed that damn patience-seeking sigh again. "You really don't trust me, do you?"

Oh, damn, now she'd turned the tables on him. How was he going to get out of this one? "I wouldn't say that exactly." Weak, man, weak, he told himself.

"I think that's exactly what it is. What are we doing to each other, Winston? I can't keep playing these games."

"I'm not playing games."

"It looks that way to me. You take me out on a double date with your mother, of all people. You bring me home and we share the sweetest kisses. You make me think that maybe you want to see if we can have something again, then you pull a stupid stunt like this. I call that playing games.''

He conceded that it looked as though he was playing games, but he most definitely wasn't. "Look, I'm sorry. Okay?"

"Not okay. You can't keep doing this me. You pull me to you with one hand and push me away with the other. I have feelings too, Winston. I can be hurt as easily as you can.''

"I'm really sorry, Marlena. I really am. Look, I called to tell you how much I enjoyed the evening''—and to ask what you were sleeping in, he added silently—"and when Marty answered the phone, I lost it. I've never been a jealous man, but . . .''

In the silence, he could hear her thinking.

"Maybe we shouldn't see each other. Maybe it's unreasonable to think we can overcome the past.''

"No," he shouted. "No, I want to keep seeing you. I need you, Marlena," he said honestly. "I've always needed you.''

"Don't do this, Winston. You don't need me. You might want me, but you don't need me. The fact is the last ten years prove we don't need each other.''

"You didn't live the last ten years with me, so speak for yourself. I can count the nights I've gone to bed without thinking about you and believe me there weren't many. I functioned without you, yes, but I haven't lived. Not really.''

Marlena curled up on the bed and hugged the phone to herself, wanting desperately to believe Winston's words. She'd thought about him, too. All the time. She'd tried to fill her schedule with work and other men, but he'd always been there taunting her with the happiness she'd so foolishly thrown back in his face.

"Do you think you can ever forgive me for walking out on you the way I did?'' she asked. "That's what all this is about, you know.''

He smoothed his hand across his forehead. "I know and every day I tell myself that I've forgiven you. I mean it, too, then something like tonight happens and it's ten years ago.''

"That means you haven't forgiven me. What will it take for you to forgive me, Winston?''

He squeezed his eyes shut. What would it take? "There's so much I don't understand. Why did you leave me? I keep thinking there was more to it than what you said."

She didn't want to get into her reasons. She couldn't tell him. The secret she harbored was not hers alone so she didn't have the right to expose it, or did she? "Why can't you accept what I told you?"

"I'm trying," he said and she believed him. She just didn't know if he could do it.

Neither did he.

Chapter 15

After calling Cheryl early the next morning and reassuring herself that her friend had made it through the night, Marlena met Marty for a continental breakfast in the hotel lounge and commiserated over the sorry status of their love lives.

"We're intelligent people," Marty reasoned. "So how did we end up in these strange situations?"

Marlena shrugged. "I don't think intelligence has anything to do with it. Our hearts did us in."

"You've got that right. It amazes me that I can still love Cheryl after what she's done. Doesn't that make me an idiot?"

Marlena shook her head. She thought just the opposite. "It means you're very much in touch with your feelings."

"Hold on a minute," Marty said, interrupting her. "You're talking to a macho man here, don't go around saying I'm in touch with my feelings. You could ruin my reputation. Hey, you could ruin the reputation of my entire gender."

"Don't make jokes, Marty, I'm serious. Anger would probably be a much easier emotion for you to handle right now."

"Don't get me wrong," he said. "I *am* angry with Cheryl. More angry than I've ever been with anybody. Last night I thought I hated her, but somewhere between the time I left your room and the time I dressed to meet you for breakfast this morning, I realized that though I hated what she'd done, I'm still very much in love with her.''

Marlena stirred her coffee idly and thought about her situation with Winston. "Then you two'll work it out."

"I wish I were as sure as you seem to be."

"With love everything is possible," she quipped, knowing that wasn't the case. If it was, she and Winston would be together right now.

Marty dumped about four packets of sugar in his coffee. "You've been reading too many romance novels. Life doesn't work that way."

"You don't have to tell me, Marty. I know. Believe me, I know."

He stopped stirring his coffee and looked at her. "How are things between you and Winston?"

"Not much better than things between you and Cheryl. Winston doesn't seem to be able to forgive me for what I did in the past."

"That's tough. What are you gonna do about it?"

She shrugged. She didn't know if there was anything she could do. She couldn't *make* him forgive her. "I'm looking for suggestions."

"You must be desperate if you're asking me. I can't even handle my own life. I still can't believe I have a seventeen-year-old daughter."

"Well, you do," she said. "And she's a wonderful girl. You should be proud of her."

"Damn Cheryl," Marty muttered. "Why did she do this to me? To us? I loved her."

Marlena could hear Winston's voice asking the same questions and she didn't have any more answers for Marty than she had for Winston. "It happened, Marty. You can't change the present situation and neither can Cheryl. You've got to deal with it, if you really want a life with her." In like manner, she and Winston had to deal with their problem if they wanted a life together.

"What about Patrice? How do I tell her I'm her father? How's she going to react to that newsflash?"

"I have no idea," Marlena said, wishing she had some comforting words to give him. "But I do know that you and Cheryl have to figure that out together."

"I have a daughter," Marty repeated with awe in his voice. "A seventeen-year-old daughter."

Marlena knew it was crazy but she envied Cheryl and Marty. Even though they had what seemed to be insurmountable problems, she envied the child they'd created together. Most of all, she envied Cheryl for having always had a part of Marty with her. She wondered how different her life would have been if she'd had Winston's child with her the last ten years. She believed a child would have helped her cope better with losing Winston.

Alone, she'd coped by taking the days one at a time. Soon the days grew into weeks, the weeks into months, and the months into years. She'd survived and she'd flourished on the outside, but on the inside, a part of her atrophied. Mike, her last boyfriend, had told her that she didn't know how to love. She hadn't corrected him even though she'd known he was wrong. She definitely knew how to love. What she didn't know how to do was stop loving.

"Consider yourself lucky, Marty," she said. "Patrice is living proof of the love you and Cheryl shared. Try to stop focusing on what you missed and focus on what you can have. That's the only way you'll make it through this." Marlena thought those were wise words even though she'd spoken them herself. Now all she had to do was incorporate them into her life and get Winston to do the same.

When Marlena walked into Cheryl's living room a couple of hours later and saw her friend surrounded by what looked to be at least a thousand squares of various kinds of fabrics, she knew all was not well.

"What's going on, Cheryl?" she asked her friend who was

at the moment pushing material off the sofa so Marlena could sit.

"I couldn't sleep," Cheryl said, "and I got tired of crying so I decided to do some quilting."

Marlena sat in one of the valleys between the fabric mountains. "When did you start quilting?"

"I picked it up after Patrice started dating. It gave me something to do while I waited for her to get home." Cheryl lips turned in a vacant smile. "Do you like quilts? I have a few I could give you, if you want them?"

Marlena nodded. "Sure, I like quilts."

"Wait here a minute," Cheryl said, getting up from her seat at the sewing machine. "I have some for you to choose from."

"You don't have to . . ." Marlena began, but it was no use. Cheryl was already off to get the quilts. She was back shortly with an armload of them. She dumped the top three on the floor then handed Marlena the remaining one, which was made of blue bandanna squares and patterned like intertwined wedding rings. "This is a beautiful piece of work, Cheryl. You're good at this."

Cheryl took one end of the quilt and the two of them spread it out on the floor. "This is one of my favorites, but you can have it."

Marlena rubbed her hand across the intricate pattern. "You shouldn't give these away, Cheryl. You should sell them. I know people who'd pay large sums for work this well done."

"I don't make them to sell; I make them to use. And I've made a couple for Patrice to take with her to school and I've started making some for the grandchildren."

"Grandchildren?"

"What can I say? Patrice dates a lot. I've had the time so I used it."

Marlena shook her head. "You have a talent here, Cheryl. You should think seriously about selling these. You'd make a lot of money at one of those regional craft shows, I'm telling you."

Cheryl sat down on the quilt and crossed her legs. "I'm too tired after working a full week to think about going to any craft shows. No, I think I'll just keep doing this for fun and relaxation.''

Marlena joined Cheryl on the quilt and patted her friend's knee. "How are you holding up, kiddo?"

"I'll be okay. How's Marty?"

"He's hurting, Cheryl, and he's very angry with you, but he still loves you."

"Humph." Cheryl dropped her head.

"Don't give up. He loves you and you have to believe that."

Cheryl looked up and she had tears in her eyes. "Then why isn't he here with me trying to work this out?"

"You know why, Cheryl," Marlena said as gently as she could. "He needs to work through this for himself. When he's ready, he'll come to you. Give him time."

"Time? I've got plenty of that." She looked around the room. "How many quilts do you think I'll have made before he's ready? One, two, one hundred?"

"Look at it this way, you can sell all the quilts you make while waiting and use the money to buy a torture chamber for him."

Cheryl smiled. "It would serve him right. You know, I thought young love was bad, but old love has it beat hands down."

"I can agree with that," Marlena said, thinking how time had only complicated her relationship with Winston.

"Did something happen with you and Winston?"

"He's acting like a jerk. He called the hotel last night and Marty answered the phone so Mr. Taylor came to the ridiculous conclusion that something was going on between us. Can you believe that man?"

Cheryl nodded. "I told you Winston came over here the first night Marty was back and warned me about the two of you."

Marlena shook her head. She wondered what she and Winston were going to do. "Winston has no reason to be jealous, and especially not of Marty."

"You know what this is about, don't you?"

Marlena knew, but knowing didn't help. "He doesn't trust me and he hasn't forgiven me." She sighed. "I don't know if we're going to make it, Cheryl. I really don't. If Winston can't trust me, we don't have a chance.''

''Have you two talked about what happened between you? I mean really talked about it.''

Marlena looked away. ''Not really.''

''Well, that's probably where your problem is. I'm going to tell you what you told me: you need to get it out in the open.''

''I wish it were that simple, Cheryl. I really do.''

''It is, Marlena. You just open your mouth and tell him. Then you wait to see whether what you've done ruins your life or gives you a second chance at the only love you've ever known.''

Winston and Marty were already in the office when Marlena arrived Monday morning. The three of them exchanged greetings then got down to work.

Around lunch time, Winston asked, ''Anybody for lunch?'' He looked directly at Marlena.

''Not me,'' Marty said. ''I promised Mrs. Hampton I'd stop by her house for lunch.''

''How about you, Marlena?'' Winston asked. ''Do you have plans or can you join me?''

She tried to read in his eyes what his mood was, but she couldn't. She wanted to have lunch with him, but she didn't want another argument. ''I don't have any plans.''

''Good,'' he said. He turned back to Marty. ''We should be back in an hour or so. When do you think you'll be back?''

Marty shrugged. ''I have no idea.''

Winston pulled a key out of his pocket and tossed it to Marty. ''Take this. Now you'll be able to get in when we're not here.''

''What about you?'' Marty asked.

Winston inclined his head in Marlena's direction. ''She has a key. We'll get a duplicate made.'' He turned to Marlena. ''Are you ready?''

She nodded and the three of them left the office. Marty got in his car and Winston suggested he and Marlena walk to the sandwich shop on the corner.

"Do you feel up to going for a ride today?" he asked after they'd gotten their sandwiches.

"Sure," she said. "Where are we going?"

He grinned that masculine grin of his and her heart turned over. "It's a surprise. Come on."

They drove north of Gaines about twenty minutes before Winston turned the Bronco off onto a bumpy, dirt road.

"A little off the beaten path, isn't it?" she commented.

He grinned at her. "A little."

After about ten more minutes, they pulled into a green meadow filled with wildflowers. "It's beautiful," she said. "How did you find this place?"

"Lucky, I guess." He opened his door, picked up their sandwiches, and got out.

She watched as he pulled a blanket out of the back seat. "You had this planned?"

He shot her a wry smile. "Not really. I knew I wanted to bring you here, but I didn't know it would be today."

She eyed the blanket, then looked up at him.

He shrugged. "I like being prepared. Now are you going to stay and enjoy yourself or do you want me to take you back to town?"

There was no pleading in his voice, just a simple question. He'd do as she wanted. "I'll stay."

"Okay, then, let's go."

She followed him across the meadow and through a heavily wooded area. She heard the stream before she saw it. "This is wonderful," she said again, throwing her hands in the air and lifting her face to sun that barely peeked out from behind the clouds. "Too bad we didn't bring our suits. A swim would be wonderful."

He spread the blanket on the bank and sat down. "The water's a little too cold for swimming, but in a month or so when the temperature is right, we can come back."

Marlena liked his reference to them being together a month from now, but she didn't know if it was realistic. She didn't plan on being in Gaines a month from now. "You know I'm going home in a week or so, Winston," she said, sitting down next him. She kicked off her shoes and wiggled her toes.

He reclined on his back and looked up at her. "Tell me about D.C. What's your life like back there?"

She began to tell him about her work, but he interrupted her. "I know about your work," he said. "I want to hear about your life. What do you do after work? What are your friends like? That sort of thing."

"Well," she began. "I've been so busy lately that I don't do much of anything after work. That's why I'm here in Gaines. My partners suggested, rather strongly, that I needed a vacation."

"Burnout?"

She looked away from him and out at the water running smoothly over the rocks in the water bed. "Something like that."

"Friends? Boyfriends?"

She looked back at him. "Not many friends. An ex-boyfriend, but no one now."

"So why are you in such a hurry to get back? Why do you even want to go back when there are people here who care about you? A lot."

She knew he was right. Gaines had what she wanted and needed on a personal level—if she excluded the snobs in Rosemont—but on a professional level it couldn't begin to compete with D.C. "My practice is in D.C."

"So D.C.'s only hold on you is your practice?"

"There is my townhouse."

"Which you could probably sell very easily and for a tidy profit."

He was right. Her townhouse was in one of the best sections of Georgetown and she knew she could sell it in a heartbeat and incur a rather large capital gains liability. "What about you?" she asked. "What's keeping you in Gaines?"

He didn't have to think about it. "It's home. Gaines is my town. I feel connected here. I've always felt that way."

She heard his unspoken, You know that. "More connected than I've ever felt."

He shook his head. "I don't think so."

"I do. I can't believe I ever wanted to come back to this bigoted town. Some of the most bigoted black folks in the world live here."

"Along with some of the best," he added. "I'm not saying the town doesn't have its faults because it does. I know that as well as anybody, but I also know that things will only get worse if everybody keeps leaving. The town needs new blood if it's going to survive and grow."

She'd heard this pitch from him before and she knew he was right. "*The Way Home.*"

"That's right. You and Marty are just the beginning. Ten years from now this town won't be the same. The bigotry will exist, but it won't be as widespread as it is now because there'll be as many people living in Rosemont, or another upscale community, whose parents lived there as people whose parents lived in Dusttown. That's when we'll know there's progress."

"You really believe that, don't you?"

He nodded. "Of course. I wouldn't be working on the project if I didn't. I don't believe in wasting my time."

Something about the way he said his last statement made her think he was referring to their relationship as much as he was referring to *The Way Home.*

He opened the bag of sandwiches and handed her one. "We'd better start eating if we plan to get back to the office by two. We've already missed the one-hour interval that I told Marty."

When she took the sandwich from him, their fingers brushed and their eyes met. "Thank you," she said, suddenly shy.

"I know I've acted badly, Marlena, but that doesn't mean that I don't care about you."

"Don't do this, Winston," she pleaded.

"Don't do what? Don't tell you how I feel or don't feel how I feel?"

Either. Both. Neither. She couldn't decide. "As beautiful and as wonderful as the past was sometimes I wish it hadn't happened."

"You can't be serious."

"I don't regret what we shared," she quietly explained. "It's just that the past keeps getting in the way of the present."

He took a bite of his sandwich. "Maybe it's the other way around. Maybe we're trying to deal with the present before we deal with the past."

"Why can't we let the past stay in the past?" she asked, more to herself than to him. It would be much easier to start fresh today than to rehash the hurt of the past.

"You tell me," he challenged. "Out of all the places in the world you could have gone to get over your burnout, why did you choose Gaines?"

Marlena looked out across the stream, then dropped her eyes to the blanket. "I was tired, Winston, and I needed to get away and think."

"That's no reason to come back to Gaines. You could have gone to one of the islands."

She looked at him and thought again how much she'd loved him and how much she still loved him. "Okay, I *had* to come back to Gaines. I felt something was missing from my life."

"And you thought you'd find it in Gaines?"

She shook her head. "I thought I'd lost it in Gaines, but I didn't really think I'd find it again. Not really."

He raked a blade of grass down her arm. "And what do you think now?"

"I don't know what to think," she said earnestly. "I know now what was missing, but I'm still not sure I can have it again."

Patrice arrived at *The Way Home* office around one-thirty and since the door was open she walked in without knocking.

"Hi," she said to the man sitting at Winston's desk. He turned around.

Marty looked up and his mouth dropped open. *Patrice.* "Hi," he managed to get out. "May I help you?"

The girl smiled her mother's smile and immediately Marty fell in love with his daughter. "Is Coach around or Ms. Marlena?"

He shook his head. This is my daughter, he thought with pride. She was even prettier than her pictures. "They're at lunch but they should be back any minute now. You can wait if you want."

"Thanks," she said, coming fully into the room. "Are you new here?"

"Yeah," he said, forcing himself not to stare at his child. The way things were going for him these days, she'd end up thinking he was a pervert. "I'm in the program."

"Oh," she said, her eyes bright. "You went to Gaines High?" When he nodded, she asked, "Do you know my mom, Cheryl Flakes? She was Cheryl Morgan back then."

Talk about your loaded questions. "Yes, I sure did know Cheryl. We were classmates."

"Boy, it seems like all Mom's old classmates are coming back. You guys ought to have a reunion or something."

"That's a good idea. We'll have to think about it."

"Did you know my dad, Nathaniel Flakes?" she asked. "I know he didn't go to Gaines High, but you might have seen him and my mother together. They were high school sweethearts. They're divorced now, though." She stopped, then looked up at him shyly. "Oops, I'm talking too much, aren't I?"

"Not too much at all." Though it took a lot of effort, he managed to give her a huge smile. So, Cheryl had told Patrice that Nathaniel had been her high school sweetheart. He wondered why no one had bothered to challenge the lie over the years. He guessed they didn't care. "And no, I didn't know your father. He and Cheryl must be really proud of you."

"I guess," she said. "But sometimes I wonder. You know how parents are. Are you married? Do you have kids?"

He opened his mouth to say he had a daughter, but he changed his mind and shook his head. "No, I'm not married and I don't have kids."

She looked as if she felt sorry for him. "Well, my mom says sometimes she wished she didn't have any."

"I bet she's joking when she says that."

Patrice laughed. "Usually she's angry. She says having me is worse than having ten kids."

He laughed with her. Marlena was right. His daughter was wonderful. He wished again that he'd been around when she was growing up. He wondered if Cheryl would show him her baby pictures. Knowing her, she had hundreds of them.

He and Patrice both looked up when they heard Winston's and Marlena's voices in the hallway. "They're back," he said with a smile.

"Sorry, we're late," Marlena said as soon as she walked in the door. "But—" she stopped when she saw Patrice. "Well, hello, Patrice," she said, recovering quickly. "It's good to see you. Have you met Marty?"

Patrice glanced back at him. "Sort of. I found out he went to school with my mom, but I didn't tell him my name and I forgot to ask his. Sorry."

"No reason to be sorry," Marty said. "It's my fault." He extended his hand to her. "Marty Jones. Nice to meet you, Patrice."

She took his hand and smiled. "Nice to meet you, Mr. Jones."

Patrice turned back to Marlena. "Do you have a few minutes?" she asked.

"For you, always." Patrice followed Marlena to her desk. "Do you want to talk here or do we need some privacy?"

The young woman looked back at Marty and Winston. Seeing they were engaged in deep conversation, she turned back to Marlena and said, "Here is all right."

"So, what do you want to talk about?"

She rolled her eyes. "What else?"

"You and Raymond?"

"Right. He wants me and Mom to come to his parents anniversary party on Saturday."

"What's wrong with that?"

"You know his parents don't want us there," Patrice said with resignation. She propped on the edge of Marlena's desk. "I don't know why Raymond keeps pushing. He makes me so mad sometimes."

Marlena sympathized with the girl. She knew Patrice wasn't

really angry with Raymond; she was angry at the situation. "So what are you going to do?"

The child sighed as if it were the end of the world. "I'm going to go and so is Mom, but we want you and Coach to come too. Raymond said his parents were inviting you."

Marlena cast a glance in Winston's direction. She hadn't received any invitation and he hadn't asked her to go with him. Maybe he was taking somebody else.

"Will you come?" the girl asked. "The church picnic was so much more fun with you and Coach there. We can have fun at this thing, too. Say you'll go."

Marlena couldn't resist the girl and she knew Winston wouldn't be able to either. "Okay, if we're invited we'll come."

"All right," Patrice said. She leaned closer to Marlena, "Do you think Marty will want to go as Mom's date? He said they went to school together."

"You'll have to ask your mother about that."

Patrice made a face. "Mom's not too swift where men are concerned. She may need a little help with this. Why don't you suggest it to her?"

Marlena thought Patrice was a smooth operator. "I'll see what I can do," she said, joining in the girl's conspiracy.

Chapter 16

Two nights later, Marlena fastened her seatbelt and watched as Winston backed the Bronco out of the restaurant parking lot. He'd treated her to a quiet dinner and now he wanted to take her by his house for dessert.

"What are you grinning about?" he asked, casting a quick glance at her before turning his attention back to the road.

"You're being rather obvious. Are you sure you aren't planning a seduction?"

He turned to her again and wiggled his thick eyebrows. "Me? What do you think?"

She smiled. She enjoyed being with him when he was like this: so open, so carefree, so tender. "I think you should take me back to the hotel," she said, but she didn't really want to go to the hotel. She wanted to see his home. Though she'd been curious about where he lived, she'd resisted driving by for a sneak peek.

He shifted gears and stopped at the stop sign. "I have Red Velvet cake," he said with a casual lop-sided smile, then shifted gears and started the Bronco moving again.

"That's not fair," she said, knowing he thought she was

talking about her favorite cake when she was really thinking of his smile.

"Did I mention that I had Martha put in extra pecans?"

"No, you didn't mention that."

"Well, she must have used two cups on the icing. The cake looks like it has brown icing instead of white."

The picture his words painted in Marlena's mind was yucky, but she knew the cake would be delicious. Everything Miss Martha cooked was delicious. She remembered the dishes the longtime Taylor cook had sent Winston during their college years. The older woman had even included a dish just for her on occasion. "Why didn't you have her bake me one and send it over to the hotel?"

He lifted a brow in her direction but he didn't answer. He didn't have to. She knew he hadn't had the cake sent over because the cake was his bribe to get her to his house. Of course, it wouldn't have worked if she hadn't really wanted to go. "It had better be good," she said and she heard him smile.

"Oh, it'll be good, all right."

She hoped he was talking about the cake, though her mind had moved to another plane, another time. It had always been good between her and Winston and she believed the timing of their first sexual encounter was the reason.

When Winston had first asked her out, a part of her had thought he'd wanted only one thing from her and she'd been determined he wouldn't get it. No, she wasn't going to let some hotshot, rich boy mess with her mind or her body.

His genuine interest in her and the simple enjoyment he'd seemed to get from being with her had surprised and pleased her. After three months of dating, she'd been convinced he wanted her and not what was between her legs. Well, that wasn't exactly right. He'd wanted to have sex, she'd felt him hard enough times to be sure of that, but he'd wanted more than sex.

Pretty soon she wanted to have sex with him, too. Resisting him became doubly hard, because she had to fight her ever increasing desire for him in addition to his need for her. Using sheer willpower, they managed to hold out until the summer after their sophomore year in college.

She came out of her thoughts as he pulled into his driveway. The motion sensor lights illuminated the house and the grounds. She wasn't surprised that his yard was well manicured and very green. The size of the house did surprise her though, and she wondered if his ex-wife had helped pick it out. Obviously, the two-story structure, much like the home he'd grown up in, had been built and bought with a large family in mind.

"Home, sweet, home," he said pulling into the crowded garage.

"What are all these boxes?" she asked. The garage looked as if he'd recently been on a shopping spree.

He cut off the ignition and shrugged. "I'm still getting settled. I'll have it cleaned out in a while." He opened his door and got out.

So Patty hadn't chosen the house, Marlena mused. She wondered what, or who, Winston had been thinking about when he'd bought this place. He'd repeatedly told her that Yolanda was only a friend, and she believed him, but after seeing the size of this house, she knew there must have been a special woman in his life when he'd bought it. "How long have you lived here?" she asked when he opened the door for her.

"Six months," he said, lifting her out of the Bronco. As he slowly slid her body down the front of his, she wondered if he'd bought the Bronco to aid in his seduction of unsuspecting women.

After her feet were firmly on the concrete floor of the garage, she needlessly brushed her hand down the soft linen of her skirt. When she lifted her head and her eyes met his, the passion she saw reflected in them made her step back and she bumped into the truck door.

"Careful," he said, pulling her to him with one arm and closing the door with the other.

His actions left her standing in the circle of his arms, so close she heard his heartbeat thump in his chest. He willed her to look up at him, but she forced her gaze to roam the garage instead. "Maybe you can get Raymond to help you clean up this mess."

He squeezed her close, but before she could give in to the need to relax against him, he laughed and released her, keeping her hand in his. "Come on," he said. "It's time I gave you that cake I promised."

She followed him to the door and watched as his strong, lean finger punched the red button that made the garage door close. He pushed a series of buttons on the door keypad and immediately the door opened. "Not bad," she said. "And I'd been thinking technology had passed Gaines by."

"Almost," he said, pulling her into the dark house behind him. He flicked a switch and light flooded the place. "Technology visited Gaines and left a few mementos, but it didn't stay."

She followed him down a long hallway into a large expanse of room that she thought was his playroom. She couldn't think of anything else to call it. It had the standard brick fireplace that occupied most family rooms, but the black faces of the high-tech gizmos that lined the walls said this was where Winston played.

"What's all this?" she asked, pointing to the electronic components along the southern wall.

He dropped her hand and moved toward the wall. He picked up a remote from the table sitting between the matching black leather couches, pressed a button, and Barry White joined them. Well, it sounded like he'd joined them.

"Since when did you become a music aficionado?" she asked.

He put the remote back down and turned to her. "Sometimes music can say what a man feels much better than he can say it himself."

The glint in his eyes told her that the best response to that comment was no response. "I can't imagine you not being able to say what you want to say," she said, ignoring the warning.

"Neither could I, but things happen and a man has to do whatever he can to make it through."

They were back to the past, but this time the trip was different. This time he wasn't blaming her or making her feel guilty. He was sharing his feelings and she appreciated his effort. She met his gaze and held it. "It's no different with women, Winston. We do whatever we can to make it through, too." She needed him to understand that their breakup hadn't been easy for her either. His slight nod made her think he'd gotten the message.

He released a sigh. "Ready for that cake?"

She grinned, feeling very lucky to be here with him tonight. "When have you known me not to be ready for Red Velvet cake?"

"Bored?" Winston smiled down at her when he heard her yawn. She'd asked for the tour but he didn't think she was going to make it to the end.

She shook her head. "No way." She patted her hand against the silk blouse covering her flat stomach. "I had too much of that cake. It'll be your fault when I weigh two hundred pounds."

I'd still love you, he said to himself, and he meant it. What he felt for Marlena went far beyond how she looked. Though God knows, tonight she looked delicious. He'd wanted nothing more than to drag her into this house and straight into his bed, but he'd controlled himself and they'd had a relaxed, nonthreatening evening. Now, though, his control was fading fast.

He looked down the hallway at the last room on the tour: his bedroom. "One more room to go," he said, leading her down the hall. He pushed open his door and allowed her to enter the room before him. "If you're sleepy, we can always—"

He stopped and his loins came to immediate attention when she started for the bed. He hadn't expected her to be so agreeable, but he wasn't going to fight fate. He followed her and almost bumped into her when she stopped suddenly at the foot of the bed and rested her hand on the footboard.

"This bed?" she asked. "Is it—"

"Yes," he answered, not needing her to finish the question. This was the bed they'd bought for the apartment he'd wanted them to share during law school. This bed represented many nights of passionate and tender, and sometimes not so tender, lovemaking between them. "It's the same bed."

She looked up at him with tear-filled eyes and his heart tightened much as his loins had. "Why'd you keep it?" she asked.

"I think you know why," he said, touching a finger to her face and wiping the single tear that slid down her satiny skin.

She covered his hand with her own. "I remember the day we bought it."

He remembered too. It was the fifth store they'd visited and she still hadn't found a bed she liked. His only request had been for a bed big enough for them to love and play in. She'd had more demanding requirements. It had taken them no time to settle on a king-sized bed and to select the mattress, but Marlena had had a difficult time finding a headboard and matching footboard.

She walked around and sat on the edge of the bed. He knew her thoughts were back to those days, too. They'd both been on edge that day because she'd turned down his marriage proposal *and* his alternative of living together.

"I want to marry you, Marlena," he'd said that morning.

"We said we'd get married *after* we finished law school," she said with what he'd thought was uncalled-for panic in her voice. "It'll only be a couple more years."

He'd pulled her into his arms then. "I want to marry you. I want you to be mine, Marlena. Only mine."

"I'm already yours," she'd said. "Don't you know that? I love you with all my heart and I always will."

Seeing he was losing the battle, he'd gone for a desperate solution. "Then move in here with me."

"No way, Winston," she'd said immediately. "You should know me better than that. I'm not living with you. I have my own place and I'm keeping it that way. I won't have people saying you're supporting me. I won't have it."

He'd known his suggestion had made her think of her mother and the distress it caused her left him with no choice but to drop the subject and pull her into his arms. She'd loved him, but she hadn't married him and she hadn't moved in with him—not then and not when they'd finished law school.

"It was so long ago, but it seems like yesterday," she said.

He sat down next to her on the bed. "Why didn't you go ahead and marry me, Marlena?"

She quickly got up and walked away from him. "You know why. I didn't have anything, Winston, and you had everything. I wanted to bring something to our marriage."

Yes, he knew it had been important for her that she go into marriage with skills to support herself. The law degree had meant so much more to her than it had to him. To him, it had been the reward for completing a course of study he'd found fascinating. For her, it had been the outward sign she felt she needed to prove to the world—she certainly didn't need to prove it to him—that she was worthy of his love.

She wanted there to be no doubt that her love for him was real and true and not based on a desire for the material things he could give her. No, the law degree was the tangible sign that told the world she was with him because she loved him. Her ideals had been endearing, but they had frustrated him to the hilt. In the end, those ideals had caused her to walk away from him.

"Are you ready to go back to the hotel?" he asked.

She turned and he saw tears streaming down her face. He had no words to ease her pain. He didn't even really know why she was crying, but he knew he wanted to comfort her. He opened his arms and she walked into them as if there was no other place she wanted to be.

He pulled her more snugly into his arms and held her as they both silently remembered the joys and pain of their shared past. The best times of his life had been spent with her and he knew the only way the rest of his life would be as good would be if she shared it with him as well.

Marlena stopped crying about fifteen minutes later. She eased back in his arms and peeked up at him. "It was the cake," she said. "It always makes me cry." She placed her hand over her mouth and covered a yawn. "It also makes me sleepy."

"We're in the right place for sleeping," he deadpanned.

She shook her head. "You're in the right place. My bed is in the Gaines Inn."

"This is your bed," he corrected. "It always will be."

She didn't contradict him. "You'd better get me back to the hotel. It's getting late. I bet your neighbors are wondering what we're doing in here anyway."

"I doubt it."

"What do you mean, you doubt it? This is Gaines, remember?"

"Hey, I know it's Gaines." He tapped two of his fingers on her nose. "They aren't wondering. They're imagining the two of us rolling around in this big old bed, all hot and sweaty."

Marlena felt heat surge through her body. If her temperature were taken right now, she had no doubt it would be off the scale. He'd done that with words; she wouldn't even allow herself to think what his touch would do. She forced herself to move away from him and stand up. "We'd better go," she said again.

He didn't say anything immediately and she tensed, knowing that if he touched her, she'd be flat on her back in that big, old bed in a matter of minutes. She relaxed when she heard him sigh, then stand up.

"How long are you going to stay in that hotel? You can come stay with me. I have plenty of room."

She didn't see a need to respond to his suggestion. There was no way she was moving into his house.

He led her out of the bedroom and down the stairs. "Want to take some cake with you?" he asked, looking toward the kitchen.

She shook her head and looked up at him, her desire clear in her eyes. "I'd rather eat it here—on my next visit."

"Damn, Marlena," he said. "I was trying. I was really trying."

Before she could ask what he was talking about, he covered her lips with his own. She sank against him, wrapping her arms tight around his waist.

She opened her mouth at his urging and he entered with

mastery. His tongue caressed hers in a ritual they'd patented together and she moaned.

"I know," he murmured against her mouth. "I know."

She didn't think he knew. How could he know how hot she was or how much she wanted him or how much she needed him? She pressed tighter against him, wanting to lose herself in him, wanting him to take her to the special place they'd discovered together long ago. She had no doubt they'd easily find their way back.

Winston's hands tightened on her waist and she thought he was going to lift her so he could caress her breasts. He tore his mouth from hers instead. "I want you so much. Do you have any idea how much?"

The fervor of his kiss left her weak and she swayed against him. "I think I can guess."

He cursed under his breath.

"What are we going to do about this?" she asked.

He took her hand and headed for the stairs. When she stopped moving, he turned back to her. "I thought you wanted this too."

"I do," she said, going into his arms and resting her head against his chest. "But not here. Not like this."

He held her close. "Why not here? This is my home."

"That's why."

He looked down at her. "What do you mean?"

"The neighbors. The town. Everybody will know we had dinner tonight and the hotel staff will know I didn't come in all night. Everybody'll be talking about us. They'll know we slept together."

"So," he said, showing how little he cared for public opinion though he knew his cause was lost. The present-day Marlena was as controlled by public opinion now as she had been when they were in law school. "I care about you, Marlena. I want more than one night . . . a lot more."

She stepped out of his arms. "I'm not going to be here that long."

"You keep saying that." He pulled her back into his arms

where she belonged. "But you're still here. I think you like it here."

"But that doesn't mean I'm not going back to D.C. next week."

"What if I asked you to stay?"

Her heartbeat quickened. "Are you asking me to stay?"

"I guess I am. Will you stay?"

"I can't, Winston. You know that."

"I know no such thing. You could have your pick of the best legal positions in this area. There's no reason for you to go back."

She looked up into his eyes. "Are you sure there's a reason for me to stay?"

He knew she wanted reassurances, guarantees, but he couldn't give them to her. She had to know for herself that their shared love was enough. "I can't answer that for you. That's something you'll have to do for yourself."

Not exactly the answer she was expecting, but it was an honest one.

"Why don't you come back to D.C. with me?"

"Because Gaines is our home," he answered without needing to think about it. "It's where we belong. Both of us."

He sounded so sure of himself that again she didn't contradict him.

"At least stay until the program gets its first relocation," he suggested, needing more time to convince her that her life was in Gaines with him. "*The Way Home* needs you almost as much as I do."

Marlena knew extending her stay wouldn't be a problem. Her partners would be thrilled since she hadn't taken a real vacation in the last six years. "I'll have to go back to D.C. for a couple of days to take care of some personal business."

"No problem," he said, hugging her. "I'll go back with you and we'll have some time away from the prying eyes of Gaines. How does that sound?"

Chapter 17

Winston watched Marlena out of the corner of his eye while he nodded his head and faked interest in Mr. Brown's limited range of conversation topics. When the car dealership owner mentioned Marlena's name, Winston gave him his total attention.

"Do you think she'd do it?" he asked, reaching for another glass of wine from the roving waiter. The Hills had gone all out for their anniversary bash.

"You'll have to ask her," Winston said. He didn't know what the man was talking about.

Brown gulped down the wine like it was beer. "I mentioned it to her once, but she didn't seem too excited about appearing in the commercials with me."

I should have known, Winston thought. Brown's conversation was limited to his car dealerships and the income derived from them.

"Well, I guess you have your answer," Winston said, looking for Marlena again.

Brown nudged him in the ribs with his elbow. "Why don't you put in a good word for me? I hear you have some pull with her." The leer accompanying the ignorant man's words made it clear where his thoughts were.

Winston tightened his fingers around the stem of his glass. "You must have your information wrong," he said. "I don't make decisions for Marlena."

The man's leer grew wider. "Come on, Winston. A little pillow talk goes a long way, if you know what I mean. Just tell her to think about it."

Winston glanced around the room, not able to look the disgusting man in the face. When he saw Marlena, he tilted his head to her and she smiled. He smiled back, then touched Brown's arm. "I want to speak to you a minute in private," he said.

The older man's eyes widened in anticipation and Winston wondered what the old goat thought he was going to say. He led Brown into the Hills' library. When Winston walked out of the room ten minutes later, he wore his best smile. He'd left Brown in the library trying to compose himself. Winston laughed when he pictured the flush that had come over the older man when Winston had told him what he'd thought of his insulting comments about his relationship with Marlena.

He brushed his hands together as if ridding them of leftover dirt, then went off in search of his date. She saw him before he saw her.

"What are you grinning about?" she asked, looking as fine as she could in her form-fitting deep purple sheath.

He leaned close to her ear and whispered, "I'm thinking about how you're going to look without any clothes." A naked and purring Marlena had been his only thought since he'd decided to go to D.C. with her.

"Who says you're going to see me without any clothes?" she teased, her eyes sparkling just for him. He wondered if she knew the power she held over him. One look into those baby browns did him in every time.

He fingered the bare skin along her shoulders. The smooth, silkiness of her flesh made his fingers tremble. "I say. Is that good enough?"

"You're sounding pretty cocky. I hope your actions live up to your words."

The challenge issued from those brightly colored lips feathered across his mind and started the replay of the fantasy he'd been having since she'd first come to town. "Count on it, sweet thing," he murmured. "I'll have you beggin'."

He watched as her quickened breathing caused her breasts to rise and fall noticeably under the thin material of her dress. "Begging you to stop or begging you not to?" she asked, determined to have the last word.

He groaned, the picture of her under him in total abandon making him wish they were in D.C. right now. "Once you start begging, it won't matter to me or to you."

She opened her mouth to speak, but he pressed two fingers against her lips. "We have to stop. If you say one more word, I'll be forced to throw you over my shoulder and carry you out of here caveman style."

"Oh," she mouthed.

"Yes, oh," he said, taking her hand. "Now let's get back to the party where we'll be properly chaperoned. You try a man's good intentions, woman."

Marlena gladly followed Winston back into the living room. The anniversary party had been a grand success so far, even if Patrice's plan for Marty and Cheryl to attend together had failed. Marlena hoped the girl missed the daggered stares the two had cast at each other all evening.

"What do you think about Marty and Cheryl?"

Winston grunted. "I think they should have come together. They aren't kidding anybody but themselves."

"They need more time. Marty's leaving tomorrow. Has he said anything more about taking the job?"

Winston shook his head. "Not to me. I don't know what he's thinking. I really hope he doesn't make his decision for the wrong reason."

Marlena hoped the same thing, but she had no idea what Marty was thinking either. "Maybe I'll talk to him before he leaves."

"Maybe you'll stay out of it," Winston said, looking down at her. "You've got your own romance to worry about."

"Jealous?"

He grimaced. "Yes, and don't you forget it."

As Cheryl watched the playfulness between Marlena and Winston, she couldn't help but wish for the same for her and Marty. She scanned the room, telling herself she wasn't really looking for him. When she didn't find him in the crowd, she moved away from the group and out to the less-crowded patio.

"Ms. Flakes," Helen Hill said.

Cheryl turned and saw Raymond's mother standing behind her with a sweet-as-molasses but phony-as-Monopoly-money smile. "Mrs. Hill," she said, acknowledging the woman's presence.

"I hope you're enjoying yourself tonight."

Cheryl, always known for giving as good as she got, matched Helen's smile with one of her own. "Call me Cheryl, and yes, thank you, I'm having a wonderful time. It was nice of you to invite me."

Helen's smile faltered just a tad. She pointed to a concrete bench in a shaded corner. "Will you sit down with me for a few minutes, Cheryl. I've been planning to talk to you about Raymond and Patrice."

Keep that smile in place, girl, Cheryl told herself, as she sat down. "What is it you want to discuss about Raymond and Patrice?"

"I don't see any point in dragging this out, so I'm going to get right to the point." She took a deep breath. "I think we need to put an end to this relationship before it goes any farther."

Cheryl balled her hands into fists in her lap, but kept her face clear of emotion. "I'm not quite sure I understand what you mean," she lied. She knew exactly what the bitch meant.

"You know as well as I do, Cheryl, this relationship won't last. I think we should help them end it now before any *problems* arise."

"Problems? You mean, pregnancy?" Cheryl wondered if

she'd misjudged Helen. Maybe the other woman was just a mother who worried about her son much as Cheryl worried about Patrice.

"Of course, I mean pregnancy, Cheryl," Helen said as if she were talking to a dim-witted child. "Teenagers experiment with sex and accidents *do* happen. Knowing Raymond, he'd feel obligated to marry Patrice and I just don't think that would be appropriate."

Reality hit Cheryl in the face like a hot dishcloth. "Appropriate?"

"Let's be honest. We both know this relationship is not going to last beyond high school. Once Raymond goes off to college and meets girls with experiences and backgrounds similar to his, he'll see that what he shared with Patrice was puppy love. But my son is honorable, if Patrice gets pregnant, he'll marry her, not knowing he'd live to regret it."

There were a thousand things Cheryl wanted to say to Mrs. Hill, but she took a deep breath and kept her thoughts to herself. She put her smile back on her face and stood up. "My lovely evening has just come to an end. I think I'll be going now." With that she turned and walked back into the house.

She searched out Raymond and Patrice and spoke with them for a few minutes to assure herself they were still in high spirits. Then she made a point of mingling with the other guests and pretending she was having a good time when all she wanted to do was stand in the middle of the room and tell all these snobs exactly what she thought of them. The knowledge that such action would only serve to embarass her daughter helped her resist the temptation.

Marlena was surprised to see Winston outside Friendship when the Sunday service was over. "I thought you were working," she said referring to his plans to put in extra hours preparing a brief so he could relax and enjoy himself while they were in D.C.

He stepped closer to her and placed his arm around her waist.

"I missed you," he whispered. "I thought I'd try to convince you to have a quick bite to eat with me."

"Sorry," she said with a teasing smile, "but I have other plans."

"I'll just bet you do and I bet I can guess who those plans are with."

She folded her church bulletin and made a production of putting it in her purse. "No need for you to guess," she said when she was done. "I'm having lunch with Marty."

"I knew it," he said, leading her away from the crowd exiting the church. "Why can't you just stay out of it?"

"Because I don't want to. They're my friends. I want to see them happy. And I know they'll be happy together."

He tried to force a frown on his face, but her sweet smile demanded one in return. "And how do you know that? I don't remember your having any physic ability."

She rolled her eyes, not seeing a need to respond to his comment. "I'll see you later," she said, turning to leave.

He stood and watched her full hips sway as she walked in the direction of the church parking lot. The knowledge that they'd soon be together kept him from running after her. "Aren't you at least going to invite me to tag along?" he called after her.

She stopped and looked back over her shoulder. "No way. You'd accept. I want to talk to Marty *alone.*"

"That's what scares me."

She laughed and waved goodbye to him, feeling secure, at least for now, in their relationship. When she reached the parking lot, Marty was waiting for her. He looked dapper in his black lightweight suit.

"Perfect timing," he said with a smile. "Are you hungry?"

She shook her head. "Not very. How about you?"

"Hey, I could eat a horse."

She laughed. "I guess that means the buffet at Miss Lil's."

"You read my mind. Where's Winston?"

"He's not coming."

"Did you have to lock him in his house?" Marty laughed. "I can't believe he didn't want to come along."

"He did," she said. "But I told him I wanted to talk with you alone."

Marty led her to his car, then held the door while she got in. "I would take that as a come-on if I didn't know how you felt about Winston."

She glanced up at him. "And how you and Cheryl feel about each other."

He gave a long, drawn-out sigh. "I suspected that's what this lunch was about," he said, closing her door.

"And you came anyway," she said once he was in the car with her. "That says a lot."

Miss Lil's was only a couple of blocks away so the drive didn't take long. After they'd filled their plates and were seated, Marlena asked, "Are you really going to eat all of that?"

Marty looked down at his plate, then back up at her. "Of course. It's not that much."

"Uh-huh." She took her eyes off his platter of corn muffins, beans, chicken, ribs, stew, cabbage, and a few other unnamed dishes, then dipped her fork into her gravy covered mashed potatoes. "So, have you decided what you're going to do?"

"Do? I'm going to eat lunch."

She aimed her fork at him and pretended she was going to launch mashed potatoes in his direction.

He laughed. "No violence in public places."

She put her fork back in her mouth.

"Have you decided what you're going to do?" he asked a short while later.

"Me?"

He picked up a corn muffin, stuffed half of it in his mouth and quickly swallowed. "Yes, you. Have you decided what you're going to do about you and Winston?"

"Not really."

"I didn't think so. Then why are you in such a big hurry for me to decide about Cheryl and me?"

She leaned toward him and lowered her voice. "Because you and Cheryl have a child. That makes your situation a lot more serious than mine and Winston's," she said, though she really didn't believe her words. Their situations were different, but one wasn't any tougher or more serious than the other.

Marty put down his fork, propped his elbows on the table, and rested his chin on his folded hands. "Patrice is not a child, Marlena. She's nearly a grown woman."

"She's still your child. I don't care if she's a hundred."

He leaned back in his chair. "Did you see her last night?" The pride in his voice matched the pride she read in his face. "I could tell she was nervous, but she handled herself well. I got the impression the Hills aren't too high on her relationship with Raymond." He shook his head. "I thought people in this town would have changed by now."

"They don't see a need to change. In their minds, they're perfect."

"Right. In their minds." He slapped his napkin on the table. "How did everything go wrong? If Cheryl and I had gotten married, things would be a lot different. If only she'd told me she was pregnant."

Marlena heard the regret and the recrimination in Marty's voice and felt some of it herself. She wondered how many people could identify the single decision in their life that had changed it most. She and Winston could and so could Cheryl and Marty. "We can't change the past, Marty," she said as much to him as to herself.

"But don't you want to sometimes?" he asked in a wistful voice.

She nodded.

"But," he said, "we can't. We have to deal with where we are now."

Marlena realized both couples were at another turning point, maybe even more life-determining than the first. They wouldn't make the same mistake twice, she told herself. They wouldn't.

"Well," Marty was saying. "I'm not going to repeat Cheryl's mistake. She kept a secret last time, but I won't keep it this time. I'm staying. I've already accepted the job."

Marlena reached over and grabbed his hand. "That's wonderful, Marty. Have you told Cheryl?"

"Not yet," he said. "I'm going by her place on my way back to the airport."

"Well, I'm glad for you."

"Now, what are you going to do about your situation with Winston? Do you still love him?"

She nodded. "I've always loved him."

"So what are you going to do?"

"It's different with us, Marty. You and Cheryl only have the past standing in your way. Winston and I have the past *and* his mother. She still hates me."

"And it still matters?"

She looked up at him and realized that it did. "Some." Mrs. Taylor could still make her feel worthless and the secret they shared was the key to the older woman's power over her.

"More than some, I'd say. Look, Marlena, you can't let that woman control your life. If you love Winston, you ought to fight for him, even if you have to fight his mother."

"You don't pull any punches, do you?"

He shook his head. "I'm too old to play around about something so important. Neither one of us has had an easy life. We've worked and fought for everything we have. Nobody's given me *or you* a damn thing. We're fighters and we're winners. Don't ever forget that."

Raymond stood up when Marty pulled his rented vehicle into Cheryl's driveway later that afternoon. The youngster had changed out of his church clothes and into the standard high school uniform of jeans and football jersey. He wore a broad grin that said he was glad to see Marty.

"Hi, Mr. Marty," the boy said when Marty reached the porch.

Marty extended his hand to the youngster. "Call me Marty," he said. "We're friends."

"Okay, Marty," the boy said and sat back down on the wood swing.

Marty leaned against the brick column in front of the door. "Waiting for Patrice?"

"All the time. I think she's getting worse."

Marty laughed at the grimace on the boy's face. "Wait till you see her. It'll be worth it."

"Patrice is beautiful already. She doesn't need to go through all that makeup stuff like other girls. I tell her all the time, but she doesn't listen."

Marty clapped the boy on his shoulder. "That's women, Raymond. Patrice isn't going to change. You'd better get used to it."

"Hey, are y'all talking about me?"

Marty turned his head to the screened door and looked at the bright, smiling face of his daughter. His daughter. His chest expanded with pride that this beautiful and sweet young woman was his daughter.

"It's about time you got ready," Raymond said, standing up and opening the door.

"Hi, Marty," Patrice said after shooting a glare at Raymond. "Mom's inside. You can go on in."

"Are you two leaving?" Marty asked.

"Finally," Raymond muttered.

Marty watched the anger flame in Patrice's eyes and was reminded of the looks Cheryl had given him when they were younger. He smiled. "You'd better watch it, Raymond. Your lady doesn't look too happy right now. If I were you, I'd try telling her how good she looks."

"See, Raymond," Patrice said with adultlike flare. "Marty knows how to treat women."

"Aw, Patrice," Raymond said, placing his hands around her waist and hugging her to him. "You know you look good. You always look good to me."

The casual manner of the young people told Marty theirs was an intimate relationship. The father in him wondered how intimate. He'd have to talk to Cheryl about the details. "Well, you two, I guess this is goodbye. I'm heading for the airport when I leave here."

Marty was pleased with the disappointment that crossed Patrice's face. "But you just got here. When are you coming back?"

"What makes you think I'm coming back?" he asked with a smile.

"You have to," she said with childlike wisdom. "What about *The Way Home* and your job?"

He smiled, glad she wanted him to stay and hoping it meant she liked him. He hoped she always would, though he knew they faced some rough days ahead. "I'll be back," he said. "I have to go home and settle some things."

"I knew it! Mom's going to be so excited. Go tell her. We have to leave anyway, don't we, Raymond?"

"We've already missed the first—"

Patrice cut him off. "But I want to get something to eat," she said, practically dragging the boy off the porch. "See you when you get back, Marty," she called.

Marty shook his head, then rang the bell. Patrice had told him to go on in, but he knew better. He turned and waved to the youngsters as Raymond pulled out of the driveway.

"I thought I heard them talking to somebody," Cheryl said from behind him.

He turned around. "Hi, Cheryl."

"Hi, yourself," she said, keeping her eyes trained on him. He wondered what she thought he was going to do.

"Aren't you going to invite me in?"

"Why?" she asked. "What do you want anyway?"

He sighed. Why did she have to be so difficult? He wanted to . . . to . . . God, he wanted to kiss her. He reached for the door and she pushed it open, then stepped back.

"Here?"

"Here, what?" she asked.

"Do I kiss you here or do we go back to your bedroom?" He was leaving and he didn't want to fight with her. They could fight when he got back. He'd dream about making up with her while he was home. The dream would get him back to her in a hurry.

She crossed her arms under those full breasts of hers . . . a big mistake. "What makes you think I'm going to kiss you?"

He moved a step closer. "I didn't say you were going to

kiss me. I said I was going to kiss you. Now where do you want it? Here, standing up, or back there, lying down?''

She dropped her arms. ''You've got some nerve, Marty. You say all kinds of awful things to me, then you practically ignore me at the Hills' party, and now you want to kiss me. You've lost your mind.''

''Yeah, I have,'' he said.

''At least we agree on something.''

He reached out and pulled her into his arms. Truth was, he didn't have to pull very hard. She was mad with him, but she wanted to kiss him. ''We'll have to decide when and how to tell Patrice,'' he said softly, brushing his lips against hers.

''She's going to hate me when she finds out, Marty. I don't think I can stand losing her. She's all I have.''

Marty tightened his hold on this woman he loved. ''First, she's not going to hate you.''

''You did,'' Cheryl accused and he saw in her eyes how much his response had hurt her.

He cupped her face in his hands. ''It hurt, Cheryl. It really hurt. And it still does. I wished we'd done things differently, but we didn't and now we have to deal with it. And we'll deal with it together.''

''But—''

He pressed his fingers to her lips. ''No, buts. I love you. Do you understand that? I've always loved you. Patrice is going to be upset, and yes, she may hate us for lying to her, but we'll love her so much she'll have to love us back.''

''You make it sound so easy,'' Cheryl said, finally relaxing in his arms and taking the comfort he offered.

''I'm not stupid. We have a long road ahead of us. I know it won't be easy.''

''What will we tell her?''

''We'll tell her how much in love we were and we'll tell her how much we love her.''

''She won't understand. I know it. Patrice can be stubborn when she wants to be.''

''Just like her mother,'' he said, rubbing his hands down her back. "She'll understand. She's in love with Raymond. She'll know exactly how you felt."

"Maybe."

"Do you think they're having sex?" he asked, remembering the embrace he'd seen.

Cheryl pulled back and looked up at his face. She smiled. "You look scared."

"I am. Sex today is a lot scarier than it was when we were kids."

"Well, rest easy. I don't think they're having sex. Yet."

"How long have they been dating?"

"A year."

Marty cursed. "A year? If they haven't done it, they're thinking about it. What are we going to do?"

Hearing Marty voice her long-held fear helped Cheryl relax. She'd raised Patrice the best she knew how and now she had to trust her. "We're going to do what I've been doing for the last year. Keep the lines of communication open and pray."

Marty grunted. "I don't know if I'm cut out to be a father. I have a feeling I'm going to get high blood pressure."

She placed her arms around his neck and pressed her body tight against his. "Let's hope worrying about Patrice isn't the only thing that raises your pressure."

Chapter 18

Marlena thought about Marty's words all the way to D.C. He was right. She was used to fighting and just as used to winning. That is, she won when she stayed in the game. She glanced over at Winston sleeping soundly beside her. She'd taken herself out of the game the last time, but she wasn't going to do that again. She was wise enough to know fate wouldn't give her another chance.

"Please return your seatbacks and tray tables to their upright and locked positions," came the voice over the intercom. Marlena lightly tapped Winston on his shoulder. "Sweetheart," she said softly, "wake up. We're about to land."

Winston came out of his sleep slowly. Poor baby, she thought. She knew he was tired. He'd worked day and night for the past couple of days to get ahead on his cases so he could spend this time with her. If she hadn't loved him before, she would have fallen in love with him because of the priority he gave this trip.

"We're almost there," she said as he pulled his seatback up. "You were pretty tired. You slept through the entire flight."

"Yeah, I was tired," he said, still coming out of his sleep. "What time is it?"

She told him the time. "It'll be dark when we get home."

"Home is in Gaines," he corrected.

"Your home. Not mine."

He yawned, covering his mouth with his hand. "All right, I won't argue with you."

"Good. I don't want to argue with you while we're here."

He leaned close to her. "And what do you want to do?" he asked, now fully awake.

"I hope that's a rhetorical question," she said, then tilted her head and kissed him softly on his lips.

When she pulled away his eyes were closed. "Hmm," he said. "Now that was good. I could wake up to that every morning. How about you?"

Marlena's pulse quickened. She refused to torture herself with thoughts of the future. "I could probably get used to it."

He opened his eyes and grinned, making her wonder what he was thinking. "I bet you could." Winston took her hand in his and lifted it to his lips for a caressing kiss. "I'm not letting you go. I hope you know that."

She didn't say anything for the rest of the flight and neither did he. He kept his word though and never let go of her hand. She told him he was being silly when he flagged a skycap to get their luggage so he wouldn't have to release her.

"This trip is for us to be together and we're going to be together. Now shut up and kiss me."

"Bossy, bossy."

He tugged on her hand until her body was flush with his. "Kiss me," he ordered again.

Determined to make him pay for his bossiness, she deliberately pressed her breasts against his chest as she prepared for her assault. She didn't care about the people around them. She wanted to kiss him and she was going to kiss him. He'd think twice before ordering her around again.

When her lips touched his, she forgot her goal. Heck, she almost forgot her name. Her only consolation was that the desperation in his uttered groan said he was as affected by the kiss as she was. She managed to pull away.

He cleared his throat. "Not bad," he said. "With a little practice, you'll do just fine."

Before she could respond, he was pulling her toward the automatic doors and out to the waiting taxi. Marlena knew she was in trouble when they got in the cab and Winston pulled her onto his lap.

"What are you doing?" she asked as he ran his hands up her leg and under her skirt.

"Nothing."

He rested his head against her breast while his hand stroked the inside of her thigh. "I've never done it in a cab," he said in a hoarse whisper. "Have you?"

No, she thought to herself. She would have spoken her answer but all her brain power was consumed with keeping his hand from doing any more damage to her senses. "You aren't playing fair," she said, trying to wiggle off his lap.

"If you don't stop wiggling, both of us are going to be in some serious trouble. Now relax and let me enjoy you."

"The cab driver," she protested.

"If you relax, he'll just think we're *in* love. If you keep squirming, he's going to think we're *making* love. Now relax. I love touching you. Your skin is so soft."

"Winston," she pleaded.

"What? I'm not doing anything."

"Yes, you are."

"What am I doing?" he asked. "Are you getting hot?"

She nodded. He knew perfectly well she was getting hot. She pushed at his hand. Unfortunately, it moved up and touched the edge of her panties. She gasped.

"I told you to be still," he whispered again. "The cabbie's looking at us."

She stopped moving. What choice did she have? "Why are you doing this to me?"

"I can't help myself. I've wanted to touch you like this since that first night at the Hamptons. When McCoy pressed his lips against yours"—his hand stroked her panties—"I wanted to kill him. I should have known then that you were mine and I'd never give you up again."

Marlena stopped resisting him. She rested her head atop his and enjoyed his touch, knowing this was a new beginning for them.

"I love you, Lena," he whispered. "I never stopped. I don't want there to be any questions about my feelings. We're going to spend a lot of time *not talking* while we're here and I want you to know what my intentions are. I want you back in Gaines, in our house, in our bed, for the rest of our lives and I'm going to do everything in my power to make that happen. Do you understand what I'm saying?"

"Winston—" she began, wanting to tell him that she loved him too, wanting to allow herself to dream his dream.

"Shhh," he said. "I don't want any proclamations from you now. I only want to love you and show you how much I love you. If you had known before how much I loved you, you never would have left me. You won't be able to leave me this time, Lena. You won't. I swear it."

She didn't contradict him because she wanted him to be right. She wanted it to work out for them. He was all she'd wanted. Marty had said she was a fighter, a winner. She hoped to God he was right.

His eyes fixed on Marlena, Winston pulled opened his wallet and handed a bill to the cabbie, then slammed the front door of Marlena's town house in the man's face. He strode toward her.

"What do you want to do first?" Marlena asked as he approached. He wondered if she were joking.

He pulled his light sweater over his head and tossed it on a piece of furniture. He'd have to tour the town house later. Now he had other, more important, things to do.

He wanted to kiss her first, but he didn't. Instead, he unbuttoned her blouse and pushed it off her shoulders and onto the floor. He placed a hand on each of her lace-covered breasts, then met her gaze. As he applied pressure to her mounds, her lips parted slightly. He groaned and pressed his mouth against hers, continuing to squeeze the breasts that filled and overflowed his hands.

When she lifted her arms around his neck to increase the pressure of the kiss, his hands slid to the hooks on the back of her bra. He quickly unsnapped them, pushed the cups up and felt the hard nubble of her breast and the satiny feel of surrounding flesh press hard against his bare chest. The touch of her skin against his made him moan into her mouth. She took advantage of the moment and slipped her tongue inside, relishing their mating as much as he was.

Marlena loved the feel of Winston's bare chest pressed against her bare skin. If only his belt buckle wasn't pressing into her belly. Keeping her lips on his, she dropped her hands from his shoulders, letting her bra fall down her arms to the floor, and reached for the annoying belt buckle. She fumbled a few times before finally getting it unbuckled, then pulled until the belt was no longer in the way. She dropped it on the floor and proceeded to unsnap and unzip Winston's Dockers.

Her hand brushed the soft material covering his arousal as she unzipped. The touch only served to make her more eager to have him fully naked against her. When she dropped her other arm from his shoulders to help push his pants down, he lifted his mouth from hers with a groan and buried his face in the side of her neck. He pressed kisses all along her neck and shoulder while his hands played with the taut tips of her breasts.

"Winston." The word was a moan.

"So sweet," he said, moving his hands down her belly to the top of her skirt. She thought he was going to remove the skirt; she hoped he would, but he didn't. He lowered his hands farther, cupping her hips and pulling her against the arousal that strained at his underwear.

His hands continued downward then began the trip back up, lifting her skirt in the process. His bare hands against her thighs made her weak and she sagged against him. He squeezed her hips again and crushed her to him. She could feel his arousal hard against her pubic region.

Winston wanted more. He rushed his hands up to the top of her panties and pushed the thin garment down her legs. Her warmth drew him and his fingers tangled themselves in the hairy covering of her mound.

"Winston," he heard her plead. His response was to slip a single finger into her warmth, causing both of them to groan with pleasure.

Figuring he'd waited long enough, Winston tried to move toward the steps, but his pants down around his ankles made him stumble and he fell to the floor, pulling Marlena down with him so she lay flush against him, her naked breasts pressed flat against his chest, her eyes boring into his.

"I guess we won't make it to the bed," he said with what he hoped was a smile. He lifted his head as she lowered hers and their lips met in an explosion of passion long denied and even longer simmering.

He frantically unbuttoned her skirt and pushed it and her panties away from her so that she was naked except for the strap sandals covering her feet. Then he uncovered his arousal and pushed his briefs down his legs where they joined the pants bunched around his ankles.

Winston's heat made Marlena squirm. The fall had been good for her. She didn't think she could have waited until they were upstairs. She wanted too much, needed too much. She pressed her lower body tight against Winston's, loving the feel of his smooth hardness against her even smoother softness. This contrast of man and woman thrilled her.

When she could wait no longer, she lifted her lower body slightly and reached down and took him in her hands, squeezing ever so lightly. His eyes met hers and his hands covered hers as she guided him to her entrance.

The look of pure pleasure on his face when his heat entered her sheath made her shiver. She knew what she shared with Winston was real. This was lovemaking: giving pleasure and receiving it in return.

When the tip of his arousal met the moistness of her inner core, Winston clenched his teeth. He wanted so much to take it slowly, but he knew that would be impossible. He instinctively pushed and buried himself fully within her.

''Ohh, Lena, baby,'' he murmured against her lips. ''So wet, so good.''

Marlena rocked against him in rhythm with his thrusts, but that wasn't enough. She pulled her mouth away from him and traced kisses along his jaw and chin, all the while watching the play of emotions across his face as he gently thrust in and out.

When she sat straight up on him, she groaned at the depth to which he filled her. Using his rhythm, she raised and lowered herself on him, bracing her hands on his chest for support.

Winston raised his hands to her breasts as their lower bodies danced. His fingers tweaked and squeezed, tweaked and squeezed, until Marlena couldn't bear it any longer. She tilted her head back, stretching her body before him, and gave in to the pleasure they shared.

The pace and the pressure of his thrusts increased, sending her over the edge and into their own paradise. With a final thrust and a loud grunt, he followed her.

Though Marlena's carpet was plush, Winston was uncomfortable lying on his back with Marlena atop him. He wished they'd made it to the bed, but he understood why they hadn't.

He idly brushed his hand up and down her spine. Her even breathing told him she was awake and alert, but he didn't say anything to her. He just continued to stroke her back.

It seemed inadequate to say their lovemaking had been fantastic. Fantastic was too tame a word for what had transpired between them. Now that he had loved her, he was even more confident he would never lose her again. Marlena was his heart. He needed her in his life as close and as tight as he had been in her body.

His hands moved to her ears and he traced them with his fingers. He was glad he'd come to D.C. with her, but he worried about Marlena's refusal to make love with him in Gaines. That she was still so concerned with what people thought didn't bode well for them. He wished for the hundredth time that she would believe what most sensible people already knew about her: that she was a wonderful woman anyone would be proud to know. Even those bigots who still had the nerve to look down on her couldn't ignore what she'd accomplished.

She stirred against him, propped her hands on his chest, and stared into his eyes, making his body grow warm. "That was wonderful," she said, her eyes shimmering with tears.

"Then why are you crying?" he asked, truly amazed that his Marlena was crying.

She tried to blink away the tears. "I'm not crying. I'm rejoicing."

"So am I," he said softly. "I love you, Lena."

A smile lit her eyes. "I bet you say that to every woman you take on floor of her living room."

"Not all," he said, pushing his growing arousal gently against her. "Only the special ones."

"So I'm special," she said.

"A little." He rolled his hips against hers.

"Just a little?" She reached down and clasped him in her hands and squeezed.

"Maybe a lot," he choked out. "Now stop that. We're too old to go at it like rabbits."

"Maybe you're too old." She slid off him and to his side, still holding him in her hands. "I'm not."

He slapped at her hands. "Stop that or you're going to be in trouble."

"I wouldn't mind," she whispered, remembering how fear of getting in trouble with an unwanted pregnancy had once ruled her life. "Sometimes I'm so jealous that Cheryl and Marty have a child. It makes me wish I'd gotten pregnant with your baby."

He pulled her into his arms. She'd voiced thoughts that had crossed his mind since learning of Patrice's parentage. The what-ifs had been endless. What if Marlena had gotten pregnant? What if they had gotten married? What if she had never left him? What if they had kept to their plan and moved back to Gaines when they graduated law school? So many what-ifs, but none mattered now. All that mattered was that they were together and, if he had any say in it, they'd always be together. "We didn't use anything. You could be pregnant now."

"I know," she said. "Are you worried?"

"About what?"

"Me getting pregnant, AIDS, you know. This is the first time I haven't used a condom."

He kissed the tip of her nose. "I'm definitely not worried about your getting pregnant. I told you I love you and I want babies. We have a lot of lost time to make up for. As for STDs, this is also the first time I haven't used a condom."

"Since you got divorced, you mean?"

Winston wished that was what he meant, but it wasn't. He sighed. "Patty wanted us to have some time together before we had children. She was adamant about it. So I even used a condom when we were married."

"You're kidding!"

He shook his head. "Not a bit. Patty was a strange woman." His using the condom without complaint also said something about him, he knew. In some ways, using the condom had given him an excuse. He could lie and tell himself that sex would be better between him and Patty when they no longer used a condom, but now he knew things would have never gotten better with Patty until he stopped loving Marlena. And he now knew just as Patty had come to know that loving Marlena wasn't something he could control.

"Why did you marry Patty so soon after we split up?" she asked, needing to know.

"I don't know," he said. "I came back home and she was there to help me pick up the pieces of my life. I needed somebody and she was there."

"Did you love her?"

"She was my wife, Marlena. I cared for her and I loved her. In a way," he clarified, knowing he hadn't loved Patty the way a man should love his wife.

"It hurt when I found out about it. It made me wonder if you really loved me."

"Well, I was wondering the same thing about you. You were the one who walked out, remember?"

"I'm so sorry I hurt you, Winston. I did love you. I did. But . . ."

"But what?"

She shook her head then lowered it back to his chest. "Nothing. It's nothing."

Winston knew something was on her mind, but he also knew now wasn't the time to push. Marlena had to trust him and herself of her own will. That was one thing he couldn't control. He knew she had the strength to do it, but he didn't know if she knew it.

Chapter 19

Marlena felt proud when she strolled into her law office the next day with Winston right behind her. She'd been eager for him to visit her office, the place where people respected her without reservation. She needed him to see her success for himself.

"Morning, Ms. Rhodes," Julie, her young secretary, said. "We didn't expect you back so soon."

Marlena noticed Julie's eyes kept moving to Winston and she smiled, understanding the woman's interest. Too bad Winston was hers. "This is Winston Taylor, Julie, an old high school friend of mine."

"Hi, Julie," Winston said, his deep voice no doubt the reason for color staining the young woman's light brown cheeks.

"Good morning, Mr. Taylor. So you went to school with Ms. Rhodes? She's my role model, you know. I started law school last year because of her. She told me I owed it to myself to give it a try."

Winston smiled at the young woman. "Ms. Rhodes is really something. You couldn't have picked a better role model. Good luck in your studies. And don't forget me. One day I may need to call on your services."

"That's nice of you to say, but I'd recommend you use Ms. Rhodes. That's what I'd do if I were in trouble."

"Stop it, you two," Marlena said, embarrassed by Julie's praise and admiration. "Julie will make a fine attorney. If we're lucky, she'll stay on with the firm after she passes the bar. Now, back to business. Is there anything urgent I need to look at, Julie?"

The young woman stepped back to her desk and clicked the mouse next to her computer terminal. "I almost forgot. Greg's back in the country. He called this morning and left his number. Of course, I told him you were still in Gaines." She scribbled the number on a slip of paper and handed it to Marlena. "That's it. I've passed everything else on to Mr. Brock."

Marlena folded the paper and slipped it into her jacket pocket. She looked back at Winston. "I guess they don't really need me around here," she said.

"That's not true, Ms. Rhodes," Julie said. "We do need you. We just want you to enjoy your vacation." She looked at Winston. "Her only fault is that she works too hard. Maybe you can help her out there, Mr. Taylor. She needs to relax."

Winston moved closer to Marlena and placed an arm on her shoulder. "I'm trying my best, Julie. It's good to know I have an ally in you."

"Hey, you two," Marlena interrupted. "I'm not that bad." Marlena didn't miss the disbelieving look that passed between Winston and Julie. "That's enough now," she said, but she wasn't angry with them. "I'm only going to be here for about an hour or so, Julie. You should be pleased to know I've decided to take some more time off."

"That's wonderful, Ms. Rhodes. Are you going some place special?"

Marlena smiled at her secretary's exuberance. "No place special really," Marlena said.

"Yes, special," Winston corrected. "She's coming back to her home town for a while. The people in Gaines are so proud of her that they can't bear for her to leave."

"I can understand that," Julie said, ready to launch into another Marlena-is-perfect routine, but Marlena stopped her.

"Not again. Julie, will you call Lester and tell him I need to see him before I leave. I want to tell him personally about my schedule change."

"Fine, Ms. Rhodes. When will you be back?"

"Two months," Winston answered for her.

Julie looked to Marlena. "Two months?"

Marlena shook her head at Winston. "Don't listen to him, Julie. I'll be away for another month at most."

"But we're going to try to talk her into staying longer—a whole lot longer."

"Longer than a month?" Julie asked. "We wanted you to take a vacation, Ms. Rhodes, but we didn't want you to desert us."

"I'm not deserting you, Julie. As I said, I'll be away for another four weeks at most."

Julie looked at Winston, then back at Marlena. "I hope you don't stay away any longer. We need you around here."

"Forget what Mr. Taylor said, Julie. I'll be back before you miss me."

"If you say so," the young woman said, clearly not satisfied that Marlena would indeed soon be back.

Marlena walked to her office door. "Don't forget to call Lester," she reminded Julie. "I want to talk to him before I leave." She motioned to Winston. "Well, come on into the inner sanctuary."

Two nights later, Winston observed Marlena over a candlelit dinner in her favorite restaurant. Again, she had him in a monkey suit, tie and all. It was worth it though to see the smile on her face and the light in her eyes. His woman, he thought. She was that, but she was so much more.

He'd known she'd become successful, but he hadn't realized how successful until he'd seen her town house and her office. Both spoke of money and success. The town house was peppered with antiques from all over the world, some she'd bought herself, many were gifts from friends. He refused to ask if any were male friends.

Her office made *The Way Home* office look like a small town bus stop. It had rich, textured wood and a gorgeous view of the Capitol. Yes, Andrews, Scott and Rhodes was at the top.

When he looked at Marlena now, dressed in a simple black strapless dress that hugged her ample breasts, bared her smooth shoulders, and exposed her gorgeous legs, he wondered for the first time if Gaines would be enough for her, if he'd be enough. When he got right down to it, whether he'd be enough was his biggest concern.

He hated to admit it, but he feared the competition out of the D.C. ranks. He hadn't missed the message from Greg, whoever he was, that Julie had given her the other day. No, he hadn't missed it. He'd waited for Marlena to tell him who Greg was, but she hadn't. He didn't know if that was good or bad.

When he held her in his arms at night, he had no questions. He was sure they belonged together. In this fancy restaurant, dressed in all their finery, he wondered. This was her world now. He didn't know if she could give it up. He didn't know if he had a right to ask her to give it up.

"You aren't enjoying your food?" she asked from across the table, her dark skin bright and soft in the candlelight.

"Who's thinking about food?"

God, she still blushed. He hardened at the thought.

"Thanks for coming with me tonight," she said. "I know how you hate dressing up. You look very handsome, though. Very handsome. I've been watching the women check you out. Maybe I should plaster a sign on your forehead that says, Taken."

Winston thought a better sign was a wedding ring on his finger and hers, but he knew now wasn't the time to make that suggestion. "Well, I see only one woman. You."

"Flatterer."

He tipped his wine glass to his lips. "I'm just calling 'em like I see 'em." He put the glass down. "I want to dance. How about it?"

She smiled. "Sure."

Winston led her to the small dance floor. When he pulled

her into his arms, he whispered into her ear, "You know this was an excuse to hold you, don't you?"

"No, I didn't know, but it works both ways. I like holding you too."

"God, Marlena, how do you do this to me?"

"Do what?" she asked, her face against his chest.

"Turn me inside out. Make me want you all the time. Make me need you. You've cast a spell over me. How do you do it?"

She looked up at him, her big, brown eyes full of emotion. "You do the same to me, Winston. You always have. You're so intense and you suck me right into your intensity."

"Is that good or bad?"

"I don't know. I just know I like it. I need it."

He leaned his head down and placed a light kiss on her lips. "Thanks for saying that, sweetheart."

She rested her head back against his chest and caressed the back of his neck with her fingers.

"You'd better stop that if you want dessert," he warned, his voice thick with passion.

She continued her smooth stroking along his neck.

"Lena, you'd better stop or I'm going to embarrass both of us when we get ready to walk back to our table."

She pulled back and looked up at him. "I don't think I'll be embarrassed. As a matter of fact, I know I won't. Excited, yes. Embarrassed, no."

"You're not getting any dessert," he told her. He kissed her lips, then took her hand and led her away from the dance floor. Fortunately, they met their waiter on the way to the door. Winston quickly opened his wallet and gave the guy a few bills, more than enough to cover the cost of their dinner and a substantial tip.

A few more bills into the valet's hand and Marlena's car was brought around. He kissed her again, then ushered her into the silver convertible. He weaved through the late evening D.C. traffic with single-minded determination. Marlena's hand on his knee reminded him of the delight that awaited him as soon as they got back to her town house.

"I thought we'd never get here," he said as soon as they were in her kitchen. "Kiss me."

She kissed him, putting all the love she felt for him into the kiss. These few days with him had been wonderful. She'd enjoyed giving him a glimpse of her world and seeing his eyes fill with pride and excitement at what she'd accomplished. She'd had no idea how much his pride in her would mean. She'd known his love in the past, but she'd never experienced his pride in her.

When she was able to step away from the kiss, she put a hand on each side of his face. "I love you, Winston," she said. "I love you so much."

It was the first time she'd said the words in ten years. She'd thought them many times since seeing Winston again, but she'd been afraid it was too early to speak her heart, afraid that speaking the words would somehow jinx what they were finding together.

"I've waited for you to say those words," Winston said. "God, how I've waited. You know what I want?"

She smiled. "I think I can make a pretty good guess."

"You're a smart woman." He wrapped an arm around her waist and led her upstairs to her bedroom.

They undressed each other slowly as if they had all the time in the world. When they stood naked before each other, Winston pulled her close. "Tell me again," he said.

"I love you, Winston Taylor. I've always loved you."

He guided her slowly to the bed and eased her down on her back. "I'll never get enough of you. Never." He placed a whispering kiss along her jaw. "You know what I think about?"

She shook her head and he felt her tremble.

"I think about going to sleep inside you every night and waking up inside you every morning. That would be heaven."

He moved his kiss to her lips and she wrapped her arms around him, needing to be even closer to him. His words moved her and made her dream of the future she so desperately wanted with him.

As they kissed, Winston's hands caressed her chest, her

breasts, her stomach, causing her desire to soar. It had never been like this with anyone.

"Winston . . ." she moaned.

"I know, sweetheart," he said, positioning himself between her open legs. "I know."

Eager, Marlena lifted her lower body against him, needing him to fill her, to make her complete. In a single thrust, he met her need. He started slowly then increased his pace when she wrapped her legs around his hips and matched his rhythm.

"God, Lena," Winston choked out.

His words coupled with his body's control of her were all she needed to make the leap from reality to paradise. Paradise was made perfect when he joined her.

"Not bad for an old man," she said when her breathing returned to normal.

Winston's chest still rose and fell rapidly. "You make me weak, woman. Do you know that?"

"I try."

He managed a laugh between deep breaths. "You succeed."

"I'm glad you came with me," she said, drawing circles around his nipple with her finger.

"I wouldn't have missed seeing you in your element, Miss Attorney-All-That."

"I do all right."

"You do better than all right. What's up with Lester Brock?"

Her fingers stopped their movement. "What do you mean?"

"He didn't look too happy to see me with you." Actually, her older partner had seemed annoyed by his presence. He'd wondered if anything had ever gone on between him and Marlena.

"You can't be jealous of Lester. He's old enough to be my father and he's very married."

"As if that matters. The guy's old, but he's not blind."

She pulled on his nipple and got an "Ouch" out of him. "You deserved that for thinking bad thoughts about poor Lester. Shame on you, Winston."

He took her hand in his. "You can't blame me. You're an attractive, successful woman. I bet you've got men coming out of the woodwork."

She did have her share of admirers, but none of them interested her. She was already taken; she knew that now. "Well, I'm with the man I want right now. I've never wanted anyone the way I want you."

"But there have been other men, haven't here?" he asked softly.

She sat up and folded her arms around her bended knees. "Why do you want to talk about the other men in my life? There are none."

"Who's Greg?" he asked.

She turned back and looked at him. "Greg?"

"Greg." He sat back in the bed and folded his hands behind his head. "Julie gave you a note from him in your office the other day."

She should have known he wouldn't let the name go unexplained. She should have given him an explanation before he asked for one, but the mention of Greg's name had so unnerved her that she'd rushed to put the note and Greg out of her mind. "He's my cousin."

"Cousin?"

"My mother's sister's child. He's a couple of years older than me, but we're close."

"Have I ever met him?"

"No," she answered, and if she had anything to do with it, the two men would never meet. The secret would be out as soon as Winston saw Greg. Though she hadn't noticed any resemblance until after she'd learned the truth, she was sure Winston would notice immediately. "We weren't that close then. It's only been since my mother's death that we've grown close."

"This Greg didn't make it to the funeral?"

"No." Marlena thanked God every day that Greg hadn't been able to get back in the country in time. All hell would have broken loose if he'd shown up for the funeral. "He was off in the Peace Corps at the time. He couldn't get back."

Winston rubbed his hand along her spine. "You know, I think about your mother sometimes."

Marlena leaned back and rested against him. "Josie was a character. I miss her."

"She never liked me, though. I never quite understood it."

Marlena hadn't either, at the time. She'd thought her mother would be impressed that her daughter was dating a guy from Rosemont, but Josie had been furious. She hadn't understood her mother's reaction then; she did now. "You know how mothers are. She thought you were going to break my heart."

He laughed a dry laugh. "She was wrong."

"I know," she said. "But there was no way for Josie to know how our relationship would turn out. I think that's why I could never really hate your mother. She believes, right or wrong, that I'm not the woman for you and she'll do anything to keep me from hurting you."

He pulled her into his arms. "Hey, you make it sound like that's the way things are now. That was ten years ago."

She looked up at him. "She's still your mother."

"But she doesn't control my life. You have to remember that, Marlena. I love you and nothing Mother says or does will change the way I feel."

Marlena wasn't too sure. It was easy for Winston to pledge undying loyalty when he didn't know the truth, but what would happen if he knew? Would he look at her differently? Would he stop loving her? "Let's talk about something else," she said. "We came here to get away from Gaines and we've had a good time so far. Let's not ruin it."

He kissed her cheek. "Fine with me. I can think of a few other things I'd rather do."

"What things?" she asked.

He pressed his mouth against her breast. "Oh, this and that."

"This and that?"

He kissed a tip. "Yes, this." His hand brushed down her stomach to the satiny treasure between her legs. "And that. Do you like that?"

"Maybe," she said.

He moved so he was lying on top of her. "How about now?"

"That's a little better."

He captured her passion center in his fingers and rubbed. "Better?"

"Hmmm. Much better."

Chapter 20

Marlena hated to part from Winston when he dropped her off at the Gaines Inn on Sunday afternoon. She stayed in his arms a little longer than necessary after he'd kissed her, refusing to let him get up and go home. "I had a good time this weekend," she said.

"So did I." He grinned down at her. "Are we going to sit here in the lobby like this for the rest of afternoon?"

She hugged him closer, resting her head on his shoulder, still reluctant to let him go. "Do you have something better to do?"

"No way. It's just that I can think of more comfortable accommodations."

She peeked up at him. "Like my room?"

"Actually, I was thinking of that big, king-sized bed back at my house."

She sighed against his shoulder, thinking of that big bed herself, tempted to let him take her there. "Sounds like fun," she whispered.

"So you want to go?"

She slowly lifted her head from his shoulder. "You know I can't. People will talk."

"So? Let them talk. I don't care what they say."

"But I do."

He cursed. "Why is what people say so important to you, Marlena? Why?"

"You know why," she shot back, wondering how he could be so insensitive as to even ask her why. "I won't have them talking about me the way they talked about Josie. I won't have it, Winston."

He pulled her back into his arms. "People were cruel, Marlena. They said some very ugly things about Josie, but, sweetheart, you're not Josie."

"I'm her daughter."

"And I'm my mother's son, but I'm not her. Look, Josie liked men and they liked her. That's a fact, but it was her business."

She wondered what he'd say if he knew everything about Josie. Would he hold her in his arms and comfort her then? She hoped so, but she wasn't going to count on it.

"You can't let the way they treated your mother back then control the way you live your life today. That's giving them way too much power."

She sighed again. They'd only been back in Gaines ten minutes and she was already tired. She hadn't faced any opposition, but she was tired of the what-ifs that continually popped into her mind. "You're right. I know you're right, but I can't leave myself open for gossip. I just can't do it, Winston."

"Does that mean what I think it means?" he asked, deceptively calm.

"It means we're going to have to be careful about when and where we sleep together," she said, then waited for his explosion.

"Marlena, I'm *not* going to sneak around like some teenager. I love you, and I want to make love to you in my house, in my bed, hell, in our bed."

She wanted that, too, more than anything, but she had to make him understand that now wasn't the time to go public with their relationship. "We need to take it slowly, Winston," she said in her calmest voice.

"Slow, my ass," he said, crushing her against him. "What do you call waiting ten years? I don't think we can take it much slower."

"But Winston—" she began.

He pulled away from her. "Maybe I've got this wrong," he said, looking deep into her eyes, daring her to lie to him. "I thought you said you loved me."

"I do love you. You know I do."

"I want to believe you, Marlena, but when you're more concerned about what people in this town think than you're concerned about me and this relationship, I can't help but wonder."

"That's not it," she began again.

"I think that's exactly it. Look at what you're doing, sweetheart."

"Just because I won't put up a banner in the middle of Courthouse Square proclaiming that we're sleeping together, you think I'm ignoring your feelings? What about my feelings? No woman wants to be gossiped about, Winston. I don't want to hear people say I'm your whore."

He cursed again. "Then marry me, and this won't be an issue. That should set all the gossips straight. Marry me and it'll shut their mouths forever."

"Marry you?" she said, not believing he'd asked her again. She'd known his mind was thinking along these lines, but she hadn't expected him to pose the question this soon.

"You heard me. You don't want to sleep in my bed for fear of being called a whore. Well, that's easy enough to fix. You'll belong in my bed once we're married."

"You're not serious."

He cursed again, then stood up and stared down at her. She saw the frustration and, yes, the love in his eyes. "Look, Marlena, I'm tired of you telling me what I feel. I know what I feel. I love you and that's enough for me. You have to decide if it's enough for you." He turned and strode out of the hotel doors. She sat there staring after him.

* * *

"Winston proposed!" Cheryl shouted. "Well, it's about time. Now what are you going to do about it?"

Marlena shook her head. When Cheryl had called her room after the afternoon program at church and welcomed her back to town, she'd gladly invited her over.

"I don't know," she responded.

"You're not sure you want to marry him?" Cheryl asked for clarification. "Well, I can answer that one for you. I *know* you want to marry him."

Marlena thought about the secret she carried. Why had she come back to Gaines in the first place if she'd known this secret would keep her and Winston apart? What had she been thinking? "It's complicated, Cheryl."

"How complicated can it be? Do you love him?"

"You know I do." God, did she love him. She loved him so much it hurt. She'd called his house four or five times since he'd stormed out of the hotel, but she'd gotten no answer. Her feelings bounced between anger at the high-handed manner with which he'd treated her to fear that something might have happened to him on the highway to pure joy that he'd asked her to marry him. No wonder she couldn't think straight.

"Okay, you love Winston. That's settled. Now, does he love you?"

She smiled as she remembered him cursing and telling her he loved her all in the same breath. "He says he does."

"Do you believe him?"

She nodded. "He doesn't have a reason to lie." Briefly, she considered that he could be lying because he wanted to sleep with her, but that didn't make sense after the weekend they'd shared. He had to know it wouldn't take a marriage proposal to get her into bed again.

"What's the problem then?" Cheryl asked, clearly not understanding Marlena's reluctance.

Marlena couldn't tell her. "Cheryl, I know what you're trying to do and I love you for it, but this is something Winston and I have to work out.''

"Don't give him a hard time about this, Marlena," Cheryl warned. "You two have been separated for ten years. Do you want to go through another ten years without him?''

Marlena could no longer dream of a future that didn't include Winston. She didn't want to. She wanted to be by his side and, yes, in that big bed of theirs for the rest of her life. She just didn't know if she could make it happen. Was she strong enough to risk losing him on the chance that she could have him forever or would she settle for having him for this short time then giving him up forever. "You're right, Cheryl. I know you're right. I don't want to lose Winston, but it just may not be in the cards for us.''

When Winston's doorbell rang, his first thought was that Marlena had come to her senses. He rushed to the door.

"It's about time you got back, Winston," his mother said as she strode past him and into the house. Dressed in her Sunday fare, which included gloves and hat, she was the picture of the genteel, southern woman. "I've been worried sick," she said, taking a seat on the blue upholstered sofa in his living room and crossing her legs. "How could you go off that way and not tell me where you were going or even leave a number so I could get in touch with you. You've never done that before.''

He sat in the matching blue club chair across from her. "Good afternoon to you too, Mother," he said, refusing to be baited by her sharp words. He was an adult and it was about time his mother realized it.

She shot him an accusing glare. "You went away with that woman, didn't you?''

He debated telling her to mind her own business, then decided it was better to be honest with her. If he had any say in the matter, pretty soon he'd be a married man. "Her name is Marlena, and yes, I went away with her.''

"She's going to make a fool of you again," she said, and

he didn't miss the emphasis on the word *again*. "Don't let her do it, Winston. Don't let her."

"Nobody's going to make a fool of anybody, Mother. I love Marlena. I always have. And she loves me."

"You said that ten years ago and looked what happened. Can't you see what kind of woman she is?"

Winston reminded himself that this woman, however much he disliked her at this moment, was his mother. "I know what kind of woman Marlena is, Mother. She's beautiful, sweet, loving, and smart. She's everything I want in a woman and everything I want in a wife."

His mother uncrossed her legs and leaned toward him. "Please tell me you aren't thinking of marrying this girl, Winston. Surely, you can't be that blinded by lust. Sleep with her if you must, but don't marry her."

Winston slowly counted to ten in his mind. It didn't help. He counted to twenty. "Listen to me, Mother, and listen well. I'm going to marry Marlena, if she'll have me, and you're going to deal with it. You're going to more than deal with it. You're going to welcome her into this family with open arms," he said, his voice rising. "Do you understand me?"

"You can't be serious, Winston. I won't welcome that . . . that low-class woman into this family. She'll never be welcome."

Winston sighed. He refused to argue anymore. "If that's the way you want it, Mother, that's the way it'll be. If Marlena is not welcome in this family, then neither am I."

"Winston, son," she said, placing a manicured hand on his knee, "you can't be serious. Surely you aren't going to let this woman come between us. You're my family. We're all that's left since your daddy died. Why, he must be turning over in his grave after hearing what you said. How can you deny your own family for that woman?"

Winston moved his leg so that her hand fell away. "For the last time, Mother. Her name is Marlena. Do you hate her so much that you can't even speak her name? What has she ever done to you?"

"It's not what's she done to me, Winston, can't you see?

It's what she's done to you. Don't you remember how torn up inside you were when she left you the first time? How do you know she won't do it again? You don't know what motivates that girl. What if she gets a better offer from a man with more money?''

Winston hated that his mother's words hit close to home. He did have a tinge of doubt that Marlena would accept his proposal. He didn't doubt her love, though. No, she loved him as much as he loved her. He just wasn't sure her love was strong enough to fight the demons that had haunted her for so much of her life. ''I can't control what you think, Mother, but I can control what you say, at least in my home. You are never to speak an ill word about Marlena again in my presence. If you do, I'll personally escort you to the door. I love her, Mother, and you're going to have to deal with it. You either accept a daughter-in-law or you lose a son. It's your choice.''

Marlena rushed to answer the knock at her door, thinking it must be Winston. Shocked didn't quite describe how she felt when she opened the door and saw his mother standing there instead. The older woman didn't bother with a greeting, she pushed past Marlena and entered the room as if she owned the place. Marlena closed the door and watched as the older woman sat down, pulled off her gloves and hat, and made herself at home.

''What are you doing here, Mrs. Taylor?'' Marlena finally asked.

''My son tells me you're getting married,'' she answered in a tone void of emotion.

Marlena sat down across from her. ''He's asked me, yes.''

''And no doubt you're thinking about accepting.''

Marlena reminded herself that this was Winston's mother and he loved her. ''I love him, Mrs. Taylor. I always have.''

''Don't try that 'I love him' routine with me, Marlena. You might have Winston wrapped around your little finger, but I see you for the slut you are. Women like you always think they can control a man with sex. Well, let me tell you, it'll be a cold day in hell before you marry my son. Do you understand me?''

Marlena straightened her back. Winston's mother or not, this old woman was a bitch with a capital B. ''I understand you exactly. Unfortunately, I don't think you have a say in the matter. Winston *wants* to marry me.''

The horrid laugh the woman gave made Marlena want to shiver, but she wouldn't give Mrs. Taylor the satisfaction.

''Winston doesn't know what he wants. How can he want you when he doesn't even know you? What do you think he'll do when he learns your mother was whoring around with his father right up until the day she died? What will Winston think about you then, Miss Hotshot Attorney?''

''Winston's not a stupid man, Mrs. Taylor,'' Marlena responded with a calm she didn't feel. ''He knows you're a cold woman who couldn't satisfy his father. He'll probably be glad my mother was there to offer him some comfort and understanding.''

Mrs. Taylor jumped up. ''You little tramp. Don't you dare threaten me.''

''I'm not threatening you, Mrs. Taylor. I'm stating fact. Tell Winston the truth if you like. It won't make a difference. He loves me, you see. He always has. Nothing that happened between his father and my mother years and years ago can change that. Your threat might have scared an insecure young woman dealing with the grief of her mother's death, but it doesn't scare me. I'm no longer that weak woman and I won't be bullied by you.''

Mrs. Taylor's lips turned down in a snarl. Gone was the genteel southern lady. The woman before Marlena now was a low-down, dirty street fighter. ''You think you're so smart, don't you? You come back here with your expensive suits, your I'm-better-than-everybody attitude and you think it makes a difference. You're a fool, Marlena. You were trash from the projects when you left here ten years ago and you still are. No amount of education and no amount of money will change that.''

Marlena stood up. ''That's your opinion, Mrs. Taylor. Thank

God, Winston doesn't share it. Actually, he thinks I'm pretty special for pulling myself up by my bootstraps, so to speak. I think I'll believe his interpretation. Now, I think you'd better go." She walked to the door and held it open. "I wish I could say this has been fun, but you know how trash is, we don't bother with common courtesy. Now, get out."

Mrs. Taylor didn't move and for a minute Marlena wondered if the older woman was going to continue standing there. She hoped not, because she didn't relish the idea of holding the door open for the next hour.

"All right, Marlena," the older woman said, making her way toward the door. "I'll leave." She stopped when she was face-to-face with Marlena. "But mark my words, you'll never marry my son. Never." With that Mrs. Taylor pulled on her gloves and strode out of the door.

"Good riddance," Marlena said, slamming the door.

She stalked to her small kitchen area and pulled a soda from the mini-refrigerator, knowing that if she drank, now would be the perfect time for a shot of something. She settled for gulping down a diet soda.

After placing the can on the counter, she wiped her mouth with the back of her hand, then slumped against the sink. Now that Mrs. Taylor was gone, so was all of Marlena's energy. The argument had zapped her strength. She'd stood up to Mrs. Taylor and she was proud of herself for doing so, but did she want to live the rest of her life fighting that woman's wrath? Did she want to subject Winston to her constant battles with his mother?

She cursed. Why did life have to be so hard? Things came so easy for some people. Why did she have to fight for everything, even love? It wasn't fair.

She sighed. Whoever said life was fair?

Chapter 21

For the fifth time in the last hour, Marlena got up from her desk and walked to the window. Three o'clock and no word from Winston. When she'd arrived this morning and he wasn't in, she'd assumed he'd had a court appearance. She'd started to worry when she hadn't heard from him after lunch. Was he avoiding her because he was upset about yesterday or had something happened to him? She'd called his house already and gotten no answer. "Where is he?" she asked herself as she looked out on Courthouse Square.

She looked back at the folders stacked on her desk. She hadn't gotten much done since lunch and she probably wouldn't until she heard from Winston. She glanced at his desk, then walked over and sat in his chair, needing to be near him.

She loved him so much and she needed to tell him. She should have told him yesterday, and not let him leave angry. What if something happened to him and he didn't know how much he meant to her? Well, she'd make sure a day like yesterday never happened again.

Winston wanted to marry her. Marriage to him was what she most wanted and what she most feared. Could they have a life together? Did she have the right and the courage to do what needed to be done so they could build a life together?

She hugged her arms around herself. Why had she come back to Gaines? What had she thought she was going to accomplish by coming back? If Winston hadn't cared for her, she would have been able to leave town and put the past behind her for good, but Winston still loved her and wanted to marry her. What was she going to do?

A knock at the office door brought Marlena to her feet and into motion. She hoped it was Winston, but she knew it wasn't. Why would he knock? "Come in," she called.

Patrice and Raymond walked in holding hands. "Hey, Ms. Marlena," they both said.

"Is Coach around?" Raymond asked.

Marlena sat on the edge of Winston's desk, facing the teenagers. "No, he hasn't been in all day. I don't think he'll be in."

"Oh," Raymond said.

Patrice turned wide eyes up at him and he caressed her shoulder. "We'll talk to him tomorrow, Trece," he said. "It'll be all right."

"Is there something I can do to help?" Marlena asked, concerned about the couple. "I've got plenty of time."

Patrice looked up at Raymond again, then back to Marlena. "It can wait," she said. "So you think Coach'll be in tomorrow?"

Marlena nodded, but she was still worried about the teens. She prayed Patrice wasn't pregnant. The child had her whole life in front of her. "I'm sure," she said. "I'll leave him a message that you dropped by. Do you want him to call either of you when he gets in?"

Again, Patrice looked up at Raymond. Marlena wondered what was going on.

"That's not necessary," Raymond said. "We'll talk to him tomorrow."

"Okay, if you're sure."

Patrice nodded. "We're sure."

"So, how are things going with the two of you?" Marlena asked.

"We're fine," Patrice answered quickly. Too quickly.

Marlena looked from one teen to the other. "You two know that you can talk to me about anything, don't you? I care about both of you very much."

Patrice looked up at Raymond, then back at Marlena. She had tears in her eyes. Marlena opened her arms and Patrice ran into them.

Marlena looked askance at Raymond, while she comforted a sobbing Patrice. "What's wrong?" she asked.

Raymond came closer and brushed his hands across Patrice's hair. "My parents don't want us to see each other anymore. They say we're getting too serious."

"They don't like me," Patrice said between sobs. "They don't think I'm good enough for Raymond. Just because my mom works in a factory and she's divorced, they don't think I'm good enough."

Marlena caught the pain in Raymond's eyes at his girlfriend's words. "That's not true, Trece," he said, continuing the brushing motion of his hand across her hair. "They just don't know you. You're the best thing that's ever happened to me. I love you so much. Please stop crying."

Marlena's heart broke for the young lovers or maybe it broke for the young lovers she and Winston had been or maybe it broke for the cruel people in the world who spoke with no care for the feelings of others. She held Patrice tighter. "Raymond's right, sweetheart. You're a wonderful girl. If I had a son, I'd want him to bring home a girl just like you."

"Please stop crying," Raymond said again. "You know I can't stand it when you cry, Trece. Please. I love you so much."

Marlena's eyes filled with tears at the young man's words. Raymond was indeed a young man, not a boy. And he was very much in love with Patrice. Marlena knew it was a love that would last forever. Why couldn't his parents see that?

Maybe they could, she reasoned. Maybe that's why they wanted to end the relationship. They probably had the daughter-in-law they wanted all picked out and were waiting for Raymond to come to his senses. Stupid, stupid people!

Patrice's sobs slowly subsided and she lifted her head. Wiping at her eyes, she said, "I'm sorry. I don't usually cry like this."

"Don't be sorry," Marlena said. "Sometimes crying helps." She remembered a time when she'd thought tears meant weakness, but not anymore. She'd given in to her tears the day she'd walked out of Winston's life and now found comfort in them.

Patrice managed a small smile, but Marlena knew the girl still hurt and would hurt for a long while. She only hoped Patrice wouldn't carry the scars for as long as she had.

"Trece." Raymond called her name softly and Patrice turned around and fell into his open arms. "It'll be all right," he cooed. "I love you and they can't keep us apart. They can't."

Marlena knew from the determination in the young man's voice that he was serious. He'd do anything and everything in his power to keep his word.

"Raymond's parents are probably worried because you two are so young and so serious," Marlena said, trying to be the voice of reason. "They don't want you to do anything to ruin your life."

"You're talking about sex, aren't you?" Patrice turned to Marlena and asked, her voice laced with disgust.

"Well, it is something to be concerned about."

"You're just like my mom," Patrice accused. "Why does everyone think we're sleeping together? Do you think sex is all Raymond wants from me—that sex is all I have to offer him?" Her eyes filled with tears again.

"No, Patrice," Marlena said calmly. "I don't think sex is all Raymond wants from you or that sex is all you have to offer, but I know how it is to be young and in love."

"So you and Coach slept together in high school?" the young girl asked.

"No," Marlena said. "We didn't." She remembered how much they'd wanted to, though.

"We don't either. We decided to wait until we graduate from high school. We've even talked about waiting until we get married, but what's the use? We may as well do it now since that's what everyone expects."

"Don't say that, Trece," Marlena was surprised to hear

Raymond say. "When we make love, it won't be to get back at our parents."

Raymond's stock climbed considerably in Marlena's opinion. "He's right, Patrice. Don't do something foolish. Talk to Cheryl, then talk to Raymond's parents and try to make them understand that you two are being mature about your relationship."

"That won't help," Patrice said in defeat. "Raymond's parents hate me anyway. It doesn't matter what I do or don't do. They still hate me."

Raymond spun away from Patrice and turned around. "And I hate them. God knows, I hate them."

"No, you don't, Raymond," Marlena said, trying to control the raging emotions in her office. "You're upset with them and you're disappointed in them, but you don't hate them. They're your parents."

"I don't care," the young man said. "I love Patrice and they won't even try to be nice to her."

Patrice rushed and put her arms around Raymond. "You can't hate them because of me, Raymond. I don't want you to hate your parents. I don't hate them. Not really. I just wish they would like me. They don't have to love me. I just wish they wouldn't hate me."

Marlena felt Patrice and Raymond's pain and she wanted to scream at the injustice of it all. These two young people should be worrying about what to wear to the prom, not about who hates whom. "Look," Marlena said, wishing she had some words of wisdom she could pull out and give them, but she didn't. "Why don't you let me drive you both to Cheryl's? It'll help if you talk over this entire situation with her."

Raymond held Patrice close. "That's all right, Ms. Marlena. My car is outside. I'll drive Trece home."

"And you'll talk with her mother?"

He looked down at Patrice. "Yes, we'll talk to her."

"It won't do any good," Patrice said again. "Raymond's parents don't like Mama any more than they like me."

Marlena was out of words. What could she say? Patrice was right. "That may be true, but you still need to talk to your mother. She's going to see that you're upset about something and it'll be good to get it off your chest.''

Patrice didn't look too convinced, but she nodded. ''All right,'' she said. ''We'll talk to Mama.''

That's all Marlena could ask. As the teens walked out of her office, their arms wrapped around each other, she felt like a failure. She hadn't said anything to help them. How could she have? She was dealing with the same bigotry and hatred Patrice was dealing with. Unfortunately, she wasn't handling it any better than the young girl was.

Marlena sat in Winston's chair for over an hour thinking about Raymond and Patrice and worrying about Winston. She needed him to hold her now and tell her Patrice and Raymond would, in fact, beat the odds that were stacked so high against them.

''Oh, no,'' she said, wiping at her tears. ''Why am I crying?''

It was important to her that Patrice and Raymond have a chance. Sure, they were young and she worried about them making mistakes sexually, but they didn't seem to be headed down that road. She hoped the pressure from their parents didn't force them to make an ''intentional'' mistake.

She should have discussed the consequences of such an action with them. She should have told them not to give in to despair and do something they'd both regret. She hoped Cheryl would be wise enough to tell them.

Cheryl. She wanted to talk to her friend, but she guessed that right now Cheryl was listening to Raymond and Patrice, so she'd have to wait until later to talk to her. Marlena hated that Marty was out of town, because she was sure Cheryl would be upset by the news and would need his support. Though her friend was afraid Patrice was getting too serious too soon, her concern didn't put her daughter down, the way the Hills' concern did.

''Hello, beautiful.'' Winston's voice reached out and caressed her and she turned around to face him.

He looked so good standing there against the door, his long

legs crossed at the ankles, his hands folded across his stomach. She wanted him to open those long arms and wrap them around her and keep her safe from the hurt of the world. "Winston," she said. "You're back."

He shoved off the door. "What's wrong?" he asked, moving to her.

She didn't answer him, she just stepped into his arms. "Hold me, please hold me."

"Always," he said, folding his arms around her and hugging her tight. This was what she needed and would always need.

"I'm sorry we argued yesterday," she said. "I love you, Winston. I do."

He caressed her shoulders and back. "I know you do, sweetheart. I love you, too."

"I want you to know I love you and I'll always love you. You believe me, don't you?"

"Of course, I believe you." He pulled back from her, tilted her chin up and kissed the tip of her nose. "Now what's wrong?"

She sighed deeply and rested her head back against his chest. "Patrice and Raymond came looking for you."

"What did they want?"

"It's so awful, Winston. Raymond's parents don't want them to see each other anymore. They think they're getting too serious."

"They *are* pretty young, Marlena. I get scared for them sometimes myself. I know they love each other, but I still worry. I don't want Patrice to end up pregnant before she graduates high school."

Marlena knew Winston was right and she shared his fears. "Patrice thinks it's because the Hills don't think she's good enough for Raymond. She's right and it makes me so mad, Winston. It made me so damn mad."

"I know it makes you mad, sweetheart," he said. "It makes me mad, too."

He continued to caress her, knowing the pain she felt was for Raymond and Patrice, but that a lot of it was for herself and the hurt she'd experienced at the hands of his mother and the other bigots in Gaines. He wanted to take her pain away, but he knew he couldn't.

"I've missed you," she said after a while. "Where have you been all day?"

He smiled down at her, so much in love with this woman his heart hurt. "I've been busy."

She smiled and it was a welcome balm to his heart. "I figured as much. I thought you were avoiding me because of yesterday. Then I thought maybe something had happened to you. It scared me, Winston. Don't do that again."

"I won't, sweetheart," he said, feeling an extra bit of warmth that she'd worried about him.

"You'd better not."

"Okay," he said with a smile. "You're the boss."

"And don't you forget it."

He pulled away from her again. "Now I have a request."

"What's that?"

"I want you to go back to the hotel and put on your sexiest dress. I'm taking you out tonight and we're going to celebrate."

"Celebrate what?"

"Being together, what else?" he answered evasively. He'd been gone all day because he'd made an unplanned trip to Atlanta to get her a gift. It was a surprise and he was going to keep it that way.

"Where are we going?" she asked.

"Oh, no, I'm not telling you where we're going. Let's just say, it's a place you've been before."

"Why all the secrecy?"

"Hey, I don't want to become too predictable. I'm trying to keep the spice in our relationship."

"Hmm," she said, then raised on her toes and pressed a light kiss against his lips. "I like spice."

He pushed her away from him. "Well, I do, too, but these kisses have to stop or we won't make it to dinner."

Talk about feeling like a teenager on a date. That was exactly how Winston felt as he straightened his tie in the mirror above the house phone at the Gaines Inn. Since this was an official evening out, he chose not to meet Marlena at her room but to wait for her downstairs. Besides, he didn't trust himself to get close to a bed this early in the evening.

He picked up the phone and called her room. "Hello, beautiful," he said when she answered. "I'm here."

"Hello, Mr. Taylor," she said. "It's so good to hear your voice. I've missed you."

He shifted his feet from side to side and stuffed his free hand in his pocket. "I've missed you, too. Now get down here so we can get this date started."

"What? You aren't going to come and get me? Josie always said a young man should come to the door and get his date."

"Well, Josie only meant that when the young woman had a chaperon behind the door with her. Trust me, darlin', Josie would be proud of my self-restraint. Now get down here before I change my mind and come up."

"Is that a threat?" she said, full of teasing mirth.

"If you aren't down here in five minutes, you'll find out that I'm not joking. What kind of underwear are you wearing?"

Winston smiled at the dial tone that was his answer. He walked to the elevator and leaned against the wall to wait for his woman. As he gazed at his reflection in the elevator doors, he thought he might get used to the monkey suit if Marlena made him wear it often enough. He shook his head. The things a man did for love.

He straightened when the elevator reached the lobby floor and waited excitedly for Marlena to emerge. When she stepped off wearing a white, shivery dress that covered her from her neck to mid-thigh and only touched her curves at her shoulders, he wondered why his body hardened. The dress wasn't tight, and the matching scarf she'd tossed over her shoulder looked like something his mother would wear, but there was something about Marlena in that dress that set his body boiling.

He let out a low whistle. "Wow."

She smiled one of her just-for-him smiles and he knew he'd never be happier than he was right now. "Thanks. You're looking right spiffy yourself. Are you beginning to like the suit and tie ensemble?''

He took her hand in his. The softness of her skin against the roughness of his added to his arousal. "I love you and you like this ensemble. That's the only reason I'm wearing it.''

"You look gorgeous. It's not fair that you should be more attractive than I am.''

He raised an eyebrow at her, clearly not believing her statement. "Flattery will get you in trouble, so watch it.''

"What if I want to get in trouble?''

He stepped back and let her through the door first. "That can be handled easily enough. Keep talking.''

When he stopped before the Lexus sedan, she asked, "Where's the Bronco?''

"I'm giving her a rest tonight. I figured you were getting tired of climbing in and out.''

He opened the passenger door and she slid in. "I was actually getting used to your helping me get out. I like the part where I slide down your body before you put me on the ground.''

"You're asking for it, aren't you?'' He kissed her softly then closed the door before she could answer.

"Asking for what?'' she asked when he was seated next to her. She raised her hand to his head and smoothed it back over his hair. "You're a very attractive man, Winston Taylor, and I love you very much.''

He took her hand in his and placed a soft kiss on its palm before resting it on his knee and covering it with his own. "I love you, too.'' She squeezed his thigh in response and he groaned. "You're definitely going to get it,'' he said.

She smiled and relaxed in the seat next to him. Neither spoke until Winston made the turn for his street. "I thought we were going out to dinner,'' she said.

"You *are* going out for dinner. You're going out to my house.''

"That's a pretty neat trick. Are you sure dinner's on the menu?''

He glanced over at her. "What else could be on my mind?

I'm a big man. I need my nourishment.'' His eyes moved to her breasts. "And how I need it.''

"If you don't have your dining room table set for dinner, I'm going to kill you," she said. "I just want you to be prepared.''

He lifted her hand to his lips again. "I do love the way you kill me. Makes me want to die nine or ten times a day.''

He heard her suck in her breath and he smiled. Tonight was going to be a long night, he knew, but the reward in the end would more than make up for the torture he felt now.

"Ready for dessert?" Winston asked from across his candlelit dining room table.

Marlena had been pleased but surprised at the care he'd taken to make the place romantic. Candles, a single white rose for her, champagne. A good meal, though for the life of her she couldn't remember what she'd eaten. Winston had consumed her thoughts. His seduction had been relentless: from the telephone call to her suite at the hotel to the ride over here to the carefully crafted mood of their dinner. Every moment they'd been together he'd let her know how much he loved her and how much he wanted her. She'd been no less open in her love and want of him. Now he asked if she was ready for dessert. She was, but not the kind you ate with a fork or spoon. "Of course," she said intentionally blurring her meaning. "I'm always ready for dessert.''

A groan escaped him and she wondered which dessert he'd give her first. He pushed his chair back and stood. "Back in a minute.''

Marlena took advantage of his absence to fan herself with her cloth napkin. If she'd had ice, she would have rubbed some of it along her skin, but she settled for fanning herself with the napkin. When she heard him coming back, she quickly placed the napkin back in her lap.

She glanced up at him and the Red Velvet cake he had on the cake plate in his hands. "You do want me to gain weight, don't you?" she said, patting her flat stomach.

He placed the cake plate on the table. "I want you happy. If you gain weight, so what? I'm not exactly skinny myself."

As he cut the cake, she studied his fit physique. Winston wasn't skinny, but he didn't have an ounce of fat on him either. She'd touched every inch of his buff body, so she knew.

He cut two large slices of cake, put them on dessert plates and handed her one, then he took one for himself.

She smiled at him, flattered by the care he'd taken for the entire evening and for her. "You've really outdone yourself tonight. Thank you."

"It's not over," he said, taking a bite of his cake.

Marlena tried to cut her cake, but her fork met a foreign object. She looked up at him. "Did you bake this yourself?" she asked, not wanting to hurt his feelings but needing to know what she was getting herself into.

"In a matter of speaking," he said. "Don't you like it?"

"I'm sure it's good," she said, lifting her slice with her fork to see what was under it. She looked down at her plate, then back up at Winston. "What's this?" she asked.

"What's what?" Winston put another bite of cake in his mouth.

She picked up what she guessed was a three-carat diamond solitaire and held it up. "What's this?"

He finished chewing, then said in his calmest voice, "Looks like a ring to me."

"Winston!"

"Okay, it *is* a ring. Do you like it?"

Marlena brushed the few cake crumbs from the ring and held it out again, just staring at it. "How could I not like it? I love it, but—"

He stood up and walked around the table to her. "No buts," he said softly, then he kneeled beside her. "I love you, Marlena, and I want to marry you. Will you stand by my side forever and be my wife?"

Tears quickly filled her eyes. Yes, she shouted inside, I want to be your wife. I want to stand by your side forever and be your wife. "Winston—"

He cut her off. "Do you love me?"

She stared into those brown, puppy-dog-like eyes and said, "You know I do."

He smiled and she felt his relief. "Then let me put this ring on your finger."

"But—"

"Shh, no buts. I love you and you love me. What else matters?"

She could think of a few things that mattered—things he didn't even know—but she didn't voice them. She just sat there and allowed him to place the ring on her finger. When he finished, he kissed the palm of her hand. "I love you, Marlena, and I'll do my best to make you happy."

Marlena felt like a fraud. She knew now was the time to tell him her secret.

Winston caressed her cheek. "I need you to say something now, sweetheart."

Tell him, Marlena. Tell him. "I love you, Winston. I love you so much."

Winston opened his arms and she slid out of her chair and into them, needing him to hold her and needing to hold him.

"We're going to make it this time, Lena. I know it. Nothing will ever separate us again. I love you." He kissed her then, a long, smooth kiss that said he loved her and treasured her.

He leaned back against the floor and pulled her with him, not breaking the kiss. After a long while, he pulled away. "Seems like we've been here before. How about we go to a more comfortable place?"

Marlena knew what Winston was doing. He was forcing her to choose to go to his bed. He could have swept her off her feet, literally, and taken her there, but he hadn't chosen that route. He wanted her to decide to go to bed with him in this house and he probably wanted her to spend the night. He wanted her to choose him over her fears.

She cupped his face in his hands, cherishing all the man he was. "Take me to bed, Winston."

He rewarded her with his, smug masculine grin. "Whatever you say, darlin'. You're the boss."

* * *

Winston woke first. He glanced over Marlena's shoulder at the clock: eleven o'clock. Eleven o'clock and his baby was still in his arms where she belonged.

He lightly kissed her lips, not wanting to wake her, just wanting to enjoy her. If he awakened her, she'd want to go back to the hotel and he didn't want her to leave their bed. He'd waited too long to get her back here to let her go now.

He closed his eyes and went back to sleep.

When Marlena woke up with Winston's arms wrapped like bands about her, she knew without looking at the clock that it would be useless to go back to the hotel now. She turned in his arms so she faced him.

She touched the stubble on his chin and smiled at the relaxed face of the man she loved. Winston Taylor. Marlena Taylor. Mrs. Winston Taylor. She mouthed the words, liking the way they felt on her lips and liking the idea of spending the rest of her life with him.

She looked at the ring he'd placed on her finger. The ring and the earrings he'd given her years ago were the only items she wore. She fell back to sleep thinking they were the only items she'd ever need.

Chapter 22

Winston eased his naked body from the bed taking care not to wake the sleeping Marlena. He looked down at the woman he loved and gratitude flooded his being. He'd been so lucky to find her again. It was nothing less than a miracle she hadn't given her heart to someone else over the years.

He wondered if his parents had felt the kind of love for each other that he and Marlena shared. His Dad had been such a passionate man—passionate about his work, about his family— that Winston could imagine him being this much in love, but his mother? He wasn't sure. She was such a controlled woman. Winston knew the passion he shared with Marlena couldn't be controlled. It had a life of its own. Even if both of them tried to deny it, their shared passion would still live in their hearts and in their minds. They'd have to fight a constant battle to keep from giving in to it.

Marlena stirred and his body stirred with her. He'd like nothing better than to crawl back in bed with her and make love to her all day, beginning the lifelong task of making up for the time they'd spent apart, but he couldn't this morning. He had an important *The Way Home* meeting in Athens and he needed to stop by the office and pick up some paperwork before hitting the highway. If there was any way for him to cancel the meeting without damaging *The Way Home's* reputation, he'd do it, but he couldn't take the risk. The project was too important—even more important than making love to his love. At least, this morning it was.

He forced himself to move away from the bed and Marlena and make his way to the bathroom. He decided on a quick shower, hoping the sound of the water wouldn't wake her.

After he'd been in the shower for about three minutes, the door opened. He turned around and saw a naked, luscious Marlena standing before him.

"I missed you," she said, stepping into the shower with him and closing the door.

He opened his arms and she stepped into them, her body cool against his much warmer and much soapier one. "Good morning," he said, running his bath cloth down her back.

She rubbed her lower body against his. "Now it is."

He sucked in his breath at the passion that soared through him. "This wasn't exactly what I'd had in mind," he said.

She pulled back and looked up at him, her eyes wide. "You don't like this?"

"Don't be stupid." He pulled her back to him. "I love it so much it's killing me."

"Then what did you mean?" She rubbed her fingers in circles along his soapy chest.

He caught her fingers in his hand and stopped her motions. "I wanted you in the bathtub."

"You can have me there, too." She kissed his left nipple. "Later." She kissed his right one. "Much later." She looked up at him. "Will that work?"

Winston's lips wouldn't open to form words, so he lowered his head and put them to their best use. The wetness of her sweet mouth combined with the slick, wetness of her smooth skin against his almost finished him. He moaned against her mouth and pulled her closer.

He felt her leg slide up his flank and wrap around his thigh. Her soft "Winston" echoed in his mind and he knew exactly what she wanted.

Keeping his lips firmly against hers, he placed both his hands on her hips and lifted her until both her legs wrapped about him. Her hand slid between their straining bodies and guided him home. Not satisfied with their connection, he turned his body slightly until Marlena's back rested into the gray tile of shower wall.

"I love you," he whispered against her lips as he found his rhythm. "God, how I love you."

A moan was her only response and it was enough. He increased his pace, holding her tight against him, not wanting to let her go, not wanting any space to exist between them. All he wanted was to love her and to have that love mean something and grow into something more.

She held him tight, keeping him close as if she felt the same emotions he was feeling, as if she needed him inside her as much as he needed to be there.

Winston wished he could make the moment last forever, but he knew he couldn't. Any minute now he'd reach a crossroads he'd have to pass. If he could only last until Marlena got there . . .

She tore her mouth from his. When he heard her call his name and felt the tremble in her body, he knew it was time. He closed his eyes and issued a final thrust. Her name on his lips and her face in his mind were the last things he remembered before he joined her in paradise.

Marlena's legs slowly slid from Winston's hips to the shower floor and she rested her head against his chest. The rapid beating of his heart matched hers.

"Are we going to start every morning this way?" Winston asked between deep breaths.

Marlena tried to catch her breath. "If you're up for it."

"Oh, I'll be up for it, all right. You don't have to worry about that."

He shifted slightly and she felt him hard against her. "I feel your point," she said. "I hope I have the stamina to keep up with you. I wouldn't want you to have to look elsewhere for your entertainment.''

He tilted her chin up and looked into his eyes. ''You'll never have to worry about me looking elsewhere. Only one woman can scratch my itch, and that's you. I'll be faithful to you, Lena. I promise I will.''

She burrowed deeper into his chest, feeling protected and loved in his arms. That his promise meant so much to her made her realize she'd needed his reassurance. Though she knew he was a man of honor, a part of her wondered how she compared to the other women he'd slept with.

''I'll make you happy, Marlena. You'll never regret marrying me. I promise you.''

She squeezed him tight. ''I'm already happy, Winston. Knowing that you love me makes me happy. If we never get married, memories of this moment will be enough to keep me happy for the rest of my life.''

''Well,'' he said with a grunt, ''this moment won't be enough for me. It doesn't even come close. We're going to have a wonderful life together as man and wife.''

Marlena fought back the fear that threatened to ruin the moment. Winston loved her and nothing else mattered. *No one* else mattered, she told herself.

''I hate to do this, darlin', but you've either got to help me shower or get out of here so I can do it. I have to be in the office in thirty minutes.''

She reluctantly stepped away from him. ''So do I.'' She allowed her gaze to slowly travel from his eyes to his feet. She looked back up at his face. ''You're right. I'd better get out of here if we're going to get ready.'' She opened the shower door.

''Don't go in today, Marlena,'' he said. ''Stay here. I want to come home to you tonight.''

She raised an eyebrow at him. ''You want me to wait for you like the perfect little wifey? I guess you want me to cook, too.''

He kissed her lips quickly. ''Don't even try it. All I want you to do is be in that bed when I get back. Food I can do without; you I must have at regular intervals.''

She looked at him as she considered his request. She didn't have to go in today and she didn't relish the idea of Winston dropping her by the hotel this morning so she could get fresh clothes.

"Will you stay?"

Yes. No. Yes. No. "Yes, I'll stay."

"Good," he said with a wide grin. He swatted her bottom. "Now get out of here, woman, before you make me late for work. I already think this is going to be the longest day of my career."

Marlena missed Winston as soon as he pulled the Bronco out of the garage and closed the garage door. Dressed in one of his old sports jerseys, the earrings he'd given her and her brand-new engagement ring, she strolled through the family room to the row of CDs in the black tower cabinet to the left of the CD player. She fingered the titles until she came to the Barry White CD Winston had played the first night he'd brought her to his house. She took the CD from its case, placed it in the CD player, then lounged back on one of the two black leather couches that dominated the room and closed her eyes.

As she listened to Barry's masterful crooning and dreamed of the life ahead of her with Winston, unwanted thoughts of Mrs. Taylor appeared in her mind. She opened her eyes and sat up straight. Winston's hateful mother would have a cow when she found out about their engagement. Yes, Marlena thought, she'd have a cow, then she'd do everything in her power to make sure the wedding never happened. She hadn't been joking when she'd made her threat.

Marlena got up and pushed off the CD player, the happiness of her morning ruined by the intrusion of reality. She turned and headed upstairs for a bath, thoughts of Mrs. Taylor having made the stickiness of her body from the early morning love-making she'd shared with Winston seem dirty.

In Winston's huge bathroom Marlena turned on the faucet in the Jacuzzi bathtub, knowing she couldn't get in that shower again. After pulling the jersey over her head and throwing it in the hamper, she stared at the engagement ring on her finger. Through vision blurred by tears, she examined the ring that symbolized the future she'd never been sure she'd experience. She still wasn't sure.

She slipped the ring off her finger and stepped into the warm water in the bathtub. After turning off the water, she eased down in the tub, allowing the water to soothe her aching heart. She'd known it would come to this. There could be no other end. She had to tell Winston. A part of her wished they could have enjoyed this moment in time for a little while longer.

As Marlena stepped out of the tub, the phone rang. She thought about answering it, then decided to let the answering machine get it. If it turned out the caller was Winston, she'd pick it up after hearing his voice.

As Winston's deep voice greeted the caller, she dried herself with one of his fluffy towels.

"Pick up the phone, girl," Cheryl's voice sounded throughout the room. "I know you're in there."

"All right," Marlena said, glad to hear her friend's voice. She quickly wrapped herself in the towel and ran for the phone on the nightstand. "How'd you know I was here?" she asked as soon as she picked up the phone.

"Hey, I know everything. Now why don't you get down here and let me in?"

"Let you in?" Marlena repeated.

"Yeah, let me in and hurry up. It's thirty-five cents a minute prime time to talk on this car phone."

Marlena heard the click and then the dial tone before hanging up the receiver and rushing down the stairs. She wondered how Cheryl knew where to find her.

Cheryl reached the front door at the same time that Marlena opened it. She quirked a brow at her friend in the towel. "I guess I don't have to ask what you've been doing."

Marlena stepped back so Cheryl could enter the house. "You're right, it's no big secret. I was taking a bath."

Cheryl laughed. "Uh-huh, that's exactly what I was thinking."

"How'd you know I was here anyway?" Marlena asked again.

Cheryl looked at her. "I called *The Way Home* office and Winston told me. He sounded pretty happy about it, too."

Marlena folded her hands across her stomach, then she realized she'd left her engagement ring upstairs. "Well, let's hope he doesn't tell all my callers where I am."

Cheryl laughed again. "I wouldn't put it past him. He might have a banner hung around the courthouse by the time you get to town."

"Don't even joke about that," Marlena said, knowing a banner was exactly the kind of thing Winston would do. "Come on upstairs. I have to get dressed. What brings you by?" she asked over her shoulder.

Cheryl sighed. "Patrice and Raymond. I took the day off work because I needed to talk to somebody about them."

Marlena walked into the bedroom she'd shared with Winston and gestured for Cheryl to take a seat. She chose the blue corduroy rocker-recliner next to the dresser.

"How are they holding up?" Marlena asked, walking into the bathroom. She pulled off her towel and grabbed what she thought was Winston's robe from the hook on the bathroom door. "They were pretty upset when I talked to them yesterday."

"And they're still upset. I finally got Raymond calmed down enough to go home last night. He was pretty angry with his parents. You know, I think he really loves Patrice."

Marlena slipped on her engagement ring and smiled at the surprise in her friend's voice. "You're surprised?"

"A little."

Marlena came out of the bathroom and sat on the foot of the bed.

"I knew they *thought* they were in love," Cheryl continued. "But now I think this is the real thing."

"I think you're right and I think Raymond's parents have figured out the same thing."

"And they don't like it," Cheryl finished for her. "Last night I wanted to go over there and slap the you know what out of both of them, the stupid bigots. I should have slapped Helen the night of their anniversary party when she as much as told me she didn't think Patrice was good enough for Raymond. Sometimes black people are a trip."

"You've got that right."

"Who do they think they are to look down on my daughter? Who do they think they are to look down on anybody?"

"It's always been that way, Cheryl. Maybe we're the stupid ones for thinking things would change. Raymond and Cheryl could be me and Winston all over again."

Cheryl nodded. "Life can certainly be a bitch, can't it?"

Marlena shook her head. "Life is what we make it. People are the bitches."

"So what do I do?" Cheryl asked, then added in a wistful tone, "I wish Marty were here."

"Have you called him?"

Cheryl shook her head. "He's only been gone a little over a week. He has a lot to do and I didn't want to bother him. You know he'd take the first plane back here if he knew what was happening with Patrice."

"What's wrong with that?" Marlena reasoned. "He should be here."

"There's nothing he can do, Marlena. I can handle things till he gets back."

"The way you handled things when you found out you were pregnant?"

Cheryl's widened eyes bore into Marlena. "It's not the same thing."

"Yes, it is," Marlena said softly, wondering why history always wanted to repeat itself.

Cheryl didn't speak for a moment, but she kept her eyes fixed on Marlena. "It is, isn't it?" she said when she finally spoke.

Marlena nodded.

"I should call him, huh?"

Marlena stood up and pointed to the phone on the nightstand.

"There's the phone. I'll go and make us a cup of coffee. Come on down when you're finished with your call."

Marlena closed the bedroom door, knowing Cheryl had passed a major hurdle in her relationship with Marty. She'd taken the first step in breaking the unhealthy patterns of the past.

By the time Marlena had prepared the coffee and put the cups on the table, Cheryl entered the room. She had tears in her eyes.

"What happened?" Marlena asked, praying everything was all right.

"Marty's taking the next plane out. He thinks we need to tell Patrice who he is. *Now.*"

Marlena pulled out a chair for Cheryl, and her friend eased down into it. She didn't have to ask if Cheryl agreed with Marty's suggestion. It was apparent she didn't. "Did you tell him how you feel about it?"

"I tried," Cheryl said with a shrug. "But you know Marty. He wasn't listening. I knew he wasn't going to listen. He thinks he knows everything. He always has."

"You sound like you're angry with him."

Cheryl looked up and Marlena saw her eyes were still red but they were no longer wet. "You bet I am. He can't come back into my life after eighteen years and start making major decisions. I've done a good job taking care of me and Patrice so far. I know what's best for her. He doesn't."

"That's not his fault, Cheryl."

Cheryl jumped up out of her chair. "Marlena! You're supposed to be my friend, but you're always taking Marty's side."

"I'm not taking sides. I'm—"

Cheryl waved her hand in dismissal. "Forget it. I know what you're doing. You think you know what's best for me, too. You and Marty. My best friend and my lover. Well, just because you two went to college and I didn't, doesn't mean you know more than I do. It doesn't mean you can raise my daughter better than I can. It doesn't mean you're better than me."

"Where's all this coming from, Cheryl? Nobody thinks that

way. I know I don't and I know Marty doesn't either. We love you and Patrice.''

Cheryl folded her arms across her bosom. "You love me? You love me?" She laughed. "Now that's a joke. You leave town for ten years and don't even bother to call or send a card. You were my best friend, Marlena. How do you think that made me feel? And I won't even talk about Marty."

Marlena felt the pain in her friend's words and, unfortunately, she also heard the truth in them. When she'd walked away from her past, she'd also walked away from Cheryl. She hadn't planned it that way, but that's the way it had happened.

"I'm sorry, Cheryl," she said. "I'm sorry I left the way I did, but I didn't know what else to do."

"Yeah, right."

"It's true. When I came home for Josie's funeral things went crazy." Marlena evaded the details, knowing she owed it to Winston to tell him first. "I left because I couldn't stand the memories here of everything I'd lost."

"You didn't lose anything, Marlena," Cheryl said. "You gave it all up: your friends, your home town, even your fiancé. You gave it all up so you could have the glamorous life."

Marlena slumped back in her chair. What could she say to Cheryl? She supposed that's how a lot of people looked at her life. She wanted to laugh at the irony of it all, but there was no laughter in her. She cleared her throat, trying to keep her tears at bay. "I know it looks that way, Cheryl, but you're wrong. What I gave up, I didn't give up freely."

Cheryl dropped her arms to her side. "What do you mean you didn't give it up freely? You make it sound like somebody forced you."

Marlena wanted to tell Cheryl how true her words were, but she couldn't. "There are things you don't know and things I can't tell you until I first tell Winston. Believe me, I didn't give up Winston or my friendship with you because I wanted to. I did it because it was all I knew to do."

Marlena remembered the devastated young woman she'd been. She'd done what she thought was best for the people she loved. Though she regretted the consequences of her decisions, she could never regret having done what she did to protect the people she loved.

Cheryl breathed a deep sigh and sat down at the table next to Marlena. "I shouldn't have gone off on you the way I did."

"Don't worry about it. We all have to let off steam sometimes. But, Cheryl, I've never thought I was more than you because I went to college. I hope you believe me."

Cheryl wiped her hands down her face. "I believe you, Marlena. I don't know why I said those things. Sometimes I regret so much the decisions I've made, especially when I see how those decisions are affecting Patrice. Maybe if I had gone to college and could provide more for her, she wouldn't be going through this trauma now."

Marlena shook her head. "Don't think that way. It wouldn't matter anyway. Some people in Rosemont still wouldn't accept you."

"They accept you because of what you've accomplished."

Marlena did laugh then and the release felt wonderful. "You've got to be joking. They don't accept me. They tolerate me. In their own way, they're using me. Sometimes I don't even think they see me, they see what I've accomplished. They accept the accomplishments. Me, they tolerate."

Cheryl stared into her cup of coffee. "I don't really care what they think. When their bigotry touches Patrice, I can barely stand it. I'd do about anything to make this whole situation go away."

"I know you would, but you can't. No more than I can." She extended her hand so Cheryl could see her ring, sensing a need to change the subject. "Look what Winston gave me last night."

"It's beautiful, Marlena." Cheryl examined the ring then got up and gave her friend a big hug. "You and Winston belong together. I know you'll be so happy. Does this mean you're moving back to Gaines?"

"I honestly don't know what it means. I love Winston and I want to marry him, but I don't know if I can. His mother hates me and she'll always be in the middle of our relationship."

''You don't know that for sure. Winston's not a child and his mother doesn't rule him.''

''I know, but she's his mother and, whatever her faults, he loves her.''

''You think he'd choose her over you?''

Marlena shook her head. ''I know he wouldn't, but I don't want him to have to make the choice. He shouldn't have to choose between his mother and his wife.''

Cheryl pointed to the ring on Marlena's finger. ''Winston's a smart man. Maybe he made his choice when he gave you that ring.''

Marlena knew Winston thought he'd done just that by giving her the ring, but she also knew he'd made his choice before he had all the data. ''We'll see,'' she said.

''What does that mean?''

''As I said before, there are some things Winston needs to know about why I ended our relationship ten years ago and I'm not sure how he's going to react when he finds out. A part of me doesn't even want to tell him.''

''But you will?''

Marlena's lips turned in a grim smile. ''Yes, I'll tell him. We may end up apart again, but this time I won't make the decision for him.''

Cheryl took Marlena's hands in hers and squeezed. ''I know it's scary, but you're doing the right thing. If I know Winston, there's nothing you can tell him that will change the way he feels about you.''

Marlena covered Cheryl's hand with her own. ''I hope you're right, Cheryl. I certainly hope you're right.''

Chapter 23

The ringing telephone interrupted Marlena's and Cheryl's conversation. "Aren't you going to answer it?" Cheryl asked when Marlena didn't move to get the phone. "It could be Winston."

Marlena looked at her friend, then at the phone. It could be Winston, she thought, or it could be his mother.

"Answer the phone, girl. You're going to be the man's wife, for goodness sake. You're entitled to answer the phone."

Marlena picked up the phone as the answering machine came on. "I thought you weren't going to answer," Winston's live voice said over his taped greeting.

"I wasn't," she said when the greeting completed. "Cheryl talked me into it."

"Well, she did right. We're practically married. I'm going to need you to tell all my girlfriends I'm no longer available."

Marlena smiled as she knew he'd wanted her to do. "I thought I was the only woman in your life."

"You are, but I can't help it if I'm irresistible to most women."

She laughed. "You're so bad, Winston. I hope you called for some reason other than to try and make me jealous."

"Are you jealous?"

She lifted her hand and looked at her ring. "Why should I be? I have the engagement ring."

Winston's booming laughter sounded through the phone. "Look," he said. "I called to give you some bad news. I'm going to be back a lot later than I'd planned. I have to pick up Marty at the airport. He sounded pretty upset when he called."

"I know," she said, glancing across the room at Cheryl. "Cheryl's pretty out of it, too. I wonder how Patrice and Raymond are."

"I've been thinking about them, too. I know we planned to spend the evening alone, but what do you think about us inviting them to have dinner with us?"

"I think that's a great idea," Marlena said. She'd find time after dinner to talk to him about the past. "That'll give Marty and Cheryl some time alone, too."

"Great, sweetheart," Winston said. "I knew you'd understand. I love you. You know that, don't you?"

"I know and I love you, too, Winston. I always have and I always will."

"I wish I was there with you now," he whispered, his husky voice caressing her skin.

"I wish you were here, too."

"Are you still wearing my jersey?"

"No."

He cursed softly. "I love seeing you in that jersey. Why'd you take it off?"

She turned her back to Cheryl and giggled. "I took a bath, then I put on your robe."

He sucked in his breath. "What are you wearing under the robe?"

"Nothing," she said.

He cursed again. "Now I really wish I were there. You know what we'd be doing, don't you?"

She twisted the phone cord around her wrist. "I think I can guess."

"Well, hold that thought. It'll be just the two of us after

dinner. I promise you it'll be worth the wait. How's seven for dinner with Raymond and Patrice?''

"Seven's fine, Winston, but let's not go out. I'd rather eat here. I think they'll be more comfortable here than in a restaurant.''

"Is that an offer to cook dinner for us?" Winston asked and she knew he had a smile on his face.

She brushed her knuckles against the front of his robe. "I think I'll be able to rustle up something in that space-age kitchen of yours.''

"Of ours," he corrected. "The kitchen, the house. Everything that's mine is yours, Marlena.''

Marlena tightened her hold on the telephone handset. This man could talk the clothes off a nun. "That was a sweet thing to say, Winston.''

"I'm not just saying it; I mean it. Now tell me those three magic words so I can hang up and get moving.''

"I love you. Be careful driving to Atlanta.''

"I will. I love you, Marlena. I'll see you tonight.''

After he hung up, Marlena held the phone in her hands thinking how much she loved him and wanted a life with him.

"Aren't you glad you answered it?''

Cheryl's voice provoked Marlena to action and she hung up the phone. "Marty called him. Winston's going to pick him up at the airport this afternoon.''

"Marty wasn't exaggerating when he said he was taking the next plane.''

"You're still angry?''

"Not angry. More like anxious.''

Marlena understood the emotion. She was anxious, too. She had as much at stake in her talk with Winston tonight as Cheryl had in her talk with Marty. "Well, we can spend the whole day dreading what's going to happen later or we can take our minds off everything and have a girls' day out. We could even drop by the school and pick up Patrice. She'd probably love to get out early.''

A smile lit Cheryl's face. "Now that sounds like a good idea. But first you have to put on some clothes.''

Marlena tugged at Winston's robe. "That's a problem. I don't have any other clothes here and I haven't washed those I had on yesterday."

"No problem," Cheryl said. "I'll run over to the hotel and get you something. What do you want me to bring back?"

"It's all my fault," Marty said for the tenth time since Winston had picked him up at the airport. "If I had come back sooner, Cheryl and I could have worked things out and Patrice would have had two parents and Cheryl wouldn't be working in that factory. She'd be living the kind of life I always wanted her to live."

Winston glanced away from the road for a second to look at his friend. He'd tried to reason with Marty, but his friend wasn't in a reasoning mood. "You can't change the past, Marty. Thinking like that will only make you sick. You have to stop looking back and start looking ahead."

"You don't understand, man. Patrice is my daughter, my flesh and blood, and I can't stand to think of her being mistreated because of something I did. Maybe Cheryl and I should pack up and leave Gaines and move some place where people aren't so bigoted."

"It's a little too late for that, man. Patrice is already in love with Raymond. I don't think she'd appreciate you taking her away from here."

Marty pounded his fist on his knee. "Man! I feel so helpless. I've never felt like this in my whole life. People have treated me wrong in the past and I've gotten over it. But when somebody does something to your kids, it cuts deeply. I feel rage as I've never felt it before. Be glad you don't have kids."

Winston wasn't. Even with all that Patrice was going through, he still envied Marty and Cheryl. He wanted a child with Marlena created out of the love they felt for each other and raised in the center of that love. "What do you plan to do?"

"I know what I *want* to do. I want to tell Patrice that I'm her father. I want to tell everybody in Gaines."

"Do you think that'll help the situation with Raymond's parents?"

Marty shook his head. "How should I know? All I know is Patrice needs to hear this from me and Cheryl, not from anybody else."

"I didn't think anybody else knew."

"What are you talking about, man? You know as well as I do that there are no secrets in Gaines. Somebody knows and I have the feeling that if we don't tell Patrice, somebody else will and it'll be too late."

"Cheryl disagrees with you?"

"She thinks it'll be too much," Marty muttered. "With all the pressure Patrice is feeling right now from Raymond's parents, she thinks the news that I'm her father may be too much for her to handle."

"She may be right."

"That's the impossible part of all of this. We're both right. I know this isn't a good time to tell Patrice, but I don't think there'll ever be a good time. If I had come back earlier, we wouldn't be in this situation now." Marty slapped his hand against the dashboard.

Winston sighed. This conversation was going no where. Marty was determined to blame himself and there was nothing Winston could do about it. "Well, you and Cheryl will have the entire evening to work this out. Marlena and I are inviting Raymond and Patrice to dinner."

Marty cursed again. "Do you know how that makes me feel? Instead of being grateful for your help, I'm jealous that you've spent more time with my daughter than I have. She's my daughter and I want to treat her like a daughter."

Winston lifted a hand from the steering wheel and placed it on Marty's shoulder. "You'll get the chance. Give it some time."

"I want the three of us—me, Patrice, and Cheryl—to be a family so badly. I hope it's not too late for us. What if Patrice decides she doesn't need another father?"

"That's a possibility, I guess, but Patrice has a big heart, Marty. If you give her time, she'll find a place in it for you."

Marty nodded and Winston put his hand back on the steering wheel. They made the rest of drive to Gaines in silence.

"Are you having fun?" Marlena asked Patrice who rested on the massage table next to her. They waited for their masseuse to come and give them their final treatment of the afternoon.

Patrice turned from lying on her stomach to lying on her side so she could look at Marlena. "Wonderful. Too bad Mama had to leave so she could get her braids redone. I keep telling her to get a relaxer put in her hair, but she won't listen to me."

Marlena smiled. She knew it would take more than missing a massage to make Cheryl give up the braids. The braids were more than a hairstyle for her friend; they were a political and social statement. "I don't see how she stands sitting there for hours while somebody braids her hair. I think I'd go crazy."

"I know I would. Give me a relaxer, hot curlers, and a blow dryer any day. In and out in less than two hours." The girl's eyes moved to Marlena's head. "I bet it doesn't take you any time to do yours."

"No time at all. I usually wash it in the shower and let it dry naturally. I see a beautician about once every two months for a deep conditioning, but that's about it."

"Well, I could never wear my hair that short. My head's too big, and anyway, I think Raymond would kill himself if I cut it. He likes it this length."

Marlena observed the girl's shoulder length curls. "I've been wearing my hair short for so long that I can't even remember having long hair."

"It's not that bad. Just relax and curl and go."

"I know," Marlena said. "But relaxers cost money and we couldn't afford the expense when I was your age. I cut my hair because it was practical to do so, not because it was fashionable."

Patrice leaned up on her elbow. "What was it like for you back then? Were the people from Rosemont stuck-up like they are now?"

The memories caused a dry laugh to spill from Marlena. "Oh, yes, they were very stuck-up."

"Did Winston's parents try to break you two up? Is that why you didn't stay together?"

Marlena sighed. She'd hoped for a chance to share her story with Patrice, but now she didn't look forward to reliving the pain. "It's a long story, Patrice, and very complicated. Winston's mother never liked the idea of Winston going out with me, but his father seemed to be okay with it."

"Why didn't she like you going out with Winston?"

"I think you know why. She didn't think I was good enough for her son."

"Because you lived in Dusttown?"

Marlena nodded. "People in Rosemont thought living in the projects was some social disease. They still do."

"Tell me about it. It goes even farther. Raymond's parents want him to date a girl from Rosemont. It doesn't matter that we don't live in the projects, what matters is that we don't live in Rosemont."

"Their thinking is not rational, Patrice," Marlena said, touched again by the young girl's pain. "I tried to understand it for years. It was worse for me when Winston and I were in high school. I could feel his mother's hatred and I could feel everybody waiting for me to come up pregnant. They couldn't see any reason other than sex for Winston's interest in me. God, how I hated that."

"Me, too," Patrice said. "Sometimes it just makes me want to have sex."

Marlena remembered the teen saying something similar before so she knew the young girl was feeling desperate. "That's dangerous thinking. You can't make a decision that could change your whole life because you're mad at a few people. The consequences of sleeping with Raymond could be far-reaching and would only serve to prove the bigots right. Do you understand what I'm saying?"

The girl sighed. "I understand, but it's more than wanting to get back at his parents. It's wanting to be closer to him. With his folks trying to pull us apart, all I want to do is get closer. Sometimes I want to stop fighting what I feel and make love with him. Sometimes I feel like I need it. Like it would complete me in some way.''

Marlena identified well with the emotions. She'd wrestled with them herself. "I know exactly what you mean, Patrice. I felt that way with Winston lots of times. Just because we didn't sleep together, didn't mean we didn't want to. But I think we were smart enough, like you and Raymond, to know that we had enough against us without adding sex to the pot. You see, I think Winston and I would've felt guilty if we'd had sex and that guilt would have tainted the act for us.''

"That's what Raymond says. You know something, Marlena?'' the girl asked softly.

"What?''

"These days Raymond is the one who puts the brakes on things. Sometimes I deliberately set out to . . .'' Patrice lowered her eyes.

"To do what?'' Marlena inquired softly though she could guess what Patrice was about to say.

Patrice raised her eyes, but she still didn't meet Marlena's gaze. "It's nothing.''

Marlena reached over to Patrice's table and placed a finger against the young girl's face, forcing her to look at her. "Sometimes you deliberately set out to seduce Raymond. Is that what you were going to say?''

"Yes, yes, yes,'' Patrice cried, then turned her face away from Marlena. "I know it's awful and you must think I'm an awful person but that's what I do sometimes.''

"No, I don't think you're an awful person; I think you're an honest person. Honey, why do you think you try to seduce him?''

The girl faced Marlena again, then shrugged her shoulders. "I don't know. Maybe sometimes I think his parents are right. Maybe I'm not good enough for him. Maybe one day Raymond will think I'm not good enough for him.''

"And?''

"And maybe making love with him will make him love me forever. Maybe I can hold onto him if I make love with him.''

Marlena's heart turned over. The tricks the mind played on a wounded soul, she thought. "You don't really think that's true, do you, Patrice?"

"Oh, I don't know what I think," the girl cried. "Sometimes I don't want to think. I just want to feel."

Marlena noticed the tears rolling down the girl's cheeks and she knew soon they would be matched by tears of her own. "Raymond is with you because he cares about you. Having sex with him is not going to make him care more. It won't. Look at your girlfriends at school. How many of them have broken up with guys after sleeping with them?"

"A lot, but a lot have stayed together."

"Well, that should tell you something. Having sex with a boy won't make him stay with you. Men stay because they want to, not because we trap them."

"I wouldn't want to get pregnant," Patrice said through her tears.

"But it's crossed your mind, hasn't it?"

The girl's tears flowed freely now. "I know you think I'm an awful person, but I'd never really do anything like that to Raymond. I love him. I wouldn't want to trap him with a baby."

"But you have thought about it?" Marlena pressed, wanting the young woman to admit her fears so she could get past them.

Patrice nodded then covered her face with her hands. "A few times. I'm so embarrassed."

Marlena got up from her table, securing her towel around her as she did so, and went over and gathered the weeping Patrice in her arms. "There's nothing to be embarrassed about. You thought about it, but you didn't do it. And do you know why you didn't do it?" After the girl shook her head, Marlena continued, "You didn't do it because you love yourself and you love Raymond. That's something to be proud of, Patrice. You're fortunate to have that love of self. A lot of girls your age don't have it, and they end up doing things that ultimately wreck their lives. You won't be one of those girls. You have a full life ahead of you. With Raymond or without him."

"It'll be with Raymond," Patrice assured her.

"Maybe," Marlena said, "but sometimes life takes unexpected turns."

"Like with you and Coach?"

Marlena smiled against the girl's head. "Yes, like with me and Coach."

Patrice pulled back and raised her tear-stained but now dry eyes to Marlena. "But you're getting back together. It was meant to be, just like me and Raymond."

"That's what I'm trying to tell you," Marlena said, deliberately not commenting on her relationship with Winston. The two of them still had major hurdles to cross before their future together was sealed. "If it's meant to be for you and Raymond, nothing will keep you apart. Not even his parents. And if you do get separated for some reason, you'll find your way back to each other."

"I hope we don't get separated though. I can't imagine not being able to see Raymond or talk with him or touch him. He's my best friend."

"You and Raymond have the best of everything, Patrice. Your love is fresh and clean and your friendship is real and deep. Don't mess that up because you're hurt by what his parents think."

"You think we should ignore his parents? What if they ship him off to another school or something?"

Marlena smiled and squeezed the young girl's shoulders. "Now, don't go asking for problems. I seriously doubt his parents will pull him out of school when he's about to enter his senior year."

"Maybe I'm getting paranoid, but I know they're going to do something. Something big and ugly to break us up. I can feel it and it scares me. I don't want to lose Raymond."

Marlena pulled the child into her arms again. "I know you're scared, sweetheart, but you have to hold on to the thought that if you and Raymond were meant to be together, no one can keep you apart. And if you're ever separated, you'll find your way back together. You have to believe that."

Patrice didn't say anything, and Marlena didn't know any-

thing more to say. She hoped her words had eased some of the
girl's fears and would make her think before doing something
that could change the rest of her life.

Winston pushed back in his chair, and clapped his hands on
his stomach. "Now that was a meal." He glanced at the almost-
smiling Patrice. Eating dinner in with Raymond and Patrice
had been a great idea, and later he'd have to properly thank
Marlena for coming up with it. "You'll have to cook a good
meal like that for Raymond some time, Patrice. You know what
they say: the way to a man's heart is his stomach."

Raymond smiled across the table at his girlfriend. "She
doesn't have to do that, Coach, she already has my heart."

"Uh-oh, Raymond," Winston said. "Welcome to the club."

Marlena stood and began clearing the dishes from the table.
"What club?"

Winston took the plates out of her hand and dropped a kiss
on her lips. "The I'm-in-love-and-I'm-glad club, so sit down.
Since you cooked, I'll clear the table, and maybe even do the
dishes."

"And I'll help," Raymond said, jumping up out of his chair.

"You don't have—" Marlena began, but Winston interrupted her.

"Come on, Raymond," he said, guessing Raymond wanted
to talk. "I could use some help."

Raymond squeezed Patrice's shoulders, then gathered the
remaining dishes from the table and followed Winston into the
kitchen. "Thanks, Coach," he said.

Winston directed the boy to place the dishes on the counter,
then sensing this was not a night to use the dishwasher, he
plugged the sink, turned on the water and reached under the
sink for the liquid dishwashing detergent.

"How you doing, Buddy?" he asked the teen.

Raymond handed him the dirty water glasses. "A little better.
At least Patrice had some fun tonight."

"I hope you did, too."

Raymond shrugged and leaned back against the counter.

"I'm not worried about me. I'll be all right. It's Patrice I'm worried about. How can my parents not see what a wonderful person she is?"

Winston heard the pain in the boy's voice and recognized it as a pain he'd experienced as well. "Sometimes people wear blinders, Raymond. They only see what they want to see. I think that's what your parents are doing. They love you and they only want the best for you."

Raymond raised up from the counter. "You don't think they're right about me and Patrice, do you?"

Winston placed the dirty plates in the dishwater. "Of course not. I just want you to understand where your parents are coming from."

"I know where they're coming from. They're bigots, Coach. My folks are bigots. I never really thought about it until Patrice and I started dating, but they are. Even when they're watching television, they talk about those 'lower-class blacks' and how they're ashamed of them. It's like they think they're members of a special class or something."

Very familiar territory, Winston thought, but he'd been more fortunate than Raymond. Though his mother was bigoted, he'd been blessed with a father whose feet were planted firmly in the soil of economic reality. His dad knew that very few blacks had *real* wealth, that as a people we were just at different levels of *making it.* His dad had always taught him to be thankful for the privileges and opportunities money afforded him, but to never think that the money itself made the difference. "Money doesn't make a man, Winston," he'd often said. "It's what we do with what we have that determines our wealth and our worth as people. Don't forget that." Winston hadn't forgotten it either. His vision for *The Way Home* had its roots in his father's words.

"Have you let your folks know how you feel?"

Raymond slumped back against the counter. "I've tried."

"What happened?"

"They listened or at least they pretended to listen, then they went right ahead and told me again how I shouldn't tie myself

down with Patrice and that there were a lot of girls in Rosemont
I could date. They just don't get it. I don't want some other
girl; I love Patrice.''

Winston shook the water off his hands, dried them with a
towel, then put them on Raymond's shoulders and led him to
one of the stools at the kitchen counter. When they were both
seated, Winston said, ''Your parents aren't all wrong, Raymond.'' The boy moved to interrupt, but Winston stopped him.
''Hear me out, first. It's parents' job to worry about their kids.''
Again, Winston had to stop the boy's interruption. ''I know
you don't think you're a kid, but to them you are.''

''That's no excuse for them to treat Patrice badly or to think
badly of her.''

''You're right, it's not, but I don't think you're going to
change them, Raymond. You can try and you should try, but
it's not your fault they're the way they are.''

The boy studied the counter for a long minute. ''I asked
Patrice if she thinks I'm like them.''

''And what did she say?''

''She said, no, but . . .''

''But what?''

''I don't know.''

''Yes, you do.''

The boy turned tortured eyes up Winston. ''But they're my
parents and I love them. How can I love them if they're bigots?''

Winston draped an arm around the man-child next to him
and knew that the next generation would be safe in his hands.
''You just said it. You love them because they're your parents
and you know they love you.''

''But I despise the way they feel and sometimes I want to
hate them. When they hurt Patrice, I feel like I do hate them.''
Raymond dropped his head. ''Oh, man, now I'm talking crazy.''

Winston shook his head. ''You're not talking crazy, Raymond. You're talking like a young man trying to reconcile his
actions with his beliefs. Don't be so hard on yourself. You and
the rest of the world are trying to answer that same question:

how to handle people we love who exhibit behaviors we find intolerable.''

"And what's the answer?" the child in Raymond asked.

Winston thought about how he dealt with his mother. "You love them, you correct them, you show them the right way by your actions, and you accept the reality that nothing you do will force them to change.''

Chapter 24

Marty rolled away from Cheryl and pulled her into his arms. "I didn't plan on this happening," he said, stroking his finger down her smooth skin.

She pressed a kiss against his chest. "Neither did I, but I'm glad it did. I needed to be with you. I guess I need you."

Her words made him complete. "I need you, too. I always have."

"I've been alone for a long time, Marty. I'm not used to depending on anyone."

"You aren't telling me anything I don't already know. You've always been that way. It's one of the reasons I love you."

She pressed closer to him and his body responded. "I'm glad you love me. Did you know that?"

"I sorta guessed it made you happy."

"Well, it does. Very happy."

He tilted her chin up so he could look into her eyes. "And I'm going to keep making you happy until the day I die. You are going to marry me, aren't you?"

She lowered her lashes. "You don't have to marry me."

He pressed a kiss against her eyelids. "I know I don't have

to, I want to. I want you, me, and Patrice to be a family. Now, are you going to marry me?''

She looked up at him and he saw the love in her eyes. ''Yes, I'm going to marry you.''

''When?''

''I don't know. We'll have to see how things go with Patrice.''

''We have to tell her who I am before we get married.''

''I know.'' She intertwined her fingers with his and held up their joined hands. ''I don't look forward to it though.''

''The sooner we tell her, the better.''

''I'm not sure, Marty . . .''

''Why not? She likes me.'' He brought their joined hands to his lips.

''I know, but—''

''No buts, Cheryl. We tell her tonight when she comes home.''

''Not tonight,'' she said and he heard the panic and fear in her voice. ''I need more time to get adjusted to the idea.''

''How much more time?''

''I don't know.''

Marty eased away from her and sat up so he could look at her. ''I'm sure we're going to disagree in our marriage, Cheryl, and sometimes I'll be the one to give in, but this issue is not one of those times. I'll give you until the end of the week. We tell Patrice on Saturday. We'll take her and Raymond to dinner and we'll tell her afterward.''

The fear in her eyes almost made him relent. Almost. ''You're sure we're doing the right thing?''

He shook his head. ''I'm sure we're doing the only thing we can do.''

''Hold me, Marty,'' Cheryl said, moving back into his arms. ''Please hold me.''

Marty eased back down in the bed and pulled Cheryl against him. His mind was on the time when he wouldn't have to watch the clock to make sure his daughter didn't find him in bed with her mother.

* * *

"Stop, Winston," Marlena said, leaning her head to the side so he could have better access to her neck. "I'm trying to talk to you."

"I don't want to talk," he murmured. "We talk too much. I want action."

She fought her rising passion. She and Winston needed to talk tonight. "Do you think Raymond and Patrice had a good time?"

"Sure," he said, pushing the straps of her soft denim sundress down her arms. "You have beautiful skin, Lena. It's so soft." He pressed a kiss on her shoulder.

"Winston, I'm serious. What about Raymond and Patrice?"

He sighed, then lifted his head. "Okay, you win. What do you want to talk about?" He pushed the top of her dress down and exposed her breasts.

She sucked in her breath when he pressed his mouth against one of her nipples. "You're not playing fair, Winston. You said we'd talk."

His hands replaced his lips on her breasts. "I'm talking, but you aren't listening. Have I lost my touch already?"

She thought he had to be kidding. He had to see how he affected her. "You don't have anything to worry about in that department. Tell me what you thought about Patrice and Raymond."

He sighed again. "Step out of that dress and we'll talk."

She raised a brow at him, but she stepped out of her dress and stood before him in the middle of the kitchen in only her blue lace panties and leather sandals.

"Now the panties," he ordered.

"I thought you said we would talk."

"We will as soon as you're naked. Now step out of the panties."

She pushed the thin panties down her legs and kicked them off. "I suppose you want me to take off the sandals too."

"That would be a good idea."

She kicked off the shoes and looked up at him. The fire in his eyes caused a burning sensation in the pit of her stomach.

"Now talk," he said, staring at her.

"What?" She couldn't remember what they were talking about. The fire in his eyes distracted her.

"Maybe we should sit down so you can think?" He picked her up and placed her on the kitchen counter. "Can you think now?" He placed a warm hand on each of her thighs.

"Raymond and Patrice? How do you think they're doing?"

He caressed her thighs with his fingers. "They're doing okay, but they're under a lot of stress. I think they had a good time tonight, but there's still a lot of tension there."

She wondered how he could make such rational sentences when her thoughts were scattered about the room. "Is there anything we can do to help them?"

"I don't think so. This is a family problem that Cheryl and Marty have to work out. All we can do is be there if they need us."

"I wish there was something more we could do."

He pressed his face between her breasts and inhaled her scent. "There is."

"What?" she asked.

"We can be examples for them. They know the prejudices we faced when we were their age. They know we were separated for a long time, and it encourages them to see us together now. Our love will keep them strong. Don't worry so much. They're good kids. They'll be fine."

She placed her hands on his head and pulled his face to hers. "I hope you're right."

"I do, too, sweetheart."

"One more thing . . ."

He shook his head. "No way. No more talking tonight. Here or upstairs?"

She looked into his eyes and decided their talk could wait until morning. "Upstairs," she said.

He lifted her off the counter. "Spoilsport," he said and strode toward the stairs with her in his arms.

* * *

The doorbell woke Marlena the next morning. She reached for Winston, but he wasn't there. She sat up in the bed and looked over at the clock: nine-thirty. They'd slept late.

The doorbell sounded again. "Will you get that, Marlena," Winston called from the bathroom. "It has to be my mother."

Marlena got up and rushed naked to the bathroom. Winston stood naked, a razor in his hand, shaving cream on his face. "Have you lost your mind? You want me to go downstairs and let your mother in? She's going to know we spent the night together."

"What I want is a good morning kiss and then I want you to go let my mother in. Of course, I think you'd better put on some clothes first."

"You're serious?"

He pressed a kiss on her lips. When he moved away from her, she wiped off the shaving cream he left on her face. "Deadly serious. She has a key. If you don't let her in, she's going to let herself in."

"She has a key?"

"Of course she has a key. She's my mother. Once we tell her we're engaged, we'll also tell her she'll have to be a bit more judicious in her use of it unless she wants to get an embarrassing eyeful of her son and her new daughter-in-law."

"You're not going to tell your mother that?" He had to be joking. He had to be.

"I won't have to tell her anything if you don't hurry. Pretty soon she'll be up here and get a firsthand account of what to expect when she walks in unannounced."

"She wouldn't come up here, would she?"

He looked at her as if she had lost her mind. "Why wouldn't she? She rang the bell and nobody answered. She doesn't think I'm home."

Marlena spun around and scanned the room. "Where are my clothes?"

"Ah, I think they're on the kitchen floor. I seem to remember you taking them off down there."

She turned back and glared at him, wanting to wipe that smile of his face. "What's so funny?"

"I was wondering what Mother is going to think when she sees your dress and underwear on the kitchen floor."

Marlena propped her hands on her hips. "You're enjoying this, aren't you?" she accused. "I don't believe it. You're actually enjoying this."

"You're wasting time. Get a jersey out of the dresser and let the woman in."

"Why don't you let her in? Why do you want me to do it?"

Winston put down his razor. "This is your home as much as it's mine and Mother needs to know that. You have nothing to be ashamed of. First, she'll take note of the jersey, then she'll see the ring. Believe me, she'll forget the jersey."

"So you want to shock her?"

"No, I want to show her where my priorities are. You're going to be my wife and she has to accept you. Now please put on some clothes and get downstairs. I'll be down as soon as I get dressed."

Marlena turned and went to the dresser. She quickly found a jersey and slipped it on. "You'd better hurry and get down there. Your mother may try to kill me." She heard his laughter as she closed the bedroom door.

Marlena raced down the stairs. She met Mrs. Taylor when she reached the bottom step. As Winston had predicted, she'd let herself in.

"What are you doing here?" the older woman asked after a moment of surprise at seeing Marlena.

"Winston will be down in a minute. May I get you a cup of coffee?" Marlena was proud of her calm. "I'm going to make myself a cup." She walked past the woman and toward the kitchen. She rushed, glad the woman wasn't close on her heels, and picked up her clothes before Mrs. Taylor got to the kitchen.

"You didn't answer my question," Mrs. Taylor said. "What are you doing here?"

Marlena delivered what she hoped was her best smile. "I think that's pretty obvious. I spent the night."

"You *are* a common woman, aren't you?" Mrs. Taylor said through tight lips. "How can you flaunt sleeping with my son like some whore? You're just like your mother, aren't you?"

Marlena felt her calm exterior begin to crumble. "Not exactly a whore, Mrs. Taylor," she said with a forced smile. "Try a daughter-in-law to be."

"Never," the older woman spat out. "Never."

Marlena felt the woman's venom, but she determined not to let it affect her. "Believe what you want. Now do you want some coffee?"

"What I want is for you to get out of my son's house and out of his life. You don't belong here."

"That's where you're wrong, Mother," Winston's deep voice said from the entrance to the kitchen. He walked over to Marlena and kissed the tip of her nose. Marlena would have laughed at his mother's discomfort at seeing her son dressed in his pajama bottoms and kissing a woman dressed in one of his old jerseys, but she was too surprised by Winston's actions to do or say anything. "She *does* belong here. This house is as much hers as it is mine."

"You can't be serious, Winston," his mother began.

"I'm deadly serious, Mother." He looked down at Marlena. "You didn't show her, did you?"

"Show me what?"

"Hold out your hand, darlin'," he said to Marlena. "I want Mother to see the ring I gave you."

"Ring?" his mother choked out.

He lifted Marlena's hand and extended it to his mother. "How do you like it?" he asked his mother.

The older woman paled. "You didn't, Winston. How could you?"

He brought Marlena's hand to his lips and kissed it. "I love her, Mother, and she loves me. We're getting married. You can be happy for us and be invited to the wedding or you can consider yourself uninvited. The choice is yours."

"But Winston—"

"No, buts. Now which will it be?"

Mrs. Taylor looked from Winston to Marlena and back again.
"Winston—"

"Which will it be, Mother?"

"I think you were too hard on her," Marlena said after Mrs.
Taylor had gone. She and Winston sat cuddled on one of the
leather sofas in the entertainment room.

"No, I wasn't. Mother's not some weakling. She can dish
it out and she can take it."

"I don't like the idea of coming between the two of you,
Winston. She's your mother."

He squeezed her shoulder. "Don't worry so. She'll come
around. She's not stupid."

Marlena didn't think Mrs. Taylor stupid for a minute. The
woman was anything but stupid. She wondered what her next
move would be. "But what if she doesn't come around?"

Winston shrugged. "Then she won't get to know her grandchildren. Trust me, it won't come to that."

"How can you be so sure?"

"She's my mother. She wants to know her grandchildren,
and she wants to be a part of my life."

Marlena relaxed against Winston. "I wished she liked me a
little."

He looked down at her with a masculine leer. "I like you
enough for both of us. Do you want me to show you how
much?"

She placed her hand on his chest when he moved to press
her down on the couch. "We have to talk."

"You talk too much. I want to make love." He wiggled his
eyebrows. "It's much more fun."

She giggled at his antics. "You're insatiable."

"So are you. You want me to prove it?" He slipped his
hand under the hem of her jersey and stroked her bare thigh.

She removed his hand. "That won't be necessary. Now sit
up and pay attention. This is important. I have to tell you
something I should have told you a long time ago."

A warning bell went off in Winston's head and he knew he

didn't want to hear what she had to say. "The past belongs in the past, Marlena. Let's leave it there."

"We can't. It'll catch up with us one day." And if your mother has her way that day will probably come very soon. "I can't live every day wondering if today's the day."

Winston's apprehensions rose with her every word. As a stalling tactic, he moved to kiss her.

"Don't," she said, moving away from him. "You have to hear this."

He lifted both hands in surrender. "All right, I'll listen."

"It has to do with the reason I broke up with you ten years ago."

"I don't want to hear this, Marlena," Winston said, his heart racing. He knew what she was about to tell him could change their lives. He could feel it. Maybe she had a child somewhere that he didn't know about. "We've been over it more than once. I don't want to rehash it."

Marlena knew he was afraid of what she was about to tell him and that made her sad. It made her wonder if their love was strong enough to survive her news. She sighed, then continued, "Your mother came to visit me the day after Josie's funeral." She remembered the day as if it were yesterday. "She said she had something she wanted to tell me. I thought she was actually coming to give her personal condolences on my mother's death. I was wrong."

She looked over at Winston. "You don't have to do this, Marlena," he said again.

"Yes, I do," she said. She knew that if she didn't tell him, his mother would, and she couldn't risk the spin Mrs. Taylor would put on the story. "You know I do."

He nodded. "What did my mother want?"

"She asked me not to see you again. When I told her I wouldn't do that, she offered me fifty thousand dollars."

Winston jumped up from the couch. His eyes blazed with something she'd never seen before: hatred. "She offered you money and you took it?" He grabbed both her arms. "Tell me. Did you take it?"

She shook herself free of his hold. "No, I didn't take it. How can you ask me that?"

"What do you mean—how can I ask you that? You did exactly what she asked you to do. Don't tell me that all of a sudden you decided you didn't want to see me anymore and the money had nothing to do with it."

"The money didn't have anything to do with it," she protested.

He looked away from her and her heart broke. "Right. I need a drink." He strode to the bar and poured a glass of something and drank it down in a single gulp.

She sat down on the couch, feeling very alone. "There's more, Winston," she said.

"More what? More money or more lies?"

She looked over at him, her eyes pleading with him to listen to her, to believe her. "Not lies and not money. I know I should have told you all this back then, but I couldn't handle it. I was at one of the lowest points in my life, and I just couldn't handle it."

"So you took the money?"

"I told you I didn't take the money."

"Then why did you leave me? What couldn't you handle?"

"When I didn't jump at your mother's money, she said there was more than one way to skin a cat. Those were her exact words. I'll never forget them." Marlena felt a chill come over her and she rubbed her arms. "Then she told me that Josie and your father had been having an affair."

"You're lying," Winston shouted.

Marlena had feared this anger and disbelief. Winston had always held his father in the highest esteem and she'd known then that this sordid tale would hurt him deeply.

"That's what I said to your mother. Do you know what she did? She laughed. She laughed and then she told me they'd been sneaking around since before I was born, before you were born."

"It's not true. Why would Mother tell you this?"

"Don't you see, Winston? She wanted me out of your life. She wanted you to see me as the slut she made my mother out to be. But Josie wasn't a slut. She loved your father, Winston. She really did.''

"This is too much," Winston said. "I have to talk to my mother."

"Not yet," she said. "There's more."

"More?"

She nodded. "I didn't believe your mother, so I went and talked to my aunt, my mother's sister."

Chapter 25

Winston leaned back against the bar and tried to absorb everything Marlena was telling him. His father and her mother had been lovers. He couldn't believe it. Josie and his father.

He looked at Marlena. She was still talking but he couldn't process the words she spoke. Her mother and his father.

"Did you know?" he asked, interrupting her.

"Know what?"

"Did you know your mother was having an affair with my father?"

She shook her head and he thought he saw disappointment flash quickly in her eyes. "I didn't know until the day your mother told me. I never even suspected."

"Your mother was having an affair and you didn't know about it?" He walked over and stood in front of her. "Come on, Marlena. You had to know something."

She looked up at him. "Josie was always seeing somebody, you know that as well as I do. I didn't want to know who. All I wanted to do was pretend I was a normal child with a normal mother." A normal mother. Those words sounded strange to Marlena's ears. How many mothers asked their teenager to call them by their first name?

Winston studied the face that was so precious to him. She hadn't known. He was sure of it. "Why didn't you tell me this back then?"

"Because I was ashamed, Winston. My mother was sleeping with your father and I was sleeping with you. Doesn't that sound ugly and dirty to you?"

Winston pushed the unappealing picture from his mind. "Did you think it would matter to me?"

"What was I supposed to think? It mattered to me. For a while I blamed your father for using my mother. I thought about all the times he'd been nice to me and I wondered if he'd been hoping I'd be to you what my mother was to him. It hurt a lot."

Winston felt her pain and at any other time, he would have moved to comfort her. He couldn't this time. "So you hated my father?"

"For a while I did, but I don't now. I was being honest when I said I was sorry to hear about his death."

"What made you stop hating him?"

She shrugged. "Life is too short to hold grudges. What was the point in hating your father? Josie was a grown woman. Your father didn't force her into a relationship with him. She wanted to be with him."

Winston sat down on the table on front of her. "At least now I understand why Mother dislikes you so much," he said aloud though he was really talking to himself.

"You think that makes her dislike of me acceptable?"

"No. I said it makes me understand it. You can understand it, too, can't you?"

Marlena shook her head. "No, I can't understand it. I can understand your mother hating my mother and being angry with your father, but I can't understand her directing that anger toward a child. That's what I was, Winston. She's treated me like dirt since high school and I didn't deserve that. Your mother's not a nice woman."

"She was hurt." Winston knew the hurt that love betrayed caused and he sympathized with his mother.

"I was hurt, too. How do you think I felt when your mother

told me all this the day after my mother's funeral? I was the most alone I'd ever been in my entire life, and she wanted me to give up the only person I had: you. She made me give you up.''

Winston shook his head. He felt anew the pain he'd felt when Marlena had left him. ''She didn't make you give me up, Marlena. That was your decision.''

''How can you say that? Haven't you heard a word I've said? Your mother is a monster, Winston. A monster.''

Winston kept shaking his head. Marlena's news had helped him understand his mother. He couldn't imagine how she'd lived with his father knowing that he was carrying on an affair right under her nose. No wonder she hadn't been affectionate. How could she have been? Maybe she had been once, before she found out. ''My father and your mother are the guilty parties here and they're both gone. You and Mother are victims and you both have to find a way to live with the past.''

''I've been victimized twice then. First by Josie and your father and then by your mother, and I think what your mother did was worse. She tried to make me pay for my mother's mistakes. She wanted me to feel dirty because of what my mother had done and she succeeded, Winston. She succeeded and I walked out of your life because of it.''

Winston didn't say anything. He didn't have anything to say. His father, the man he'd loved with all his heart and respected beyond measure, had been cheating on his mother for years. He'd thought his mother was the cold, uncaring one. How many times had he felt hatred for her and her ways? How many times? If only he'd known what she was going through, maybe he could have helped her. Why hadn't she told him? Why hadn't Marlena told him when she first found out?

He knew Marlena hadn't told him because she'd been ashamed and afraid. She'd been afraid he'd think less of her because of what her mother had done. She hadn't trusted their love enough to know it could survive anything and she still didn't trust it. He could tell by the stiffness of her back and the fear in her eyes. She still thought he'd walk away from her because of what had happened. She still didn't know him and how much he loved her.

He knew she wanted him to rail about the injustice his mother had heaped on her and a part of him wanted to, but another part of him couldn't. He knew how his mother felt. He imagined she felt just as he'd felt when Marlena had walked out of his life. He'd had to live with loving someone who wasn't there. His mother had had to live with loving a man who was there, but who loved or, at least, made love to, someone else. There was no doubt in his mind that his mother's burden was heavier.

"Aren't you going to say something?" Marlena asked, interrupting his thoughts.

He looked at the woman he still loved, but didn't really know or understand. "This is a lot to digest."

Her lips curved downward. "There's more."

"More?"

She took a deep breath, preparing herself to tell him everything. "I told you I went to see my aunt after your mother came to see me."

"What did your aunt say?"

"She said it was true. She said Josie and your father had been lovers, but that they had stopped seeing each other when you and I started dating. Josie didn't tell my aunt whose idea it was, but my aunt said Josie was pretty broken up about it."

"How did the relationship start?"

She shrugged. "Who knows? My aunt wouldn't say."

"What else did she tell you?"

Marlena looked straight into his eyes. "You and I have a brother."

Patrice wasn't looking forward to brunch with the Hills, even though Raymond was going to be there. She much prefered spending the school holiday catching up on her sleep, but she'd been so surprised to hear from Mrs. Hill that she'd accepted the invitation without much thought. She regretted the hasty decision as soon as she reached the Hills' home and found out Raymond wasn't there.

"He had to make a quick trip to Athens for me," Mr. Hill said. "He should be back soon. Come on into the dining room."

Patrice reluctantly followed the adults to the formal dining room. The sideboard was covered with an array of breakfast dishes. "We're pretty informal this morning, dear," Mrs. Hill said. "Just help yourself."

Patrice looked from the older woman to the sideboard then back to the older woman. Something wasn't right; she could feel it. "I'd like to wash up first, if you don't mind."

The woman gave what Patrice was sure was a fake smile. "Of course. You know where the facilities are."

Patrice turned and headed for the bathroom. She should have known this wasn't going to be a pleasant visit.

She quickly washed her hands and went back to the dining room. Raymond's parents were already seated at the table, their plates in front of them. She smiled, grabbed a plate and helped herself to fruit and cereal. She didn't think her stomach would take much else.

After she was seated, Raymond's parents began to eat and so did she.

"How is school these days, Patrice?" Raymond's mother asked.

"Okay," Patrice said. "Finals are coming up, but they shouldn't be too bad."

"Good. Raymond has told us what a good student you are. Where do you plan to go to college?"

Patrice began to relax. Maybe this visit wasn't going to be so bad after all. "I've applied to Spelman and the University of Georgia."

"Oh, Spelman's nice," Raymond's mother said. "All the women in my family have gone there."

"Raymond told me. He also said that a lot of the men in your family went to Morehouse."

"Mine too," Raymond's father added. "I'm a Morehouse man myself, but I'm sure Raymond told you that."

"Yes, sir," Patrice said. "He wants to keep the family tradition."

"Has anyone else in your family gone to Spelman?" Raymond's mother asked.

"I'll be the first," Patrice said with a smile. She'd be the first member of her family to go to college and she didn't know who was more excited, her or her mother.

"Good for you. What school do your people usually attend?"

Patrice took a swallow of orange juice. "Actually I'll be the first to go. They're pretty proud of me."

"Oh," both adults said at the same time.

"That is something to be proud of," Raymond's mother added, but Patrice knew she didn't mean it.

"I thought your father went to Stanford," Mr. Hill said. "I'm sure that's what he told me."

Patrice shook her head. "I didn't know you knew my father."

"Of course we know him," the older man said. "Why would we invite him to our anniversary party if we didn't know him?"

Patrice looked from the older woman to the older man. "I think you've gotten my father confused with someone else. Nathaniel Flakes is my father. He lives in Leeds and works at the factory there."

"He's talking about your *real* father, dear," Raymond's mother said. "Marty Jones."

Patrice lowered the glass she was bringing to her lips. "What are you talking about? Marty Jones is not my father."

Raymond's mother covered her mouth with her hand and looked at her husband. "Oh, dear, I don't think she knew." She turned to face Patrice. "We thought you knew, dear. Marty Jones is your real father."

Marty Jones is your real father, the words bounced off the walls of Patrice's mind. "You're wrong. Nathaniel Flakes is my father. Marty and my mother went to high school together, that's all."

"Now, dear," Raymond's mother began, "we know this is a surprise for you, but it's true. It's why we wanted to talk to you this morning. You know there'll be a lot of talk once everyone in town finds out and we don't want our Raymond in the middle of it."

Patrice pushed her chair back from the table. So this is what the brunch invitation was all about. They'd found a way to break her and Raymond up. "What are you saying Mrs. Hill?"

"I'm saying that Raymond has a great future ahead of him. A future that having a wife—or a mistress—with a shady family history could destroy. Now you wouldn't want to do that, would you, dear?"

Patrice's mouth dropped open, but she couldn't say anything. What could she say? The two people sitting before her were the parents of the boy she loved and they hated her. She'd known that they didn't like her, but it was only now that she realized how deep their dislike went. How could they hate her when all she wanted was to love their son? She felt tears well up in the back of her eyes and took a deep breath to keep them from falling.

"Of course," the older woman continued, "once Raymond finds out, he may not want to go out with you anymore. There's always that chance."

Patrice removed her napkin from her lap and gently laid it on the table. "Why are you doing this? Why are you lying like this?"

"We're not lying, dear," Mrs. Hill said.

"Stop calling me 'dear,'" Patrice said, ignoring the voice in the back of her mind that told her to respect these people because they were her elders. "I'm not your 'dear.'"

Mr. Hill jumped in. "There's no need to get upset, dear."

"I said, stop calling me dear." Her voice was louder this time. She was tired of hoping these people would come to like her. She knew now that would never happen.

"Calm down, Patrice," Mr. Hill said.

"Don't tell me to calm down," Patrice said, near tears. "All I've ever wanted was for you to like me. That's all. But you couldn't even do that. And you know what? I just don't care anymore whether you never like me or not. You think you're so much because you have a nice house on the good side of town and a little money in the bank, but you're nothing and I hate you."

She stood up and pushed her chair to the table. "Thanks for

inviting me to brunch.'' She turned, her head held high, and left the room and the house.

When she got to her mother's car, the tears began to fall. It couldn't be, could it? she asked herself. Marty couldn't be her father.

She started the engine and backed out of the driveway. There was only one way to find out for sure.

''Brother?'' Winston shouted. ''What do you mean we have a brother?''

Marlena's gaze didn't waver. She had to tell him everything and she'd known it wasn't going to be easy. ''Your father and my mother have a son. We have a brother.''

Winston rubbed his hand across his head. ''I can't believe this. What are you talking about? Did Mother tell you this?''

Marlena shook her head. ''My aunt told me. I don't think your mother knows.'' Marlena didn't want to risk her finding out either. Who knew what the woman would do if she knew Josie and her husband had a child together.

''A brother?'' Winston stood up and walked back to the bar. He picked up a bottle, then he put it back down without pouring a drink. ''You and I have a brother?''

''It's a disconcerting thought, isn't it? It doesn't mean we're related, I know, but it feels strange.'' Marlena shivered though the air in the room was still. ''Back then, it felt ugly and dirty.''

''How do you know your aunt was telling the truth?''

She knew Winston wanted to believe it wasn't true. She'd wanted to believe it wasn't when she'd first heard the story. ''What reason would she have to lie?''

''I don't know,'' he said, clearly blindsided by the news. ''I can't believe this.''

''Believe it.''

''A brother. Tell me it's an older brother. I pray it's not a younger brother.''

Marlena knew that feeling, too. It was much better to think of her mother and his father making a baby *before* she and

Winston were born. She didn't know if she could have handled a younger sibling. "He's older. Two years older to be exact."

"Where is he?"

She took a deep breath. This was the news that would hurt the most. "He lives in D.C., but he's out of the country a lot. He works for the State Department."

"You know him?"

She nodded. "Yes."

"How long have you known him?"

She dropped her eyes then, no longer able to look at the hurt in his. "I've always known him. I just didn't know who he was."

"What exactly is that supposed to mean?"

He came and stood in front of her again and she forced herself to look at him. The strain etched in his face tugged at her heart. She hated to be the one who put it there. "It means I've known him all my life, but I didn't know he was my brother."

"Come on. Spit it out, Marlena. There's no sense beating around the bush now."

"He's my cousin. He was adopted by my mother's sister." There. She'd said it.

He dropped down on the table with a thud. "This is ridiculous. Your cousin is our brother? Which cousin?"

"Greg."

"Greg? The cousin who called you when we were in D.C.? That Greg?"

Marlena didn't like the accusation in Winston's voice. She understood it, but she didn't like it. "Yes, that Greg. He's our brother, but he doesn't know, Winston. His mother never even told him he was adopted."

"But you knew? You've known all this time?"

His accusation hurt, but it was true. She focused her eyes on the painting on the wall behind him. "I've known since my mother's death."

"And you didn't tell me? You didn't think I deserved to know? What kind of woman are you, Marlena? I thought I knew you, but now I'm not so sure."

She turned her gaze back to him. "What good would it have done, Winston? The news would have broken your heart the way it broke mine. So many people would have been hurt. Greg, your father, you, my aunt, even your mother."

"My mother?"

"Yes, your mother. It's one thing for her to know about the affair, it's a whole other thing for her to know there's a child out there that belongs to her husband and my mother. The scandal alone would have killed her."

Winston missed her sarcasm. "You're telling me you kept this secret to spare my mother's feelings. Give me a break, Marlena."

Marlena told herself to ignore Winston's attitude. He was in pain and she was the closest target. "I couldn't tell you, Winston. My aunt begged me not to. She wasn't sure your mother knew. She didn't want to put Greg at risk. If your mother was awful to me, how was I to know what she'd do to Greg if she found out about him? He's innocent in all of this."

"Are you sure he doesn't know?"

"Positive."

Winston shook his head. "Doesn't it bother you—all the lying?"

"I didn't lie. I just didn't tell everything I knew."

"It's the same thing. You lie every time you talk to your brother, your cousin, whatever. You lie every time you make love with me."

Tears stung the back of Marlena's eyes, but she wouldn't let them fall. "You know that's not true."

"How do I know anything anymore? I didn't know about your mother and my father. I didn't know about my brother. And apparently, I don't know you as well as I thought I did."

"What are you saying?" Marlena asked prepared for the worst. She'd known ten years ago her relationship with Winston couldn't survive this revelation. It seemed nothing had changed.

"Look, I don't know what I'm saying. I need to get out of here. Get some air. Think. See my mother." He got up from the table without looking at her. "I'm going to get dressed."

Marlena kept her seat on the couch, though she wanted to

rush after Winston and beg him to tell her he still loved her. She'd told him the truth. A little late, but she'd told him. She'd done what needed to be done if they were going to build a life together.

She twisted the engagement ring on her finger. She still wanted that life. She hoped he did, too.

Chapter 26

Winston drove around for over an hour thinking about Marlena's revelation: his father had had an affair with her mother that lasted over twenty years. How had his father managed a secret life for all that time? More importantly, how had his mother dealt with his father's duplicity all those years? Why hadn't she left him? There was only one way to get the answers he needed. He made a quick U-turn and headed for his mother's house.

Fifteen minutes later, he pulled into her driveway. All the times he'd been angry with her filled his mind and his guilt overtook him. Though he'd always thought he was a good son to both his parents, now he wasn't so sure. Maybe what he'd been was the stereotypical only child—so self-absorbed that he'd missed what was going on in his family.

He took a deep breath, then opened the door of the Bronco and got out. He found his mother in the kitchen drinking a cup of coffee.

She looked up. "Winston," she said, "I didn't hear you come in."

He walked over and hugged her. He held her too long, he knew, but he felt she was much overdue for a hug.

When he pulled away, she asked, "What was that all about?"

He smiled at her and realized that though she was still a beautiful woman, she was getting older: her eyes weren't as bright as they used to be. "You're my mom and I love you. What's wrong with a hug?"

"There's nothing wrong with it," she said. She picked up her cup and held it with both hands. "So you're getting married?"

"She told me," he said, seeing no need for chitchat.

His mother's eyes widened, and she tried to hide her surprise by sipping from her coffee cup. "Who told you what?" she asked after she swallowed.

He sighed. She was going to make this difficult. "Marlena told me what happened between the two of you."

"I don't know what you're talking about. What did she say happened between us?"

"She told me about Dad and her mother."

The color drained from his mother's face and she stood up, turning her back to him. "I don't know what you're talking about. There was nothing between Albert and Josie."

Winston got up and went to his mother. He placed his hand on her shoulder and she turned around. She had tears in her eyes. "Don't cry, Mom," he said.

"I'm not crying," she said, wiping at her tears. "What do I have to cry about?"

Winston's heart contracted upon seeing the pain written all over his mother's face. His father had been dead five years and his mother still hurt. He wondered if she'd ever allowed herself to cry, to heal. "Maybe I'm wrong. Maybe you need to cry. Sometimes it helps."

"Oh, you," she said, then stepped past him, still brushing at her tears. "I don't have anything to cry about."

"When someone you love betrays you, I think you have a right to cry. I know. I've been there, remember?"

She turned back to him. "Oh, I remember, all right. I thought you'd forgotten."

He shook his head. "I haven't forgotten, but I've forgiven. I still love her. Love's funny that way. Just because the person you love hurts you, doesn't mean you stop loving them. You hurt because they hurt you, but you still love them and that only makes the hurt worse.''

"He never loved me, you know," she said. "I thought he did at first, but he didn't.''

"You can't know that, Mom. He wouldn't have married you, if he didn't care for you.''

His mother shook her head sadly. "You don't understand the relationship he had with Josie. It was sick, but he loved her. He never loved me the way he loved her.''

Winston was at a loss to contradict her. He didn't know his father well enough to comment. "When did you find out about them?''

She wiped her eyes again. "The night she had the baby. Somebody called here and he rushed out. He was gone for two days. When he came back, he was drunk and he stayed drunk for a week. It was the first time I'd seen your father drunk. And all he did was talk about Josie and his son and how he'd messed up his life.''

"Why didn't he leave? Why didn't you leave?''

His mother sat down at the table again. "I didn't leave because I loved him and I didn't have anywhere else to go. Your father was the best thing to happen to me. He was my knight in shining armor. He drove into my dreary life on his big black stallion and swept me off my feet. I could never have left him. He was brightness and life. I needed him as much as I needed air to breathe.''

Winston realized he'd been wrong, his mother *was* passionate. She'd just been unfortunate enough to marry a man whose heart belonged to another. "Then why didn't he leave. If he loved Josie so much, why didn't he leave?''

His mother laughed a dry laugh. "I ask myself that question all the time. I think he married me to spite her. Maybe Josie didn't want to get married. You know how she was.''

"That doesn't sound like the dad I knew," he said aloud though he was talking to himself.

"Oh, he was different with you. Maybe he would have eventually left if you hadn't been born, but after you were born, I knew he'd never leave. He loved you too much.'' Her lips turned in a half-smile. "And I think he even came to love me more than he had."

"What about his other son?"

"Josie gave him up for adoption. That was another reason your father was drunk. He wanted her to keep the baby, but she wouldn't do it. He stayed angry with her for a long time after that and didn't see her again for years, but he finally forgave her and they started up again after you entered elementary school."

"And nobody knew? I can't believe nobody knew."

"Of course, people knew, Winston, but since Josie saw a lot of different men—single and married—most people thought your father was just one of many. Only his closest friends knew how he felt about her and they accepted Josie in his life as much as they accepted me. It was strange. I never heard any of them mention her name except Herman."

"Mr. Sanders knew?"

She nodded and a weak smile crossed her face. "He knew and he didn't like it. He and your father argued about it all the time. He even visited Josie once, but he didn't do that again. Your father was furious with him."

Winston felt they were talking about a man he didn't know. How could the father he'd loved and respected have been so cruel to his mother? "This sounds like something out of a soap opera."

"I wish it had been a soap opera, but, no, this was very real. I lived it."

"I don't see why you didn't hate Dad," Winston said, trying to understand his own feelings for his dad. He loved him still, but . . . "How could you live with him?"

"Don't be childish, Winston. I told you. I loved your father. I focused all my hate on Josie."

"And Marlena."

She looked down at her cup. "Well, you can do better than that girl."

"She's not a girl. She's the woman I love."

"That's what scares me. You love her the way your father loved her mother. She's going to break your heart, just like her mother broke your father's heart. I know she will, Winston. I know it.''

His mother's words triggered understanding in Winston and he found peace amid his confusion. He shook his head. ''No, Mom, I don't love Marlena the way Dad loved Josie. I love her the way you loved Dad.''

Marlena grew weary waiting around Winston's house for him to call or return home, so she dressed and took a taxi back to the hotel. After a fresh shower and a change of clothes, she went to *The Way Home* office, hoping work would keep her mind off her problems.

After about an hour, her lack of concentration forced her to give up. All she could think about was Winston. She wondered what he was doing, what he was thinking. Did he still love her or would he ask for his ring back?

She didn't know what his decision would be, but she knew he'd have to ask her to get out of his life because she'd never again leave freely. She loved him too much to ever give up on them again.

The phone rang and she picked it up on the first ring, hoping it was Winston.

''Marlena,'' Cheryl's tight voice said.

''What's wrong, Cheryl?'' Marlena asked, hearing the fear in her friend's voice.

''It's Patrice. She's run away.''

''What?''

''She's run away!''

Marlena grabbed the edge of her desk with her free hand. ''Are you sure? How do you know?''

''They told her.'' Marlena could barely make out the words.

''Who told her what, Cheryl? Where's Marty?''

''I can't believe they told her. How could they be so cruel? She's only a baby.''

What was Cheryl talking about? Marlena asked herself. Someone had told Patrice something, but what? ''Calm down, Cheryl. Now who told her what?''

"Raymond's parents told her about Marty. Can you believe they told her?"

Marlena couldn't believe it. What would the Hills have to gain by telling Patrice this information?

"You should have seen her, Marlena. She was so hurt. So hurt. I've never seen her that upset. And Marty. He tried to reason with her, but she wouldn't listen. I don't know who's hurt worse, him or her."

"Where's Marty, Cheryl?"

Cheryl sniffled. "He went after her. She raced out of here in my car and he got in his rental and went after her. They were going so fast. What if there's an accident?"

"Don't let your imagination run wild. I'll be right over."

"No, don't," Cheryl said quickly. "She may come over there. She may want to talk with you."

Marlena knew Cheryl could be right, but she knew her friend needed support too. "Are you by yourself?"

"No," Cheryl said. "Raymond's here. He suggested I call and see if Patrice was with you and Winston."

"How's he doing?" Marlena asked, knowing how much the young man loved Patrice.

"Not too good. He had a big argument with his parents. They've called here, but he won't talk to them. I think they're coming over. I don't want them here, Marlena. I don't."

Marlena couldn't much blame Cheryl. The Hills had been way out of line telling Patrice what they had. It would have been different had they made their pitch to Cheryl, but they'd gone after the child and that was wrong. "Look, Cheryl, I'm going to find Winston and have him come over there."

"That's not necessary."

Marlena knew it was. She didn't trust Cheryl to be under the same roof with the Hills. Hell, she didn't trust herself to be under the same roof with them. "It *is* necessary. I'm going to hang up and try to find Winston. Are you going to be okay?"

"I'll be fine," Cheryl said, but Marlena didn't believe her. She knew her friend wouldn't be fine until her daughter was safely back at home.

Marlena pressed the switchhook and dialed Winston's number. When the answering machine came on, she hung up. She took a deep breath and dialed his mother's number. Mrs. Taylor answered on the second ring.

"Mrs. Taylor, this is Marlena. I'm looking for Winston."

"He's not here," was the short reply.

Marlena took another deep breath. "Look, Mrs. Taylor, this is important. I have to find Winston."

There was a long pause before the woman spoke. "Hold on a minute. He just walked out of the door. I'll see if I can catch him."

Marlena gave thanks and prayed Winston was still there.

"What is it, Marlena?" he asked, his voice full of concern. "Are you all right?"

"I'm fine, Winston, but Cheryl's not."

"What's happened to her? Where's Marty?"

Marlena explained the situation to Winston.

"I don't believe they did that," he said.

"Well, they did. Will you go over to Cheryl's? Raymond's there and she's expecting his parents to come over, too. I don't want her alone with them, there's no telling what she might do. I'm scared for her, Winston."

"Don't be afraid, sweetheart," he said. "I'll head right over there. Are you coming, too?"

"Not yet. Cheryl wants me to stay here in case Patrice comes by. Hurry and get to her, Winston."

"I'm on my way," he said and hung up the phone.

"What is it?" his mother asked.

Winston quickly explained what had happened as he rushed to the front door.

"Maybe I should go with you. I know Raymond's grandparents. Maybe I can help."

Winston hesitated. He wasn't sure if his mother would be welcome and, he admitted, he wasn't sure if she wouldn't do more harm than good.

"I won't go if you don't want me to, Winston, but I think I can help. I know what Raymond's parents are trying to do and now I know it won't work. I can tell them that."

Winston studied his mother's face, then nodded. "Okay, let's go."

Patrice sped down Athens Highway. All she wanted to do was get away. How could her mother have lied to her all these years? How could she?

Tears streamed down her face making it hard for her to see. She knew she should pull over, but she didn't want Marty to catch her. She looked in her rearview mirror and saw him close behind her. "Damn him," she said.

Marty Jones was her father. He and her mother had been high school sweethearts, not her mother and Nathaniel Flakes. She couldn't believe her mother had told so many lies.

Marty said he hadn't known about her, but Patrice didn't know if she could believe him either. What if he was lying so she wouldn't feel bad?

There was nobody she could trust except Raymond and she was beginning to think a life with him was impossible. How could she have a life with him if his parents despised her and everything she was? If she couldn't have Raymond, she didn't know if she wanted to live.

The tears continued to flow and her vision became blurry. The road curved ahead of her a bit more quickly than she'd expected and she lost control of the car.

Marty's heart stuck in his throat when Patrice's car ran off the road and struck the embankment. He quickly pulled his car to the side of the road, got out and ran to his daughter, praying she was all right. She had to be all right. God couldn't be so cruel as to give her to him and then take her away before he had a chance to know her.

"Patrice," he called when he reached the car. She sat with her hands on the steering wheel and her head resting back on the headrest with her eyes closed. "Patrice," he called again. "Are you all right?"

When she didn't say anything, he wondered if she was unconscious. He pulled open the car door, thanking God it wasn't locked, and shook her shoulder. "Patrice," he said again. "Please be all right, sweetheart. I love you so much and I'm so sorry this had to happen. I'd give anything to make all this right for you. You're my little girl and I want you to be safe and happy."

Patrice stirred and Marty's heart pumped faster. He wanted to stay with her and he wanted go get his car phone and call for an ambulance. When she opened her eyes, he asked again, "Are you all right?"

She shook her head from side to side as if to clear her mind. "I'm fine."

He knew she wasn't fine, so he assumed her words meant she wasn't physically hurt. "Be still. I'm going back to my car and call 911. We'll get an ambulance out here."

"Don't do that," she said. "I don't need an ambulance. I'm not hurt."

"You can't be sure of that, Patrice," he said, stepping easily into the parental role. "I had to call your name four or five times before you answered."

"I heard you," she said, staring at him as if she'd never seen him before. "I heard you. I just didn't want to answer you."

Her honesty surprised him, but he still wanted to call for an ambulance. "Did you hit your head or anything when you ran off the road?"

She shook her head. "Nothing. I only lost control for a moment. I'm fine."

He squatted down next to her open door. "You're not fine, Patrice. You can't be after what you've learned today."

She looked away from him. "It doesn't matter."

"It does matter," he said softly. This young woman was his daughter and his first gift to her had been pain. He promised himself he'd never hurt her again. "It matters to me, it matters to your mother, and I think it matters to you. Cheryl and I should have told you. You shouldn't have found out the way you did."

"Why didn't you tell me? Why did she lie to me all these

years?'' Patrice pounded her fists on the steering wheel. He could see the tears in her eyes. ''I hate her. I hate her.''

''You don't hate her,'' Marty said, wishing he could endure her pain for her. ''You're angry with her, but you don't hate her. You love her, but you don't understand why she lied to you and that makes you angry.''

Patrice wiped at her tears, then turned dry eyes to him. ''How do you know how I'm feeling? You don't know anything about me.''

He smiled, content for right now that she was talking to him. ''I know because I wanted to hate her when she told me about you. You're my daughter and I never knew about you. I was angry when I found out.''

''How did you find out?''

''Cheryl told me.''

''When?''

''Right after I came to Gaines.''

''So you knew that day in *The Way Home* office?''

He nodded. ''I knew and I wanted so much to tell you, to call you my daughter.''

She turned away from him again. ''Well, it takes more than sperm to make a father. All you are to me is sperm.''

Her words hurt, but Marty was prepared for her anger. ''I know that's what I am, but I'd like to be more. If you'll let me.''

Patrice didn't say anything. She stared straight ahead, her hands tight on the steering wheel. Marty wondered what she was thinking. ''Patrice,'' he said, then he tentatively reached his hand out to touch her.

He breathed a relieved sigh when she didn't push his hand away. It wasn't much, he knew, but it was a start. He'd take it.

Chapter 27

Marlena pulled into Cheryl's driveway about fifteen minutes after Winston called and told her that Marty and Patrice were on their way home.

Cheryl met her at the door with a hug. "My baby's fine," she said. "My baby's fine."

Marlena held her friend tight and let her cry out her relief. When Cheryl pulled away and wiped at her tears, Marlena noticed the other occupants of Cheryl's living room: Raymond and his parents and Winston and his mother.

She smiled her greeting and everyone nodded, except Winston, who stood up and pulled her into his arms. "Are you all right?" he asked.

"I am now," she said, needing the comfort he offered. "It's been a rough day."

"Let's go outside," he whispered. She nodded and allowed him to lead her out the front door.

He sat on the swing and pulled her down next to him. "Are you sure you're okay?"

"About as well as I can be given the circumstances. How about you?"

He placed his arm around her shoulders and pulled her close.

"I'm better now that you're here with me. I talked to Mother this afternoon."

"How did it go?"

"She knows they had a baby."

Marlena tensed next to him. "What does she know? What's she going to do about it? Did you tell her? Tell me you didn't tell her."

"Don't get all excited. No, I didn't tell her, but I would have if she hadn't known. There have been too many secrets, Marlena. Look at all the hurt they've caused."

She knew he was right, but she still wasn't sure the truth wouldn't cause even more hurt and pain. "But what about Greg? He's innocent in all this."

Winston had done a lot of thinking about his brother. He wanted to get to know him. "We'll talk about Greg later. Let's finish this first."

"But—"

"But nothing. Mother has known about the baby since he was born. She knows your mother gave him up for adoption, but she doesn't know that your aunt adopted him."

"And you didn't tell her?"

He shook his head. "I want you to tell her."

"No, Winston. You can't ask that of me. Who knows what she'll do to Greg if she finds out."

Winston sighed. He really couldn't blame Marlena for not trusting his mother, but the lies and the hating had to stop somewhere if the two of them were going to have any chance at happiness. "She won't do anything."

"How can you be so sure?"

"Because she knows she was wrong. What do you think she's doing here?"

"Why is she here? I bet this is the first time she's stepped foot on this side of town."

"You may be right, but she's here now and she's here because she wanted to help. She thought she could talk to Raymond's parents."

"For what?" Marlena gave and unladylike snort. "To give them pointers on keeping Raymond and Patrice apart?"

Winston hated the mistrust in Marlena's voice and he knew his mother was going to have a hard time winning that trust back. "No, she wanted to tell them how futile their efforts were."

Marlena pulled back and looked up at him. "She wanted to what?"

"You heard me. She wanted to tell them how futile their efforts were."

"So, did she?"

He nodded.

"And what happened?"

"There was a lot of screaming. Mostly Raymond. But I think he and Mother finally got through to them."

She shook her head. "Come on, Winston. You expect me to believe that all of a sudden Raymond's parents have seen the light and decided Patrice is acceptable daughter-in-law material? Get real."

"No, that's not what's happened," he said. "Raymond's parents have agreed to sit down and talk with Cheryl and Marty. After the parents talk, they're going to talk to Patrice and Raymond. All four of them want what's best for the kids."

Marlena leaned her head against his chest again. "I guess that's a start."

"That's exactly what it is."

"It's sad it had to come to this," Marlena said. "It's going to take Patrice and Raymond a long time to forgive his parents for what they did today."

Winston knew Marlena was also telling him it would take her a long time to forgive his mother, but that she was willing to try. That was enough for him. "It's going to be hard for Mother too, Marlena. For almost all of her married life she had to live with the knowledge that she loved my father and he loved your mother."

"And I remind her of my mother." She sat up again. "Who are we kidding, Winston? This is not going to work between us. How can it?"

"Do you love me?" he asked.

"Love is not enough sometimes." Her lips turned down in a frown. "It's not."

"Does that mean you *do* love me?"

She looked into his eyes. "Of course I love you. I've always loved you."

"Then we'll work it out."

She stood up suddenly, presenting her back to him and crossing her arms. "You make it sound so simple. It's not."

He stood up and pulled her back into his arms. "And you make it sound impossible. It's not. I wish you and Mother were best friends, but that's not the case. So, we'll work with what we have."

"What if things never change?"

"They will."

"How can you be so sure?"

"Because they're already changing. Mother is here because she wants to be and she's here for you as much as she's here for me. It's her olive branch, Marlena. You can accept it or you can reject it to pay her back for the way she's mistreated you. It's your choice."

Marlena sat on the porch long after Winston had returned inside. Her thoughts went over her situation, her life, what she had and what she wanted.

"May I join you?"

Marlena looked up at Winston's mother. Her first instinct was to ignore the woman, but she scooted to the end of the swing. "Help yourself."

Mrs. Taylor sat down. "I know we haven't gotten along in the past," she began.

"That's an understatement," Marlena muttered.

"I've done some things that I'm not proud of and I don't expect you to forgive me, but I would like it if we could find some place to build a relationship. You're going to marry Winston and you're going to be the mother of my grandchildren. I want us to be a family."

Family, Marlena repeated in her mind. Her mother was dead;

she never knew her father; and she couldn't claim her brother. Now this woman who'd made her give up the only man she'd ever loved wanted to be a family with her. She didn't know if she could do it.

"You have every reason to hate me, Marlena, but I know you love Winston. Can't we find some middle ground for his sake?"

Marlena turned and looked at the woman she'd alternately wanted to impress and to kill. "Will you ever be able to look at me and not see my mother?" she asked. "Will you hate it when I tell your grandchildren about their Grandma Josie? Josie was my mother, Mrs. Taylor, and I loved her. I still do."

Mrs. Taylor studied her hands. "I know you love her and you should."

"You haven't answered my questions," Marlena reminded her.

Mrs. Taylor looked at Marlena. "I didn't dislike you because you reminded me of your mother. I disliked you because I thought my son loved you the way my husband loved her and I didn't want you to hurt him the way your mother hurt his father. Taylor men love real hard, Marlena. They give everything they have and when it's not returned or when it's misused, they hurt for a long time. I don't want to see my son hurt. I want to see him happy and I know now that you make him happy."

Marlena was suspicious of Mrs. Taylor's sudden change of heart. "And what made you see the light all of a sudden?"

"It was something Winston said."

"What did he say?"

"He said that I had it wrong. He said he didn't love you the way his father loved your mother. He said he loved you the way I loved his father. I knew then that there was nothing I could do to come between you. I have to accept you or I lose my son, and I don't want to lose my son."

Marlena respected Mrs. Taylor's honesty. She wouldn't have believed the older woman if she'd said she had developed a sudden fondness for Marlena. "Well, Mrs. Taylor, that's one thing we have in common. I love Winston, too, and I don't want to lose him either. I guess that means we have a truce."

Later that night when Marlena climbed into Winston's king-sized bed and into his arms, she was tired, but very hopeful.

"I love you, Marlena," he whispered in her ear. "I've always loved you and I always will."

Now that there were no longer any secrets between them, Marlena could accept Winston's words of love without reservation. She brought his strong hand to her lips and kissed his palm. "How could I be lucky enough to find you again?"

"It's not luck, sweetheart. It's fate. We were meant to be together." He intertwined his fingers with hers. "Long before we were born, we were destined to complete each other's lives."

She felt the tears form in her eyes at the beauty of Winston's words. "I feel complete," she said, "as if everything is my life has been set right. I've never felt like this, not even when we were together before."

He squeezed her to him. "I know what you mean. They say that love has to be tested. Well, ours has been tested and it's survived. It's a much stronger love now than it was back then."

Winston's words rang true in her heart. Theirs *was* a stronger love for all it had endured. It was a love she could depend on, a love she knew would stand up under the harsh realities of everyday living, a love that could face the challenge of their new brother and her new mother-in-law. She smiled the happiness she felt deep in her soul. "I guess this means you want me to move back to Gaines."

"I want you to be happy, Marlena. Where we live is not important."

She pulled back so she could look into his eyes. "You're saying you'd leave Gaines and move to D.C. if I wanted you to?"

"I'm saying I love you and I can be happy anywhere you are." His baby browns echoed the sincerity of his words.

"What about *The Way Home?* I know how much it means to you."

''When I first came up with the idea for *The Way Home*, I thought Gaines was home. Now I know Gaines is where I grew up, where we grew up. It's a place. Home is in my heart and my heart is where you are. We'll work out *The Way Home* together.''

Marlena knew there could be no happier woman in the world than her. She had Winston and she was loved. ''Gaines is where I want to be. I've spent too much of my life running and trying to prove to everybody that I belong. I don't want to run anymore and I no longer have anything to prove. All I want is to live a very long life with you and the children we'll have.''

He yawned and she knew he was as tired as she was. ''I think we're going to have to wait until tomorrow to get started on those children,'' he said.

Marlena didn't mind. She and Winston had the rest of their lives. She snuggled closer to him, happy she'd finally found the way home, and enjoyed the intimacy of being in his arms.

ABOUT THE AUTHOR

Angela Benson is a former engineer who now writes full-time while she pursues her second graduate degree. She's the author of six novels and a novella. Her titles include *Between the Lines, For All Time, Bands of Gold,* and *Friend and Lover,* her contribution to the Holiday Cheer anthology. October 1997 brings Angela's next Pinnacle title, *The Nicest Guy in America.*

To receive Angela's popular newsletter, Angela's Corner, write to her at P.O. Box 360571, Decatur, GA 30036, or send e-mail to abenson@mindspring.com.